HEARTS OF SMOKE and STEAM

The
SOCIETY OF STEAM
BOOK TWO

HEARTS OF SMOKE and STEAM

ANDREW P. MAYER

an imprint of Prometheus Books
Amherst, NY

Published 2011 by Pyr®, an imprint of Prometheus Books

Cover design by Nicole Sommer-Lecht

Cover illustration © Justin Gerard
Interior illustration by Ted Naifeh © Andrew P. Mayer

Inquiries should be addressed to
Pyr
59 John Glenn Drive
Amherst, New York 14228–2119
VOICE: 716–691–0133
FAX: 716–691–0137
WWW.PYRSF.COM

15 14 13 12 11   5 4 3 2 1

Library of Congress Cataloging-in-Publication Data

Mayer, Andrew P.
    Hearts of smoke and steam : a novel / by Andrew P. Mayer.
        p. cm. — (Society of steam ; bk. 2)
    ISBN 978–1–61614–533–0 (pbk.)
    ISBN 978–1–61614–534–7 (ebook)
    1. Steampunk fiction. I. Title.

PS3613.A9548H43 2011
813'.6—dc23

                                                                    2011028714

Printed in the United States of America

To my mother, June Mayer,
living proof of the virtues of good manners, common sense,
and just the right amount of righteousness

Contents

Prologue

The rest of the Paragons had arrived—scouring the empty park and trying to make sense of the remains of the battle they had missed.

Their show of force would terrify and delight the frightened tourists peeking out the nearby hotel windows, watching the scene below. Seeing the city's greatest heroes in action would be something wonderful to tell the people back home, but it was meaningless—the real threat had already escaped.

The hot air blasting out from the vent had kept him warm while he watched the tragedy through a pair of opera glasses he had modified so that they could be strapped to his head. He had seen it all: the Automaton being torn apart under the arm of Liberty, the arrival of Sarah Stanton, her confrontation with her father.

But he couldn't interfere. There were still too many questions left unanswered for him to betray Eschaton now.

The only moment that had truly pulled at his conscience was when he had witnessed Lord Eschaton ripping the heart out of the mechanical man. Anubis had failed to stop him achieving the single greatest step in his plan, and it had taken all of his willpower not leap down and confront the madman then and there.

And even if he could have saved the clockwork man, it would have made no actual difference. The Paragons were still doomed by their own hubris, and whatever the Automaton was, he was not human.

From his rooftop vantage point he watched the Paragons frantically scurrying around—angry, but without purpose. The Industrialist screamed loudly enough that Anubis could hear his cries as the harpoon was pulled from his arm.

Where there had once been seven Paragons, now only four remained, one of them confined to a wheelchair . . .

Anubis had already made one attempt to involve himself with their affairs. The end result had been the death of the Sleuth. Giving the old man the information he had wanted had ultimately simply been another futile action piled on top of all the others that he had already made. He would need to be more careful in the future.

Watching the heroes running through the streets helpless and confused only confirmed what Anubis had decided on the day that Sir Darby died; if there was any hope that he would be able to put a stop to Lord Eschaton's plans, he must work alone. He could only betray the villain once, and he would need to be sure he could destroy him.

But there was also the girl. "She has fire," he whispered to himself. Her passion was still undiminished by cynicism. It would be worth keeping an eye on *her*.

He had noted the direction she took when she ran off into the darkness of the city. She had left her father and the Paragons behind. It would be worth seeing where she would go . . .

Slipping his mask back over his head, Anubis hooked the end of his staff onto the edge of the rooftop, and lowered himself down on metal wire toward the streets below.

Chapter 1
The Burning Bush

Alexander Stanton had always found the Hall's main courtyard gloomy and a bit useless. He had even disliked the idea of it, and when Darby had presented him his original design for the Hall of Paragons, Stanton had responded by asking if they might be able to use the garden space to increase the size of the gymnasium instead.

Darby had objected, of course. He had pointed out that there were activities which it would be better for them to hold outside, in the fresh air—not the least of which would be his daily breathing exercises. "That," he had told the Industrialist on more than one occasion, "might be something you could join me in." Stanton had never managed to find the time, and now it was too late.

And there was some sense to the argument that a group of gentlemen adventurers might need some open air space, especially when you had some members who were able to take to the sky, while others wore costumes that produced large volumes of noxious fumes and fire.

So, after losing yet another argument to Darby's superior intellect, the courtyard had been built as originally planned, and that was where the Paragons sat now—seated on particularly uncomfortable stone chairs behind the center of the thick granite slab that Darby had named the "philosopher's table." Alexander's nickname for it was "the pain in my arse."

The rest of the dreary yard stretched out in front of him: floored mostly by concrete, walled on all sides by granite, and decorated with a number of sad-looking trees and bushes that were regularly replaced by the building staff after they inevitably turned brown and died from lack of direct contact with sunlight.

Tryouts were always a sedentary activity for the active members, and even though the sun had finally managed to burn wanly through the cloud cover, the north end of the courtyard received none of it. He supposed that spending enough time in the cold shade would turn any man a philosopher.

And April had been quite chilly. Mrs. Farrows had, with her usual efficiency, already packed away most of his winter woolens for the season. Alexander had been forced to wear a black evening coat over his dress costume.

Standing in front of them was one of the few men who had managed to seem impressive enough to bother seeing in person: the Hydraulic-man. His real name was Chadwick Prescott, and he was currently doing his best to prove that his claims of superhuman fighting prowess were genuine.

The costume that he had put together was actually far more impressive than Alexander had imagined it would be, and the design had clearly been significantly upgraded since the one he had described on his initial application to the Paragons.

The outfit had a snake theme, the motif playing off the fact that the word *hydra* was contained within *hydraulic*. Alexander found the wordplay a bit too forced to be clever, although it was far less ridiculous then some names he had encountered.

By manipulating a series of levers that sat on a metal panel on his arm, Chadwick could raise and lower the different snake heads arrayed on his shoulders. Attached to the bottom of each was a cloth-wrapped hose leading to a metal canister strapped to his back. These containers provided the liquids spat out by the heads, keeping them at pressure so they could travel over a distance.

With serpents standing on either shoulder, the mask had been fashioned to make him look as if his own head was the largest snake of all. Alexander smiled to himself as he wondered if Prescott could, if necessary, spit at his opponents with his toxic saliva.

Acid sprayed from one of the Hydraulic-man's snake heads and landed on the concrete with a hiss, burning a long scar across the ground where it fell.

Stanton felt his nose curl from the smoke. The fumes were acrid and probably most unhealthy. He felt thankful for their quick dissipation into the plentiful outdoor air, and then grimaced as it dawned on him that Darby's foresight had once again proven far better than his.

Grüsser began clapping loudly at the Hydraulic-man's ridiculous performance. Stanton had guessed correctly that the round Prussian would be thrilled by the idea of having another liquid-themed hero in their ranks, but his enthusiasm alone wouldn't be enough to make the Hydraulic-man a Paragon.

Grabbing another one of the levers on his sleeve, Chadwick lowered the acid-spitting head and began to shift a new snake up into position.

Alexander audibly sighed and sat up in his chair. "Thank you Mister Chadwick. I think we've seen quite enough."

"Industrialist, if you could just give me a chance, I think you'll find that this last Hydra-head is not only the most effective, but also my most entertaining!"

"Ya, Stanton, I vant to see it!" Grüsser interjected with dramatic enthusiasm.

"Thank you, Herr Submersible," Chadwick replied. As it locked into place, two small points of flame appeared in front of the snake's mouth, giving it a pair of flickering fangs. Turning to face away from the crowd, he pressed another lever, and a jet of liquid fire arced spectacularly across the courtyard, then splashed against the far wall.

As it struck the stone, it bloomed into a large fireball, enveloping a half-dead shrubbery nearby. The bush ignited instantly, and then began to burn with such enthusiasm it almost appeared joyful to have been put out of its misery.

A blush crept up and over the man's face. It wasn't until that moment that Stanton noticed how young he appeared to be, although his application had placed him in his early thirties. "Oh my goodness! I'm so sorry." He clutched at the levers on his wrist, desperately trying to bring up the next snake head. "I'll put it out!"

Stanton looked across the table at Nathaniel and gave him a smile and a wink. "A most impressive use of a biblical theme!"

"Now if he can only make it speak," Nathaniel chimed in.

"I apologize." Prescott blushed and Stanton actually found his nervousness quaint, although it was something the boy was going to need to lose if he was ever going to be ready to go into the field. "I hope my demonstration was satisfactory."

Stanton tried to reassure him. "We all make mistakes, sir. It's how you handle them that truly matters." A calm head would be doubly important for someone with high-pressure canisters of fuel and acid strapped to his back.

Hughes looked up from where he had been quietly gnawing on his thumbnail. Ever since the incident at the Darby house the man had a disturbed, far-away look in his eyes, and his words came out without emotion, as if he was being woken from an unpleasant dream that he couldn't quite puzzle out. "Interesting technology. Of course, you'd need a significant upgrade to your apparatus before we'd be able to make you a full member."

Stanton had hoped they would keep their reviews to themselves until after the demonstration, but it seemed clear that Hughes had no intention of playing along. "And what would you suggest, Hephaestus?" The fire had robbed Hughes of what remained of his ability to walk, his legs having been so badly burned during the battle against the Automaton that the doctor's only option had been to amputate both of them above the knee. All that was left were a pair of wriggling stumps—still wrapped and healing.

The last vestiges of his red hair had also vanished. What was left was entirely gray, except for a few stray wisps of orange that were the only reminders of the man he had once been.

Unable to continue as a fighting member of the team, he had turned his hands to invention. Although he had shown only a limited aptitude for it before, it seemed that he had a previously hidden talent that was now flourishing. "Increase the power of the sprayers, find a more rapid way for him to raise and lower the snake heads. Better control and more accurate aim." He rattled off the phrases like a shopping list.

Although he was nowhere near the level of genius that Darby was, Hughes had quickly proven himself to be a capable engineer, showing skill with old man's work. Not only had he helped to complete work on Nathaniel's Turbine costume, he'd followed the gas lines in the wall to uncover a previously unknown store of fortified steam.

Without Darby's amazing gas, their devices would become nothing more than complicated hunks of metal. There was still a question as to how they would come by more once this supply was gone, but the hidden cache had been a godsend when they needed it most.

Clearly there were more reserves to be had in Darby's main laboratory, but so far they'd been unable to figure out a way to unlock the massive gate in the basement that sealed the way in. For now, they could afford to be patient while Hughes attempted to pick the lock. But when the steam started to run out, they would have to resort to more desperate measures to gain access.

Hughes began to rise up on the device that had acted as his chair. The frame lifted him up with a hiss, a metal plate rising against his back and pulling him into place as he rose. His harness sank down into the machine's "chest," essentially a set of padded metal ribs that held him in place. Underneath him were a pair of mechanical legs, and they began to walk.

Having lost his battle suit in the ruins of the Darby mansion, Hughes had built himself this new machine and rechristened himself as "Hephaestus." The irony wasn't lost on anyone familiar with Greek mythology—he had named himself after the blacksmith god who had created two mechanical assistants to make up for his crippled legs.

But even if the design didn't make him appear fully human, it was still a masterpiece. The machine was beautiful, the limbs showing many of the elegant hallmarks of something Darby might have built. The top half, where Hughes was held in place, was far more utilitarian. If you stared at it long enough, it almost appeared as if Hughes was being swallowed up by the decapitated torso of a mechanical man.

The device crossed the floor with a waddle, Hughes swaying slightly from side to side as it took each clanking step forward. It seemed like a somewhat precarious situation, but even after only a week's practice using his new lower limbs, it was already clear that he was becoming more agile with their use with every passing day.

Even though he had managed to find a mechanized solution to make up for the loss of his legs, Stanton felt as if the man's personality had also been burned away in the blaze that had destroyed the Darby mansion, and there was no prosthetic that could replace it. Hughes had previously been quick to anger and always looking for confrontation—now he was quiet and grim.

Alexander didn't miss the challenges and confrontations, but whatever transformation the man he had once called Iron-Clad had gone through in the flames, he was convinced that it wasn't for the better.

He looked up to see Hughes staring at him. "Will that work for you, Stanton?" The face was an emotionless mask.

Alexander hesitated for a second, letting his thoughts come together. He had always considered himself to be a man of focus and action, but lately he found himself easily distracted, his thoughts constantly headed in ten different directions at once.

He wondered how the others regarded him, since. "That's a very good idea." He stood up from his chair and walked up to the candidate. Chadwick was clearly nervous at having the two Paragons examining him so closely.

"So, Hephaestus," said Alexander, drawing out the name as he pretended to examine the equipment with authority, "what else do you think we could do for him if he joined us?"

Hughes's frame clanked as he walked around him, small wisps of fortified steam released from the hips with each step. "Hydraulic?" he snapped at the man. "Kept under pressure?"

"V-valves," the man replied, stammering slightly. His eyes darted back and forth between them. "The central canister powers all the heads separately."

"You considered a single snake?" Hughes stopped right behind him. The legs leaned forward and he hung halfway out of the chassis, leaning hard against the ribs. He looked intently at the equipment.

"I did, but I was concerned at what might happen if the liquids were to combine. The acid and the fuel are both highly volatile."

"Yes, you'd want a reliable valve," Hughes replied in an absentminded tone. He paused for a moment, and then made a rhythmic clicking sound against his teeth.

Stanton tapped one of the snakes that lay flush against Prescott's shoulder. "And he wouldn't be much of a hydra, would he?"

"Yes, er . . . no," Chadwick responded with a shake of his head.

"I'm sure that we could make improvements," Hughes said, "but your basic design seems sound enough, if overly simplistic to be useful in battle. If damaged . . ."

"I can fight with my fists if that's a problem." He had directed the answer at Hughes, but it was Stanton who responded.

"It's not a problem, Chadwick. And yes, a man needs more than fancy gadgets to win a fight. But it isn't his fists that turn the tide—it takes bravery and nerves of steel."

He could see the man's brows knitting underneath his mask. "Are you accusing me of something, sir?" His nervousness has been replaced by an air of indignation.

"No need to get angry." Alexander gave him a quick smile. "And it's good to see that you're capable of defending yourself when challenged. I think you have great potential." He paused for a moment before continuing. He actually liked the man on some level, but the Paragons were supposed to be the best of the best. They couldn't take just anyone, and this man seemed only half baked . . .

"I think we've seen enough for today, Mister Prescott. You've given us a great deal to think about." Alexander nodded at the door. "Thank you very much for showing us what you can do. We'll let you know our decision as soon as possible."

The Hydraulic-man nodded his head. "Thank you all very much," he said as he left, but the tone in his voice wasn't a happy one.

As soon as the door had closed, Nathaniel spoke. "I'm not sure, but I'm getting the sense that William didn't like him."

Alexander grimaced. "Is that what it was, Bill?"

Hughes clanked his way back over to the table, then lifted his head. "I think we're learning that the game is changing." The look in his eyes was terrifying, as if he was holding back an avalanche with sheer force of will. "Since the death of Darby, this has become a war. You've fought in a war, Stanton, you know what that means." Again he started to suck on his teeth, and then let out a click. It was an annoying habit that seemed to have come with his new persona.

"I do, Bill. But our goal has always been to prevent destruction. Even if we are at war, it's still our duty to protect the innocent."

"First you have to protect your own." He turned to face Nathaniel. "Isn't that right, Turbine?"

The young Paragon reached up to touch the back of his head where the battle with the Automaton had left a permanent scar, but said nothing.

Instead, Grüsser broke the silence in his usual clumsy way. "Vell, if anyone cares to know vat I zink, I liked him."

"I like him as well, Grüsser, but this isn't a popularity contest." Alexander turned to the other men at the table. "The man clearly needs more time to come into his own. We can put it to a vote once we've seen all the candidates . . . Let's take a moment to gather our thoughts and then we'll see King Jupiter."

He turned and pointed to the still-burning shrubbery. "And can we get someone to please put that out?"

Chapter 2

A Tale of the Heart

When she had first undertaken to run away from her life as a young lady of society, Sarah had steeled herself to the fact that however challenging she imagined the world outside of the Stanton mansion might be, the reality would be worse. And yet no amount of preparation had managed to stop Sarah from still finding herself regularly driven to the verge of tears by the random cruelties that the world seemed determined to inflict on her.

It wasn't that anything in *particular* was more difficult than she had expected. In the case of work, for instance, Sarah had never been one to shy away from hard labor. It was that simply *everything* seemed to be more complicated than she could have ever imagined: cooking, cleaning, shopping, working, and even simply getting around town, were an endless cycle of effort and time—made all the more difficult by the fact that every penny needed to be counted before it was spent.

But this morning she had made a vow to stop the tears, and today it seemed something had changed; from the glorious sunrise to the golden hue of the early evening, this fine spring day had conspired to show her that life could occasionally offer possibilities beyond toil and failure. Perhaps the world wasn't always as full of doom, gloom, and strife as she had begun to fear.

Her father had often scolded Sarah that she was clueless when it came to money, but as she walked up the street toward her house with her salary in her purse and a smile on her face, she was sure that she had gained a much deeper understanding of finance now that she was forced to earn every penny, rather than simply having had them placed into her hands by a servant.

Her entire week's wages were now less than she would have once spent on a single piece of fine French ribbon, but considering how perilously close she had come to being destitute in the first few weeks of life on her own, the paper in Sarah's pocket now seemed like a fortune. And it would be good to finally be spending money without draining away the last few dollars that remained in her bank account.

Her time at the department store had been no less demanding today than it had been on any other day. Sarah was still constantly at the beck and call of women who seemed to think that she was there to be abused at their pleasure, but she had given a smile to the shy boy who cleaned up in the restaurant on the ground floor, and later he had handed her a good-sized slice of roast chicken wrapped in wax paper. And when she had gone to buy a sugar cookie, the friendly old man at the pastry counter had demanded that she take an éclair as a present for simply "blessing an old man with the pleasure of her company."

It all made Sarah blush to think about it, but at least she wasn't an old maid yet . . .

As Sarah climbed her front stoop, the sun peeked out from the clouds, bathing her in a sudden feeling of warmth. She stopped to bask in it, and felt a wave of joy wash over her. For an instant she felt so good it made her want to burst into song, but she decided it might be better to simply hum instead. There were still so many tasks to do, but things were finally looking up!

Reaching the landing, Sarah slipped her key into the lock of the front door. Her building wasn't anything special, but it was clean and relatively bright. Compared to the dark, dingy holes that some of the other girls had told her they lived in, Sarah had begun to think of her little tenement as positively palatial.

As the door swung open she was greeted by the strong scent of whitewash. A fresh coat had been painted onto the hall just a few days ago, and despite the strong odor the whole place seemed more bright and cheerful for it.

It seemed that the owners had recently been seized with a fit of pride in the place, and they had been adding a number of improvements, including cleaning up the halls and putting in window boxes under the front-facing eaves. Sarah was already imagining that perhaps she could use hers to grow a few fresh herbs once the weather warmed up a bit, although beyond sticking the seeds into some dirt and pouring water on top of them she had little idea how that would be accomplished.

Normally after a long day on her feet she felt like the only thing she had the energy left for was collapsing onto her bed, but Sarah seemed to float up the stairs today. When she reached the third floor, she ran down the hallway towards her door as fast as she could, eager to get a chance to eat her dinner before the remaining sunlight vanished behind the rooftops.

She had already reached a hand into her purse, and had begun to pull out her key when she saw that someone had placed a large iron padlock on the door. The tune she was humming died on her lips as she looked up to make sure that this was indeed her apartment. The painted number nine on the door left no doubt about it; someone had locked her out of her home.

Trying not to let an obvious mistake ruin her day, Sarah put her shopping bag down in front of her door, took a deep breath to clear her head, and headed back down the stairs to the superintendent's room. Her feet felt decidedly heavier than they had on the way up.

Arriving back at the ground floor, she rapped lightly on the door to the superintendent's apartment. There was no reply.

She gave a harder knock, this time using enough force to make the door rattle in its frame. "Mr. Grieves?" she said loudly, "It's Susan from 309!"

She could hear the sounds of someone stirring in the apartment. She rapped again, still harder, and this time was rewarded with a mumbled shout, "Just a minute!" After a few seconds there was the clank of a bolt being pulled back, and a small crack opened between the door and the frame.

The man who peered out at her was quite disheveled and was wrapped in a tattered silk robe of red and black. The long whiskers on his face were not only uneven but contained numerous unidentifiable crumbs trapped in the patches of hair. He looked up at her through red-rimmed eyes. "Whatcha want?"

"I hope you could help me," she said, trying to retain a bright and positive tone. "I think there's been a mistake."

He licked his lips, and then opened his mouth with a terrible, wet smacking sound that made Sarah think of someone kissing a frog. Not content to do it once, he made the noise a few more times before he started to speak. "And what kind of mistake would that be, Miss Standish?"

"It's my apartment. I'm afraid that someone has put a padlock on the door and I'm locked out." She gave him the best winsome smile she could muster under the circumstances. "I don't suppose you could get the key and open it up for me?"

"No mistake there, Miss," he said and then slipped his left hand down into the pocket on the front of his robe. The pouch lay right over the top of his potbelly, and when he lifted up his fingers, the sound of jingling keys rose up from it as if they were laughing at her. "Mrs. Brooks is planning to sell the building to the church, and she don't want the priests seeing fallen women hanging around, so she's throwing you out."

Sarah understood what the words meant, but it took a moment for her to fully comprehend everything that had been implied in Mr. Grieves's sentence. She felt a flush of anger as she realized that her perfect day now had a large crack running straight down the middle of it. "Fallen Woman?" she said, the tone of her voice rising in both volume and pitch as she spoke. "That's *my* apartment Mr. Grieves, paid for through the middle of this month!"

"Ain't none of my business, I'm afraid," he said, shaking his head sadly, as if he was somehow sympathetic to her situation but helpless to take any action to actually improve it. "Me, I just do what I'm told." He started to shut the door. "You want to argue about it, take it up with Mrs. Brooks."

Sarah could see that her window of opportunity was also about to close with the door, and inserted her boot into its path. Wood hit leather with a thump. "Now see here," she said, her voice taking on the commanding tones that she could remember her mother using when she ordered the servants around, "all the things in the world of any value to me are in that room—in *my* room—and I won't let you steal them because some old biddy has decided to try and impress the clergy!"

Grieves gave the door an exploratory pull, determining that he had indeed been effectively stopped from closing it, before responding. "I don't care about your *things* one way or the other. I was told to lock it up and I did." He pulled on the door again, harder this time, still looking surprised that it wouldn't simply smash her foot. "If you could please move, Miss."

"I won't!" Sarah replied sternly, managing to somehow wedge the boot even a little further in.

Realizing that the door was going to remain open, he took the opportunity to take a long look at Sarah from top to bottom. "You seem like a *nice* young lady . . . pretty, too. And things being what they are, perhaps we could work something out between us."

Sarah knitted her brows together, wondering if what he seemed to be implying was what the man was actually trying to say. "Now see here . . ." she began softly, fully intending to unleash her outrage by the time she reached the end of the sentence.

Instead, Mr. Grieves cut her off. "Don't matter anyway. Mrs. Brooks was very clear about all of it, and there's nothing I can do no matter what. She said she'd get you your rubbish in due time, so why don't you toddle off and talk to her?"

Sarah could feel the heat rising up into her cheeks. A little anger might be useful, but she didn't want to unleash the full Stanton temper on the man unless she was given no other choice, as it left little opportunity for retreat. "Clearly sir, you don't know me very well. It may be that you can lock me out, but I know that I have *some* rights, and if you don't get up there and open the door for me this very minute I shall be forced to call the police!"

"The police?" The grizzled man chuckled and nodded condescendingly. "You go ahead and give those greedy bastards a call, and then we'll find who has the deeper purse. I'm guessing it isn't a delicate little harlot like yourself!"

Fantasizing for a moment, Sarah let herself imagine the look on the old lecher's face if she called on her father to throw this giggling simpleton out onto the street. The Industrialist would follow that by breaking down the door to her apartment with a single swift kick. Then, all sins forgiven, they would take her things and go back to the mansion. Sarah would return to a soft, clean bed and a comfortable life . . .

She pushed the thoughts out of her head. It was a delicious dream, but still a fantasy. The life she had known was gone for good, and her powerful father with it.

Her next option was to call Grieves's bluff and actually contact the police, but the truth was, from what little contact she'd had with the constabulary in the last few months, the man was most probably right—in New York, justice was something that seemed inevitably to go the way of the highest bidder.

Grieves scowled, allowing some of the looser crumbs to escape from his beard. "Are we done here? I'd like to get back to my dinner."

Sarah felt her frustration rising. Maybe she couldn't call her father, but she could at least summon the Stanton *spirit*. Leaning backwards, she raised her hand up to her brow, as if she were feeling faint. It was hardly uncommon for a woman under stress to become woozy, and as she expected, the superintendent relaxed the pressure to allow her foot escape, and to perhaps prepare to assist a damsel in distress.

Taking advantage of the moment, she leaned forward and rushed the door, bursting it open and throwing the man off his feet.

As he tumbled backwards, his hand came up from his pocket in an attempt to steady himself. Looped around the index finger of his left hand were the keys that he had been mocking her with a minute before.

Sarah grabbed his wrist, managing to steady him just before he tipped so far over that he would have crashed to the ground, then plucked the key ring off of him. It made a jingle as she slipped the metal circle over her wrist.

The superintendent's red eyes were wide open now, clearly in shock that this tiny, unassuming girl not only had managed to steal away his keys, but had also become the only thing keeping him suspended above the ground. "Leave me alone!" he howled.

"You mean, let you go?" she responded with a satisfied smile. Her perfect day had been *ruined* by this man, and Sarah was fighting off an urge to punish him not only for his own sins, but for all the other slights she had been forced to endure over the last few weeks. But she recognized that would not only be unladylike, it would be un-*Paragon*-like. With a grimace, she hauled him back to his feet.

His balance restored, Mr. Grieves hunched over and stared at her out of the corner of his eye. "You've gone mad!" He looked like a whipped dog, trying to play for sympathy now that the tables had turned. "Don't kill me!"

"What a pathetic bully you are, Mr. Grieves. I won't hurt you."

"Mrs. Brooks was right! You're a whore and a monster!"

The name-calling made the anger rise up in her, and for a moment Sarah's vision seemed to disappear behind a curtain of red. When it cleared an instant later, her hand was already up in the air, only a moment away from slapping the rudeness out of him. Grieves responded by cowering, letting out a rabbitlike shriek as he wrinkled up his nose with fear.

For a moment Sarah stood there frozen, her mind split in two. One half of her was angry and out of control, the other half stood watching in terror and disbelief at what she was about to do. For an instant the darker forces won, and she raised her hand up higher. Grieves dropped down to his knees, placing his arms over his head to protect himself from the rain of blows that was sure to come.

"No," she said out loud, and lowered her hand. Sarah had stopped herself, but only barely.

But if she couldn't beat this little tyrant who had stolen away her perfect day, at least she'd put the fear of God into him. "You said it yourself, Mr. Grieves—the police only care about money. And while I'm sure you'd be happy to pay them to haul away the brute who beat you, once they saw it was a tiny little thing like me that had terrified you so, they'd be far too busy laughing to take your money."

Realizing that the expected blows weren't going to come, Grieves put down his arms and peered up at Sarah. His eyes narrowed and he opened his mouth wide, screaming at her through rotting yellow teeth. "Harpy! Demon! Trollop!" He balled his hands up into fists. "Get your things and get out!"

Sarah lifted her arm again and the old man flinched, but it was clearly less of a threat than it had been a moment ago. She backed through his door. "I won't be long."

As she walked up the first flight of stairs, the keys jangling in her hand, Sarah wondered how many other lone women there were in the building who might come to face the same unfair circumstance, but without the spine to stand up to the troll downstairs.

As she reached the first-floor landing, she walked down the corridor, using the stolen keys to unlock two padlocks she found there. On the second floor there were another two, and three on the fourth. Finally she undid the lock on her own door.

Picking up the sagging bag of groceries, she opened the door and looked inside her apartment. The space was the same as she had left it this morning —small, simple, tidy, and clean. The two rooms were sparsely furnished, with a large stove taking up most of the main room. The only furnishings she owned were a battered wardrobe that she had found on the street, a wobbly wooden table with a single chair, and a decent (if lumpy) straw-filled mattress that she had purchased the same day she had gotten the apartment, and so far seemed to have remained free of insects.

Sarah placed her bag down on the table and removed the parcel with the roast chicken. She cut the twine with a knife, and then pulled out one of her two plates, a cloth napkin, and her single fork, placing them all on the table to make a setting for herself.

Lastly she poured herself a glass of water into a chipped mug. She put it beside the plate and sat down at the table.

Sarah took a bite. The food was delicious, although she found it incredibly difficult to swallow. It seemed that there was a large lump in her throat. She took a sip of water and then spoke to the air. "Absolutely delicious," she remarked loudly and with exaggerated conviction.

Once the chicken was all gone, she sat quietly for a minute, breathing deeply until the urge to cry had passed. Giving her nose a blow into a piece of lace, she decided to save the éclair for later, then stood and brought the dirty dishes over to the tiny sink.

Looking up, she caught her reflection in the window, backed by the view of the grime-covered light well that had been built between the buildings. "Come on young lady, there will be no tears," she said, trying to summon up the ghost of her mother. "You're better than this. Now let's have an upright chin and a smile!"

"No tears," she repeated, more forcefully this time. Sarah wiped away the last tear with a damp hand, took a good long sniffle, and then nodded to herself before she turned around and walked to her tiny bedroom.

The space wasn't much bigger than the bed. And at the far end, beyond the small mattress, was a small, doorless closet. Pulling apart her meager collection of clothing that hung from the rod, she reached to the back wall and pulled out a section of the lath that she had sawed away. She had seen hideyholes like this one in Nathaniel's adventure books when they were children. Although it had always been the villains who had them in his books, Sarah also found it amusing to think of this as her own version of the secret chamber at the back of her father's office, where he kept the Industrialist's guns and costumes. But this space was only big enough to fit an old suitcase and a small rosewood box, and contained no secret passage to the outside.

The luggage rattled and thumped as she pulled it free and dragged it over to the battered kitchen table. She had purchased the leather case from the secondhand store. She had chosen the shop because it was so scandalous that she was absolutely sure she would never run into anyone she knew there, and so she frequented it often. There were often good bargains to be had if one had the patience.

Sarah unbuckled the luggage straps, and the brass hinges on the back squeaked as she flipped open the lid.

Inside was a large, hexagonal object wrapped up in paper and twine, surrounded by the different bits and pieces of her Adventuress costume along with a battered leather notebook. The garments were slightly wrinkled, unworn since she had taken off into the night after confronting her father. They were a reminder of the world she had left behind—probably forever.

Sarah put her hands around the paper bundle in the middle of the luggage and lifted it out. It was made of metal, and she winced slightly as she felt something inside of it shift around. For some reason the heart felt heavier now than when she had lifted it out from Tom's shattered body.

Sarah had tried using the key she wore around her neck to replace the one that Lord Eschaton had stolen, but Tom's metal heart had been badly damaged when he had fallen under Lord Eschaton's attack, and it had no effect.

And she had been a little relived by that: if, by some miracle, inserting the Alpha Element had brought Tom back to life, he would have awakened to find himself reduced to a shattered ruin. It would, she imagined, be a most painful and unpleasant existence to return to.

That was not to say that she had given up. Sarah had—discreetly, she hoped—brought the broken heart to a number of jewelers, hoping to find someone who might be able to help her repair it. But the few whom she had judged safe enough to show the object to had always asked the same question once they saw it: "What does it do?"

When she had explained to them that it would be impossible for her to tell them its function, most of them had replied that without such information there was nothing they could do. One had colorfully suggested that she use it as a paperweight.

But in the shop she had visited yesterday, she had finally been given a glimmer of hope. Rather than simply handing it back to her, the old man behind the counter had put his loupe up to his eye and taken a closer look. He had marveled at the precision work it contained, and then turned it around in his hand, giving puzzled looks at its shape. He told her it was like something out of a Jules Verne story—an object from the future.

"It doesn't look like it does much. Are you positive it isn't just meant to be a piece of art?" he asked her.

When Sarah had assured him that it was indeed an object with a purpose, he had hemmed and hawed a bit, but finally told her there was a man out in Brooklyn who might be able to help her. "He's a Frenchman, and a bit . . . well . . . mad, really," he had said. "I'm not sure that he could actually do anything. But if you're willing to take the trip out there to see him, his store is open Saturday afternoon . . ."

Sarah had assured him that she was, and that the jeweler, who also lived in Brooklyn, should let the Frenchman know that she would be taking the ferry out to see him in the late afternoon.

She had actually been given hope that someone could help her. The fact that he was available on her day off was one of the many things that had made today seem so miraculous—right up until she had found the padlock on her door.

Sarah hadn't visited Brooklyn since the disastrous events at the bridge, but part of her was quite excited to return. She had never ridden the ferry across the East River before, and even that journey was something she was quite looking forward to.

After giving it a final squeeze, Sarah placed the metal heart back into the suitcase and pulled out the leather-bound notebook. She ran her fingers over the image of a magnifying glass that had been embossed into the cover.

The journal had belonged to the Sleuth, and for the most part the notes in the book were as cryptic as Wickham himself had been. But it was the final scribble that she had spent hours poring over since she had lifted the book from the Automaton's shattered body: "Section 106—Darby had made Sarah's dream come true. Alexander lied."

Sarah had found a note in her father's closet with the same reference, and the Sleuth had clearly taken that clue and uncovered something more about it. Sarah frowned as she once again realized that she would never see

Wickham or Darby ever again . . . The shocking feelings of loss that came with the remembrance of their passing came less frequently now than they had, but the feelings had yet to diminish. In fact, their infrequency made them all the more intense.

She supposed that soon enough they would fade, and her memories of the old men would be like those of her mother—faded faces and a longing ache for a world that she could never return to.

Written in the pages above the note were a number of other cryptic scribbles including addresses and references to the Automaton's "ascendency." She knew that Darby had intended for the mechanical man to take over as leader of the Paragons after his death, and it was her father's own ambitions that had led to Tom's downfall and eventual destruction.

And somewhere out in the world there was still the unsolved mystery of what had become of the Automaton's other body. It had been the theft of that device from Darby's lab that triggered the events that had shattered Sarah's life.

A commotion in the corridor broke her concentration. She put the book back into the case and closed it before she stood up and walked to the apartment door. When she flung it open she found, as she had suspected, Mr. Grieves standing in the hallway. He had changed out of his robes and was wearing something almost respectable enough to be called clothing.

He was still stooped over, and obviously worse for wear from having dragged himself up three flights of stairs. He had collected the open padlocks on his way up, and they sat on the floor nearby.

Sarah tried to make herself look threatening. "What do you want?"

"I want you out of this building, trollop," he replied, shaking a fist at her.

"Well, I'm not leaving. I've paid up through the middle of the month. That's this next Thursday, and it's mine until then, no matter what either you or Mrs. Brooks have to say about it."

"And you'll have to take it up with the old lady. She's tougher than me, I can tell you that. But in the meantime I'll have my key ring back."

Sarah slammed the door shut without a word and went to the kitchen counter. The key ring was sitting there, and Sarah unscrewed the bolt and began to pull off the padlock keys, letting them clatter onto the table one by one.

When she had cleared them off the ring, Sarah closed it up again and opened the door. Grieves was standing right outside, and she was startled slightly to find him staring directly at her. "Here you go, Mr. Grieves."

He closed one eye so that he could get a better look at what it was that she had just handed to him. "You've stolen my . . ."

Sarah gave him a glare, and he scowled in return. "God will damn you for your wicked ways, Susan Standish."

Sarah tried not to smile when he said the false name she now lived under. She was fairly sure that pretending to be someone else was a damnable offense all by itself. But she had been to church often enough to know that no matter how grave her offenses, redemption still remained open to her.

"Give them back," Grieves said, holding up the ring and dangling it at her.

"I know that there are other girls in this building who would be equally upset to discover that Mrs. Brooks had an attack of extreme piety in the name of profit. I'm keeping them safe so she won't have to embarrass herself with an explanation." The shocked look on Mr. Grieves's face was, she had to admit, rather gratifying.

He stared at her, and then turned around. "Hellion, sinner," he muttered to himself. "Whore!" he spat out loud enough for her to hear. "We'll see what's what!"

"That's as may be," she yelled after him, "but I'd better not find another lock on my door when I return, or I'll be coming after you for those keys as well."

Sarah shut the door and slid the bolt closed. Her heart was beating hard in her chest, almost as forcefully as it had been after she'd faced Lord Eschaton and her father in the park.

She reached into her bag and pulled out the battered copy of the Louisa May Alcott book she had purchased from a street vendor on her way home. It was one she had read previously, and not one of her favorite stories, but at least it was something familiar, with a simple, bright view of the world that she could most definitely use at that moment.

"And the sun is still out," she said to herself as she opened the book and sat down in her kitchen chair. She might as well relax when she could. After all, tomorrow had every chance in the world of being worse than today.

Chapter 3

New Paragons to Consider

Although Nathaniel had already been somewhat impressed by the drawings and photographs that had accompanied his application, seeing King Jupiter in the flesh was still something to behold. The man was not only staggeringly tall, standing a few inches over six feet, he was also massive. His body seemed to have been constructed from something even more dense than flesh.

The costume that he wore was primarily purple, sewn from finely spun silk that had been woven with a golden thread that seemed to shimmer even in the cloudy light. The main portion of it had been constructed to form a single piece that buttoned down the back and sides in a close-fitting manner, along with a series of straps and panels that gave the whole thing a slight Oriental feeling as well.

The front was low cut, clearly intended to show off the muscles of his physique. They were insanely large, built up to almost comical proportions. At the neck, a collar sprouted up and back, circling his head in a manner that mimicked the hopelessly old-fashioned Regency style. But beyond that, it was covered with some kind of rich animal fur, and it gave him a sort of lion's mane, making him appear almost ludicrously regal.

As if that wasn't enough, sitting on the top of his head was a golden circlet, clearly intended to be a crown. Hanging down in front of it was a mask, also formed from gold, that completely covered his face. And at the bottom of it, carved into the metal, were rows of stylized ringlets. Nathaniel recognized them from ceremonial beards that had been used to denote royalty in ancient Mesopotamia. He had seen them when Mr. Stanton had taken him and Sarah to the American Museum of Natural History, years ago.

He smiled at the realization that the long, dull hours spent gaining an education *were* occasionally useful, just as his teachers had always told him they would be.

But there was, thought Nathaniel, something very wrong with the color of the man's skin. "Are you a negro, sir?" he blurted out, earning a harsh stare of rebuke from the Industrialist.

"We've barely even given him a chance to introduce himself, and already you're questioning the man's racial heritage?" Alexander shook his head and sighed. "I must apologize for the boy's rudeness, sir."

King Jupiter laughed. "No no, it's quite all right. The color of my flesh is something I've had to live with for a long time now." He lifted off his crown, revealing a bald head underneath. "I'm not embarrassed by it anymore." Like the rest of him, the skin was the color of black smoke, his eyes pure white. The features of his face were broad and heavy like someone of Saxon descent.

He walked up to the table and placed the golden crown in front of Nathaniel. "And the answer to your question young man, is no." His wide smile revealed a row of teeth that shone out so brightly against the darkness of his skin they seemed to glow, "I am not a negroid. My family was French aristocracy. The Revolution forced them to relocate to the United States or face the end of their bloodline by guillotine."

So much for his theories of Germanic heritage . . . Nathaniel looked at the headpiece. It was enormous. He reached out a hand to touch it, and then stopped. "Do you mind?"

Jupiter shook his head. "Not at all. Feel free."

When Nathaniel wrapped his hand around the metal circlet, it was warm to the touch. He lifted it up to feel the weight of it. "That's real gold, isn't it? It's heavy." And it was clearly too big to fit on his head.

"Shakespeare said, 'Heavy is the head that wears the crown.' But to be honest, you quickly get used to it."

Nathaniel looked up into his eyes, and the man held his gaze easily. He had to admit that even if Jupiter might not be a real king, he had the natural charisma of royalty—and the bloodline! "So then the color of your skin has something to do with the origin of your miraculous powers."

"If I may say so, you're as clever as I've been told, Mr. Winthorp." King

Jupiter stepped back a few feet and pulled off one of his thick purple gloves. Revealing the dark hand underneath, he held it out for Nathaniel to examine—the fingernails were moon white. "As you can see, my skin is normally gray in color, except for my eyes, teeth, and nails." He took his index finger and pressed it into the exposed skin on his chest. As he did so, white lines began to radiate outward from around his fingertip, creating an aura of crackling light. "But I can actually gather the energy under my skin, which turns it white." He pressed harder, and the field began to grow in size. "Until recently, I have to admit, it all came with unpredictable and rather painful results."

He slowly lifted up his finger, and as he drew it away, the energy jumped out from his flesh, crackling back and forth between his fingertip and the surface of his skin. But at the same time the circle was growing smaller, clearly being consumed by the sparks. "Over time I've begun to learn how to draw out and manipulate the energy." He moved his entire hand in a waving motion, and more white energy leapt out from his chest, turning his fingers entirely white and leaving behind a black spot on his torso.

He held out his hand for Nathaniel to view once again. Now it had turned white from the tips of his fingers down to the middle of his palm. "Having discovered these new abilities, my natural instinct was to explore how to channel them." He clenched his hand into a fist and squeezed it so tightly that it began to shake. White lines climbed up his arm until the entire limb had changed to a bright white, as if it were being lit from within.

"And seeing their power I wanted to know if I could do more than simply move the energy around within myself." As he pulled his fingers apart, lines of light danced between them, riding up and down like a Jacob's ladder. "Perhaps I could find a way to move it outside of my body, and use it in more *interesting* ways."

When he clenched his fingers, the energy crackled around the outside of his fist. He turned to face the blackened bush that the Hydraulic-man had ignited earlier. "With practice I began to discover that it is not only desire, but intent that allows me to control the lightning within my body."

King Jupiter knit his brow into a look of intense concentration, then he flung out his arm, releasing a blinding arc of lightning that leapt from his fingers to the bush. Nathaniel's eyes shut reflexively from the bright spark. When he opened them again, the shrubbery was once again on fire.

"No one likes that plant," Hughes said dryly.

The Industrialist was leaning back in his chair, and Nathaniel knew the next two words that his step-father was going to say before he even opened his mouth. He had heard them many times, growing up in the Stanton household. "Impressive," and then the caveat that always followed. "But," he said drawing out the word, "does it always take that long for you to be able to do that?"

"At first it did, but not anymore." He held up his hand in the air. The light was climbing up his arm into his hand, and the white lines rapidly snaking upwards filled the entire limb in a matter of seconds. "Since those early days of discovery I've begun to perfect my control."

King Jupiter whipped his arm forward to let loose another blinding bolt. This time a loud cracking sound followed the white light, and even with his eyes closed, Nathaniel could see the outlines of the flashing bolts of power.

When he opened them again, he saw that the bush had disappeared entirely. Only the stump remained, burning like a sad candle.

King Jupiter put his hand back down at his side. "I hope that proves there is at least one way that I might be an asset to the mighty Paragons."

Grüsser clapped his hands together. "A lightning man! I have never seen der like."

"Nor I," said Hughes. There was some enthusiasm in his voice, but it was hard to discern it from sarcasm in his tone. "You are a genuine marvel of the modern age."

Jupiter took a small bow. "Thank you very much."

Alexander looked down at the papers on his desk. "You've told us that the origin of your powers is related to your abilities, but your application doesn't mention where these miraculous powers have come from."

"No sir, it does not."

Nathaniel leaned forward now. "Would you care to enlighten us?"

There was a grim smile on his face. "It's an interesting story, I'll admit, but not one I'm planning on revealing to anyone today."

Stanton stood before he spoke. "You do understand that, if you are allowed to join us, we will be trusting you with our very lives. Certainly you can see how important it will be for us to know everything possible about the abilities of our allies? We must determine how they can provide us with both strengths and weaknesses."

"Yes, I can see how you might think that I wish to keep secrets from you, but it's not that." He coughed deeply to clear his throat. "It's simply that I have made promises to other men that I would not reveal their secrets. It is not myself that I'm protecting, but others who might be harmed."

"Hmmmph," Hughes interjected. "That seems highly convenient to me."

"Oh, leave him alone," Nathaniel said. "I'm sure that when it comes down to it, King Jupiter will tell us everything. You have all kept enough secrets from me."

"All right then," the Industrialist said, flipping over a page. "Your skin is supposedly 'impervious to most ordinary objects' and 'much like stone.' That all sounds very good, but just *how* impervious are you?"

"Am I impervious to bullets? Is that what you're asking?"

Alexander looked up at him. "There's no need to keep trying to second-guess my meanings, King Jupiter. Just answering the questions as I ask them will be fine."

"I'm sorry, Industrialist, but it's a question I've pondered myself. Perhaps a practical demonstration would be in order. I would be honored if you would participate . . ." He held out his hand palm-up and then flipped it over to point at the open space nearby. "If you don't mind."

"Not at all," Stanton replied, standing up.

Nathaniel got a sudden queasy feeling in the pit of his stomach. He didn't like where this was going. As far as he was concerned, King Jupiter had been behaving as a perfect gentleman, and Alexander Stanton seemed intent on proving himself to be a perfect ass. "Is this necessary?"

"Yes, I think it is."

"We'll need your weapons," Jupiter informed him.

The Industrialist's gun was slung over the back of his chair. Stanton picked it up and slid the harness on over his shoulders in a single, smooth motion.

He walked out from behind the philosopher's table and faced off against King Jupiter. "I assume that this was what you had in mind?" he said, holding up his gun.

Jupiter nodded as he began to open the buttons on the side of his costume, revealing more of the gray skin of his chest underneath.

"These aren't normal bullets."

"I would hope not," the gray man replied.

"And I can select the strength of my shots, within reason."

"Then I ask you pick something rational." The smile vanished from Jupiter's lips as he stared straight at Alexander. "As long as your goal is to test me, not to try to kill me."

"Quite right, sir." Alexander lifted up a leather flap on his belt. Revealing a dial underneath of it, he twisted it to the left. When he was done, he raised up his gun and pointed it directly at the gray man. "Are you ready?"

Nathaniel wanted to believe that King Jupiter had superhuman powers, but the idea that he could actually stop bullets with his flesh was utterly preposterous. But the man had suggested Stanton shoot at him . . .

"Are you ready?" Alexander asked again. As much as he wanted to stop what was clearly about to be an execution, Nathaniel found himself so excited by the prospect that the other man could actually survive a close-range attack from the Industrialist's weapon that he couldn't bring himself to move or speak.

For better or worse, the Paragons had, up until now, been primarily composed of men who used technology to augment their natural gifts. There had been a few villains with unexplainable abilities, and even heroes who claimed powers beyond mortal men, but if King Jupiter could do what he claimed, their world was about to change irrevocably.

King Jupiter's head was bowed in concentration, and on his chest there was a circle of white that began to grow bright and larger.

The Industrialist flexed his fingers and brought the gun to bear with a steady hand. "I asked if you're ready."

"Just another moment," Jupiter said with the sound of strain in his voice.

"You're either bulletproof or you aren't."

"Maybe . . . I just want . . . to give you a better . . . target," he grunted through gritted teeth.

"Alexander," Hughes interjected, "I think that we've taken this quite far enough."

Stanton didn't turn his head as he spoke, his eyes remaining fixed on his target. "I'm grateful for your opinion, William, but while I'm still the leader of the Society of Paragons, I believe that the final decision rests in my hands." A bead of sweat trickled out from underneath the Industrialist's mask and ran down his face.

"Are you ready *now?*" the Industrialist asked again, louder this time.

Nathaniel found himself swallowing hard as Jupiter looked up at them and lifted his right arm straight up into the air. His chest was pure white now, pulsing around the edges where it frayed off into lines of light. "Yes!"

The gun fired with a crack and a puff of steam. An instant later there was an explosion of light that filled the courtyard as a bolt of lightning shot up toward the sky from King Jupiter's outstretched hand.

This time Nathaniel hadn't closed his eyes quickly enough, and for a moment there was no color in the world, just a blinding contrast of pure white and the darkest black.

As the echo died off, it left behind a stunned silence as everyone blinked away the images that had been painted onto their eyes.

The quiet was broken by a rumbling sound that came up from King Jupiter's massive body. When it stopped, he dropped down to his knees as if someone had cut invisible strings holding his shoulders up. Slowly he brought his arms up over his head, and tipped forward onto the ground.

Nathaniel half rose from his chair, but the Industrialist had covered the distance before he could finish getting up. The rumbling started again, and, clearly concerned, Stanton knelt down in front of him as the sound grew louder. "Are you all right, sir?"

Jupiter lifted up his head to reveal a smile and the fact that the sound had been the beginnings of laughter. "Yes. *Quite* all right!"

Alexander rose up and took a step back, as if King Jupiter's good humor was some kind of infectious disease. "Good God, man, I thought I'd killed you!"

The gray man rose to his knees. "No," he tried but failed to stifle his whoops. "I feel totally alive!" He exhaled heavily and wiped his brow.

Finally getting his humor under control, King Jupiter continued, "I had a theory that I might be able to channel the energy of a bullet from movement into electricity."

"*Wunderbar!*" said Grüsser with a clap.

"What are you talking about?" Alexander snapped.

"Amazing!" Nathaniel said. "You hit him at point-blank range with a bullet, and he didn't move an inch! All its power was transformed into lightning!"

King Jupiter held his hand out toward Alexander. "The boy seems convinced, but what do you say? Will you let me join?"

"I say," Alexander sounded angry, and then he paused. Nathaniel knew just how stubborn he could be . . .

Stanton took a moment to look at his fellow Paragons. "I can see that I'd be outvoted, no matter what I thought." He reached out and lifted the man's hand up into the air, "So I say, welcome King Jupiter, the newest member of the Society of Paragons!"

Chapter 4
Crossing Over

Emilio slouched down into the hard wooden seat, his thumbnail jammed between his front teeth. He was surrounded by dozens of people, but his gaze was fixed on a single spot on the linoleum floor in front of him where a piece of it had worn away. *"Perchè qui?"* he mumbled to himself.

The only outward expression of his frustration was the rhythmic tapping of his foot on the floor. The tip of his leather shoe struck the ground precisely once per second, releasing a sharp snap that could be heard above the vibrations of the grinding of the ferry's steam engines as they chugged along, driving the massive ship across the East River.

Emilio was still youthful in appearance, although some of his soft edges had been worn away over the last half decade of his life, leaving behind the hard edges of an older man. But age had done nothing to make him any less handsome. His features were classic in the European sense, but under his nose was a mustache that had been groomed upward into a modern pair of delicate curlicues that landed on either side of his rather generous nose. His eyes were tipped with heavy brows, clearly comfortable being knitted together in intense concentration as they were at this very moment, although the left one rose slightly higher, giving him an unintentional look of surprise. Not too far above them, Emilio's hair sat black and straight on his head, chopped and shaved on the sides, the front of it pomaded back to reveal his high forehead.

His suit was made from brown worsted wool, well tailored, with the dark red vest brightened up by a incongruously sky-blue silk kerchief that stuck straight up from his pocket on a tower of starch.

With every few beats of his foot, he garnered the attention of another of his fellow passengers. Occasionally one would glance up, his tapping breaking them out of their own trances. They grimaced at him with weary looks of annoyance and disapproval, some angry, but others looking almost grateful for anything unusual or interesting that might distract them from the dull journey.

Emilio was a fellow traveler, but unlike most of them, the trip to and from Brooklyn was not one that he made every day, six days a week. The journey was still novel for him, although he had chosen to give his attention to the floor, and not the skyline that usually entranced the less regular passengers.

If he was aware of the attention he was getting, then he chose to ignore it, squinting his eyes so that he could focus even more deeply on the tiles in front of him, noting to himself how the wood that had been revealed underneath the worn linoleum was splintering from the unseen forces that had driven so many feet to focus their steps on that single spot.

After another half minute he began to suck on his thumb, alternating the "tick" of his shoe with a "titch" as his tongue rubbed against the nail.

"*Basta*, Emilio!" a female voice exclaimed, accompanied by a jab to his ribs. He jerked up and out from his reverie; the quick movement caused the large round sack at his side to fall over, landing with a clatter and a thunk on the floor.

Still dazed, Emilio turned to his sister. It seemed to take him a moment to recognize her, and then another to realize what it was that had just happened to him. When he had overcome the shock, he lifted up his hand and shook the back of his fist at her. "*Calma*, Viola!"

"*Calma* to you as well," she replied, slipping half into English, and spinning her hand back at him. "I've had more than enough of your brooding today," she told him in Italian.

"I'm not brooding." Emilio reached down for the bag. "I hope you didn't break anything."

"Me?" the girl replied, curling her mouth into an outlandish sneer that could only hide half of her smile. "I only break hearts, Emilio." Her lips, like the rest of her, were not so much large as luscious.

Taken one by one, every piece of Viola seemed like it shouldn't work: her nose was aquiline but oversized, her eyebrows black and rough, and her hair was a shining red. She was too round in some places, and too flat in others. But the way everything came together created something so uniquely exotic that she seemed to be able to make men all around her blush simply from the way everything moved when she walked. Viola Armando was beautiful was because she was constantly revealing herself to be more than just the sum of her parts.

Even those few males who claimed that they were immune to her physical charms seemed unable to completely prove their lack of interest when she engaged them with her full attention. The only living man who could genuinely claim to find no lust in his heart for Viola's almost painfully quirky beauty was her brother, Emilio, and he proved it by jabbing the blade of his hand hard into her ribs.

Viola gasped, squealed, and then jumped to the side, managing to shove her bottom into the man next to her. The codger let out a surprised harrumph from somewhere underneath his thick white whiskers.

"*Scuzi! Scuzi!*" she replied, and shifted herself back, using the momentum of her hips to nudge her brother just a bit.

Emilio shoved her back, sending her over into the old man's chair once more.

After letting out another grunt, the white-haired man turned to look at her, mouth open to unleash a tirade. But the moment he saw her, he stopped, clearly thunderstruck. "That's all right my dear," he mumbled by way of a reply, but having already apologized, Viola's attention had returned to her brother, whom she was berating in her native tongue.

"What are you thinking about that you have to annoy everyone on this boat with your tapping?" She waited only a moment for a reply before poking his shoulder with two fingers. "Eh? Eh? Or do I have to ask?"

"Why did you even make me go out there to see them? There was a line out the door, and I told you that they'd never talk to me."

"You said you wanted to be one of the Paragons. And they make money!"

"They *have* money!" He sighed. "There were dozens of men waiting there, and they didn't want some foreigner, they wanted a hero."

"Foreigners can be heroes!"

Emilio shook his head. "Maybe if you're English or German . . ."

"Why are you always looking for the reasons why *not*, Emilio? You're smarter than any ten of those idiots that were standing in the room."

"But I have no costume, just this." He tapped the bag next to him, and it let out a muffled clank in response.

Viola sighed, then grabbed his arm and rested her head on his shoulder. "In America you can be anyone you want to be. You just have to show them that you're the smartest man in the world!"

"You say that because you're my sister."

Viola tilted back her head and laughed, her curls falling back around her shoulders. As she glanced around the cabin, men's eyes darted back to their wives, or dived into their handkerchiefs and newspapers. "You know me better than that!"

Emilio smiled and rolled his eyes. "Perhaps I do."

"Anyway," she said, sliding her arm around his shoulders in a show of warmth that clearly made some of the people around them uncomfortable, "our money problems aren't as bad as you think, and if you did get that job, it would mean leaving me all alone in that junkyard all day."

"Ha! I'm sure by the end of the week you'd have charmed ten of our neighbors into building a whole new house for you."

"I don't know what you're talking about," Viola replied, batting her eyelashes with a look of mock innocence. "And anyway, I'm thinking that it isn't only the Paragons that have you feeling sorry for yourself."

"Maybe, maybe not." He tried to keep his tone light, but the darkness in his mind felt like the beginning of a storm that had already begun to pull in memories best left forgotten.

"It's been many years now, Emilio. If you could let yourself move on it wouldn't mean that you loved them any less."

He turned away from her and stared out through the dirt-smeared windows behind him. Outside, New York was sliding by, the buildings clearly outlined in the yellow light of the late-afternoon sun. "I don't like the way this city looks."

"We've come a long way from Tuscany, brother."

"Too far, I think."

"There's no going back now."

"Not for me anyway."

Viola frowned, then jumped up from her seat, spun around, and took his hand. "Come on, Emilio. Let's go look at the engines. You can tell me all about how poorly made they are."

He stood up and grabbed the round sack by the two thick leather handles along the top. "Which only shows you never listen to me! Those engines are beautiful, it's the lack of maintenance! Americans always build amazing machines, then hand them over to inattentive barbarians who let them rot. It's a wonder anything in this country still runs at all."

Now it was her turn to roll her eyes. "That's because Americans have better things to do than fall in love with hunks of metal."

"America invents everything and cares for nothing!" he replied defensively, and fell back into his seat. "The world is doomed!"

"You're doomed to be an idiot." She started to pull him up and off the chair. "What would fix *you* is a woman—someone pretty who can listen to your horrible whining so that your sister can get on with her life."

"I'm protecting the world *from* you!" But Emilio had already relented, and he allowed himself to be dragged along behind his sister, a smile on his face. Going down to the engine room might not be such a bad idea after all.

On the other side of the cabin, his eyes landed on a site that took his thoughts away from machines entirely.

Most people on the boat wouldn't have bothered to notice the young lady. She was wearing an unassuming shopkeeper's dress, and a simple black hat covered most of her hair, but Emilio could see that a few blonde ringlets had slipped free from underneath of it. To him they spoke of a mystery that he would love to solve.

The woman's head was turned downward, and she clearly trying to avoid the attention of anyone around her. Her desire to hide her face only made her more enticing.

His curiosity was rewarded when the blonde girl finally turned her head toward him, revealing a mouth fixed in a frown so sad, delicate, and truthful that it made him catch his breath.

Emilio slowed, and then stopped in his tracks, his arm quickly rising up to cover the distance between himself and his sister, who was still marching forward with his hand in hers.

There was something about the girl that seemed familiar . . . But if he'd met her before, he couldn't quite place when, where, or how.

Clutched against her chest was a battered brown suitcase. She held onto it in a way that made Emilio imagine that it must contain the most important thing in the world.

He could feel Viola's fingers tearing away from his as he stood and stared, his mouth slightly open. His eyes followed the blonde girl as she opened the far cabin door. She stopped for a moment, looking wistfully at something up above them, and then slipped up the stairs.

Once again he felt a jab in his side, but this time he didn't jump. "What's the matter with you?" Viola said to him with frustration in her voice. "Are you losing your mind?"

He turned to his sister and smiled. "I'm fine. Let's not go to the engines," he said as he pulled on his coat. "I have a better idea! Follow me!"

They stepped outside, where the chill spring air was a shocking contrast to the humid warmth of the passenger cabin. "Where are we going?"

Emilio looked around, trying to see what it was that must have interested the girl. When he looked up and out in front of the ship, he saw it. *"Ponte di Brooklyn!"* he said, pointing up at the massive bridge standing a few hundred yards ahead.

"Since when do you care about bridges more than engines?" Viola asked with annoyance in her voice.

"Let's go," he said, and began to scamper up the metal stairs.

"Idiot," Viola muttered in English as she lifted up her dark velvet skirts and followed her brother.

When they reached the top deck, they found only a few rugged souls who had decided to brave exposure to the chill weather on their journey down the East River—foolhardy tourists, parents with over-curious children, a few old men taking an impromptu constitutional, an artist with sketchbook in hand, and the blonde-haired girl. None of them seemed to be happy with their choice.

Viola tracked her brother's gaze to the girl. "Now I know what it was that got you up here. It is nice to see you didn't leave your manhood back in Italy, but really, Emilio, she's far too skinny for you."

He frowned. "Hush or she'll hear you!"

"Do you think that little thing speaks Italian?" she said with a laugh. "Girl! Look over here!" she said, raising her voice. "My brother has fallen in love with you!"

No one bothered to glance their way, and if anything the girl made a concerted effort to ignore them.

Emilio thought it must have been the bridge that she had come up to look at, but as they passed beneath the steel girders of the unfinished structure, the blonde girl's gaze moved around and faced behind the boat. Whatever she saw there had clearly shocked her. He saw the word *no* forming soundlessly on her lips, the same in either language. "Impossible," was what she said out loud.

When he turned around to see what had caused the girl to react with so much fear, he saw a black object hanging in the sky behind them.

It was round, with a ribbon of black smoke trailing out of the back of it. "*La mongolfiera!*" he said loudly, pointing it out for his sister to see, although it was unusual enough that it seemed almost impossible that *anyone* would miss it.

It was moving rapidly, heading directly toward them, and after a few seconds Emilio could make out two large propellers sticking out from either side, pushing it in their direction at rapid speed.

The blonde girl seemed frozen in place, unable to decide what she should do. She had already pushed herself back to the railing, and there was nowhere else for her to go. She looked down at the case and clutched it even more tightly to her chest.

She stood up and bolted toward them, clearly intent on heading down the stairs. Emilio and Viola were standing directly in her way.

He looked into the girl's eyes, hoping to catch her attention. The girl was clearly terrified, but there was also a determination in her gaze that he couldn't help but admire. His heart skipped a beat, and Emilio knew it wasn't just admiration that her beauty had triggered inside of him. If she was in trouble, surely they could help.

"Excuse me," she said, her tone clearly hovering between desperation and frustration. "I need to go downstairs."

"You need help, pretty lady?" Like almost every time that he tried speak to someone in English, Emilio found himself regretting the attempt an instant after the words came out of his mouth. He may not have ever been a poet or an orator, but at least when he spoke to someone in Italian they didn't give him a look as if they had just met the world's first talking horse.

But the blonde woman didn't seem to notice his terrible grammar, or anything about him except that he was in her way. "No, no thank you," she replied, shifting to one side and then the other, clearly trying to find a path between the siblings that would let her escape down the stairs. But Emilio and Viola had created an impenetrable wall.

"Are you afraid of the baloney?"

This time his words did get the look he had expected. "What are you talking about?"

"Baloney!" Emilio replied, pointing up at the sky for emphasis. They had almost completed their journey past the Brooklyn Bridge now, and even though the black ship was going above the cables, it had also moved appreciably closer to them.

Viola shook her head. "It's called a *balloon*, you idiot!" Maybe it had been because she was younger than he was, or because she'd spent more time actually talking to people and not working on machines, but since their arrival, Viola's English had quickly become much better than his. "Now, lady," his sister said to the girl in a tone shockingly reminiscent of their sainted mother, "maybe me and my horse's ass of a brother can help you with whatever is bothering you."

"You can get out of my way!" the girl yelled, and then dove toward them with an outstretched hand. The startled siblings parted, and she stumbled down the stairs.

"We sorry, miss! Please let's help you!" Emilio shouted after her, but if she understood his words, they didn't slow her down.

From somewhere in the sky above them there came a chuffing sound, as if a gigantic locomotive had started to move. A second later, the ship rocked as a large metal harpoon sank through the surface of the top deck with a screech of tearing metal. Screams rose up from the people on the deck around them, and after another moment passed, Emilio could hear muffled shouts of terror coming from the passenger compartment below.

Looking at the lance that had penetrated the ship, Emilio could see a thick cable that ran out from the back of it. It trailed away in an arc that led all the way up to the balloon in the sky above them. The wire lay slack for a moment, and then tightened up with a thrumming sound. The deck jerked underneath his feet, as the ship slowed down from the effort of dragging the balloon behind it.

He looked up to the ship in the sky. It was continuing to move closer. Clearly there was some sort of mechanical winch on the other end rapidly winding it down toward them.

Emilio tried to think about what he should do next. His peaceful afternoon ride back to Brooklyn had been turned into an assault, and the beautiful blonde girl who had captivated his attention was at the center of it.

Emilio had been caught in the middle of a battle before, and experience had taught him that the best way to stay alive when such things occurred was to try to gather enough information to remain one step ahead of whomever—or whatever—was trying to kill you.

Now that it was coming closer, he could see that the balloon was larger than he had imagined. The steaming gondola that hung directly underneath the massive gasbag was easily the size of a small house.

The balloon dropped altitude, lowering the angle on the wire, and a man climbed out of a hatch, working his way down to the nose of the gondola. When he reached the end, he attached something to the metal wire and jumped.

"Out of the way sir!" screamed a voice behind him, and a forceful hand shoved him up and away from the stairs, pushing Emilio in one direction, and Viola in another.

A group of seven men boiled up from the stairway and onto the deck. The leader was a policeman, and four uniformed members of the boat's crew followed. The final two were a pair of burly fellows who simply seemed to have decided to lend their fists to the fight against whatever it was that had attacked the ship.

The policeman brandished a gun, and the rest of the men were holding different objects clearly intended to be used as clubs. Some of the crewmen were stained with blood, a sign of the carnage that must be occurring below the deck, where the harpoon had pierced the ship.

The men charged into action. The two civilians immediately began trying to free the ship while the crewmen began directing the women and children down the stairs to safety.

Emilio looked up at the man who was rapidly descending towards them from the balloon. Whatever device he had attached to the wire, it clearly had some kind of brake built into it, and it was letting off an impressive shower of sparks as he slid down toward the boat.

Emilio pointed and shouted. "He's coming to us!"

The policeman looked upward at his yell. He pointed his revolver up at the figure, and there were five quick cracks as the bullets fired. If any of them hit their intended target, they didn't do any visible damage to him.

The policeman brought down the gun and began to reload it. "Let him come," he said with a well-practiced voice of authority, "we'll deal with him when he land—" An instant later, he collapsed to the deck, a thick silver rod sticking out of his neck.

"Emilio, watch out!" Viola grabbed her brother's hand and pulled him backwards. Losing his balance, he dropped his bag and stumbled down the steep stairs, barely managing to grab the rail before crashing to the lower deck. Viola, who had always been far stronger than she looked, grabbed him around the waist and tried to stop his fall.

Emilio found himself slammed backwards into an iron support beam by the weight of his sister. It crushed the air out of his lungs, and as he gasped for breath he felt a moment of pure terror, his heart feeling like it would explode out of his chest.

From up above them there was a series of whistling noises and a rhythmic "thunk, thunk, thunk" across the surface of the deck. It was followed by the screams of men in pain.

As Emilio's lungs attempted to rediscover their ability to breathe, the scent of gunpowder reached his nostrils. For a moment he contemplated flinging himself and his sister over the side of the boat, plunging into the cold, black waters of the East River to free himself from his terror. But he had to know what had happened to the girl . . .

It took a few seconds before he could once again draw in a decent lungful of air. As the ability to breathe returned, the terror began to pass, although he could still feel his hands shaking from the surge of adrenaline that had just passed through him.

"C'mon, Emilio!" Viola grabbed his arm and tried to pull him further down the stairs. "We need to go!"

Without a word, he tugged his arm free and marched back up. When he reached eye-level with the deck, he could immediately tell that things had gone very poorly for the seven would-be heroes.

Scattered across the deck were small steel rods that stuck up like shining porcupine quills. Most of them had landed without striking anything more than pitch or wood, but that left plenty to pierce human flesh, and they had done their work with grisly efficiency. Every man who had remained on the deck was dead or dying.

Before he could stop himself, Emilio scanned around to see if any of the women and children had been killed, but the innocents seemed to have escaped without harm. He felt blessed—if he had witnessed that kind of tragedy, he might not have been able to go on.

Standing over the bodies of his victims was the grizzled figure who had travelled down the wire. He was dressed in a worn tweed greatcoat, with a battered old kepi cap pulled down tight on his head.

The most striking thing about him was the machinery he wore: both his arms were encased in metal tubes. The one on his right ended in a menacing steel barb.

The frame on his left covered the entire limb down to the hand. It ended in a circle of metal that contained a series of holes that appeared to have fired the metal quills. Strapped to his back was a complicated device that provided the power for the machinery. Emilio found himself admiring its design.

Even though he had always been interested in the Paragons, Emilio had never seen one of New York's legendary villains in the flesh before. In the last few years there had been fairly few actual attacks—until Darby's death. And this particular villain was clearly Bomb Lance, the very man who had killed the Paragons' leader . . .

"Not so fast, lad." The Irish accent was thick, but he clearly had a far better command of English than Emilio ever would. When Emilio looked up, he saw that the villain's gleaming harpoon was aimed straight at him.

Emilio waved a hand at him and took a step back. "I sorry. I no problem." For once he was grateful for his poor speech. Perhaps sounding like an idiot would gain him some sympathy.

"No problem, eh?" the man said, waving the harpoon at him. "Then what's in the bag?"

"Here?" he said, "Is nothing. Ahhhhh . . ." he held onto the end of the word as long as he could, trying to use the time to not only come up with a suitable excuse, but to put it into words that the Irishman would understand. "Is my family."

"What does that mean?"

"Is Pica-tures." He sent up a little prayer that his sister wasn't in earshot. If she heard the nonsense he was spouting, surviving might not be worthwhile after all.

"Why don't you show me yer 'pica-tures.'"

"Isa okay then, yes? I go." As Emilio took another step back, the man's left arm rose up and fired a single metal quill. It landed in the ground a foot in front of Emilio's feet.

"Not okay, wop. You stay." The sound that rose up out of the Irishman was the rasp that served him as laughter. Emilio noticed that black smoke was leaking out from the hole that had fired the metal rod. "Now let's see."

Emilio dropped the bag to the deck. It let out a metallic clunk. The look on the other man's face turned more serious. "That don't sound like pica-tures to me."

He knelt down, wondering how long he'd be able to keep playing the fool before the Irishman decided to simply shoot him and get it over with. "No. Is okay! Is box! I show you!" He pulled the handles apart and reached inside.

"I'm looking for a girl," the Irishman continued. "Blondie with pale skin." The man took a deep breath and spat. "Did you see her?"

"A blondie? I no understand." But it wasn't hard to conclude that the girl the villain was looking for was the same one who had caught his attention earlier. If she knew that this man was coming for her, it was clear why she had fled with such determination—it would have been obvious that Emilio's abilities as a protector were sorely limited against such a man.

"A blondie," he said, pointing up at his hair.

Emilio's hand groped down into the canvas bag. His fear was so pure now that it felt like time itself had stopped—this would be his only chance.

It wasn't much of a plan, and even then there were a million tiny things that could go wrong. But as his hand found the cool brass grip at the bottom of the bag, Emilio breathed a sigh of relief. Finally something had gone right today.

"Hell, I'm all out of patience," the Irishman said. He raised his left arm, clearly preparing to fire.

Emilio pulled his trigger finger tight, releasing the mechanism. There was a rough popping of cloth as the bag shredded, destroyed from within by the razor-sharp plates that were spinning open inside it.

That sound was immediately followed by the loud "tunk" of metal against metal as the rod that had been fired directly at Emilio's chest instead impacted with steel. The force of the attack was still enough to knock him off his feet and throw him backwards. He landed rudely on a puddle of something wet and sticky.

"Now, that's something new," the Irishman said, moving closer. "And pretty, too."

Emilio held the shield up in front of him, peering over its edge. The device was constructed from a series of fan-shaped plates that spiraled around a center spindle and then locked together to form a solid metal barrier. The surface of each one was etched with ornate floral patterns that caught the light and made the polished steel glimmer and shine. The device had been crafted with as much artistry as Emilio could put into it—inspired by the creations of Sir Dennis Darby, he had intended it to be as much a piece of art as it was a weapon. But its aesthetic perfection had already been ruined by a large dent from the steel rod. It would now be unable to close with the same elegance that had managed to open it a few seconds before.

The Bomb Lance fired again without warning. The rod whistled past Emilio's head, then careened off the railing before it spun off into the river.

Emilio's best option was retreat, and he used his feet to shove himself backwards toward the stairs. Then there was a shocking jolt of pain in his leg: the Irishman had stuck the barb of his long harpoon directly into his calf. Emilio refused to let out a scream.

"Now I've got yer attention," he said, pulling the point out from his flesh. "Tell me about the blonde girl."

"I no know the blondie."

"If that's true, it's going to get very bad for ya very quickly." He raised his harpoon and pointed it directly at Emilio's chest. "Now I'll ask ya one more time, and if ya tell me no again, I'm going to stick this lance someplace that yer not gonna like. So, if ya know where the girl is, and I think ya do, ya should tell me."

"She's right here." It was a woman's voice, and it came from behind them. Emilio looked up, expecting to see the blonde girl from earlier. What he saw instead was a vague female form swaddled in layers of leather and cloth, a black mask over her face.

The Irishman breathed out what sounded like a sigh of relief, and a smile spread across his face. "Ah. There you are, Miss Stanton," he said as he swung the harpoon up to face her. "We've been lookin' all over for ya."

Chapter 5
Angry Young Men

Alexander stared at the White Knight in disbelief. "Couldn't find another way, sir, or simply wouldn't?" Was it going to be the job of every candidate they saw to challenge his authority?

He had to admit that despite the happy outcome, the confrontation with King Jupiter had left the Industrialist with his feathers ruffled.

The nature of their engagement had left him with little choice but to accept the man, even though he knew that bringing someone with so many mysteries into the Society was bound to end badly. But King Jupiter had, at least, shown genuinely incredible abilities—powers that none of them had ever seen before. As much as Alexander might be uncomfortable with him, it also made sense to keep a man like that where he could keep an eye on him.

Today was becoming, he thought to himself, a slightly off-kilter version of *The Three Little Pigs*. They had met a man of wood, and then a man of brick. And now the White Knight was turning out to be the man of straw.

"Either way, it was what needed to be done," Clements replied.

It was clear to Alexander from the moment the third candidate had stepped into the courtyard that inviting him had been a mistake.

Clements was the kind of man who believed that the best way to fortify his courage for a confrontation was to douse his fears in liquor.

To his credit, the man had only staggered once as he walked out in front of them, but being able to hold your drink was a prerequisite to joining a gentlemen's club, not the Society of Paragons.

And after only a few minutes, it was obvious that Jordan Clements was claiming to have superhuman powers he clearly didn't possess, and had been reciting a history that was, on reflection, equally as suspect as his claims of exceptional strength and reflexes.

But despite his subterfuge, Clements seemed to be of the opinion that the simple fact that he was standing in front of them entitled him to their time and attention.

Alexander didn't know what made him angrier: the man's attitude, or the fact that he actually thought he'd be able to get away with it.

In person, the White Knight's costume was more ludicrous than terrifying, although it was clearly offensive to anyone who remembered the bad days that had followed directly after the end of the Civil War. The whole thing was baggy and poorly fitted, and managed to showcase a protruding belly that clearly spoke to a life of indulgence and poor self-discipline.

Currently the man was subjecting them to a drawn-out tale of some nonsensical adventure where he had single-handedly managed to chase away a gang of "marauding negroes" who were terrorizing the city. Not only did Alexander doubt that there was much truth to his story, but Clements told it while wearing such a self-satisfied sneer on his face that Stanton was practically aching to wipe it off of him with a fist.

As the White Knight pulled the noose off from around his neck and held it up to explain how he had used it to "subdue" one of the "subhuman trespassers," the whole scene took on an unreal quality. Was this what the Paragons had been reduced to?

Stanton wasn't sure about his own stance on the negroes, but this was clearly over the line. Besides that, there was only so much nonsense that a man could take.

He looked around at the other members of the Society to see if their reactions were in any way similar to his. Grüsser seemed bored, as if he had already made up his mind that this man was not Paragon material, and was simply waiting for the moment when they could tell him to be on his way.

Hughes was shaking his head, as if he'd expected something more from the man and was sorely disappointed by what he saw in front of him.

Lastly was Nathaniel. He almost chuckled when he saw the young man sitting there with his mouth open, his eyes wide with what must have been disbelief. It was as if the boy could hardly imagine that a man such as the one who stood in front of them now was even possible, let alone actually real.

Stanton swallowed and took a deep breath. His admittedly small reservoir of patience had been utterly drained, and it was time to take action.

But what should he do? He had already had a confrontation with one of the candidates today, and while it had ultimately resulted in a new Paragon, he felt no satisfaction from it.

The Industrialist couldn't confront every man who attempted to join them, but each word that came out of Clements's mouth only served to make him angrier. The White Knight's blow by blow description of an attack against unarmed men seemed intended to make a direct mockery of everything that the Paragons stood for—it undermined their most fundamental ideals.

Alexander Stanton was well aware that his temper was considered to be legendary, even though it was something he worked very hard to control. But in moments like this, his anger was like a caged beast inside of him—something that must be set free on occasion or the greatest victim of its fury would be himself.

And maybe, like King Jupiter, Clements would turn out to be a better man than he first appeared—someone who, when confronted, would give them a genuine display of both humility and power.

The Industrialist began to roll his knuckles back and forth against the granite table, the exposed metal tips in his gloves letting out a set of rhythmic tapping sounds. It must have been annoying, but it didn't seem to be loud enough to interrupt the White Knight's enthusiastic storytelling. "And that's when one of them pulled out a machete!"

"What's a machete?" Nathaniel asked.

"Well, son, it's a kind of jungle knife that savages use to cut off the heads of strong white men." The White Knight said it so matter-of-factly that his ridiculous definition sounded like something he'd read in an encyclopedia.

"What it is," Stanton mumbled, "is enough."

When the White Knight turned to look at him, the cloth mask slipped over his eyes, and he had to readjust it to look through the holes. "What did you say, sir?"

Alexander raised his voice. "I said that we are done here." He slowly placed both hands down on the table. "You can leave."

The other man visibly stiffened, standing quietly for a moment. "That's not right! I'm not finished! I haven't even shown you my steel lasso!"

Stanton refused to make eye contact, instead concentrating intently on the table in front of him. "I've seen all I need to see. Thank you, sir, we're done. We'll let you know."

Hughes's machine took a single clanking step, turning to face in Stanton's direction. "Alex . . . Industrialist, don't you think we should at least give this man a chance to prove himself?"

"I think," he said, and then paused to take a breath. Perhaps he'd waited too long. His temper seemed poised to boil over, and every time he opened his mouth the anger inside of him seemed as if it were about to gush out. He needed to get it under control. "I *think* that this man is a hateful blowhard, a drunken buffoon, and an affront to everything that the Paragons represent." Still, sometimes it felt good to let go.

Hughes knitted his brows together. "Well, you're not the only one making the damn decision here, Stanton!" It was good to hear some of the old fire back in Hughes's voice, but it wouldn't be enough to make a difference: the dam had burst.

"That's right. I'm not. But last time I checked, we needed to make a unanimous decision in order to induct a new member, and I wouldn't give this man a yay if he were the last hero left in the world. Which, incidentally, he isn't."

Grüsser chimed in next, as he always did. "Industrialist, ist only fair to give ze man his say."

"Thank you, Helmut. I'll take that under advisement." He quickly rose from the chair. "Now, if you could kindly get the hell out of here, the Paragons will continue with the business of finding men of worth."

The White Knight reached up and pulled off his mask, revealing a round, red face underneath. The hair on top was a blond thatch of thinning curls. His face was puffy and his eyes were wide and dark, sitting above small nose and an almost lipless red slash that acted as a mouth. Taken all together, it appeared to Alexander as if they were being addressed by an enormous baby, and from the look on his face, Alexander wouldn't have been at all surprised if the man were about to cry.

Instead, he finally managed to speak. "I'm offended by your accusation, sir."

"Are you trying to tell me that you're not drunk, or that you aren't a buffoon?"

The man stumbled with the false choice for a moment until Alexander decided to help him. "Or maybe the word you're struggling to find is *idiot*? Either way, you're clearly not cut out to be one of us."

As crimson as Clements's face already was, Stanton could see the red growing even deeper as the man slowly absorbed the meaning of his insult. Staring at his face, he wondered what it must be like to go through life with a range of expression so limited that it had become necessary to use the exact same look for both anger and embarrassment.

The reply came out in a manner that could only be described as sputtering. "I, I, I am a *gentleman*. I will not be treated this way!"

Stanton drummed his fingers across the table. He felt a moment of doubt pass through his chest, but the momentum of the anger was pulling him forward now, and there were times when it was necessary to let the inexorable happen without trying to step in its way. "When you're ready for it to stop, the door is over there." He pointed at the exit.

"There's no need to be that insulting," Nathaniel chimed in, stating the obvious in his own obtuse way. Of course there was no *need* for it. The boy still had far more heart than sense, especially considering everything he had been through recently.

"My point exactly, Turbine. And the moment Mr. Clements vacates this room, we can stop being insulted." He was still the president, and sometimes power was there to be exercised.

"I demand satisfaction!" Clements shouted, throwing his mask to the ground in an attempt to add weight to his pronouncement. The cloth landed in a limp pile.

"Of course you do," Alexander replied. If the man wanted a fight, then they were in perfect agreement.

Hughes rose forward and up, the legs of his frame giving him impressive height. "Now Clements, there's no need for that! I'm sure that the Industrialist only means to test you."

"Hughes, I remember when you used to be a man whom I could rely on to *fight* the enemies of justice." The words were just tumbling out of his mouth now. There was something refreshing about being honest, no matter what the consequences turned out to be. "I was hoping that maybe we'd see some of that man come back to life, but instead you're making excuses for villains." Often when his anger began to spin out of control, the visage of his dead wife would appear before him, still the powerful woman that she had been the day she died. This imaginary woman would give him the stern look she had always used with him when his temper threatened to get the better of him.

And although Amelia Stanton had never been willing to back down from a fight, she had always been a woman of peace. She had died before Alexander had ever been given a chance to properly reconcile his secret life as the Industrialist with her pacifist views.

But this time, oddly, it was not his wife's face that appeared in front of him, but Sarah's. And in his mind's eye she was wearing the Sleuth's mask, just as she had on that last night that he'd seen her, except that the leather veil had been torn away, revealing tears streaming down her face. Her lips were pressed together in angry line of recrimination.

Was it his anger that had driven his daughter away? It had been terrifying to see his own dark side reflected back at him through her face that night. All he had ever wanted for her was the best, and somehow in trying to ensure that she had it, he had managed to lose her altogether.

"No," he mouthed back at her, and her face disappeared, replaced by the visage of the quivering charlatan in front of him.

"When would you like to meet, sir?" the White Knight asked him.

"We Paragons are men of action." When he stood up he realized that he was still wearing his gun, and he laughed as he pulled at the straps on his harness to undo the belts that held it onto him. When he was finished, he placed the weapon, along with the steam bottle that powered it, down onto the table in front of him. "Since you won't leave, I propose to take care of you here and now."

Clements's eyes widened. Whatever he had expected coming into the courtyard, it had not been a battle with the Industrialist. "Whatever you want," he replied, clearly trying to push some courage into his voice.

"Since you called for the duel, I assume that you'll let me choose the weapons."

"As you say, sir." Even beneath his thick jowls it was clear that the man's jaw was clenched.

He started to pull off his heavy gloves. "You claim to have both strength and reflexes beyond those of a normal man. I say we put that claim to the test, and engage in a round of fisticuffs." The metal-lined gauntlets landed on the table with a heavy thud.

"Zis should be güt," Grüsser said with a laugh.

"Whatever you'd like," the Southerner replied. "But it is customary for me to have a second."

Hughes was quiet for a moment, but the fact that he'd balled his hands into shaking fists made it clear that he was unhappy with the direction that things had gone. "Don't be a fool, Stanton. The man is ten years younger than you are."

"Do you hear that, Mr. Clements? Mr. Hughes is concerned for my safety. But if you're capable of it, sir, you can beat me to death." He heard Nathaniel let out a gasp. "That way you can be sure that you've removed the most vocal opposition to your membership in the Society while simultaneously proving that you have the strength needed to actually deserve the role. And if you don't think yourself capable of at least breaking a few bones, I'd suggest that you simply leave now." Alexander let himself smile. To be honest, no matter what happened, it would simply be nice to have a chance to hit something again.

Clements pulled off his white gloves and began to roll up the sleeves of his shirt. "I'm not afraid of you, sir, and I'll gladly accept your challenge."

Stanton pointed to Nathaniel. "I'll need you to second for me."

The boy stood up and took off his jacket. "I don't think this is a good idea, Industrialist."

"You don't have to. Your job is to make sure that this gibbering coward doesn't pull out a hidden weapon in the middle of the battle. And if he does, it will be your job to take revenge."

Nathaniel blinked a few times. "I'm not sure that . . ."

"Yes," Alexander asked him, letting his voice drop a bit, "or no?"

"Yes."

"Good. And Hughes, since you seem so concerned with the welfare of our applicant, why don't you go ahead and second for *him*?"

"I object to your behavior." Hughes rose up on his frame and began to clank around the side of the table. "But if you are determined to go ahead with this foolishness, far be it from me to dissuade you."

"Thank you, William." He slowly unbuttoned his leather jacket. It did provide protection, but he'd only just had it cleaned, and it would be a shame to soil it with another man's blood.

As he stretched to pull off the sleeve, he felt the pain from where the Bomb Lance's harpoon had pierced him and winced slightly. The wound was mostly healed, but not entirely. It would certainly slow him down a bit. Trying to hide his discomfort, he slid the coat off the rest of the way and handed it to Nathaniel. He carefully unbuttoned the collar of his shirt and rolled up his cuffs.

Properly prepared, the two men took up their positions in the courtyard with their seconds standing beside them. "You can end this by simply calling surrender."

Clements narrowed his eyes. "I thought you said I could beat you to death."

Alexander nodded and raised his fists into the air. "I've never admitted defeat."

The White Knight came at him like a freight train, barreling forward with the clear intention of planting one of his slablike fists directly into Stanton's stomach. Instead, Alexander stepped out of the way and jabbed at the man's head, managing to knock him off course.

Now that the fight had begun, a thrilling feeling of satisfaction flooded through him. Darby had always been their conscience, always trying to steer the Paragons away from violence in pursuit of a more "honorable" path. But there was only so far down that path a man—a *real* man—could travel, before he needed to stop being righteous and start doing what needed to be done.

The man in front of him might not be a villain by the standard definition, but he had all the attributes of one: a blowhard, a liar, someone who believed that the world *owed* him all the things that he couldn't work to get for himself. And in the end, it had felt good to hit him, and that *made* it right.

The blossom of pain in his side was as disorienting as it was surprising, and it forced him to let out a shout. Clements had seen an opening and used it to make a low blow to his back. Stanton hadn't even seen it coming, and it proved that his opponent was surprisingly quick for a man of such meaty stature.

He danced away and tried to clear his head. "Good, Mr. Clements. Well done." This wouldn't be as easy as he first thought. "Better than expected, in fact."

There was an ugly sneer on the other man's face now. He had tasted blood and he obviously liked it. "Call me all the names you want, Industrialist, but you're about to find out I'm no liar." He jumped forward, and before Alexander could react, he'd been struck twice, once in the face and once in the chest. It felt like he had been hit by metal instead of flesh, his rib cage flexing from the force of the blow. "I'm not an ordinary man."

Knowing that the coming pain might rob him of his strength at any second, Stanton struck back hard. His attack was wild, but some of the blows landed directly on the White Knight's neck, throwing him off balance.

The two men broke apart, both gasping and coughing.

The mask of civility that Clements had been so loosely wearing before was completely gone now. Sweat poured down his face, plastering his hair to his skin. "I'm going to send you straight to hell, you pompous son of a bitch!"

"Calm down, Jordan," Hughes said to the man in half a whisper.

The tone made it seem as if they knew each other, and for an instant Stanton wondered if there was more going on here than he realized, but his reply was certainly not a friendly one. "You can go to hell, cripple. I don't need to be lectured by you." His eyes flicked to the right as he talked, and Stanton saw a clear opening where he could move in. But instead of damaging his opponent, he found that it was Clements's fist that had impacted with *his* chin.

His head snapped back, and there was a sound in his ears that made him think that perhaps all his teeth had come loose and were suddenly rattling around inside of his brain.

As Stanton stumbled backwards, another blow struck him in his chest, faster than he would have thought possible. This time there was a definite snap as one of his ribs gave way. "That's the broken bone you asked for," Clements said, and followed it up with another punch to the face that seemed to do something terrible to his nose. Stanton could taste the blood in his mouth.

He tried to raise up his hands to protect himself, but instead he tumbled to the floor, his legs no longer willing to cooperate with his commands. As the other man loomed over him, he found himself simply trying to cling to consciousness.

"That's enough, damn it!" The voice was coming from behind him. It sounded like Nathaniel, although he could no longer be sure.

"It's enough when *he* says it is, *boy*, and he hasn't said anything yet."

Stanton felt himself trying to speak, but he couldn't push the words out through the blood in his mouth. Instead he just gurgled and moaned. He felt like laughing—he should have never taken off his damn jacket.

The next voice that reached his ears came from Hughes. "Whatever he told you, Stanton is the leader of the Paragons, and we won't allow you to beat him to death in our Hall."

"Who's going to stop me?" Clements replied, his voice rising to a yell. "You? The boy?"

"If that's what it takes," he heard Nathaniel say. Alexander forced his eyes open and watched as the young man leapt out in front of him.

At some point, the boy had slid on the Industrialist's leather gauntlets, and his youthful speed combined with the metal-studded fists quickly over-whelmed the other man.

Whatever superhuman speed and strength the White Knight might have had, it vanished under the attack, and Clements became little more than Nathaniel's punching bag. After a few solid blows to the head, he joined Alexander on the damp concrete floor.

"We are the Paragons, you sad bastard, and when you take on one of us, you take on all of us!" Nathaniel shouted.

The yells of triumphant rage ringing in Alexander Stanton's ears were familiar—something he hadn't heard since he had left behind the blood-soaked battlefields of the Civil War. And as he fell into unconsciousness, he realized that his anger had, once again, led him into a terrible mistake.

Chapter 6
In the Eye of the Beholder

N ot being a believer in bad feelings or otherworldly intuition, feminine or otherwise, Sarah had convinced herself that it was simply a desire to see the Brooklyn Bridge again that had pushed her to leave behind the warmth and safety of the main cabin and head out into the cold spring air on the upper deck.

The sky outside had been gray and threatening when she boarded the boat, but the weather on the East River was worse than she had imagined. Not only was the day cold, but a bitter wind seemed to penetrate every part of her—exposed or otherwise.

As she looked up to the incomplete structure of the span, it seemed even more unfinished than when she had been on top of it. That dizzying view had, for a moment at least, made her feel as if she were standing on Mount Olympus. Now she had fallen from those great heights and was riding the river Styx into the underworld, trapped beneath pointing girders and dangling wires.

As she looked up to the tower where Darby had died, Sarah wondered if any traces of his blood still remained. But even if there was still a red smudge to mark his passing, it wouldn't last long. Only stone and steel survived in New York.

Looking across the gray sky, her eyes caught on a black object hanging in the air. There was a moment of curious familiarity that turned to frozen shock as Sarah remembered seeing a similar spot before: the black balloon that they had seen on that January morning before Darby had been killed.

Sarah laughed at herself for being so hysterical. Every trip to Brooklyn couldn't be followed by a villainous attack. But her smile faded with the realization that there was a long smudge of dark smoke trailing out across the sky from behind the black object. "Impossible!" she blurted out, but there was no doubt left in her mind that this was the same flying machine that she had seen before.

A jumble of thoughts attacked her at once: who was piloting this ship, and how could they know she was on this ferry? She'd been so careful, but clearly not careful enough!

Sarah stepped backwards, cowering until she could feel the cold iron bars of the ship's railing pressing into her back. Shocked by the sudden press of metal, she turned and looked over her shoulder. She could make out the lip of the lower deck below, a firm line against the gray and unforgiving waters of the East River that lay just beyond.

Sarah tried to compose herself. The how and why of it could wait for later. Right now she was trapped on this ship, and the only thing she could be sure of was that whoever was on the balloon had nothing good planned for her.

She lifted up her small suitcase and clutched it to her chest, feeling the objects inside banging against the leather and cloth. If she was going to survive, she wouldn't be able to do it by running away. And if the Children of Eschaton were coming after her, she should at least be dressed for the occasion.

But if she was going to face her enemies as the Adventuress, first she'd need to find a place to change—the deck of a ferry was certainly no place for a lady to disrobe.

Sarah charged for the stairs only to find herself blocked by a young couple standing in her way. The man was tall and somewhat swarthy in complexion. He was clearly foreign, although he was not quite foreign enough that her friend Jane would have referred to him as "exotic." Still, there was no doubting that the word *would* be a perfect description for the woman standing next to him.

Her skin was so olive that it almost glowed, and her black hair bounced around her head and shoulders in a cascade of springy curls.

"Excuse me," Sarah said, trying to sound as resolute as possible. "I need to go downstairs."

"You need help, pretty lady?" The man's accent was enticingly strange, and she immediately recognized it as Italian.

Sarah glanced up and almost gasped when his bright blue eyes caught hers. Perhaps she had been too quick to judge . . . But the last thing she had time for was pointless flirtation with strangers. "No, no thank you."

She leaned first to one side and then to the other, trying to find a way between them. As she took a second look, she realized the two of them must be related—cousins, perhaps? The girl looked almost like something out of a fairy story, although Sarah thought that she would be better cast in the role of the witch, casting a glamour on an unsuspecting prince.

"Are you afraid of the baloney?" the man asked her, his fractured English falling to pieces.

Why were they stopping her? Sarah felt the Stanton anger rising up in her. "What are you talking about?"

"Baloney!" he said, emphasizing his gibberish as he pointed up to the sky.

"It's called a *balloon*, you idiot!" The girl's frustrated tone reminded Sarah of the way she might have spoken to Nathaniel. "Now, lady," the witch-girl said to her in surprisingly well-formed words, "maybe me and my horse's ass of a brother can help you with whatever is bothering you."

For a second Sarah considered taking their offer. It would have been a relief to share her burden with someone, and something about this woman looked surprisingly strong. But any thoughts of finding an ally were wiped away by what had happened the last time. In her mind's eye she saw an image of Darby, half dead, and Nathaniel screaming, pinned to the stone tower by a shining metal barb. Her eyes glanced up to the nearby tower where it had all taken place. "You can get out of my way!" she said, and pushed past them, rushing down the steep stairs.

"We sorry, miss! Please let's help you!" the man with the blue eyes shouted after her. She ignored his charmingly naïve plea and concentrated on navigating the remaining steps without losing her balance or the suitcase.

Once she reached the bottom of the stairs, she ran for the corner. She had made it as far as the main cabin door when the entire ship shuddered around her.

The shock made her drop the case, which bounced off the railing before landing miraculously upright next to the edge of the boat. For a moment it seemed safe, and then it began tipping over, heading toward the water. A shock ran through her from head to toe as Sarah desperately fumbled to keep it from falling into the river.

Unable to reach it with her hands, she brushed her foot against it. It tipped back toward her and fell flat onto the deck by her feet.

Before Sarah could breathe a sigh of relief, she heard screaming from nearby. She turned, and saw the source of the sound through the main cabin window. It took a moment for her to resolve the mayhem she saw on the other side of the glass. Then it all became clear: the shaft of a massive metal harpoon had penetrated the main deck and plunged down into the passenger cabin below, mangling anyone inside unfortunate enough to be caught in its path. Men and women alike were desperately trying to help a man who had been squarely penetrated by the device, but from the amount of blood that surrounded him, it was clearly hopeless.

A moment later, both the lance and its victim were pulled up into the air. The ship lurched as the hook pulled tight against the cabin ceiling, eviscerating the harpooned man completely. The would-be Samaritans screamed as they were drenched in a shower of the victim's blood.

Unable to witness any more, Sarah turned away from the horror and continued forward. If she had harbored the slightest doubts as to what villains might be riding the airship, the appearance of an enormous harpoon had wiped them all away.

As terrified and sickened as she was, a small part of her relished the idea that she might have an opportunity for revenge against the villain who had caused her, and so many others, so much pain. At the very least, she could stop him from killing anyone else.

Moving forward, Sarah came to the stairwell to the lower deck. She pushed herself against the wall as a number of uniformed crewmen rushed past her, clearly intent on discovering what had happened to their ship.

When she reached the bottom of the stairs, she stopped for a moment. The noise of the engines was almost painfully loud, and she could feel the vibrations of it through the soles of her feet.

This area wasn't forbidden to passengers, but it was hardly inviting either: the paint was old and chipped, the wood decking rougher, unfinished, and stained with pitch and oil.

Sarah had only walked a few feet before she found an entrance with the words "Crew Only" marked on it in bright yellow paint. The door had been left ajar, and Sarah stopped to look inside.

The corridor beyond was cramped and dark, and it stank of musty seawater and lubricant. Sarah stopped for a second, trying to listen for any signs that some of the ship's crew might still be around, but if they were, it would be impossible to hear over the chugging and hissing from the nearby engines. It sounded to her as if they were straining, and Sarah guessed that the ship was struggling as it dragged the balloon behind it.

As she stepped through the doorway, the sound of the engines was muffled slightly, the thick metal absorbing the thundering noise. Sarah had only walked a dozen feet before the distinctive tap of shoe leather against the iron decking became clear. She jumped into an open door to her right and hid as the footsteps grew closer, holding her breath for the moment they passed by. Whoever it was, he was clearly more concerned with the emergency up above than with any possibility that there might be a young woman stowaway.

When the threat had passed, Sarah looked around and discovered that she was in a changing room of some sort. Clothes were strewn all across it, and it stank of sweat, smoke, and general maleness.

It made her wonder how it was that creatures as different as men and women ever found happiness together under the same roof. Certainly it hadn't been possible between herself and her father, and their house had allowed them to remain utterly separate.

Still, it seemed an appropriate place to do what she needed to do. Sarah flipped open the suitcase and began to undress.

She began to pull out her costume. The Adventuress's outfit was still the same hodgepodge of clothes that it had been when she first put it together, but at least it was no longer a bulky mess. Sarah may have been hopeless with a needle and thread, but if there was one thing that was not in short supply in New York, it was capable seamstresses.

It seemed that hidden behind every tenement wall were dozens of women doing ironing and piecework. And no matter how odd the looks had been when she first laid out her clothing, she had found that compared to the penny or two they could earn for churning out collars and sleeves, most girls would gladly take a nickel to rework a man's shirt and coat to better fit a young woman's frame.

Sarah had also replaced the original riding pants with a rugged pair of canvas leggings. Not only were they stronger, but she hoped they would do a better job of keeping out the cold. Either way, as she pulled them on, she couldn't deny that simply putting on a pair of men's trousers somehow made her feel more like a hero.

She had also had the bodice reworked so that it could be quickly hooked up the side. It didn't fit with anywhere near the same snugness that it would have if Jenny Farrows had been pulling the strings with her usual efficiency, but there were also no friendly housemaids to be found in the stinking bowels of an East River ferry.

Sarah slipped on the leather coat and felt the weight of the pneumatic gun in the pocket. She was tempted to fire it now and see if it still worked, but she could only imagine the damage it might do in close quarters if it did.

It had been an incredibly effective weapon when she'd used it against Lord Eschaton, but that had been months ago. The Automaton had warned her that there was only a limited supply of fortified steam contained within it. Who knew how well his hasty modifications had effectively sealed in the gas? Perhaps all she would hear the next time she fired it would be the sound of a villain's laughter . . .

But it was the only weapon that the Adventuress had besides her wits—which she honestly wasn't sure were in good enough condition to be facing men who could fire harpoons and shoot lightning bolts from their hands.

Sarah wrapped the wide belt tight around her waist, almost completing the costume. Once all the pieces had been adjusted to her specifications, she took a look at herself with the help of a dingy shaving mirror that was hanging on the wall.

Even in the murky light, Sarah had to admit that Jenny was right—there was something slightly scandalous about her outfit, although she had done her best to retain a demure look.

Lastly, she pulled down the mask over her face. She had removed the curtain of leather that hung over the lower half of the face, leaving only her eyes and nose covered. Sarah had considered replacing it with a lace veil, but that had somehow seemed horribly old-fashioned—like something a grandmother might do.

And even the original mask had done nothing to hide her identity from her father. She prayed that most people would not have the facility to guess who she was simply from the color of her eyes.

Sarah threw her dress back into the suitcase, wedging it around the paper-wrapped object and notebook that were still inside. When she had swaddled the contents as best she could, Sarah closed the lid and buckled up the straps.

"And now what?" she asked herself. The case was big and bulky, and could certainly be a fatal encumbrance if she were to engage in battle with a villain while holding it. At the same time, it contained the remaining piece of Tom—possibly the most important one. Sarah had already failed him once. If he somehow ended up at the bottom of the river, or in the hands of a villain, she would never forgive herself.

She sat for a long moment in the quiet of the ship, pondering what to do next, when it dawned on her that the pounding vibrations of the engine had stopped. The ferry was now adrift on the East River.

There was clearly no more time to think—she had to act! Sarah grabbed the suitcase and headed back outside. She had almost reached the stairwell when she ran directly into one of the ship's crew. He was a strapping fellow, around her age, if not a bit younger. His shirt and pants were streaked with grease and soot, and he must have been a member of the crew coming to check on how or why the engines were no longer working. For a moment they were both speechless, and then Sarah realized that if she was going to dress like a Paragon, then she needed to act like one. "What's going on here, lad?" she said. Somehow, in a moment of panic, she had instinctively tried to adopt the low, authoritative tone that her father used when he was dressed up as the Industrialist. It sounded twice as ridiculous coming out of her mouth as it ever had from his.

"We . . . It's . . . There's someone attacking the ship, sir!" the engineer said. "We need to hold on the water."

Had he called her 'sir'? Perhaps there was something to this costume business after all. "Good work. I'm going up to see what's going on."

She started up the stairs when she heard the voice of the man behind her. "But you're a lady!"

Grabbing onto the railing, Sarah swung backward. As she rolled her head back to look at him, she swept out her other arm. "I'm no lady," she said, and gave him a wink that was probably invisible behind her mask. "I'm the

Adventuress!" She pulled herself back around, and bounded up the steps with a wide grin on her face.

Her sense of self-satisfaction at her performance was short-lived. As she passed by the passenger-cabin windows she could hear the moans and desperate shouts of pain coming from the injured inside. Sarah kept her head down and avoided looking in. She already knew what the Bomb Lance was capable of, and if she stopped to help the wounded she might not be able to stop another attack.

A hand reached out and grabbed her wrist. Sarah yelped and spun to greet the attacker, her fingers already reaching down into her pocket to grab hold of the gun, although she wasn't sure it would be of much use to her at such close range.

"Where you think you're going?" said a voice with a heavy Italian accent.

When Sarah looked up, she saw the exotic witch-girl who had blocked her way previously. "It's you!" Sarah started to say, and then cut herself off before she could finish the first word. If she was going to all the trouble of masking her face, it was probably be a bad idea to start telling the people she had only ever seen while unmasked that she knew who they were. Instead she simply replied, "Upstairs."

The woman's dark features pulled down into a look of concern and anger. "My brother is up there."

Sarah looked up the stairs and saw that there was blood dripping off the landing.

She could hear his voice now, drifting down from above. It sounded desperate.

"Emilio!" The Italian girl tried to run past her, but Sarah grabbed her hand before she could climb the steps.

"Stop!" Sarah said.

"My brother!" She said, tugging at her arm. The girl was strong. "He needs help!"

Sarah nodded. "But if you try, you may just end up dead."

There was a loud pinging from up above—the sound of metal against metal.

"Let me go!" the woman said, twisting in Sarah's grip, but the leather glove held her tight.

"Just wait."

"What are you going to do?" asked the woman.

Sarah held up her hand. "I'll show you."

Sarah pulled off her glove and reached into her pocket. When she pulled it out, she was holding the gun, and it clearly had the intended effect on the girl.

Even if Sarah doubted whether it would work, at least the weapon *looked* impressive in the dark eyes of a foreigner, especially one who had never seen Sir Dennis Darby's handiwork before.

"Are you going to use that as a gun or a hammer?" the girl replied with a sneer.

Before Sarah could reply, her attention was grabbed by another pinging sound, and they both looked up to see a metal rod spinning off toward the river.

If she couldn't impress this woman, she had only one option left. "Stay here!" Sarah said, pointing at the woman with her index finger, and mustering up every bit of her father's courage and her mother's stern authority. She held her gaze tightly on the girl's dark eyes until they turned away.

Sarah started for the stairs and then turned back. "Hold this for me," she said, and roughly shoved the suitcase in the witch's hands.

"What is it?" she said, putting her ear to it, and then sliding it back and forth. The metal heart bumped around inside.

"Everything I have in the world," Sarah said, stopping her. "Be careful with it, and wait for me here."

Sarah turned and climbed the steps carefully, her gloved hand holding the rail tightly as she tried to step around the cooling blood on the steps.

The sound of a familiar voice sent a chill down her spine. "If that's true, it's going to get very bad for ya very quickly." The Irish accent's sneering tone brought back a flood of bad memories. How was it this man managed to be at the center of every tragedy in her life, and how could she stop him?

As she rose up above the landing, the Bomb Lance's ugly face was the first thing she saw. He was still wearing his threadbare and misshapen kepi cap, along with the patchy red and gray beard that grew on his face like Irish moss. The last time she had seen that lopsided grin, it had been celebrating the fact the man behind it had just punctured her father's arm with his harpoon. "Now I'll ask ya one more time," he said to the figure in front of him, "and if ya tell me no again, I'm going to stick this lance someplace that yer not gonna like."

Sarah lifted up her gun and finished climbing the stairs. Her heart was pounding in her chest, and it sounded like a roar in her ears. She took a deep breath, feeling doubly glad her bodice wasn't laced with its usual constricting tightness.

Sarah's eyes flickered over to the man on the ground, and she recognized him as the girl's brother. He was holding up some kind of metal shield, and with his Italian features he appeared for all the world like a mythological Roman hero—all he lacked was a sword. Except for that and the mustache, he was a figure so classic that her father would have gladly etched him onto the front door of the Hall of Paragons.

"So," the Irishman continued, waving his harpoon menacingly at the man's chest, "if ya know where the girl is, and I think ya do, ya should tell me."

Sarah pushed down her fear, and stepped onto the deck. The gun in her hand was pointed directly at the Bomb Lance. "She's right here."

The Irishman smiled and sighed. "Ah. There you are, Miss Stanton," he said as he swung the harpoon up to face her. "We've been lookin' all over for ya."

As she took in the carnage all around her, her teeth became too tightly clenched to reply. There was no need for words anyway. You didn't talk to monsters, you slew them. She pressed the trigger on her gun.

The weapon fired with a loud burp. In her nervousness, she had forgotten to check the weapon's settings, and the force of the blast spun her around. She landed violently against the railing, the steel bars driving the air from her lungs. The pain of the impact spread across her chest.

Sarah gasped and tried to determine just how much damage she'd managed to do to herself. With the waves of pain and panic, it was quite possible that she could have broken a rib, or worse, and Murphy was a man to take every advantage.

As she waited for the pain to pass and her wind to return, Sarah felt something like a moment of clarity pass over her. She was, for better or worse, still alive—her goal was to stay that way. And the gun still worked!

When she could breathe again, it came in gasps. Now that she was drawing air, she touched her chest, but there was no telltale pain of a broken rib. The terrible sensation of that was a story her father had often told his guests when recounting his adventures.

Although she couldn't begin to imagine the bruises she would have, it seemed as if she was mostly undamaged. Every part of her cried out to simply lie down. But there was no time to rest or to even begin to worry about her wounds—the most murderous man she had ever faced was only a few feet away. She dialed down the power on her gun and whispered a small prayer to herself as she turned to face the Bomb Lance.

She felt sick when she saw that the gun's blast had blown the bodies of the dead men about the deck. For a moment she couldn't pick out the Irishman from the disturbed corpses, and it wasn't until he stirred that she could discern the living figure among the dead.

The young Italian man had also been swept up in the weapon's blast, and he lay face down, unmoving. Had she managed to kill him instead of saving him?

"That's twice, and the last damn time yer going to use that on me, lass." The Bomb Lance had risen up to his knees, his clothes stained red with the blood of his victims. He swung his left arm directly at her and fired. His weapon shuddered and let out a click, but no deadly metal emerged from the end of it.

"Damn," the Irishman swore as he dropped his arm. A metal rod slid out pathetically from the end of the weapon and landed on the deck with a clunk. There was a pleading look in his eyes as he turned towards Sarah.

She raised her gun, taking care to aim it slightly higher this time, intent on not disturbing the tangle of bodies around his feet—one of them most assuredly the Italian. She pulled the trigger, but this time the gun sighed instead of barking, the force of the blast managing only to knock the hat off the Irishman's head.

Sarah felt her heart drop. She'd used up too much power with the previous shot. The gun was empty now, and another small piece of Sir Dennis Darby had died with it.

Murphy opened his eyes and smiled. "Looks like we've both got a bum gun." He lifted up his other arm, the harpoon at the end of it sharp and gleaming. "Lucky for me, I always carry two."

Sarah stared at the tip of the weapon. There seemed to be something awfully unjust about a universe that would let her fall to the same weapon that had killed Sir Dennis, instead of letting her use Darby's weapon to get revenge on the man who had killed him.

She tried to will her eyes closed, but they refused. Instead, her gaze remained utterly transfixed on the tip of the sharp metal shaft pointed directly at her.

"*Cazzi!*" yelled the Italian boy, throwing his arms around the villain's legs.

Sarah watched breathless as the harpoon flew by her head, missing her by inches. It seemed to travel in slow motion as it passed, and she could clearly see that it had been modified from the version the Bomb Lance had used earlier, a ribbon of steel wire trailing behind it. The barb sunk into the main smokestack of the boat, easily piercing the thin metal tube.

She approached the Irishman, almost but not quite completely ignoring the man who had saved her as he pulled himself up to his feet. He seemed to be basically unhurt, although it was hard to tell the true state of someone covered in blood.

As she closed the last few feet between them, the Bomb Lance started laughing. "Seems like everyone's out of luck today."

Transferring the gun to her left hand, she curled her right into a fist and used her momentum to drive it into the Bomb Lance's face. She felt something a great deal like satisfaction as she watched his look of shock crumple underneath the metal-lined glove.

He stood dazed for a moment, weaving slightly. "You're a fiend and a murderer," Sarah proclaimed, and then struck him again. This time he collapsed to the ground, pulling taut the wire that trailed from his right arm.

Surprisingly, instead of her rage dissipating, she felt it continue to grow. Sarah put the gun back into her hand. "Are you going to use that as a gun or a hammer?" the Italian girl had asked her. Now she knew it would have to work as both.

She raised the weapon up high over her head. "You killed Darby, shot my father, and have stolen the lives of God knows how many others." Her father would have yelled the words, but Sarah spoke them softly, almost like a prayer, just making sure she was loud enough for the old Irishman to hear.

Her tone was flat and bitter, and she barely recognized the sound of her own voice. "Now I'm going to make you taste their pain."

She took a deep breath and heaved back, tensing her muscles so that she could put all of her strength into the blow. A voice cried out, and a hand gripped the lower half of her arm. "No, no, no!"

She turned to see what fool had interfered, and stared straight into the Italian man's blue eyes. This time she did yell, letting her fury pour out on him. "How dare you!"

"No, *bella donna*. You don't want this."

With a sense of alarm, frustration, and shame, she felt traitorous tears welling up in her eyes. "You don't know what he did to me!" she shouted, using her anger to hold back the flood. There would be no crying.

She slowly lowered the weapon down and handed Emilio the gun, too exhausted to trust herself to hold it any longer.

"Such a weapon!" He said, looking at the gun in his hands. "You make this?"

Sarah shook her head and stared down at her feet. "Darby."

"Dennis Darby?" he replied. There was genuine awe in his voice.

He stepped towards her. "And who are you?" He reached out toward her, and as his hand brushed against her face, Sarah gasped and closed her eyes. She could feel that he was gently lifting the mask away from her face.

"No!" she said, turning away, but it was too late.

"I'm sorry," he said, letting his fingers trace down her cheeks. They felt cool against her skin, leaving a trail of sensation as his hand settled under her chin. He lifted up her face to gaze back into her eyes. "I know you. You are that girl! He called you Sarah! S-s-s-Stander!" He said the wrong name proudly, as if he'd won a contest.

Sarah twitched free from his gentle grasp and stared out over the water. "Stanton," she sighed as she glanced back up at him—so much for her masterful disguise. It was stupid to have removed the veil. Clearly the mask alone was useless. She should have covered her entire face like the women of the East. "Now you know my name. What's yours?"

The Italian boy (man!) opened his mouth to reply, but before he could say another word, there was a stirring at their feet—the Bomb Lance had begun to recover, and something would have to be done about him.

He had activated something in his harness, and the wire that connected to the harpoon to his arm began to retract, rapidly dragging him across the deck towards the smokestack.

Sarah glanced up and saw that the balloon had positioned itself directly above the ship. Something toppled down from it, and an instant later a large weight slammed into the top of the ship's bridge, denting the roof. It was an anchor at the end of a thick rope that led back up to the balloon.

Sarah tried to grab the Irishman as he slid away, but her gloves made her clumsy, and she only managed to snag the edge of his coat. The cloth pulled free from her hands almost as soon as she caught it.

Murphy twisted himself around and brought his feet in front of him as he struck the wall of the wheelhouse. Using his momentum along with the power of the retracting cable, he walked straight up the side of the wooden shack, then grabbed onto the waiting rope.

She ran after him, but he was out of reach.

"Damn it! He's getting away!" she shouted.

The Italian boy stood ran up next to her. "Is okay. We're okay."

Sarah shook her head, trying to clear the anger that was flooding her thoughts. "It's not okay. We have to stop him!" She desperately tried to think of something, anything she could do to prevent the villain from escaping.

In frustration she reached down and grabbed at one of the metal rods sticking out of the roof nearby. The shaft was stuck deep in the pitch and wood, and by the time she had worked it free, the Irishman had already managed to steady himself on the anchor.

"Not again!" Sarah shrieked as she ran toward the end of the deck. She threw the metal stick at him with all her might, but it was only enough to send it spinning through the air for a few yards.

But it was too late—the villain was already rising rapidly into the sky, and there was nothing she could do to stop him.

Chapter 7

Family Matters

By the time the doctor's assistant told Nathaniel that he could see Alexander, almost three hours had passed. For most of that time he had been sitting with Grüsser.

The Prussian had seemed desperate for company, and had asked Nathaniel question after question about why he thought Stanton had been so eager to get into a fight with the Southerner.

Nathaniel had suggested that perhaps it was the man's murderous attitude towards negroes that had been the final straw, but Grüsser seemed unconvinced. He believed that the Industrialist's temper alone had been the cause of it.

"Something set him off," he had replied. "I've never seen him hit a man without a reason."

"Zen I very much hope zat Herr Stanton never finds a reason to hit me, Ja?"

Later on they had taken dinner in the dining room. As disgusting as he found Grüsser's noisy eating habits, he found the slurping to be a definite improvement over his incessant chatter.

Truth be told, Nathaniel had little or no idea what Clements had done that could make Stanton so angry. The White Knight's costume made it obvious that he had some strong feelings when it came to the negroes, no matter how much he protested that he wasn't involved with the Klan "in any official capacity," as he had so politically managed to describe it.

But that would have hardly been reason enough to set him off. And even if the Stanton temper was something of a legend, he had never seen him resort to goading and needling his enemies the way he had with Clements. He had lost both decorum and control.

It left the most likely reason as the most obvious: that between his taking on responsibilities as the new head of the Paragons along with the disappearance of Sarah, Stanton had been under too much pressure and had finally cracked.

Nathaniel had tried to talk to his step-father about his step-sister's fate, but the old man had refused to discuss her with him. The Industrialist hadn't searched for her, or even spoken her name since the night she had run away.

For his own part, Nathaniel wanted to believe that she was still well— that Sarah had left the city and carved out a life for herself someplace where she might escape the responsibilities of modern life that she seemed to detest so much.

The only thing that his step-father had revealed was that she had been wearing a costume when she had tried to save the Automaton.

It made Nathaniel laugh to think of her battling criminals and villains. The whole concept was completely ludicrous, and yet according to Stanton not only had it happened, but Sarah had succeeded in driving off the two attackers, even if it had been too late to save the mechanical man. And in retrospect, it did seem like the kind of ridiculous enterprise that she would attempt.

Ever since the events at the Darby house, Nathaniel had been coming to the realization that she had never been the girl he had imagined her to be. And, to her credit, Sarah had tried to tell him as much.

Things had not gone well between them since Darby's death, but siding with the machine over him during their battle had been unforgivable. Luckily the burns and cuts had mostly healed, but he still felt wounded by the betrayal.

But no matter what else may have happened, and despite all the questions that surrounded her disappearance after the mysterious events in Madison Square, he was glad to hear that the Automaton had finally fallen that night.

The metal man had been the most dangerous foe he had ever faced, and just the thought that it might still be prowling the streets of the city sent a shiver up his spine.

The infirmary was housed in between the living quarters and the offices, and as he walked down the hall, he decided that the wood and plaster walls were far more welcoming than the austere granite that had been used to construct the rest of the building.

He rounded a corner and saw that the door was already open. Alexander lay sprawled out across one of the operating tables, the doctor still hovering over him. He was bare-chested, a massive bruise blooming across his scar-covered torso, clearly marking out where the White Knight had broken a rib.

"You're getting too old for this kind of ridiculous nonsense," he heard the physician say grimly.

Alexander choked out a chuckle before he replied. "You've been telling me that for ten years."

"And every year I mean it more than the last." Doctor Josephs grabbed the point of his white beard and shook his head. He was rail thin, his lean physique only intensified by the long, black jacket he wore. "You've been a lucky man, Mr. Stanton, but even your legendary good fortune seems to be slowly running out."

Stanton turned, and seeing that someone new had entered the room, he smiled. "Nathaniel! Come in!" His jaw was as black and blue as his chest, and his attempt to sound jovial made him slur his words.

As Nathaniel started to walk forward, the doctor turned and gave him a hard glare that froze him in his tracks. "You can just stand out there for a minute while I finish binding up this old fool."

"Don't be such an old fusspot, Josephs," Stanton said.

"And you should try not to talk," the old man said, putting on his spectacles. "There's no telling what else might come loose in your head."

Nathaniel wondered how it was that some men could instantly command enough authority to make everyone else feel like children, while he seemed only to be capable of having people continually treat him like one.

The doctor pulled out a gleaming metal tube from his bag. It was fluted on either end, and he pressed the wider horn against Stanton's bare chest, putting his ear up against the other side. "Now breathe deeply."

Alexander started to take in a lungful of air and then coughed it out again. "It hurts."

The doctor stood up and frowned. "That's what you would expect to happen when a gentleman your age decides to start playing fisticuffs with a man half his own."

"He wasn't half my—" Stanton began to protest, but the doctor cut him off.

"You're an expert at blowing hot air out, now let's hear you take some in! And raise your arms up this time."

Stanton did as he was told, managing to put himself through the entire exercise with only a few winces.

Nathaniel stood quietly, deciding that it was far better to err on the side of caution than it was to risk the wrath of the prickly doctor.

"All right, you can put them down now," Josephs said after having him complete a few breaths. "You've clearly fractured a rib or two, and you didn't do that other wound of yours any good."

"And your face looks like you lost a fight with a road," Nathaniel added.

"Thank you, young man," the doctor replied without looking at him. "I'm sure Mr. Stanton appreciates your unnecessary jocularity at his expense."

Alexander laughed, then winced. "It's okay, Nathaniel. He's just a spoilsport."

Ignoring their discussion for the moment, the doctor stacked his arms together, put a hand on his beard, and tapped his shoe rhythmically against the floor. "Hmm," he said, letting the end of the sound trail out almost like a purr. "What I would normally prescribe is two weeks of bed rest, but I know you won't do it, so instead I'm going to give you some more morphine and ask you to take it easy for the next few days."

"Thank you doc—" The old physician cut him off before he could finish.

"And I'd like you to seriously think about finally putting away that ridiculous hat and costume before I'm left standing in front of your grave."

"I'll consi—"

"Lift your arms again," the doctor said, pulling a roll of fabric out of his bag. "I know you think I fuss over you too much, but there are few men your age capable of taking the punishments that you've been given over the last few months, not to mention the stress of losing Darby and your daughter." He began to wind the fabric tightly around Stanton's chest as he spoke. "You may think that you're invulnerable, but I don't need to be a doctor to know that any man who acts as you do will end up paying a terrible price for his behavior." As he said the last few words, he turned and gave Nathaniel a hard stare, "And it doesn't matter what age you *are*, or who you pretend to be."

Nathaniel glanced up in time to catch the doctor's eyes. There was no doubt that Josephs was the right man for his job, but that didn't make him right about everything. "Am I allowed to talk to him now?"

The doctor continued winding the material around the Industrialist's chest, tugging on the end to keep it tight. "I'm a firm believer in the fact that children should be seen and not heard. But you, Mr. Winthorp, are clearly no longer a child, and I'm afraid that any opportunity you might have had to reap the benefits of a proper upbringing have passed us all by." Finishing the roll, he pulled out a few safety pins and used them to tack the end of the fabric into place.

"Now Alexander, try to take care of yourself," he said, putting his top hat on his head. "I know your temper can get the best of you, but perhaps you can leave the actual punching to younger men."

Stanton nodded, but it was an unconvincing gesture. "I'll do my best, Doctor."

"See that you do." Josephs snapped shut the medical bag smartly, sliding closed the two clasps that held it in place in a single smooth gesture.

"Thank you," Alexander said, holding out his hand.

The doctor took it and gave it a curt shake. "You're welcome, Stanton. Just remember that while you're out there making more work for me, that there are actual sick people who could also use my help." He turned to face Nathaniel. "All right, young man, the grumpy old doctor is leaving now. You may commence with your costumed tomfoolery."

He walked out and Nathaniel shut the door behind him. "He's got a point."

"About what?" Alexander grabbed his clothes from the table next to him. "That I'm too old? It's nonsense."

"Being in the Paragons will probably get us all killed."

"We're all going to die someday," Stanton said matter-of-factly. "At least this way it's a choice and not an accident." When he tried to move his arms in order back to put on his undershirt, he couldn't hide the pain. "Ungh . . ." he grunted.

Nathaniel moved in closer, taking the shirt from his hands. "That's one way to think of it."

"I know you've had a rough few months, boy. You'd be a fool *not* to be worried after what's happened to you."

"And Sir Dennis, and Sarah."

Stanton paused for a second at the mention of her name. "*She* decided to run away."

Without saying a word, Nathaniel picked up the starched shirt and held it open. "I'm not an invalid," Stanton complained. But he took the offered assistance and pushed his arms up through the sleeves. Once the shirt was on, he quietly began doing up his buttons, and then paused to pat the open space on the table next to him. "Have a seat, Nathaniel."

As he sat down, he realized that it had been a long while since he had been so close to his step-father. "Why did you fight with Clements? What had he done to you? Wouldn't it have been enough to just tell him no?" For a moment he felt like Grüsser—asking one question after another.

"It was a mistake, but in the end . . ." A slight smile appeared on Alexander's lips as he shook his head. "Men like that don't understand the meaning of the word *no*, anyway. They just need to be taught a lesson."

"Don't you need to win for that to work?"

"You don't think we won?"

Nathaniel stared at him for a moment, and then looked down at his own bruised hands. He didn't know what to say next.

Stanton laughed, and then winced. "That's what being a Paragon is all about. We call ourselves a *society* because we work *together* to do things we could never do alone. And perhaps we don't always do them well, and we argue with each other, but when we need to, we win *together*."

Nathaniel had been around the Paragons for so long that what he was being told seemed blindingly obvious, and yet it was something no one, not even Darby, had ever bothered to actually say out loud: they fought to *win*. "I think I understand."

"No, you don't—not fully—because you've never been on a battlefield before."

"I've fought!" he said reflexively, embarrassed by the defensive tone of his voice before the words had even finished leaving his mouth.

"But not in war . . ." Alexander looked into his eyes. "And that's not something I would wish on any man. Imagine being surrounded by hundreds of strangers, all of them screaming, shouting, and dying. Your only chance to live is if you can figure out who is trying to kill you or protect you." He sighed and went back to buttoning up his shirt.

"You make it sound horrible. But there's glory too."

"Only after the fighting is over. And the worst part is that some of the men who want you dead are inevitably on your side." He looked down at the ground. "And you also find allies in the strangest places."

He shifted on the table and looked up into Nathaniel's eyes. "I pray to God that you'll never have to face it yourself. But there are lessons that *surviving* war teaches you—the most important one is that whenever possible, you need to surround yourself with men you can *trust*. That's the only way you can safely get back home to the ones you love."

Alexander put his hand on Nathaniel's back. "I know that since your parents died I've been a poor substitute for your father, and I'm sorry about that. It was always Amelia who I relied on to raise the children, and once she passed away . . ."

Nathaniel felt overwhelmed. He had grown up with Alexander Stanton, been raised by him, but he had never felt this close to him before. "I think I've turned out all right."

"Maybe you have, although you still have some growing to do." It made Nathaniel feel good to hear him say that, and Alexander nodded and brightened. "Where are you living now? I mean, since the Darby mansion burned down?"

"I've taken a small apartment nearby. It's a place that a friend's father owns. The house is modest but comfortable. And honestly, I spend most of my days here at the Hall anyway."

"In those dark stone rooms? That's nonsense," Stanton said. He slipped off the edge of the table to stand, swaying a bit. The pain made him hunch over and move stiffly, like an old man.

Nathaniel grabbed his shoulders to help, but Alexander shrugged him off. "Don't baby me, boy!"

"I'm sorry, sir," he replied, and quickly let go. Alexander Stanton was a proud man, but all the pride in the world wouldn't help him heal any faster.

"No no. It's all right. I'm sorry as well. I lose my temper sometimes, you know that."

"I do."

"But that's beside the point," he said, and began tucking the tail of his shirt down into his pants. "I want you to move back into the house with me."

Nathaniel was shocked. "Back in the mansion? I thought . . ."

"It's just me in the house now, and it's ridiculous to waste all that space on one old invalid. Besides, you'd rather be there than some filthy apartment, wouldn't you?"

A million thoughts raced through Nathaniel's head. As much as he disliked his cramped home, there was also a certain freedom that came with being on his own that he quite enjoyed: no one told him what to do, or where to go. And even better, no one tut-tutted about his late-night drinking or the mornings spent sleeping in . . .

Then he felt a rising sensation of shame. Had he been angry at his stepfather for so long that when the hand of friendship was finally being extended, he was too proud to take it? "Of course, sir," he said, extending his arm, "and gladly."

"Good, good," Alexander replied with a slightly hazy tone. Clearly the opium that the doctor had provided him was doing its work. "You can move in on the first of the month. I'll let Mrs. Farrows know. Now, if you could just help me on with my tie, I think I'll spend the rest of the evening back at our home."

Nathaniel picked up the ribbon of black cloth and began to tie it around his neck. "Of course, Father."

Chapter 8

Something in the Air

Emilio had been spent years protecting himself from any emotional complications, and yet it had taken only a single moment of attraction to this blonde-haired woman for the entire dam to collapse, and now he was drowning in her life.

The girl stood there, her face twisted into a mask of rage and frustration. "Not again," she repeated as she watched the villain rise up into the sky.

"Is okay, Sarah," he said to her. When he touched her shoulder, the girl wrapped her arms around him tightly, and then crushed herself into him.

He felt her quivering with anger at all the injustice of the world, helpless to express anything but rage. His sister was like this from time to time, but it seemed to fit this girl far more poorly than it did Viola.

"Is okay," he repeated, rocking her slightly. She was clearly not used to the kind of endless anguish and pain that the world could so easily deal out, even to the most innocent and loving of people. Emilio wondered if this was what he had been like the day that he discovered that his wife and children were gone . . .

Somehow he doubted it. He had already seen and done so many terrible things by that time . . . But he hadn't been completely empty at that moment. And yet so much of his heart had been scooped away that when fate came for the last small piece of it, it had barely felt like losing anything at all.

And here he was, being embraced by this beautiful woman, and he found himself feeling grief and sorrow instead of joy and passion. It reminded him of something his grandfather had told him when he was a boy. "Sometimes," the old man had said, grinning with a mouth full of missing teeth, "life will give you everything you want, just to prove how wrong you are for wanting it."

There was sharp thump, then a groaning sound nearby. Emilio could feel a vibration underneath his feet, and when he looked up and over the girl's shoulder he saw that the harpoon cable had been pulled taut. It was being tugged so hard by the balloon that it would soon rip out of the deck.

"You like me?" he asked her quietly.

Sarah pulled away. There was a puzzled look on her face. Her eyes were red but tearless. "I barely know you, sir!"

Emilio shook his head and rolled his eyes. He'd gotten the words wrong again. "No no, *fidati di me!!*" The words obviously meant nothing to her. English was such a ridiculous language, full of tricks and traps to make you sound like a fool, even when you were only trying to express the simplest things.

He tried to clear his head. If this was going to work, they would only have a moment. "Trust! Trust me, yes?" As he said it, he looked into her eyes. "Please?"

"I still don't . . ." Emilio took her confusion for consent, and grabbed her hand. As he pulled her toward the teetering harpoon, he saw his shield lying on the deck, dented and spattered with blood. He slowed for an instant to pick it up. If his plan worked, they would need it.

He squeezed the handle and gave it a twist, hoping against hope that it hadn't been damaged too badly to work. The blades attempted to spin closed, the device making a nasty klunk as it stuck on the biggest dent.

At least it was *mostly* closed, and there was no time to fix it now. He used the clip he had placed onto the back of it to hang it off of his belt. There was no doubt that he'd need both hands free, and hopefully the exposed edge wouldn't cut its creator.

Just above where the harpoon had caught in the deck there was a round flange, making a tiny platform around the edge. Emilio decided that it had been placed there to allow the device to punch through something before locking itself down, making it more of an anchor than a weapon.

It seemed small, but perhaps it was big enough . . . Emilio stepped up onto it, wrapped his arms around the shaft, and held out his hand. "C'mon!" he said just as the whole thing shifted ominously beneath him. He found himself wishing that the surface beneath his feet was bigger, but the fact that he hadn't slipped off was a good sign.

As he thought about the journey he was about to undertake, he felt the old familiar fear rising up in him. And before he even had a chance to try to calm himself, he heard a voice confirming his terror. "Are you mad?" the girl said. "We'll fall to our deaths!"

Somehow hearing his distress mirrored in her voice made it seem smaller. "No, I help!" Emilio nodded his head and shook his hand more forcefully. "Come!" he said. There could be only seconds before the entire thing ripped free.

"I can't!" she replied, but took another step towards him. Then she stopped. "No, I can't!"

Emilio was shocked. He was a commoner, and as far as he knew there wasn't a drop of noble blood in his body. His own failings he could under-stand, but this was Sarah Stanton, the daughter of the Industrialist—a Paragon! Was she that terrified, or was he truly being insane?

Maybe he could convince her if spoke English better—there must be something he could say. What would his sister do? She was always so good at manipulating people, perhaps he could . . . "Not again!" he yelled out to her.

"What did you say?"

"Not again!" He shouted her words back at her in a tone so dramatic that it was close to mocking her, and then he held out his hand. "Now come!"

He couldn't help but smile a little bit as he watched the desperation on her face turn to anger. "Damn you, sir!" she said, and flung herself at him.

He had barely wrapped his arms around her when the harpoon tore free.

There was a terrible sensation in the pit of his stomach as they swept up and across the deck like a pendulum, veering towards the pilot's tower. For a moment it seemed as if they would smash straight into it. Emilio clutched Sarah as tightly as he could, crushing the pole in between them. His grip on her felt wrong, and he knew he was relying too much on his feet to hold him steady. If only they had been given a moment more to prepare. Perhaps they could still jump off . . .

Emilio looked up and saw the horrified face of one of the ferry's crewmen as they swung rapidly toward the window of the bridge. Underneath his white hat, the man's eyes were wide and his mouth was open. Emilio imag-ined that his own expression must have mirrored his as they careened toward each other.

Just before the inevitable impact, there was a gut-churning lurch as he and Sarah were jerked up into the air. The tip of the spear scraped the roof, tilting them over sideways. And then, the moment before Emilio realized that this might be their last chance to let go, it swung free.

They rose up and away from the boat, hanging above the open water as the damp wind whistled past them. As they rose into the sky and the world beneath them shrank, Emilio could feel the terror inside of him growing. He looked around the shaft of the spear and over at the girl, giving her what he hoped was a reassuring mile. This had all been a huge mistake, and now they were both going to die for it.

"I find myself in your arms a second time," she said. Her voice was calm, and almost cheerful. It sounded like she had gotten over her own trepidation. "And yet I still don't know your name!" He broke his gaze away from the dark water beneath them and turned to look up at the girl's face. He was shocked to see that Sarah was grinning. Perhaps he'd misjudged her; it seemed she was a genuine Paragon after all.

"Is Emilio Armando!" His voice was trembling and high, and he barely recognized it. Hoping to salvage some of his manhood, he tried to widen his own smile.

"Hello, Emilio!" she replied with a weak smile. "I can tell by the look on your face that we both think you came up with a spectacularly bad idea!" Neither one of them laughed, but he appreciated her effort to lighten the mood.

Emilio nodded up toward the balloon, although he couldn't bring himself to actually look. Not yet anyway. "We are going to be up there!"

"Yes." Sarah looked up to their destination and squinted. He could feel her arms underneath his, clenching him tightly. He supposed the thick gloves on her hands might do a poor job of hanging on. "And soon, with a little bit of luck!"

Pulling together all the courage he could muster, Emilio tilted his head upwards. She was right—the balloon wasn't very far away, and the black gasbag loomed larger with each passing second.

This close, the machine appeared to be far larger than he had originally thought. The gondola was tapered in the front and back like a boat, and it seemed as if the balloon grew straight out of it. The construction of it was mostly metal, with steel plates along the bottom, probably intended as armor—although they wouldn't protect the balloon.

Protruding from either side were a series of long struts. Each had a series of propellers attached to them, with a larger one at the end. The spinning blades pushed the ship through the air.

Sticking out from the back of the gondola was a mad jumble of pipes in all different sizes and shapes—belching out smoke and steam.

Emilio was no stranger to the fear he felt. It was as if someone had stuck pins into the tips of his fingers and traced the pain back through his body with shards of glass. His joints were locked into place as if he were a statue.

He had always been terrified of heights, and his father had spent days working to make his son unafraid of what scared him. In the end, he had been mostly successful. And yet, when the time came to prove his bravery, he had failed to act. He had been a coward and his loved ones had all paid the price for it.

Emilio forced himself to look down. He could see that they were now hundreds of feet above the river and still rising straight up. The balloon wasn't only winding in the cable, but climbing higher as it went, and they were flying well above the towers of the Brooklyn Bridge. He was higher in the sky than he had ever been before. His father would have been proud.

When he looked up again, they were only fifty feet or so away from the bottom of the ship. Emilio could clearly see where the cable was being reeled back in through a hole under the nose. It was impossible to judge the size of it perfectly, but he doubted that both he and the girl would fit.

"I wonder," Sarah said, speaking his thoughts more clearly than he could ever hope to, "if we shouldn't figure out a plan for what we do when we get up there."

"Yes, I see," were the only words he could manage to say.

Sarah tried again, "What do you think we should do, Emilio?"

It seemed more likely that the girl would fit through the hole. She could ride the spear all the way into the ship, although it was impossible to say what waited for her inside. It would be tragic for them to have made it all this way only for her to be mangled by some hidden mechanism. Even so, he envied her compared to the fate that the plan which had just formed inside his head spelled out for him. "You stay, I jump."

"What? That's ridiculous."

The end of their ride was coming closer very quickly now. There would be little time before he had to act. "I'm okay! *C'è una scala . . .*"

"I don't speak Italian!"

Emilio couldn't help but roll his eyes a little bit. Why were women constantly worried about the details of things they couldn't control? "Stairs!" he shouted.

They were only a few yards away now. The hardest part would be flinging himself toward the right direction.

"When it comes to falling, three meters, ten meters, a hundred meters," his father had used to say, "it will all kill you just the same when you touch the ground." But it *did* make a difference to the young Emilio—because the higher he went, the longer he would have to ponder his death before the end. And right now they were very, very high.

As he tensed himself to jump, he felt something brush against his lips. The girl had kissed him . . . "For luck!" she shouted. "Now go!"

A feeling of pleasant surprise muted his terror, and Emilio felt lighter as he threw himself into the air. Then, an instant after he met the void, the feeling melted away. The rungs, which had been zooming towards him just a moment before, now looked dangerously remote. He felt disconnected from his hands as he watched them claw through air, desperate to find something to grab onto before gravity asserted itself.

Just as he was beginning to fall, he felt his fingers finally wrap around one of the metal bars, but momentum was still on his side, whether he wanted it or not. The ship slammed into his chest, knocking the wind out of him and breaking his grip.

As he began to drop, Emilio realized that his worst fear had come true. Now only empty air lay between him and the dark water far below.

Chapter 9
Dangerous Voyages

If the hole in the nose of the airship was any larger than Sarah herself, it wasn't by much. She hugged herself to the shaft of the harpoon as tightly as she could, willing herself to be as small as possible, but it would only take the slightest brush of metal against flesh to peel her off the shaft and send her broken body tumbling down.

As she passed through from light into darkness, she felt light pressure against her shoulder, but there was no flash of pain or damage. Her eyes popped open as the spear began to tilt upwards, her feet sliding off from the small flange she had been standing on. She tried to hold on, but her arms, already tired, could no longer hold her as she swung downwards.

Sarah was falling through the air, and worse—she was dropping directly back toward the hole she had come in through. The idea that she could have made it this far only to end up falling *back* out of the ship was as ridiculous as it was likely.

She slammed into the hull at the edge of the void, her legs crashing into the metal sheeting of the deck with a bang while her torso hung out over open space.

For the first instant she was too stunned by the fall to react—it was all she could do to try and hold herself in place, and not slip out of the ship. Cold air rushed by her face, the wind clutching at her like a thousand pairs of tiny hands, all of them intent on dragging her outside. As she slid forward, Sarah realized just how precarious a position she was truly in—only the weight of her legs was keeping her from sliding out of the ship, and it was only just enough.

Sarah felt Wickham's mask dangling down from around her neck, blowing and twisting in the breeze as she slipped slowly forward with every breath. If she was going to pull herself to safety, she had to do it quickly.

Her hands reached behind her, scrabbling for purchase against the smooth metal of the deck, but her thick gloves, so useful for punching villains, were unable to find any grip.

Desperate for any way to drag herself back from the edge, she clamped her fingers tightly around the sides of the hole. Her gloved fingers slipped off as she pulled, but with concerted effort she was able to shove herself backwards until the daylight slid out of view.

Sarah rolled over onto her back and fought back a rising urge to be sick by taking a few deep breaths. Above her she saw the tip of the harpoon she had ridden up to the ship. It was safely locked back into the cruel-looking device that had been used to launch it against the ferry, ready for its next moment of mayhem.

The harpoon launcher itself was massive—easily twice as long as the shaft it launched, but the springs, gears, and other mechanisms were all exposed, the large mainspring locked back into place. She wondered who had invented it.

Thinking of the spear reminded Sarah of Emilio, and she said a little prayer for him, hoping that he had managed to make it onboard as well.

Underneath her, Sarah could feel the wind thrumming and rattling against the metal of the hull. The surface was cold and hard, and something was sticking uncomfortably into her back.

When she sat up to take a look around at her environment, she saw that there were hinges on either side of the "floor" that she had landed on. What had been bruising her was a latch. She looked down and saw that the entire floor was actually a large hatch, held closed by a mechanism that seemed uncomfortably frail.

She stood up, but was still forced to hunch over. The space was dark and stuffed with machinery, the walls just large enough to allow someone to slip around to work on the devices while the ship was flying, if the need arose.

She headed toward the back of the ship. With every step, the ship's engines and the hum of the propellers became louder and louder.

Without warning, the ship lurched underneath her feet. Sarah's head banged painfully against a metal rod hanging down from the ceiling in front of her. At the bottom of it were a series of mirrors that twisted back and forth, focusing on a porthole cut into the floor of the ship. It was obviously a viewing system of some kind, the mirrors designed to carry the image up to another part of the ship. She moved, hoping that whoever was responsible for controlling the craft hadn't seen her face reflected in them.

Taking a moment to rest against the wall, Sarah examined the craftsmanship all around her. The framing had been constructed from strips of metal bolted together, creating a complicated scaffolding from which everything hung.

The structures made everything appear unfinished and insubstantial: more the "shape" of a machine than a machine itself. Compared to the solid, chunky, and deeply crafted designs of Darby, the work here was almost ethereal, as if it had been built by a very talented spider who spun his inventions together like a web.

But as impressive as it was, what Sarah needed most was a way forward. Peering down the hull, she saw a shaft of light trickling down a few yards ahead. As she pulled herself closer, she saw that the illumination came from a hatch cut into the ceiling. She searched around, but there were a number of barriers between her and the exit, and there didn't seem to be any way to actually climb up to it.

Sarah had almost given up before she suddenly noticed that the scalloped "ribs" that rose up the walls were designed to act as ladders. She grabbed one of them and gave it an exploratory tug. When it seemed sturdy enough, she started to climb upwards to the hole. "A very clever spider indeed," she remarked to herself.

When she reached the hatchway, she carefully poked her head up through it. The new space was gloomy, but not too dark, as there were glass plates sealed into the walls at regular intervals. It was also larger than she had imagined—the dimensions of a good-sized ballroom.

The gas-bag rose up through the center of the room, the thick canvas curving up from the floor to form a broad, sloping ceiling above them.

Her eyes continued to adjust as she peered around, and with a shock she saw the squat form of a man standing right behind her!

Before she could dive back down the hatch, a pair of rough hands grabbed her shoulders and yanked her up. Her knees banged painfully against the edge of the hatch as the stranger pulled her through.

Sarah found herself flung against the "wall" of the ship—essentially a series of metal struts laid out against some kind of treated canvas. The wall rose up and held onto the bag with a series of rope hooks that were laced through the grommets that had been stitched into the canvas.

She looked up at the man who had thrown her and saw a familiar smile. "Look what we have here—it's a flying rat." The Bomb Lance had removed his frame, and was holding some kind of gun in his hand. The weapon looked complicated, but the shining metal barb that stuck out of the business end of it sent a simple-enough message. He smiled when he noticed Sarah looking at it. "Did you bring yer special gun as well, girlie?"

Sarah could feel the weight of the useless weapon in the pocket of her coat. "Yes," she said meekly. She had come all the way up here to try and stop this man, only to be taken prisoner by him within minutes of her arrival.

Murphy laughed, and turned to speak to someone she couldn't see. "Look at her, Monsieur. You wouldn't think such a little mouse could be so dangerous, but she managed to knock down both myself and Lord Eschaton."

"Size, she iz not important," said a voice from within the darkness.

Sarah turned to look for the man the Bomb Lance had referred to as "Monsieur." She saw his silhouette at the other end of the gondola, and realized that by calling her "little," Murphy was having a joke at the other man's expense. The man was tiny, perhaps an inch or two shorter than she was. He hunched over in a way that made him appear to be someone of advanced age.

"I am not unawawe of ze barbs of ze Bomb Lance." The man spoke with a heavy French accent and a lisp. Even so, he punctuated his words with sarcasm. "But you should always wemember who it was who constwucted your new hawness."

As he stepped into the light, Sarah was shocked to see just how old the Frenchman truly was: his hair was pure white and stuck out from his head in thick tufts, revealing patches of bright pink skin underneath. His shoulders were deeply drooping, and his hand clutched a cane, which he leaned against heavily. She could just make out, underneath his fingers, that the head of the cane was a sliver globe. His eyes were covered by a pair of thick spectacles, held in place by a leather cord.

His clothes were bunched and ill-fitting on his withered frame—a strange mix of a leather apron, suspenders, and thick rubber boots. There was also a large belt strapped around his waist, from which hung a variety of tools and gadgets, some of them familiar, others twisted and strange.

The wizened figure walked over to her with an odd gait that landed firmly between a hobble and a run, as if he were in a terrible hurry even though he was constantly on the verge of falling over. The cane banged on the metal deck with every step, and the objects attached to his belt jingled as they swayed. After each movement he had to pause as he pushed his cane out in front of him before taking another step forward.

When he had covered half the distance between himself and Sarah, the wizened figure stopped and yelled back in the direction he had come from, "Fwancis, please bring ze ship back around."

"*Oui, oui, Monsieur.*" When she followed the source of this voice, Sarah saw that there was a platform in the front of the room that sat high up off the floor in front of a large glass window. Numerous panels, handles, and dials sprouted up from the deck to form a control panel in front of the ship's operator.

Standing in front of the bouquet of devices was a small bear of a man with the demeanor and build of a boxer. He wore a pair of grease-covered overalls and a bowler hat so tight around his head that it seemed almost screwed on. The band around the hat brim showed off colors of the French flag—red, white, and green.

From his accent, Francis was clearly American, although the French theme was continued in the large silver brocade patch of the fleur de lis sewn onto the arm of his white shirt. "*Bon,*" the old man replied, and turned his eyes back to Sarah.

"So little girl, what iz eet that you thought you would accomplish by invading my airship? And where, may I ask, is your fweind who caused Mr. Muphee zo much twouble down below?"

"I honestly don't know." Sarah replied.

The Bomb Lance narrowed his eyes and waved his gun menacingly. "Watch it there, girlie. Yer full of tricks, but I'll skewer you before I let you put any more holes in me, or blow me around again with that gun of yers."

Sarah ignored the Irishman and took a small curtsey in the direction of the old man. "We haven't been properly introduced, Monsieur. My name is Sarah Stanton."

"Ah yes well, you must forgive Mr. Muphee, madame. He has been wendewed incapable of mannews by an unfortunate act of birth." The Frenchman bowed his head slightly. "You can call me le Voyageur." He took another step closer to her and slowly examined her with his eyes. "But zis costume?" He lifted up his cane and pointed it at her. "You fancy yourself a hero?"

Murphy chuckled. "She thinks she's a Paragon, like her father."

His reply was as loud and angry as he could muster, and his voice quivered as he spoke. "I did not ask you, you Irish simpleton, I asked *her*!"

"I call myself the Adventuress."

The Frenchman laughed. While everything else about the man was ancient, his laughter still had the haughty, mocking quality of a schoolyard bully. "Oh, I am sure your fazer must be very pwoud of you."

Sarah could feel her cheeks blushing with a mix of shame and anger, but knew she needed to stop herself from responding to their taunts.

"And now you have nothing to say. Maybe zat is good since I need you to tell me where ze heart of your mechanical man is. I assume you did bwing it wiz you."

Sarah's breath caught in her throat. She had left Tom's heart back on the boat with Emilio's sister! And if the woman's brother hadn't survived the journey, how would she ever find her again? "It's still on the ferry," she replied.

"Zat is unfortunate. Lord Eschaton will be vewy disappointed if we do not bring back his pwize." He closed his eyes and slowly rocked back and forth on his cane. When he opened them again there was a smile on his lips. "I am sowwy if I am being wude, but now, young lady hero, ze time has come for us to say good-bye." He looked up at the control booth. "Fwancis. If you could be so kind, I think that Mr. Muphee may need your help escorting zis young lady *off* of my airship."

Sarah's eyes opened wide. "What?"

"*Le Ciel Noir* is an attack ship, not a passenger cwaft," he said in a deeply condescending tone. "You were not invited, and I have discovewed you have nothing I want. In fact, my dear girl, I think zat everywone will be most pleased zat you have been taken care of." The Frenchman grabbed a nearby lever and gave it a good pull. Down at the far end of the gondola, a trap door fell open. As it slammed down into place, a set of stairs and a railing sprang up from the flat surface, locking into place with a sharp snap.

When she was younger, Sarah had spent a great deal of time imagining how she would react when facing a maniacal villain bent on her destruction. In her fantasies, she had always seen herself facing death with a calm dignity that would leave a lasting impression on her enemies, possibly with a clever quip to show how utterly unafraid she was. It would be important that they realize just how futile their actions had been when she somehow managed to miraculously escape. Now that the moment was actually here, the clever words she was sure would come so easily to her were nowhere to be found.

"I can tell you where the heart is," she said meekly. Had she really given up so easily? What would stop them from killing her once they got what they wanted?

"What was that, my dear?" the old man said, making a grand gesture of putting his hand to his ear. "I'm afwaid I could not hear you begging for your life."

Murphy stepped forward and roughly grabbed her hands. "You should save yer breath, girlie. That old piece of gristle has got no mercy left in him. And it doesn't matter—if we couldn't take the heart, we were supposed to sink the ship and find it later."

For a moment Sarah thought he might actually be showing a moment of mercy, himself—until he spun her around and then pulled her arms tightly and painfully behind her back.

"And zis ship is more zen capable of sinking ze little fewwy with *everyone* aboard."

Sarah wanted to scream at the old man, call him insane and a fool. But she also knew that villains were most likely to respond to accusations and threats with maniacal laughter. And le Voyageur, it seemed to her, would be exactly the kind of man to do that sort of thing.

Instead she kept quiet, biting her lip and trying to figure a way out of her fate. The Irishman was far stronger than she was, and her grease-covered shoes were already sliding across the deck as she tried to resist. Her only hope, it seemed, rested in the hands of Emilio, a man most likely dead.

But her despair was washed away in a wave of nausea when the entire floor shuddered. As the metal decking twisted and buckled, she realized just how delicate the construction of the ship really was. And Sarah wasn't alone—she could see that the old Frenchman had also been unpleasantly surprised. "Fwancis!" he yelled up to the man in the control room, "what iz going on?"

From somewhere below them came the sound of metal grinding against metal.

"Something's wrong with the engines. We're losing pressure." The burly engineer grabbed the railings that led from the control room to the gondola floor, and slid down them in a single bound. "I'll go take a look."

"Be careful," said Murphy. "This one," he said spitefully, and shook Sarah's arms, "didn't come up here alone, and that guinea may still be crawling around down there somewhere."

"I'll be careful," Francis replied with a smile, and held up a brutish-looking wrench.

Reaching the far end of the room, the engineer reached out and pulled up another hatch in the floor. As he lifted it, a pair of hands shot out from the hole and grabbed his ankles, yanking Francis forward and throwing him off balance. He landed on the metal decking hard enough to send out a ringing sound across the gondola, along with an audible "ungh" as the air was forced out from his lungs. It was followed by a strangled cry of pain as the hatch crashed back down onto the engineer's knees.

"*Il Volano ci sta!*" Emilio said as he shoved open the hatch and bounded onto the deck. Francis made a feeble grab for him as walked by, but he was too slow, and Emilio danced out of his way, following it up with a kick for good measure.

"There you are," the Irishman said with a low rumble of satisfaction.

"Let her go," Emilio replied with a tone of cool seriousness in his voice, his words calm and clear.

"All right, lad."

The villain gave Sarah a brutal shove that sent her stumbling across the gondola until she crashed painfully into the metal frame of the wall.

Sarah stood up, testing to see if the sensation of her entire chest having caved into her body was genuine, or simply a side-effect of the burning pain that she was feeling.

"C'mon boy!" she heard Murphy saying behind her as she tried to steady herself. "Let's see what yer made of."

As breath returned to her lungs, Sarah was relieved to discover that she was mostly intact, although she would probably wake up tomorrow to find bruises in numerous unmentionable places—if she survived.

As she turned around, Sarah caught a glimpse of the Bomb Lance firing his weapon at Emilio, the silver barb glinting in the gray light. Emilio's shield was opening even as the projectile travelled across the room towards him.

The harpoon let out a "tang" as it ricocheted off the metal and spun off into the air. Emilio smiled grimly. "*Ora sai la forza del il Volano!*" he shouted out, and held up his shield in front of him.

The grin vanished into a look of concern as he looked down and saw that the device had only opened a quarter of the way.

He gave his arm a flick, and the plate let out a screech as it scraped over the dent before it finally sprang free and the shield locked into place.

Even from a distance, Sarah could tell that the device looked a bit worse for wear now, with the plates no longer fitting together as tightly as they had before.

Emilio tried to regain his triumphant attitude and yelled again, "Il Volano!" He lifted up his shield and it began to spin, quickly gaining speed until it was a humming blur.

"No matter what tricks you come up with, that flimsy platter isn't going to save yer guinea arse." As he spoke, the Bomb Lance fitted another barb into his weapon. "Sooner or later I'm going to skewer you, and then I'm going to laugh while you die."

As the pain began to clear, Sarah saw that Emilio and Murphy were circling around one another. Murphy had reloaded his gun and was attempting to line up a shot that would eviscerate the Italian, moving his gun up high, and then down low, Emilio trying to both match his moves and keep an eye on the other man. The spinning shield, while clearly ingenious, was also primarily a defensive device. It was only a matter of time.

Emilio's movements were almost comically broad, like a circus clown's. He seemed to be trying to goad the Irishman into taking a shot. There was something about his demeanor that was fundamentally foreign, and Sarah found it rather charming—even in these deadly circumstances.

As the men continued to dance around each other, Sarah saw the old Frenchman sneaking up behind them. He stopped and tilted the cane forward, until his hands were down near the bottom tip. When he lifted the silver globe up above his head, it was clear to Sarah that he was intending to use the metal planet as a bludgeon on Emilio when the opportunity presented itself.

Sarah mustered her strength and began to move quickly in the opposite direction. If she could reach the Bomb Lance quickly enough, she might be able to help—but Emilio was rapidly coming into range. It was odd to think that she was risking her life for a man she had known for such a short time, but there was rarely a story that her father had told of battle that didn't end with a lesson in knowing who your allies were, and Emilio was the only one she had right now.

Seeing her opportunity, Sarah dove to try to cover the remaining ground, her hand outstretched. She only managed to land a tap on the old man, but it was enough to throw him off balance. When his cane came crashing down, it crashed harmlessly against the metal deck.

The Frenchman turned toward Sarah and gave her a narrow stare. "Mr. Muphee was wight. You are a twue nuisance!"

As Sarah got back to her feet, she watched le Voyageur flip the cane over, catching the globe in his hand with a surprising amount of grace. He gave it a twist, and two nasty-looking silver blades sprung out from near the tip, locking into place with a click. "Your fwiend is not ze only one who can make zings spin!"

He twisted the globe again and the blades began to turn, slowly at first, then with increasing speed until they had become a silver blur. "You may soon wish zat you had let us thwow you out of ze balloon."

Sarah took a step back and waited while the Frenchman poked the whirring gadget at her menacingly, closing the gap between them.

Worse still, she and Murphy were standing almost next to each other, as the Irishman continued circling to try to catch Emilio.

Desperate plans were forming in her head: perhaps she could use her gloves to catch the blades. But she had no idea how powerful they were, and the price of failure would be too terrible to contemplate . . .

"Then *pardonnez-moi, Monsieur*," she said, nodding to the Frenchman, "while I try a different option." Sarah threw herself sideways into the Bomb Lance.

Her already-battered body responded with a shocking wave of pain as she collided with her target. Her attack had less impact than she had hoped, but it caused Murphy to jerk his hand upward as he fired his weapon. The harpoon tore through the gas-bag almost effortlessly, and a blast of warm air streamed down into the gondola from the hole.

The Frenchman let out a loud, wavering whine that landed somewhere between crying and screaming. "Aiiiieeeeaaahh! Don't puncture ze balloon, you fool, or we'll all fall out of ze sky."

Murphy turned his attention to Sarah. "You'll pay for that." As he swept his arm out at her, she balled up her fist and punched at his jaw with the greasy glove. It knocked him back a bit, and left a black mark on his face, but the jolt it sent up her arm seemed to be more shocking than anything she'd done to him.

Clearly she'd been lucky with her previous attack, and Sarah wondered if her father would have given her more training and fewer platitudes if she'd been born a boy. Thinking about Nathaniel, she realized the answer was most likely yes.

She could hear Emilio and the Frenchman conversing in the background, but she was far too focused on her new adversary to pay attention to what they were saying.

Murphy smiled at her. "You seem to be losing yer touch . . ."

For her second blow, Sarah came up from underneath and landed her fist directly beneath his jaw. Murphy's head seemed to vibrate from the blow. "Tha thaaaa . . ." he said, followed by a slurred mash of sounds that could barely count as words.

His eyelids fluttered, and a moment later he was toppling towards her like a felled tree. Before she could move out of his way, the unconscious Irishman had landed on top of her, his weight knocking her down and slamming her to the ground.

Chapter 10
Kissing Victory

As his hands clutched at the empty air, Emilio kicked outward, adding a little more energy to his momentum. He felt his foot catch against the bar, and his body jolted to a stop, his boot feeling dangerously loose as it clung to the metal.

As he hung there, dangling by a single limb, he could feel the adrenaline coursing through him. It had been a long time since Emilio had tried anything so ridiculous, but his father had trained him from the moment he could walk, and he had spent years more using his skills as an aerialist to earn his living. His fear of heights had always been his greatest motivation, and it was not the first time that the skills he despised the most had saved his life.

He muttered a small curse at himself in Italian for being foolish enough to get into this position in the first place. What had made him think he would ever want to be a Paragon? Hadn't he had enough of heroes and villains?

Staring down into the vast emptiness beneath him, Emilio felt fear vibrating in the tips of his fingers. They tingled for just a moment, and then terror seemed to evaporate completely.

"*Il Acrobato sei ancora idiota*," he muttered to himself. He had been glad to feel the fear again. It meant that sense was finally returning to his head. Using the strength of his legs, he locked his other foot into the ladder, swung himself back up to the rung, then began to climb upward.

Where the ladder ended, there were a series of depressions that ran down the side of the ship. The steep curve of the hull meant that travelling across them would leave him hanging over empty space. He reached inside a hole to find a small bar inside of each one, and a matching foothold below. They had clearly been designed to allow someone to move easily about the exterior of the ship, although perhaps not at such great altitude.

Grabbing a hold, he began to work his way slowly down the gondola, holding on tight as he shuffled from one set of holds to the next.

Halfway down the ship there was a metal plate that sat beneath an access door. Finding his footing, he lifted the handle. The door swung open with a reassuring metallic squeal and a blast of warm air that stank of smoke and oil. There was a loud, rhythmic thumping that came from inside.

Reaching in he found another crossbar, and Emilio pulled himself up and into the ship.

What he saw as his eyes adjusted to the darkness made him smile. In front of him were the long pistons of the aircraft's engines, noisily chugging back and forth from the power of a large boiler hidden somewhere nearby.

Emilio let his eyes follow their endless circles until he was almost dizzy. The pistons were quite unlike the usual iron bars that he was used to. These shafts were long and spiderlike, bolted together from a patchwork of brass, shining steel, and iron.

They were, in a word, ridiculous. But even more ridiculous was the fact that the machinery hadn't torn itself to pieces. What he saw in the spindly and elegant machines was the design of a madman, but a work of genius nonetheless.

He actually felt a twinge of regret when he realized that in order to save Sarah it would be necessary to damage these gorgeous moving sculptures. But this was the machine of the enemy, and he (and hopefully she), were now high above the earth, riding on the same ship that housed the evil men who had caused the massacre down on the ferry. If they were going to have any chance of stopping them, then disabling this machine would be the best place to start.

It took Emilio a few moments to follow the gears and get some idea of how the whole engine had been put together. As he traced the design, he laughed again at the ridiculous fragility of its construction. His eyes landed on a gearbox that had been strapped to the wall. A series of cogs rotated behind a small sheet of glass.

He moved to examine it more closely. The tiny machine was a regulator of some kind, and he gave himself a second to commit the general design to memory—some of the concepts might actually be useful in his own work.

The fragile mechanism would, he decided, also be the perfect place to commit an act of sabotage.

Lacking any tools, he pulled off his shoe and gave an exploratory tap at the glass with his heel. The first smack did nothing. He knocked it a few more times, hitting it harder and harder with each strike until the heel finally left a crack in the glass.

The gears seemed unaffected by his attack, and he smacked at it again. The glass splintered further, and this time one of the gears was thrown off its track, dropping down into the jaws of its neighbor. Everything froze for a moment, and then another gear spun sideways, becoming snarled in the teeth of the two cogs next to it.

The machinery ground to a halt, the gears bulging on their springs and pressing hard against the glass. It took Emilio an instant for his survival instinct to overcome his fascination, and he ducked out of the way just as the window exploded outward.

Shards of metal and glass flew past where he had been standing a moment before. One of the cogs careened off a nearby wall and smacked him in the back of his head. "Ow!" he said loudly, and reached up to rub the wound. Finding the offending piece of metal still entangled in his hair, he pulled it out and threw it to the floor.

As he stood, a deep shudder went through the ship, sending his feet sliding out from under him on the greasy floor. His bottom landed hard against the back of his shield.

If they hadn't known he was here before, they would certainly be aware that someone was here now . . .

Whatever damage the destruction of the regulator had done to the engines hadn't been fatal, and the patchwork pistons continued to turn, although they were moving at a much slower rate than they had been before.

With the engine noise diminished, Emilio could hear footsteps and concerned voices from the deck up above.

Looking around the cramped compartment, he saw a hatch in the ceiling. As he clambered up the metal machinery to reach it, he could hear a heavy gait moving quickly toward his location. Someone was coming to find out what happened to the engines . . .

Emilio crouched down beneath the hatch just as the wheel above him began to turn. He wasn't sure what he was going to do until the hatch began to open and he saw two ankles, clearly male, standing invitingly in front of him. His days on the trapeze made it almost instinctual—he reached out, grabbed them, and gave them a yank.

There was more resistance than he had expected, but he had managed to pull hard enough to send his target crashing to the ground. An instant later, the hatch slammed back down on Emilio's back, but his own shout of pain was drowned out by the heavy grunt that came from the man he had toppled as the metal cover slammed into his shins.

Gathering his wits, Emilio pulled his shield off of his belt and gave it a quick once-over before slipping his hand through the strap.

It didn't look good. The prototype had been built as an exercise in showing off the kind of weapons he *might* be capable of creating, but it hadn't been intended for battle. "Hold together," he whispered to it. It was the same tone that his father had used to when trying to convince his terrified son to give a particularly dangerous trick one more try.

The fact that he'd chosen to construct the shield in the first place had come from his boyhood fascination with the legendary warriors of Roman myth, and a quote from Dennis Darby that he had once read where the inventor had stated that technology was always at its best when it was fashioned into a tool to protect mankind, not destroy it. He hadn't bothered to mention that it was always the best for the poor fool wielding it . . .

Taking a deep breath, Emilio shoved open the hatch, pushing the man's legs out of his way as he launched himself onto the deck. "*Il Volano ci sta!*"

The downed man made a feeble swipe at him as he passed by. Realizing just how big his fallen enemy was made Emilio feel better about having ambushed him. He gave the fellow a kick to the ribs to make sure that he would stay down for a while longer.

Before he even had a chance to take in more than a quick glimpse of the ship's main cabin, he heard the Irishman's voice. "There you are!" The man was holding Sarah's arms out behind her, and she was clearly in pain.

He could feel the anger rising up in him, but he didn't want to do anything rash. "Let her go."

"All right, lad." He shoved her hard, and Sarah careened into the wall.

Emilio considered running to her side, but the Irishman would have none of it. "C'mon, boy! Let's see what yer made of."

Emilio nodded, and the Irishman returned the gesture. It was only the instant before he fired it that he noticed that the Bomb Lance was holding a weapon.

Emilio brought the shield up as quickly as he could, and breathed a sigh of relief when he felt the shaft bounce off the steel plates.

Emilio narrowed his eyes. *"Ora sai la forza del il Volano!"* As he looked down, his eyes widened again with surprise—his shield had opened only a quarter of the way. The mechanism had jammed against the panel that had been dented in the last attack. He'd been very lucky that the lance had been deflected at all.

He shook his arm at the wrist, and the device finished opening. "Il Volano!" he repeated, hoping the bravado would cover his fear.

Emilio had avoided activating the shield's other ability before now, but he needed some kind of advantage against the Irishman, even if it was only a mental one.

As he pressed the second control with his thumb, he knew there was a very real chance that if his shield was too badly damaged, it would tear itself to pieces.

He once again thanked God as the device quickly began to spin. After only a few seconds, it had reached full speed. He could feel it wobble slightly as it turned, but for the most part it seemed to be working well.

"No matter what tricks you come up with, that flimsy platter isn't going to save yer guinea arse," the Irishman said as he reloaded his weapon. "Sooner or later I'm going to skewer you, and then I'm going to laugh while you die."

Emilio considered charging the Bomb Lance before he could finish his taunt, using the spinning shield to strike his opponent. But if it came to it, he wasn't sure that the weapon could take down the Irishman.

Instead, he weaved around his opponent, using the skills he had been taught by his father to try and keep his enemy on guard. If nothing else, it certainly seemed to confuse him.

But their stalemate wouldn't last long. If the villain fired again and missed, Emilio would have to try to take him down, no matter how horrible the outcome might be.

To make matters worse, he could hear that Sarah and the old madman were fighting somewhere nearby. She sounded as if she needed his help, but the moment he glanced away would be the moment that the Irishman would strike. It wouldn't take much to find a gap with a shield that he now realized was far smaller than it should have been. The ancient Romans had constructed theirs larger, and he should have as well.

From out of nowhere, something whizzed by his head and slammed onto the ground only inches away. His glanced over and saw it was the silver globe of the Frenchman's cane.

The Irishman had been distracted more thoroughly, and Emilio lunged toward him, forcing him back.

"Mr. Muphee was wight," said the Frenchman's voice from somewhere disturbingly nearby. "You are a twue nuisance!"

Somewhere on his forehead Emilio could feel a rogue bead of sweat forming and he shook it off. He had a hard time imagining what would be worse: dying from being momentarily blinded by sweat or being forced to tell everyone in the afterlife that it was a single drop of perspiration that had killed him.

"Your fwiend is not ze only one who can make zings spin!" he heard the Frenchman say.

The words reminded Emilio of another problem: the shield's rotation was powered by a small spring that would quickly unwind.

"You may soon wish zat you had let us thwow you out of ze balloon." The Frenchman said to Sarah, and let out a short, nasty laugh to punctuate his words.

"Then *pardonnez-moi, Monsieur*," she replied, "while I try a different option." And then Sarah appeared in front of Emilio, flying through the air, and crashing straight into the Bomb Lance. The Irishman didn't fall, but instead managed to fire his weapon straight up into the gas-bag above them.

The old Frenchman let out a terrible screech. "Aiiiieeeeaaahh! Don't puncture ze balloon you fool, or we'll all fall out of ze sky."

Emilio's attention was instantly focused on the ridiculous spinning cane in the mad Frenchman's hands as he moved it toward Sarah, intent upon attacking her with it while she faced off against the Irishman.

"Look here! Look here!" Emilio shouted. There was no doubt that his shield would at least make an effective counter to the cane.

"Oh, is zat *your* device?" The Frenchman seemed disappointed.

"My wheel," he said, lifting it slightly, "is better than your stick."

"Look awound you boy," he said, raising up his hand. "I build so much more zen just toys." Emilio realized that he and Sarah had both traded one weapon-wielding opponent for another. At least this one might have slower reflexes.

From somewhere behind him there was a crash and a thud. A moment later he heard Sarah scream.

"Sarah, you good?" Emilio yelled over his shoulder.

There was no response for a few long seconds, "I'm fine . . . mostly" she said, obviously in some kind of discomfort. But even just the sound of her voice brought him a wave of relief. "But I could use your help when you have the chance."

Le Voyageur had no intention of giving him one, and poked at Emilio with his buzzing stick.

Emilio deflected it with his shield, and as they struck its surface, the spinning blades stopped for a moment. He lifted the shield away, and they started up again the moment they were back in the air. "The power is spring?" Emilio asked.

"What are you saying?" the Frenchman sneered in reply. "I can baw-ely understand your tewwible Engwish."

"You use a spring?" He spoke slower. He may not like the man, but had to admit that he did have some respect for his skills.

"Oh my boy," he chuckled in reply, "Ze fawces at work here are quite beyond your imagining."

As the two of them danced around each other, Emilio discovered that the shield was getting easier for him to maneuver. But if the gyroscopic force of the spinning disc was putting up less of a fight, that also meant it was slowing down.

Feeling both tired and desperate, he intentionally stepped in and lowered his guard, trying to present himself as a target too irresistible for the Frenchman to resist.

The old man took the bait and swiped at him, managing to catch the edge of Emilio's coat and shredding the fabric.

Instead of simply batting away the old man's attack, Emilio turned, bringing the shield straight down onto the cane. *"Sacredieu!"* the Frenchman shouted as it was ripped from his grasp.

The buzzing blades stopped as they hit the floor, and Emilio stamped down onto the cane with the heel of his shoe. The wood shell shattered, freeing the spring inside. The coiled metal wriggled frantically as it unwound like a dying snake, spewing an impressive number of pins, cogs, and a puff of black smoke.

"Cos'è?" Emilio stared down at the object. In an instant he was so fascinated with the shattered technology that when a shadow rose up over the pieces, his first instinct was to tell whomever it was to get out of his light.

"Watch out!" Sarah screamed, and some instinctual part of Emilio reacted, allowing him to dodge just as the steel spanner came hammering down where his body had been. But he wasn't fast enough: the blow he received was only a glancing one, but the contact of metal against flesh sent a spasm of pain out across his shoulder and back.

Emilio spun with the attack, barely managing to keep his balance, and realized that Francis the engineer had come back from his nearly unconscious state.

There was some blood on the huge man's pants where the falling door had struck his legs, and it was a maddened look that stared out from behind his grizzled beard and bloodshot eyes. Francis was clearly very upset at having had been hurt by Emilio.

When he opened his mouth to try to reason with the man, he heard le Voyageur's voice instead of his own. "Kill him quickly, Fwancis. We have much work to do."

The engineer nodded and stepped forward with a look of anticipation on his face. There would be no dancing away from this attack. Emilio barely had time to lift up his shield before it caught a blow so furious that it bent one of the metal plates and sent a spasm up his arm. The shield was spinning, but the wobble was clearly worse.

Emilio tried to catch his breath, but another blow came down, then a third and a fourth—each one more impossibly powerful than the last.

Somewhere nearby he heard Sarah yell out. It was a sound born of fury as much as of fear, and the fact that Emilio was torn between saving himself and protecting her meant that he was either more heroic than he realized, or that his feelings for this girl were, against all sense, deeper than he knew. If he could somehow survive the devastating assault he was under, perhaps he would be given a chance to figure it out.

Maneuvering the shield as he went, Emilio took a step backward with each attack. The ceiling was rising out of the edges of his vision—he was getting close to the wall. But running out of room was hardly his only problem. The damaged shield was beginning to disintegrate under the relentless attacks. The spinning mechanism had jammed, and the metal panels were twisting and buckling, barely able to hold together under the stress.

"Stop toying with him, Fwancis." The old Frenchman's tone made him sound like an angry parent.

"Yes, sir."

As the next blow came, the burly engineer shifted his motion halfway through the attack, allowing his weapon to come up from underneath just as Emilio lifted up the shield to protect himself. The spanner caught the underside of the platter and tore it to pieces.

Emilio watched in terror as his creation disintegrated, the spinning plates flying apart, violently propelled in different directions by the force of the spring he had used to power the shield.

The plates zipped in all directions around the room, some of them pinging off the floor, the others making loud whispers as they tore through the fabric of the balloon.

Emilio, now defenseless, tensed himself for the final blow, but instead of hitting him, Francis dropped his wrench and grabbed his neck as if he had been stung by something. For a moment, Emilio thought that his opponent had simply been grazed, but then a stream of blood gushed out from the engineer's throat.

Emilio stepped to the side as Francis stumbled towards him, but the engineer managed only a few stumbling steps before he let out a stream of strangled gurgles and crashed to the deck. He kicked only twice, his last breath escaping in a wet hiss.

"Some help, please!" Emilio looked up to see that Sarah had been pinned to the deck by the unconscious Irishman, and that she was desperately trying to struggle free.

Shaking the broken remains of his shield off his arm, he ran to her side. "Get him off me."

"Yes." He stuck his hands underneath the Irishman and rolled him away from her. The Bomb Lance tumbled over and let out a moan. That meant he'd be waking up soon, and Emilio didn't want to get caught off guard again.

Reaching out his hand, he pulled Sarah to her feet. "You were amazing!" she said. "But where did you learn how to move like that?"

Emilio was shocked that she would be impressed. "*Il circo.*" If anything, he had moved like a wounded slug, and his lack of confidence had almost allowed the Bomb Lance to kill her.

Sarah looked up at him, and in an instant, Emilio found himself as entranced by her gaze as he would have been by any machine. The world became suddenly silent, and Emilio could feel himself leaning, pushed toward this girl by an instinct he had not felt for a very long time.

Just as his lips were about to reach hers, there was a loud tearing sound. The ship jerked downward, and they stumbled into each other's arms.

"*Heure d'aller,*" came a voice from across the room. Emilio looked up to see that the Frenchman had slipped on a leather harness of some kind and was standing near the open stairs. "Good-bye, young lovews. I hope zat you will embwace ze passion of a shared death with the zame enzuziazem you showed fighting me."

"You're not leaving me here to die with them, you crazy frog!" the Irishman said as he stood up and stumbled across the room.

"Muphee! If you wish to live, grab ze deceleratuer and follow me." Pulling a pair of goggles down over his face, the Frenchman threw himself out of the ship and vanished into the wind. Murphy pulled another pack off the wall and began to strap it on.

"We need to stop them!" Sarah yelled as the ship lurched again.

The two villains tumbled out of the ship and into the sky.

"Too late," Emilio said, pulling himself out of Sarah's embrace with no small feeling of regret. "Follow me."

The two of them ran toward the control platform and sprinted up the ladder.

The view out the thick glass window was not a comforting sight. The ship had already lost a great deal of height, and they were floating somewhere over the unforgiving outline of the city . . . but where? He looked around desperately for something familiar, and saw the towers of the Brooklyn Bridge standing less than a mile away.

With that landmark to guide him, the buildings underneath him became familiar. If they were in Queens, that meant he could try to take them home.

Emilio looked at the controls and dials, trying to make sense of the forest of brass in front of him. He *had* disabled the engines, but their descent had given them speed, and the propellers could still give them control.

"Hold on!" he yelled at her. An instant later, he could feel her arms wrapping themselves tightly around his waist as he grabbed one of the long levers. It wasn't a random choice exactly—more of an educated guess. He squeezed closed the release, and gave it a pull.

The ship swayed frantically in response, and Emilio felt the floor trying to slide away underneath him.

After a moment, he eased it back. They were heading in the right direction, but the balloon was losing lift too fast. They needed to drop ballast.

His eyes scanned the controls for anything familiar. Near the top was a horizontal lever under a sign that read "*Détachez*."

"What's in English?" he said to Sarah, pointing at the word.

"Um. Undo! Pull apart!"

He nodded and grabbed the lever. It pulled up halfway, and then stopped. For a desperate moment he didn't know what to do, until Sarah's hand reached out and pushed it sideways.

As it pressed down into position, there was a series of clicks in the room all around them.

For a moment, nothing happened, and then a series of small explosions made both of them jump with shock.

As the booming faded, there was a single instant of silence before the struts began to snap apart, each one breaking with a distinctive "ping" followed by the tearing of fabric.

"Is that good or bad?" Sarah asked. Before he could answer, the bottom of the gondola fell away. Instantly, a cold wind began to roar, although they were still protected by the control panel's window. And the balloon, freed of the gondola, except for the small bit of metal they were standing on, lurched back up into the air.

The only other remaining pieces of the ship were a single bank of propellers and a small engine that poured out greasy black smoke through a pipe. It was clearly meant to allow for some control of the ship in an emergency just such as this. "*Mi dispiace, cittadini,*" he mumbled as he imagined the damage the falling gondola might do to the unsuspecting citizens below.

Turning his attention to the controls, he grabbed the wheel, using it to try to control their progress as they crossed over the city. Then there was another unhappy tearing sound, and they began to fall again.

He looked over the dials, praying that there was something there that would give them what they needed to land safely.

"It's beautiful," he heard Sarah say from behind him.

"*Cosa?*"

"The city," she said, pointing her finger to the side of the platform.

Emilio took a moment to look around. The gray clouds had begun to disappear, letting the rays of the setting sun strike their edges and turn the sky into a brilliant palette of ochres, reds, and purples that bathed the city in color. He took it all in, trying for just a single instant to ignore their predicament.

He moved around to face her, keeping one hand firmly on the panel's edge.

Sarah's arms remained wrapped tightly around his waist as he turned. "Very pretty," he said.

"A Tuscan sunset," she replied.

He smiled at that. "You've been?" They were both a mess, covered in blood and grease, but she was no less gorgeous than the first moment he had seen her.

"Never," she replied.

"Ten times more beautiful."

"I'd want a balloon, it's so quiet up here." Almost as if in response, one of the propellers made a coughing, sputtering sound, and died.

Sarah crushed her arms around him and pressed her cheek hard against his chest. It was the kind of warm embrace that Emilio hadn't felt in years, and the memories that came with it were overwhelming. He breathed in deeply, trying to control his feelings, but a single tear escaped from his eye and rolled down his cheek.

She looked up at him. "I suppose there's nothing we can do . . ." There was resignation in her voice, and for a second he believed it, too.

Emilio shook his head, and tried not to look into the eyes of the girl who was holding him. "I try to save us, okay?"

"Look at me," she said in a soft but demanding tone, "just one more time."

When he stared into her eyes, he could feel himself getting lost. His sister claimed he was afraid of women, but he'd never had trouble speaking to, or even charming, girls. He simply was a true man of passion. If he did something, he did it fully, and it was far too easy for him to lose his heart. So after he had lost his wife, he avoided women. There was only so much sadness he could take. And now here it was again—love and loss all rolled together into a single instant.

Sarah turned her face upwards and covered the remaining distance between them by standing on her toes. Once again they were kissing on the brink of death, but it was different this time—less electric and more romantic. And it lasted longer.

When he opened his eyes, he could see that they were getting very close to the ground. Spires and rooftops loomed threateningly just below them.

When they broke away, Sarah smiled at him. "All right, Emilio. Maybe we have something to live for. Go save our lives."

He began to turn, and then felt his confidence melt away. "I don't know . . ."

"You remind me a little bit of a man I used to know, I think." Sarah's hands grabbed his waist and began to spin him around the rest of the way. "He was a genius, and I'm guessing you are, too."

"I try," he said, looking back over his shoulder. Scanning the board, his eyes fixed on a control labeled "*Quatre*." He turned it slowly and was rewarded by a blast of flame from the engine that shot up directly into the balloon. Their descent slowed.

The buildings underneath them began to give way to the shipyards and empty flats of the shoreline. Emilio was amazed that they'd made it this far. Maybe they could at least crash into the river.

He turned the control further, and they rose—just for a instant. From directly above them there came the sound of disintegrating fabric. They began to fall rapidly, dropping as if someone had cut their strings from the sky.

"That's bad, isn't it?" he heard Sarah say from behind him.

"Very," he replied.

And as the ground leapt up to meet them, Emilio told God that if he was going to steal away someone *else* whom he cared about, that this time he must do him the courtesy of taking him as well.

Chapter 11
A Seat of Power

King Jupiter stood, slightly hunched, in front of the massive laboratory gate. He wasn't wearing his golden crown, but the ceiling was still slightly too low for him, and he kept his right hand resting lightly on the stone roof to remind him not to stand up straight. A metal key dangled from his wrist. He turned to Hughes and smiled. "It's taken me years to reach this place, but I'm finally here."

"I thought you wanted to be on the *other* side of the door." Hughes said the words with a tone so flat it was almost impossible for Jupiter to tell if he was being mocked.

The mechanical frame walked Hughes a few steps back from the gate, giving the gray man room to work.

Jupiter pulled the loop off of his wrist and slipped the key into the lock. It turned easily, and there was a satisfying sound from somewhere deep inside the wall. A moment later, the key slipped out of his fingers, drawn into the hole. "What? Is that supposed to happen?"

Hughes shrugged. "I stole this from Wickham's office. It's got to be the right one . . ." He stroked his beard. It was impossible for King Jupiter to ignore the fact that in a matter of only a few weeks, the streaks of white now outnumbered the remaining red. "But I don't know how to use it—I've never been down here without Darby."

They both waited in silence for a few long moments until it was clear the door was not about to open, nor was the key coming back. "It has to work!"

"Maybe it knows."

"Knows?" Jupiter replied, a clear tone of annoyance in his voice. "Knows what? That Darby is dead?"

"That you're not the Sleuth."

King Jupiter took a deep breath, closed his eyes, and willed his anger and frustration into his hands, concentrating until he could feel the living energy flowing down his arms.

When he opened his eyes again, his fists were glowing white with power, and he smashed them hard against the iron fittings of the massive door with all the strength he could muster.

He could tell that it had been a thunderous blow, but as hard as he had hit it, the wall only rewarded him with a dull, echoing thud as the shock-waves were absorbed by the wood.

The arcs of living energy continued to race across the iron and brass of the gate for a few seconds until they finally disappeared down into the floor.

The incandescent bulbs that ringed the chamber brightened as they absorbed the power and converted it to light. One of them flickered for an instant and then flared out, leaving the room slightly darker than it had been before, but the door remained unmoved. "Damn you, Darby!" Jupiter muttered.

"You already sent him to hell, *Lord Eschaton*," Hughes said. It was hard to tell if his use of the term was genuine or intended to mock him.

"I told you to never use that name inside these walls."

"There's no one else around."

Eschaton turned and glared at him in the harsh electric light. "I know that familiarity breeds contempt, Mr. Hughes, and after all the time you've spent in the company of those self-important so-called *heroes*, I'm sure your contempt for them must be very great indeed, but they are *not* fools. Under-estimating your fellow Paragons would be a very bad idea. As is," he said with great emphasis, "underestimating *me*."

Hughes's face tightened. "And what's that's supposed to mean?" he muttered. Eschaton recognized his expression as the mask the half-man wore when trying to conceal the rage that was seething inside of him.

From the first time they had met, Lord Eschaton was aware of the endless battle that Hughes fought to control his fury. And as his infirmities took a greater and greater hold, it was a war that he was obviously losing.

"Things are continuing to move forward, despite," Eschaton said, smacking the flat of his hand against the gate, "some small obstacles. So if we fail to achieve our goals, we do so because of our *own* incompetence and impatience. That would be a great tragedy."

"If you say so."

Although he would not consider himself a compassionate man, it was hard for Eschaton to not to feel some pity for this pathetic figure. The Iron-Clad had once strode across the world making Hughes a giant among men. Now the parts of him that remained were growing weaker by the day.

And beyond feeling sorry for him, Eschaton did owe him at least a small debt: no one had been more instrumental in helping him to undermine the Paragons than Hughes, even going so far as to personally kill the Sleuth when he had become too great a threat.

But after the fire, Hughes had turned inward, his emotions constantly threatening to turn him from a great asset into an intolerable liability. But it was his capacity to channel that almost-limitless anger that Lord Eschaton genuinely admired about the man. It certainly made him more tolerable than Stanton.

Becoming hobbled had forced Hughes to reveal a surprising capacity for science and engineering that he had not let on he possessed when he had been the brawler in an iron shell.

That said, there was little creativity or vision in the man. He could take orders, however, and he was a more capable builder than the Jew had been, although he lacked Eli's vast knowledge and knack for genuine invention— nor did he have his steady hands and almost endless patience when it came to the detailed work.

But Hughes was *motivated*. His will to regain his lost strength and stature was inexhaustible, and he had been working almost without stop to find a way to replace his lost flesh with mechanical equivalents. He had even allowed Eschaton to run a few experiments on him with fortified smoke, although they seemed to have had no effect.

Ultimately it was a battle Hughes couldn't possibly win; the wasting disease would take him eventually. Meanwhile, there were rewards to be reaped from his desperation, because beneath it all was still a growing hatred for humanity that not only kept the man alive but also made him the perfect ally in Eschaton's attempt to cull the human race and build a better world.

"You want to open this gate, right?" Hughes asked him.

"You cannot know how badly. Beyond this door lies the secret of fortified steam."

The bearded man looked down at the floor. "I thought fortified smoke was better than fortified steam." Eschaton imagined that underneath that beard, he was smirking at him.

"Better for my purposes, yes. But the smoke is a wild, uncontrolled substance, and with the steam we might even be able to cure—"

Hughes cut him off and continued. "It also has a tendency to eat through anything that isn't lined with metal."

Eschaton didn't like be interrupted. He turned the anger into energy and let it crackle out across his skin. "It made me who I am." After he had gained his powers, it had taken him only a few days to begin to discover that the key to controlling his abilities lay in properly focusing his emotions, but sometimes they were beyond his control. "Are you trying to make me mad?"

"I know you're a madman, I want to make sure that you're the right kind of madman."

"And have I disappointed you? I've given you a new body, haven't I?"

Hughes's frame turned slightly and walked closer to the corner of the room. "A body which *I* stole out from the same lab we're standing in now. And I killed a man to cover it up."

"You did. But you needed me to redesign it so that it could act as your new legs. You're many things, William, some of them quite impressive, but you are not Dennis Darby."

"Well, *you* didn't create these legs, and you can't open that door. Seems like you may be losing a fight against a dead man."

Eschaton felt the rage boiling up inside him. "That's *enough*!" he shouted, and let the energy stream out through his hands towards the gate. It scorched the wood and sent bolts of living electricity racing along the wall.

"What's that?" Hughes held up a hand and pointed over to the corner of the wall.

"What?" said Eschaton. He looked around, but couldn't see what it was that captured Hughes's attention.

"Can you do that again?"

"Of course I can."

Hughes stared at him for a moment and then shook his head. "Okay, then do it. And this time look up there."

Anger, he had discovered, wasn't the only emotion capable of igniting his abilities on command. Fear, need, even desire—anything, as long as it was intense enough to bring about the intense physiological changes in his body chemistry that could generate his unique electric powers.

But there were limits. The more he used his abilities without recharging himself, the more his own body would turn against him. His muscles were in constant tension. It took a great deal of concentration to relax his flesh and control the pain. Each blast of power left him a little more drained—one step closer to the brink of no return.

After his display with the bullet in the courtyard, Eschaton had been in a bad enough state that he had been concerned he might have damaged himself permanently. It had taken until yesterday before he finally felt he'd managed to completely shake off the loss.

He was sure that there had to be some more efficient way to recharge and repair himself than simply patience. He had tried bathing in fortified smoke, but the original incident seemed to have made him immune to any further effects. He had also begun to experiment with electrical power, but there would be better tools for that in Darby's laboratory than in his own meager workshop.

But until he unlocked those secrets, it was only time that seemed capable of returning him to full strength—not that he was about to reveal that to Hughes.

Letting himself focus fully on his frustration at Darby's ridiculous tricks and traps, he gathered energy into his arms. When he felt the tingling that told him he had reached his capacity, Eschaton clapped his hands together and slammed them hard against the iron bindings. The living electricity exploded out of him and into the steel. This time, as it arced across the wall, he managed to see what Hughes had been pointing at: a small iron bolt on the wall sparked to reveal the energy that was shooting upwards through it.

"And I suppose you . . . think you know where that goes, Mr. Hughes?" he said, trying not to gasp for breath as his lungs spasmed and his heart thudded in his chest.

"Not for sure. But since you asked, I do have a theory, Lord . . . King Jupiter." The clanking machine turned and began to walk out of the room. "Follow me."

As he watched him go, Eschaton looked at Hughes's waddling frame. Hughes was correct when he said that Darby had surpassed him in some areas. While they might have been equal in terms of invention, there were places where the old man's abilities had excelled far beyond his own, including two-legged locomotion. Despite many attempts, the ability to create something that actually walked had always been one thing that he had never quite seemed able to master elegantly.

Most of the devices that Eschaton had created over the years relied heavily on wheels or broad, flat feet designed to maneuver up stairs and the like. He'd come up with some machines that mimicked the human stride, but they had a bad habit of toppling over whenever their movement was interrupted.

He had also struggled with mechanical locomotion, and had finally determined that in order to create true two-legged ambulation it was necessary to have some kind of rudimentary integrated intelligence that regulated balance. Tom had been the proof that he was right.

But even knowing Darby's secrets hadn't been enough, and no matter how he tried, Eschaton hadn't been able to fully solve the problem. In the end, it had taken Darby's technology to allow Hughes to walk.

He and Hughes had tried to be careful when they rebuilt the frame, but many of the pieces that they had removed had been a mystery—most likely elements designed to integrate with the original Automaton.

Even beheaded, the frame integrated some kind of intelligence of its own . . . The proof of Darby's genius was walking up the stairs right in front of him.

But genius wasn't everything. As he followed Hughes into the granite-lined halls of the main building, Eschaton couldn't help but feel a flush of pride at having successfully managed to infiltrate the impenetrable Hall of Paragons! (And did his cramps loosen just a bit? Did positive emotions have a beneficial effect? He would have to experiment further . . .)

His plan had been simple and straightforward—chop off the head, and the body would fall. But even that was easier said than done, and this was far from the first time he'd hatched a scheme to kill Dennis Darby. The difference was that this one had finally *succeeded*. In retrospect, it was clear that it had been his own hubris that had been getting in the way of his success all these years.

For so long, he had been obsessed by the need to show Darby the error of his ways *before* he killed him. He wanted the old man to admit his inferiority before he sent him off to meet his maker. And that had been the seed of failure in every plan: the old scientist truly was every bit as clever as his reputation suggested, and no number of intricate puzzles and carefully laid traps had been able to prove his undoing.

What it had taken to win was being able to finally admit that Darby had been the greater genius. Maybe not by much, and certainly not in every way, but it was the truth.

It hurt to admit it, but that realization had also been his moment of transformation into Lord Eschaton. If he couldn't be Darby's equal in pure intelligence, then he would use ruthlessness to make up the difference.

"King Jupiter . . ."

No amount of genius could act as a shield against the simple sharpened piece of metal that had ended the old man's life. And ruthlessness had other advantages: it not only allowed him to get his revenge, it had let him build a tool of destruction that he could use to remake the world.

And now, having smashed Darby's mechanical man to pieces with his bare hands, he stood on the verge of completely dismantling Darby's greatest legacy—the Paragons. True, he didn't have the Automaton's clockwork heart, but it was only a matter of time.

"Jupiter?"

Before he was through, he would tear down the walls of this granite hovel and turn the building into a tomb for these idiots who called themselves heroes.

He would purify the planet, and when a refined and enhanced humanity was all that was left, he would build a monument to his vision on this place. An edifice so great that no one would ever forget the sacrifices he made to help the world escape its sad fate.

"Damn it, *Eschaton*!" said Hughes impatiently next to him, piercing through his introspection and destroying his rising sense of elation.

"What is it?" he asked angrily, frustrated that he had been so rudely torn out of his vision of a better tomorrow. But he did seem to feel much better . . .

"I've lost the line." They were standing outside the door to the meeting room now. "I need you to use your charge on the wall again. And if you want me to use your alias, you can at least do me the courtesy of responding to it."

Lord Eschaton grimaced and shook his head. Grabbing Hughes's metal frame, he gave it a hard shove. The machine tilted backwards, the metal feet clanking as they tried to find some purchase against the polished floor.

The look of terror on Hughes's face as he stumbled was priceless. His hands scrabbled for the controls as the frame began to fall, the device almost tipping over completely before it bounced against the walls and stopped. Some combination of Hughes's panic and the innate ability of the device to keep itself upright managed to allow him to find balance.

Eschaton walked up to Hughes. His face was red, the bushy gray brows above his eyes knitted together in obvious anger. "Damn you, Eschaton!" he hissed at him.

"Damn me?" Without thinking he gave the man a hard slap across his face, only remembering at the last instant to soften the blow so as not to rip his head from his shoulders.

The frame was immobile, but the blow was still hard enough that Hughes rocked in it. "And I told you *not* to use my real name."

The crippled man's mouth hung open in an obvious expression of pure surprise. His face was still red, but the flesh where he had been struck was a darker shade of crimson.

Eschaton watched in amusement as Hughes's lips begin to twitch, stopped, and then twitched again. He was clearly on the verge of saying something, teetering on the brink of rebellion, with the lesson of a fresh sting from Eschaton's hand on his flesh holding him back.

He'd faced this breaking point with so many men—Eli, Jack, Murphy. The moment came often when you worked with poor souls who simply wished that they were more than they really were. In every relationship came the time where a true leader needed to exert his will over others to prove to them that his position was no accident, but something as irrevocable and undeniable as nature itself.

And now that moment was here with Hughes. Before the man could finally spit out his angry words, Eschaton grabbed his frame by an exposed bar and flung it through the entrance.

This time Hughes was ready for the assault and managed to pilot the machine with some grace as it stumbled along the floor.

Eschaton followed quickly, taking just a moment to throw the doors to the conference room closed behind him. Hughes had only begun to turn around when he pushed him again, shoving the frame with enough power that he crashed into the meeting table. "Do you really think that you have the right to challenge me?" he said with a shout. There was still a chance that someone outside might hear, but in a perfect moment of crisis there were always risks that need to be taken.

"I, I, I . . ." Hughes said.

"It's a simple question, Mr. Hughes. Do you think you have the right to challenge Lord Eschaton? Yes or no?"

"N-n-no." The half-man's hands were balled into fists now, his eyes closed tight.

"Look at me when I'm talking to you!" He smacked his hand hard against the frame, rattling it and sending a mild electric jolt through the metal. "I want to know what I did that gave you the impression that you are my equal. I want to know because I want us both to be very clear on where we stand going forward."

"Y-y-yes." His stutter was more pronounced now. Hughes had been successfully pushed to the edge. Now there was just one more step.

"But since you're so eager to use my name, I want to hear it."

Eschaton leaned down over the crippled man. Now that they were face to face, he realized that Hughes was weaker than he'd thought. The frame he wore would have been more than capable of fighting back if the man wearing it had the will to use it. "Es-Eschaton," Hughes said feebly.

This man had once been the most powerful Paragon, and now he was a whimpering child. Eschaton let the rage flow through him, feeling the current rising inside of him. He grabbed the frame with his hands and felt the charge flowing out through the metal. Hughes's muscles went rigid as the current cascaded through him. "Say *all* of it."

"L-l-l-l-l . . ."

"*Lord* Eschaton! Say it!"

"L-l-lord Eschaton!"

He released the frame, stepped back, and smiled. "Good." Now was the moment of truth. It was in this next instant that he would find out if he had actually broken the man, or had only just begun the process.

He lifted Hughes out of his frame. With the absence of his legs, it was almost too easy—like plucking a worm from an apple.

Without their pilot to guide them, the metal legs seemed to sag down, as if they had somehow lost something from having Hughes's consciousness removed from them. "Now say it again!" He dropped him onto the table. The living energy flowed directly from his arms into Hughes, making the legless man twitch.

"Lord Eschaton!" Hughes screamed back at him.

"Again!" He jabbed at him with his fingers, reminding him of his power.

"Lord Eschaton!"

"Very good," he said, letting the words slip out in a soft purr. "Now we understand each other." But his attention was already slipping away. When he had sent out that last shock, he had seen something strange happen on the table beneath him.

Hughes sagged down against the granite tabletop and breathed heavily. "I'm sorry."

Eschaton nodded solemnly and placed his now inert hand against the other man's chest like a priest giving a benediction to a lost believer. "I forgive you." In the world he was building, the purified humans would be made of stronger stuff.

He picked up Hughes and dropped him back into the frame. The response was almost imperceptible, but the machine definitely *did* respond. There *was* something different about the way it stood now that a man inhabited it. He'd need to look into that—later.

"Look!" Eschaton said, nodding at the table.

"What is it?" Hughes replied, his voice a dreamy slur. His eyes were wide and unfocused, as if he were staring at an invisible monster in the distance.

Eschaton leaned down and placed his hands against the metal inlay in the granite. Good mood or not, he would pay for the amount of energy he was putting out today. But if they succeeded in entering the laboratory, it would be well worth the cost.

He sent another bolt out through his skin. It circled around the metal inlay on the table, and then vanished. "Now look at that chair," Eschaton said, pointing to the wrought iron throne sitting up above the rest of the room. A moment later, he could see the power crackling in the golden wreath that stood above them.

Hughes shook his head and tried to concentrate. "You did that?"

Eschaton nodded and smiled. "There's something else going on here. What plan did Darby have in mind?"

Hughes's hands shook as they moved across the frame's controls. "What should we do?"

He grinned widely as he stared at Hughes's metal body, letting his white teeth appear between the dark grey of his lips. Darby may have been a genius, but he was also predictable. "I think you should go sit in that chair."

Chapter 12
Soft Landings

Sarah woke to the familiar feeling of crisp linen sheets. A warm slash of bright morning sun cut across the fabric and warmed her toes.

It seemed like it had been ages since she had woken up in her own bed, and even longer since Jenny Farrows had let her sleep in, but she was finally safely home.

As she started to roll over, her dreamy sense of satisfaction was quickly overwhelmed by the burning sensation that prickled across her skin. Had she been in some sort of accident?

Giving up her attempt at sitting, she instead tried to lean back down and was rewarded with a fierce pain in her right arm.

The veil of sleep was lifting quickly now, and stray thoughts began to invade her dream: if she was back home, when exactly had her father forgiven her?

And then the memories came flooding back, "The balloon over the East River, the mad Frenchman!" She gasped. "We crashed!" she shouted out as her eyes opened wide.

This time Sarah ignored the pain and bolted upright. She tried to take in her strange surroundings, but wherever it was she had landed, it wasn't the Stanton mansion.

The room she sat in was a large space, roughly constructed from wooden frames and fabric walls. It was, she realized, like she had woken up inside a junk shop: the floor was covered in what seemed to be a maze of chairs, tables, and rugs. On every flat surface someone had placed lamps, statuary, and other bits of colorful bric-a-brac. Most of the objects were chipped and broken, with some of the statues so badly battered they would have been envious of the Venus de Milo.

Sunlight was streaming down through a circular glass skylight that had been built in the ceiling. It had clearly been cobbled together from numerous bits of stained glass, with a large, clouded bull's-eye at the center that gave the viewer a warped and shattered vista of the clouds above.

Sarah leaned back and looked up at the riot of colors until they seemed almost to swim and swirl around her. As she closed her eyes, Sarah could feel a painful throbbing in her head—and when she reached up to touch her aching brow, she discovered that it had been bandaged. "What's happened to me?" she said out loud.

"You almost died," a woman's voice replied from just out of sight. "But your head isn't broken."

Sarah turned her head slightly, and could see that Emilio's sister was standing nearby.

She held a tray in her hands, and on the top of it were a bowl of soup and a cup of tea, both giving long strings of steam in the chilly morning air. Normally Sarah would have been anxious for her morning tea, but today it was the cool glass of water that stood next to the other items that Sarah had her eye on.

"That stupid brother of mine, he almost got you killed," she said, setting the tray down on the bed next to her. The settee was like something that she might have seen at her father's home; a slab of Italian marble chased with patterned silver around the edges.

The whole object was dreadfully old-fashioned—a faded piece of tableware from another time and place. It was something that her grandparents might have used, although no tray in the Stanton mansion would last long with a dirty crack running straight through the middle of it.

Remembering her savage thirst, Sarah picked up the water glass and gulped the contents down, consuming almost the entire thing in a series of noisy gulps. The sounds made her feel guilty, and she set the glass back down onto the tray even though she still wanted more—it was the ladylike thing to do.

"Your brother saved my life," Sarah said, trying to continue the conversation.

Viola turned her head and mimed as if she were spitting at something. "Pfhh."

"Up in the balloon."

"In the balloon, yes." She waved her hands and rolled her eyes. "He told me *all* about it. Fighting and shooting, and kissing and falling."

"This smells delicious," Sarah said, as the scent of whatever it was in the bowl reached her nose.

"I saw you jump onto that thing with my brother. Why would you go up there, anyway?"

Sarah picked up the spoon and took a closer look at it. It was pure silver, and huge—clearly something intended for serving and not eating with. "That man, the one with the harpoons," Sarah said as she dipped the massive implement into the thick red liquid, "killed my friends and attacked my father."

The woman frowned at her with a look of disapproval so deep that it was almost motherly. "That seems like a reason to stay *away* from him."

"I've fought him before." Sarah said as she brought the spoon up to her mouth, once again dispensing with etiquette in the face of need. "And last time I managed to . . . Oh!" Sarah found herself overwhelmed by the flavor that unfolded on her tongue. She'd had Italian food before, of course. There had been a period during her childhood where she had been obsessed with spaghetti, although her father described the noodles as "food for commoners."

But the soup was something else entirely. She could taste the tomatoes, the spices, the beef broth—everything together and separate at the same time. And there were potatoes, carrots, garlic, along with something mysterious and slightly spicy—her mouth felt like it might explode. "This is amazing!"

"Just minestrone. But I'm glad you like it."

"I love it."

"My sister, good cook, no?" Emilio peered through one of the curtains, revealing that a doorway was hidden behind it.

Sarah felt her cheeks blush deeply, and her eyes darted away from the handsome man who had just entered her room.

Viola shook one hand at her brother as she spoke. "*La hai bel imbarazzato, Fratello.*"

"I am sorry." He spoke slowly, clearly trying to concentrate on the words. "But," he said as he stepped in and came closer, "I want to make sure you're okay."

She could see now that Emilio hadn't managed to make it through their adventures entirely unscathed, and two jagged stitches held together a small cut on his face. Sarah felt stupid and childish as she clutched the covers tightly (but not *too* tightly) around herself and averted her eyes. She was only wearing—what was she wearing? Some kind of white nightdress . . . And who had dressed her, or undressed her?

And her hair! She had only just begun to overcome the damage from the fire, and now her head was wrapped in a bandage . . . Her head began to swim again and she lay back into the sheets.

Reacting to Sarah's distress, Viola jumped up and walked over to her brother, her hands moving in a sweeping motion. "*La fai sentire piu male! Parta!*"

"She's awake. I just want to make sure."

"You saw, now go away. You've already done enough damage."

Emilio retreated back through the curtains as his sister gave him a series of sharp shoves in the chest and shoulder to direct him more rapidly out the door.

Sarah felt a pang of guilt for forcing him out of his own room in his own house, even more so for the sense of relief it brought when he was gone.

She had always thought of herself as forward-thinking, but there was no doubt that whatever desires she had toward being a more modern woman, her mother's lessons on what it meant to be a lady had a deeper hold on her.

Sarah propped herself up and took another sip of the soup. The huge spoon she had been given forced her to make a loud slurping sound as she tried to suck in a large chunk of potato. It was a noise that she was sure any one of a number of her family and friends would have found quite shocking. She smiled to herself and then did it again, on purpose, suddenly feeling *most* unladylike.

Viola smiled back. The grin looked mostly sweet, but there was something behind it that appeared calculating, as well. "You're a lady, aren't you?"

Sarah supposed that she must be, despite her occasional dalliances with rude behavior. Then she remembered how she had tried to knock over the Bomb Lance by throwing herself into him and shook her head. "I'm not sure I'd go that far . . . but I do have manners."

Viola nodded. "You're a rich girl." She pointed to her hand. "You need the right spoon, the right bowl."

Sarah felt like she had turned transparent as glass. How had the woman read her thoughts? "I'm just not comfortable having strangers in my bedroom," she said, trying to turn the conversation in another direction.

"Strange *men*," she said. "You don't mind me."

Sarah took a deep breath. This girl was infuriating! "Strange men, then—yes."

"And it's not your room, it's *ours*."

"That's true." Sarah felt her impatience growing. "I don't like boys seeing me when I'm not at my best." There was no doubt that this woman was a handful, but she needed to keep her temper. And she reminded her of Jenny Farrows in a way—a child of the streets, but also something more.

"You think it's yours because you can always choose who comes and goes, and when they come and go." It sounded like an accusation.

"Certainly I don't think that strange boys should be able to barge into my bedroom whenever they like. Don't you agree?"

"I don't spend time with *boys*," she replied. "I like men." She said it in a lusty tone that spoke to volumes of experience with the opposite sex that Sarah hadn't even read the forewords to. "And the men I know go wherever they want."

Viola stood up and walked a few feet away from her. She picked up one of the chipped statues off a wobbly oak cabinet. It was a bust of a woman looking dreamily off into the distance. She stared at it while she ran her finger back and forth over the rough surface where the nose had once been. "You live in a big fancy house?"

For a moment she considered lying, but the idea of denying her past made it feel like she was wiping it away. "I used to."

"And why did you run away from your big fancy house?"

Sarah tried to think of an answer. It was a question she had asked herself every day since that night in the park, and every time the answer she gave herself was a bit different. The answers were all equally unsatisfying. "I wanted to see the world."

"So, how is it?" she said with a low tone in her voice. The girl seemed sad now, as if she remembered something upsetting, and her thumb continued to work over the broken plaster face she held in her hands. "You like the world that you've seen?"

"I haven't seen it all yet."

"Maybe that's lucky for you."

"I'm not as innocent as you seem to think I am," Sarah said with a touch of resentment in her voice.

"I think you're like this girl," she said gesturing to the bust in her hands. "Once she was very pretty, then someone was not careful. And once she got broken, the rich people didn't want her anymore, so she ends up here, with Viola and Emilio."

There was a sinking feeling in Sarah's stomach, and her head began pounding a bit harder than it had been before.

"And one day . . ." Viola said as she turned over her hand, sending the bust tumbling to the floor. It exploded on contact with the ground, shattering into a thousand pieces. "That, I think, is what happens to the porcelain girls who run away from home."

Sarah gritted her teeth and narrowed her eyes. If this woman had been like Jenny once was, she also had never learned to be more.

The Italian woman lifted her head and returned her gaze. "My brother is a fool, but I think this is a game for you. Many men died on that boat, and then you put on your costume, and get my brother to fight your little wars for you."

Sarah swallowed, the aftertaste of the soup suddenly bitter in her mouth. "I think you underestimate him. He's a brave and clever man."

"No, he's a fool!" she shouted back at her. "He wants to make toys for people like the Paragons—silly weapons for fake wars." There were tears shining in her eyes. "He played those games back home, and we lost everything!" The woman put her hand up to her face, hiding her eyes, clearly ashamed of her tears.

Sarah felt her guilt rising again. How was it she managed to end up in over her head time and time again? "I'm sorry. I didn't mean to put him in danger. He wanted to help . . ."

To Sarah's surprise, when Viola pulled her hands away from her face, not a single drop of moisture had escaped from her eyes. They looked at her with a hardness that Sarah had only seen in women twice her age. "I think you used him, rich girl!"

There was something about this woman that Sarah found both incredibly noble and utterly terrifying. Part of her wished that she could pull Viola out of her pocket the next time she was having an argument with Nathaniel. "I found you both on the beach, in that crashed balloon. I thought Emilio was *dead*!"

"I'm sorry, I didn't . . ." A blinding spike of pain shot through her head from front to back. She groaned and lay back.

"You're not sorry enough." She took a step closer, and squinted with one eye shut. If it was a gesture meant to menace her, it was working. "If he had been dead, I would have left you out there to rot on the sand as food for the birds."

The words penetrated the pain and left her breathless to respond. She remembered what her mother said to her father a thousand times after he had revealed his identity to them: "What happens to us when you die out there?"

Another memory flashed by: her tiny hands clinging to the edge of the Industrialist's leather coat, pleading with him not to leave, sure that this would be the time he never came back. The richest irony was that it had ultimately been Sarah's mother who had paid the price for her father's adventures as a Paragon.

And now, here she was—battered and bruised, sitting in a stranger's bed, slowly realizing that she had been so wrapped up in seeking revenge that she had never bothered to think of the consequences of her vendetta: it had almost cost a man his life, and a sister her brother. "I'm truly sorry, Viola."

But somewhere out there the families of the men that the Bomb Lance had killed on that boat were also mourning. Wives, sisters, mothers and fathers, sons and daughters, all of them innocent and devastated by the news that the person they loved the most in the world was never coming back.

Sarah had been one of them the day Darby died—a victim. And when she had put on a mask, she had made a choice. "Sometimes you have to fight back."

Viola stared into her eyes. "Then don't be sorry, rich girl."

"What?"

"Don't be sorry." Something inside the other woman had changed so quickly it seemed like the clouds had parted from above her head. "My idiot brother—I can tell he will do anything for you."

Sarah could feel the heat of another blush rising up from her chest to her cheeks. "I'm sure you're mistaken. He was just helping out a lady in distress."

"If you believe that, then you know *nothing* about men." Viola's laugh was loud and scornful, and she followed it by pursing her lips and making a kissing noise.

Sarah was about to respond, and then she realized that she was entirely unsure of what she should say next. It seemed like every way she went with this woman, somehow it was the wrong direction. "A lady always opts for discretion." It was one of her mother's sayings—a useful one in this case. Sarah turned her eyes away and slurped up another spoonful of the soup.

"I kept your suitcase," Viola said, shifting the conversation.

The suitcase! Clearly the blow had rattled her brains more than she realized. How could she have forgotten?

The Children of Eschaton had gone to all that effort just to retrieve Tom's heart, and whatever these madmen wanted with it, it was surely for a plan of great evil. There was more than just their own lives at stake here, there were the lives of all those that Lord Eschaton would kill once he got what he desired. "Did you open it?"

"My brother did." Viola grabbed one of the nearby chairs and sat down on the badly faded velvet. Sarah almost expected a cloud of dust to rise up from it as the red-haired girl dropped down onto it, but even if the things in the house were old and broken, they were also well cared for. "All I saw inside was girl's clothes and old junk."

Sarah felt her stomach shift. "You didn't get rid of it?"

"I said *I* saw junk. My idiot brother, he said he saw a masterpiece."

If Sarah was woozy before, she was waking up now. "What did he do with it?"

"He wanted it, so I let him have it."

Visions of the Automaton's heart dissected into a thousand pieces danced in Sarah's head. "Tom!" she shouted, and threw back the covers.

Sarah began to lift herself out of bed, but felt Viola's hands grip her arm. "You need to stay in bed, rich girl. You're not better yet."

Sarah yanked herself free, rocking the bed. A bright red dollop of soup leapt over the side of the bowl and began to run toward the edge of the tray.

"Aiee!" Viola let go of Sarah to dive for the spill before it could reach the sheets. She almost made it.

Sarah used the confusion to try to dash for the curtains, but the instant that she stood up, her head began to revolt, descending into pain and dizziness. She put her hand to her brow and tried to steady herself.

There was no doubt that Viola was right—she should have stayed in bed. But the decision had already been made. Emilio was clearly technically gifted, possibly a genius. He was *exactly* the kind of person who could do something irrevocable to what remained of Tom. If he had taken the heart, then she needed to talk to him as soon as she could.

"Here, rich girl," Viola said, throwing a ratty pile of faded silk at her, "put this on."

Sarah unfolded it and realized that it was some kind of Oriental robe. The intricate Asian threads and dyes were mostly faded and worn away, but it had once been covered in exotic flowers and brightly colored birds.

She slipped it on, and wrapped the red belt tightly around her waist. She weaved her way across the room, avoiding tables and chairs until she reached the curtains. She passed through a short hallway, and then wandered through a second set of burlap curtains. When she pushed them back and passed through, Sarah entered into another world.

If the bedroom was a junkyard, then this was the scrap heap. There were bits of machinery everywhere: metal and porcelain lined the walls, hanging down from the ceiling were bales of wire, and strewn across the floor were bits of steel, sheets of leather, and all kinds of brass objects, from hinges to cogs.

The space itself was narrow and dark—like a train compartment. Light came in from a series of casement windows at regular intervals near the top of the wall, along with some gas lamps beneath them, their bright reflectors doing their best to bring light back down into the room. Somewhere in the distance she could hear the familiar sound of a boiler building pressure. Nearby, an old Franklin stove, heavily modified with baffles and pipes, blazed merrily away.

She could see Emilio at the other end, facing away from her and bent over a worktable, clearly engrossed in his project. "Emilio!" Sarah shouted out as she entered. She yelped as something bit into her foot. When Sarah lifted it up, there was a screw pressed sideways into the flesh of her heel.

She brushed it away, sending it bouncing across the floor to finally disappear underneath a pile of brass scraps and wire.

Now that her eyes had adjusted, she could see that the floor was littered with shards of metal—this was clearly no place for bare feet. Nearby a pair of badly beaten work-boots stood on a slumped pyramid of metal ingots. Keeping an eye out for any other dangerous bits, and there were several, she tiptoed over to the shoes and pulled them off the pile. She stepped back from the small avalanche she had started and slipped them on. They were huge, and her feet rattled around inside of them as she walked, forcing her to take odd, unladylike steps.

As she leaned against the wall to steady herself, she saw a sign attached to it, listing out directions for proper packing. Sarah realized that her initial impression had been totally correct—not only did this space look like a train car, it actually was one.

Listed in red print at the bottom of the message were some helpful, if menacing, directions on how not to lose a limb while closing the main door, or when coupling the cars together.

Sarah clomped across the floor. The distance from one end to the other in a straight line would have only been a few yards, but Emilio had done his best to maximize the use of the space, turning it into a maze. Projects in various states of completion had been placed on stands, and Sarah wound her way around any number of works in progress, including what seemed to be earlier versions of the shield he had used on the balloon.

When she neared the end of the car, she stood and watched Emilio for a second. He was clearly still unaware that she had invaded his sanctum, and was bent over his table, deep in concentration, poring over whatever fantastical object was in front of him.

Seeing him like this reminded her of time she had spent in Sir Dennis's laboratory, quietly observing the world's greatest inventor as he stared for hours at some mysterious object, intent on solving a tiny portion of an intricate puzzle of creation that was wholly mysterious to anyone locked outside of his mind.

When she had been a child, she had been trying to discover the old man's secret, thinking that maybe she could become like him if only she knew how. But she soon realized that there was little she could glean from seeing Sir Dennis slowly turning a screw, or shaving the tiniest bit off the edge of a brass casing. But even if the science had remained a mystery, what she *had* begun to learn from him was focus. That he could continue to patiently turn that same tiny screw back and forth for an entire afternoon was almost beyond belief.

The man in front of her was different than Sir Dennis in so many ways, but Emilio had some of the old man's intensity.

Sarah felt a warmth rising up in her chest, and she realized that her heart was taking her into strange and dangerous waters. For the first time, remembering Darby was making her smile. Maybe losing someone didn't mean you had to lose everything about them forever.

She let out a small cough in an attempt to capture Emilio's attention without upsetting him, but there was no reaction. Perhaps he hadn't heard her over the thrumming of the steam engine . . .

She tried again, clearing her throat loudly with an audible "Eh *hem*," but once again it seemed to have no effect.

"Excuse me," she said, beginning to feel frustrated, and then yelled out his name, "Emilio!"

"What?" His head rose up as if he had just awoken from a dream.

As he turned around to face her, Emilio smiled, and she felt her face flush again when he said her name. "Sarah!" Her heart was fluttering in her chest, a potent mix of excitement and fear threatening to wipe away any common sense she had left in her bandaged head.

She swallowed hard and attempted to push the feeling down to her toes where it wouldn't get in her way. "Viola says that you opened up my suitcase. There's something inside of it that's very valuable to me and I . . ."

"This?" Emilio said, holding up his hand to show her what he was working on.

Sarah gasped. Her worst fears had come true; he held a piece of Tom's heart in his hand. "What have you done? That wasn't yours!" Peering over his shoulder for a closer look only made her more upset.

The rest of the mechanism was laid out on the table in front of him, and the gears had been placed in tidy rows. The hexagonal frame that had once surrounded it was broken down into a series of small rods and joints. "What have you done?" she asked, but the answer was all there in front of her.

"I sorry Sarah. Is so beautiful! I had to look."

Her head was pounding again, the pain almost blinding.

Emilio clearly saw what was going on, and his smile vanished. "No, no, Sarah! I sorry. I fix it! I am fixing it!"

"What?" she said.

He pointed to a bent gear. "Broken!" He pointed to a metal rod that was cracked in two. "Broken too! Not by me! I fix it. It will be okay."

It was devastating to see Tom reduced to tiny pieces. The Automaton had once been a man—mechanical, to be sure—but far more than just the sum of his parts.

She had watched helplessly as he had been brutally shattered by Lord Eschaton, torn to pieces until only his heart remained. Now even that was gone.

Could she even begin to hope that the bits and pieces on the table in front of her might be reassembled back into the Tom she once knew? Which one of these gears and rods was the part that gave him his soul?

Sarah felt the pain in her head growing stronger, and Emilio was looming closer and closer. For an instant she thought he might be trying to kiss her again, until she realized that *she* was falling toward him.

"Bella!" He leaped up and grabbed her, and she sank into him, every muscle in her body seemingly incapable of assisting her. "You are still sick!"

"No." But she hoped that she was, because the alternative was that Sarah had just transformed into some silly character from one of her novels; the kind of girl who would tremble at the knees, and then "unintentionally" tumble into the men they desired, in hopes they would finally notice them and then take them to the ball.

Emilio softly guided her down until she was sitting on his stool and he was standing over her. Somewhere along the way he had also used his foot to pull the seat a safe distance away from the desk. "Four days, and still you need more sleep."

Every bit of her was aching now. Whatever had happened to her in the crash, it clearly needed more time to heal . . . Her eyes widened, "Four days?"

"A very bad crash for you. Viola found us and she save you."

"Then what day is today?"

"Is Wednesday."

"Wednesday?" Sarah felt sick and faint all over again. At least this time there was no chance anyone could claim that it was anything but nerves. "Mr. Grieves!"

She stood up woozily, one hand locked around Emilio's arm, trying to ignore the fact that the muscles underneath his shirt were pleasantly firm . . . "I have to go!"

"Go? You go to bed." She noticed the scent of alcohol on his breath. She looked down and saw a chipped mug sitting on the workbench, half full with a clear brown liquid. It was still the morning, surely too early for a temperate man to be imbibing. But she also knew that foreigners could have very different ways. "You too sick to go out right now."

He was right of course, but if Tom could be brought back to life, it would take more than just his heart . . . "I have to get something, and there's no time to wait." She pointed at the pieces on the table.

"Is a *cuore*, yes?" He placed a hand on the center of his chest, and then began to lift it up and down, rhythmically (and adorably) thumping out a beat.

"A heart," she replied with sudden comprehension, "yes."

"So very beautiful."

She couldn't imagine how he had begun to puzzle out the object's purpose with so little to go on. "How did you know?"

He pointed excitedly at the pieces laid out on the table as he spoke, "Valve, timer, pump . . . You see? For *L'Automa*, I think?"

Sarah was amazed. Everyone else she had shown it to had reacted only with curiosity and confusion, but Emilio had seen it for what it was.

She supposed it helped that he knew whom it had belonged to, but his skills clearly lent themselves to more than just weapons and shields.

Her father had always told her that you could take the measure of a man by staring straight into his eyes and seeing how he reacted. She looked at Emilio straight on, and wondered why no one had had ever mentioned to her that there were blue-eyed Italian men.

As she held his gaze, his smile softened. He seemed uncomfortable, as if she had invaded some hidden, private part of him. "I sorry, Bella," he said turning away. "You didn't want me to help . . ."

Sarah felt a pang of guilt rise up in her stomach. Perhaps she shouldn't be using her father's advice for matters of the heart. He had always been ready to judge anyone and everyone, and he mostly found them deficient. The world of Alexander Stanton was, on the surface, always very simple: up or down, good or evil, black or white.

Not only did the Industrialist view the world in simple terms, but it seemed to her that he had spent his life making sure that it *stayed* that way, no matter how much more convoluted the reality often was.

But Sarah couldn't accept such a negative view of the world, let alone defend it. It seemed to her that even if there were shadows lurking in every corner, there was also a ray of hope to be found in all but the darkest despair. It was that common belief that had drawn her to Darby as a girl, and it seemed to be drawing her to this man now. "Emilio," she sputtered out, "I do want your help." She pointed down to the table. "If you think you can do it."

The Italian's soft smile returned, and this time she didn't try to fight the feeling that it made blossom inside of her. If she was, as Viola had said, a chipped statue, then maybe she should start trying to embrace her new life. "The Automaton was my friend, Emilio, and I need you to try to bring him back to me."

"To fix Mr. Darby's work . . ." He nodded solemnly, as if he were a knight who had just been given the quest to find the grail.

"Yes," she continued, "but there's a piece missing. The piece that made him come to life, and I need to go get it—*now*, before it's too late."

"No, Bella," he said shaking his head. "You are still too hurt. You can't go alone."

Sarah thought of trying to navigate her way quietly around New York with an immigrant boy on her arm—every eye would be turning her way. She might as well parade down Fifth Avenue as the Adventuress. "No. I can't take you. And anyway, you need to work on Tom."

"What if another baloney comes?"

With his accent, she couldn't tell if he was joking or not, but either way it made her laugh. "I think we're safe from baloney for a little while."

"And she won't be alone, idiot," said Viola from the other side of the room. She stood there with her arms crossed, somehow managing to give them a stare that was both angry and amused. "I'm going with her."

142

Chapter 13

An Improper Evolution

T he Hall of Paragons had been constructed so that the members' quarters all faced the central courtyard. Having rooms designed to act as both an office and a vault had seemed like a stroke of genius when they had first conceived of the place, but in hindsight the problems with the idea were obvious: the rooms were dark and poorly ventilated, and the only source of natural illumination were three roundels that had been cut into the two-foot-thick granite slabs that made up the exterior wall of each one.

What little light trickled in through the stone tubes only served as a reminder that there was a brighter world outside the cold walls.

There had been plans to drill skylights into the roof soon after the Hall had opened, but there always seemed to be something more important to do.

Alexander Stanton referred to his quarters as "the dank cave," and for years he had made every effort to occupy them as infrequently as possible. But after his ascension to the leadership of the Paragons, it had become far more difficult to avoid spending at least some of his time dealing with the paper-work that kept piling up at his desk.

Besides the standard headaches of managing a team of costumed exhibitionists, there were constant issues and responsibilities that arose from their celebrity and special status as agents of the law.

It seemed that most of New York either wanted them to forcefully subdue family members and neighbors, or show up at "once-in-a-lifetime" events such as birthday parties and weddings. The rest wanted to either take the Paragons to court or run them out of town on a rail.

But love them or hate them, if the Paragons insulted them by refusal to comply with their requests, it turned out that everyone had a famous or powerful relative to complain to.

As Alexander Stanton struggled to come up with a diplomatic answer for each issue, it became harder to imagine that this was the same job that Sir Dennis Darby had relished for so many years. Especially considering that the old man's mind seemed to always have been either on his next project, or chasing some mechanical flight of fancy.

The Industrialist had a suspicion that it was the Sleuth who had been responsible for the lion's share of the social work. This kind of meticulous nonsense was precisely the sort of thing that Peter had thrived on. But it was a suspicion that would be impossible to confirm now that both men had left this world behind.

Either way, this was work that needed to get done: a thousand signatures to scrawl on a thousand different documents in order to keep the Paragons alive. And Alexander Stanton was the man responsible for all of them. "I'm going to need to hire somebody to take care of all this before I go mad," he mumbled to himself.

And then the building began to shake. It was subtle enough at first, and Stanton wondered if perhaps he already *had* lost his mind. But by the time the books started jumping down from their shelves, it was obvious that it wasn't *all* in his head.

A wave of relief washed over him as he put down his pen and went to strap on his gun. Action was something he understood well.

The protocols they were supposed to follow in cases of dire attack inside the building were clear—in fact, he had written them himself. Rule number one: in case of invasion, exit the Hall and gather outside.

Pleased that he was following his own advice, Stanton headed to the stairs, fully intending to leave the building. It was only when the distant sounds of someone screaming reached his ears that he stopped. The pathetic noises were loud enough to be clearly heard over the rumble, and as he listened, they switched from yells to a long, powerful moaning. It was a sound that men only made when they were suffering excruciating pain.

By the time he reached the bottom step, he could hear maniacal laughter mixed in with the terrified whimpering.

For a moment he turned toward the front doors, and then he stopped and looked back. He couldn't begin to count the number of times he had told the other members of the society that the point of having *rules* was to follow them *unquestioningly*.

More than that, he had written them expressly to protect the Paragons from succumbing to a ruse in exactly these kinds of dilemmas. He could remember Darby nodding in agreement as he had presented the plan. "In all things," Darby had said during that meeting, "we must remember that we are always more powerful as a group than any single man, no matter how clever or skilled we believe our abilities to be."

And yet the threat was *here*—so very close by. If he could assess what it was and bring that information back to the others, it would surely allow them to properly prepare.

The voice returned to screaming again, and this time he recognized the owner: it was Hughes. "God's wounds," he muttered, turning towards the sound. He had written the rules—he could damn well break them.

Drawing his gun from the holster, Stanton held it tightly in his hand as he crept down the corridor. Bits of granite cracked and fell from the ceiling as the building shook, the crumbling rock masking any noise that he could possibly make. And as loud as it had seemed before, the rumbling continued to grow louder as he moved closer to the main council room.

"Excellent! Excellent!" boomed a familiar voice from out the door. "Don't worry, Hughes, it will be over soon. Comfort yourself in the fact that you sacrifice yourself in the name of all humanity!"

Stanton took another step forward. He knew he should leave. He would have told any other Paragon that attempting to try to deal single-handedly with whatever lay beyond the meeting room door was an act of utter folly.

The rules were the rules for a *reason*. Trying to outsmart the system they all had lived under for the past two decades was childish and selfish. He had repeated the message to the new members only a week ago. "We're a team," he had said to them, "and without the people you see here around you, you are nothing more than a man in a costume. How are the others supposed to rely on you if you aren't willing to rely on *them*?"

But Stanton had already made his decision at the bottom of the stairs. The voice in his head, the one screaming at him to leave, was simply justification for cowardice.

As he took another step toward the meeting room, a huge gust of white steam blew out through the door. It was cold and wet, like a billowing version of the London fog. The cloud rolled past him and settled across the floor, melting away into the ether.

As he breathed it in, Alexander could taste a familiar hint of metal on his tongue. This was a cloud of fortified steam.

"Help me!" screamed Hughes. Stanton began to run, and then stopped short when he heard his next words. "Help me, Lord Eschaton!"

"Eschaton is here?" he whispered to himself. How could a villain have infiltrated the Hall? It seemed impossible. But if he was here, he'd be no match for the Industrialist's bullets.

Another cloud of fortified steam billowed out the door, and Stanton stumbled into the room. It took him a few moments to make out what was going on, although when he finally made sense of it, what he saw was almost beyond comprehension.

The president's throne and the dais it stood on had slid forward from their original position. They now stood in the center of a gaping pit in the floor where the meeting table had once been. Sprouting up from the hole was a mix of steel rods and tubes.

Sitting in the throne was Hughes, twitching with panic as a metal forest grew up around him. Some of the shafts pierced his body. Stanton watched in horror as one of the brass rods impaled the poor man's throat. It silenced his screams and emerged from the other side of his neck, covered in crimson blood.

From somewhere unseen an arc of electricity ripped through the air, striking the metal chair. Hughes silently twisted and squirmed, his open mouth twisted in agony.

Stanton caught a flash of purple and gold before another cloud of steam obscured his view. "Jupiter, is that you? You need to help me! This man is dying!"

"The Industrialist," a voice boomed back at him. "I'm so glad to see you've decided to join us."

"What's going on, Jupiter?" he shouted back. Their first real crisis, and already the new man was falling to pieces. "I heard Hughes say that Lord Eschaton is here. We need to stop him!"

The dais was sinking down into the floor now, taking Hughes with it. The impaled man let out a choking groan as he descended, and Stanton realized that the frame Hughes wore appeared to be growing around him, reaching up to his shoulders, bands of metal wrapping around his body almost like a living thing.

The shaking paused, and as Hughes vanished out of sight, the only sounds Stanton could hear were a mechanical clanking and the hiss of steam.

The moment the clanking stopped, the rumbling began again, but softer this time, and the pit closed as the two halves of the table slowly rejoined over it.

There was an instant of quiet when the two sides met, and then the skylights shattered, glass falling down to the floor in a crystal rain. Stanton's striped leather top hat was knocked off his head as he dived under one of the tall chairs.

He could feel shards of glass battering his costume and could hear it hitting the stone floor all around him. None of the pieces were large enough to pierce his jacket, but the wounds he had received from the battle with the White Knight started to complain from the exertion. He could only imagine what the doctor would say if Alexander managed to pull muscles that were on the verge of healing.

Looking out into the room, he saw King Jupiter emerge from the steam cloud. The giant stood in the center of the room, his arms spread wide as the glass rained down and bounced harmlessly off his flesh.

From out of thin air, a new voice began to speak. The tone was scratchy, and it sounded far away, as if it were an echo that had travelled a great distance. But the words were understandable, and it took only a few syllables for Alexander Stanton to recognize who was doing the speaking. "This is Sir Dennis Darby," the disembodied voice said. "If you are hearing this audio image, please, I ask that you not let yourself become alarmed. It simply means the following events have occurred: firstly, I am dead.

"That is most unfortunate, although it was inevitable that it would happen to me one day, as it must happen to us all eventually. I only hope I left this world with dignity.

"Secondly, and more importantly, the activation of this audio impression means that the Paragons have decided to follow my instructions as they were laid out in my will. Not only have you placed Tom's heart into his new body, but he has ascended the dais as the new leader of the Paragons. Congratulations!" Darby sounded pleased as punch, as if these events were a foregone conclusion. Stanton wondered how shocked the old man would have been to find out that his old brother-in-arms had done everything in his power to make sure that Sir Dennis's desired outcome would never come to pass.

So then, why was this message playing? The Automaton had been destroyed, the mechanical man's heart stolen. Why was it accepting Hughes instead of Tom? And more importantly, what was it trying to do to him?

The recording continued, the voice of the dead man blissfully unaware of just how badly his plan had failed. "I know that it cannot have been easy for you to follow through on what must have seemed like the scheme of a madman, but I knew that the Paragons would be able to overcome their prejudices and realize that for such a powerful group of men, there could be no better leader than an impartial machine."

"It *was* madness," Alexander whispered. The rain of glass seemed to have stopped, and the Industrialist crawled out from underneath his chair.

When King Jupiter turned to look at him, Stanton could see the gleam in his eye. "Hello, Mr. President. Welcome to the beginning of the end."

"The end?" Realization dawned on the Industrialist, opening up a pit in his stomach that felt wider than the one that had just swallowed Hughes. "Eschaton . . ."

Jupiter held up his hand. "Be patient. I think we're about to hear the best part!"

"I have," Darby continued, "unbeknownst to the other members, secretly designed a series of improvements into the structure of the Hall of Paragons."

Stanton reached for the gun on his waist.

"Mostly these are minor cosmetic changes, but my primary goal was to make sure to offer a mechanism whereby *all* the members of the Paragons could have unlimited access to the fortified steam they needed without having to store large amounts of it in my laboratory." A panel opened in the wall, revealing a shining brass nozzle in a small nook. "These units are placed throughout the building and will provide fortified steam to any member of the Paragons who requires it, provided you have access." Steam poured from the nozzle, and Alexander shook his head, amazed that Darby's flair for the dramatic could reach so far beyond his death.

"But, you may ask, how will we keep those who might be undesirable or unworthy from tapping the bounty of what, I admit with some sadness, must remain my greatest discovery? In answer to that I ask you to please stand back." The floor began to rumble once again, and a few remaining shards of glass gave way from the ceiling. Stanton shielded himself, but they fell harmlessly to the floor.

"Eschaton!" Stanton shouted.

The gray-skinned man turned to look at him with a smile. "*Lord* Eschaton." Stanton realized that all his suspicions had been confirmed. "I'm a little surprised that you didn't recognize who I truly was when you saw my powers in the courtyard . . ."

Darby's voice cut off Stanton's reply. "The Automaton's consciousness has now been integrated directly into the Hall of Paragons." The edges of the meeting table didn't just part this time, but flipped upwards and disappeared directly into the floor, revealing the pit. "Tom will not just be the leader of the Paragons, but will literally become the heart and soul of our headquarters."

"I give you my greatest creation, the Paragon!"

The shaking became more violent. "Eschaton, what have you done?"

"I've made Darby's dreams come true," the gray man said, laughing. "That man always had a delightfully perverted sense of progress."

Stanton looked down into the pit, but could see nothing but blackness.

"Hughes, are you down there?" Eschaton shouted out.

He was rewarded with a scream as the dais rose back into the light, birthing an abomination into the middle of the meeting room.

The thing that came back up through the floor was twitching and grasping at the air as it ascended, obviously in incredible pain.

Its mechanical legs were gone now, and instead the torso was fully integrated into a metal pylon that had replaced the throne. Oil and steam leaked out of its sides, mixed with what seemed suspiciously like blood.

Hughes's face was entirely hidden, covered by a silver mask. A slit in the middle of it allowed his terrified eyes to stare through.

It reminded Alexander of an iron maiden, with Hughes as the tortured prisoner, forever trapped inside the metal body.

"Hughes, you're alive!" Eschaton yelled out. "And you thought my smoke had made no difference! You see, Stanton!" the giant said, holding his hands out towards the pathetic figure. "Working together, Darby and I have given birth to a new entity! We have created a fusion between man and machine."

Darby's disembodied voice pierced the air once again. "And now, gentlemen, I must say my good-byes to you for the final time. I leave you, and the future, in the capable hands of my creation."

"Very good, Darby." Eschaton said, clapping. "Truer words have never been spoken."

Hughes raised his arms, and the rumbling grew louder, the nozzle on the far wall spewing out a cloud of steam. Cracks appeared in the walls around it, and a moment later the entire apparatus disappeared under a pile of stone.

"Hughes, you need to stop, or you'll tear the building apart." But Stanton doubted that the poor man could still be reasoned with.

Eschaton walked closer to the monstrosity that had been the Iron-Clad. "Give him a moment to adjust. I'm sure there's a great deal for him to try to understand."

"Can't you see that he's dying in there?"

"I don't think so, actually."

A jolt underneath his feet sent the Industrialist tumbling to the floor.

Stanton felt a surge of panic. He was sure that both Nathaniel and Grüsser had been in the building somewhere . . . Surely they must have gathered outside by now. Didn't they realize that something terrible was going on?

The rumbling grew louder than it had ever been—powerful enough that the members' chairs were toppling and bouncing across the floor. He could see that pieces of his own chair were cracking and falling away. Dangerously large cracks had appeared in the walls.

Eschaton took another step towards Hughes. "Look at me!"

The mechanical head turned, and the rumbling seemed to diminish a bit. "You need to regain control! I need you to obey me!"

The creature reached out an arm towards the gray man, the limb oozing ichor and steam through the metal skin. Stanton couldn't begin to imagine what form of alchemy was keeping the man alive, but death would be a mercy.

"Good!" Eschaton shouted at him. "I need you to move beyond the pain, and concentrate!"

The figure gave an almost imperceptible nod, and the rumbling began to subside. Whatever hold the villain had over the man, it seemed to be working.

Stanton sat up and began to reel in his gun. The weapon had been thrown out of his hand when he fell, but it was still attached by the wire that secured the feed belt to his waist. He looked it over to be sure that nothing had broken, but the only way to truly test it would be to fire it.

Eschaton had walked up to the dais and pounded his hand against the shaft that held the monstrous creature in place. The metal rang out in response. "Now tell me my name!"

The Paragon twitched and jerked a few times. "Focus, damn you! You've come this far."

The creature slumped over and let out a long wheezing sound that seemed to echo around the room.

As the rasping continued, Stanton realized that the noise wasn't coming from Hughes directly. Instead it seemed to surround them, piped out of the same hidden places that Darby's message had been generated from. After a moment, it began to form into something recognizable. "L-l-l-ord. Es . . . Eschaton."

"Good God!" Stanton blurted out.

The giant turned towards the Industrialist. "Perhaps you begin to truly understand what has happened here: the Hall is mine! The Paragons are mine! And now I have moved beyond even what Darby was capable of! I've given birth to the first true child of the new humanity!"

"The bastard whelp of your insanity, more like it," Alexander said, attempting to stand. The polished granite bit hard into his knees, and the wounds he had taken from the White Knight were complaining loudly. He could feel blood seeping into his costume. Perhaps some of the glass had managed to pierce him after all.

Eschaton smiled at him. "It's taken me years to get to this point, Stanton. I'm so glad you could join me at both the beginning and the end of my journey."

Alexander pulled himself up into an empty chair, barely noticing that it was Nathaniel's throne of smoke that he was sitting on instead of his own shattered seat.

For a moment, he considered shooting the gray man and being done with him, but after his display in the courtyard there was no guarantee that his bullets would even pierce the skin. Besides, the villain seemed in an expansive mood, and the others would be along any minute. "The beginning? Who in the blazes are you?"

"Of course you don't remember *me*. Not at all . . ." Eschaton took a step toward him.

Stanton lifted his weapon and aimed it at him. "That's close enough."

The gray man smiled, revealing a row of startling white teeth. "I made your first gun."

"Darby made my gun."

Eschaton's brow furrowed, leaving deep cracks along his face. "As always, Darby took the credit. But," he said as he held up his arms in front of him, "it was these hands that did the work!"

Alexander narrowed his eyes. "Wait . . . That man whom I hired . . . The one from the accident . . ."

"Accident?" he said in a mocking tone. "You think it was a simple mistake that found me in that chamber?"

Memories began to return to him in bits and pieces. "Harris, was it?"

"Harrington," Eschaton said, correcting him. "That's who I was once, but it's the name of a man long dead."

Hughes sighed. "You were the Clockwork Man. We fought you, beat you, and I thought we killed you . . . It must be ten years ago now."

Eschaton stepped closer. "You fought me and lost."

"That's not how I remember it."

"Because I realized it was better for me if you *thought* I was dead. And once I had vanished, I could supply your enemies with the machinery they needed to fight against you."

Stanton and Darby had often been puzzled by how the villains had managed to keep up with them for all those years without the power of fortified steam. The Sleuth had postulated a supplier of some sort, but they'd had nothing more than the vaguest of clues to go on. It turned out that Wickham had been right again. "For all the good it did you."

"Oh, Alexander, you defeated my customers, but at what cost? The Crucible's incineration gun—the one that took the life of your wife and orphaned the Winthrop boy? That too, my dear Industrialist, was built by these hands."

Alexander could feel himself squeezing the trigger, but it was a distant and disconnected sensation, almost as if someone else was doing it. He hadn't even realized that his other hand had dialed up the power of his weapon to maximum until the shot rang out loudly and he felt his arm snap back.

Eschaton, Stanton, and Hughes all screamed in unison as a shower of living electricity exploded out from the gray man's body. It moved from point to point around the room, jumping across exposed metal.

Bolts touched the gun and his belt, shocking Stanton in his chair. Every muscle in his body contracted and shook.

Nearby, Hughes's amplified moans were barely audible above the sounds of shattering stone as the building began to heave again.

A shockwave ripped through the floor, leaving a crack in its wake as a metal pipe rose up from underneath the ground.

The shock passed and Stanton felt his arms return to his control. He lifted up his gun and aimed it at the shaft that attached Hughes to the dais. He pulled the trigger and the force of the blast toppled him on the floor.

"Pain!" the half-man screamed, and when Stanton pulled himself up, he saw that the Paragon had disappeared into a cloud of steam that was billowing out from the bullet hole.

The shaking increased, sending a large chunk of the ceiling crashing to the floor. The Hall had been built from pure granite, and Darby had intended it to be able to take the worst abuses, but Alexander imagined that there was no building built by human hands that could withstand these forces for long. If he couldn't stop Hughes soon, the entire structure would collapse on their heads.

"What have you done?" Eschaton shouted as he fell to his knees. It was impossible for Stanton to tell just how much damage he'd done, but at least for the moment the gray man seemed unable to act.

"Hang on," said Stanton, his voice surprisingly steady as he rose back to his feet. "I'll deal with you next."

Peering through the steam, he waited for a moment until he could see a recognizable shape inside the mist. His fingers rotated the dial at his belt, turning down the power to his gun by a single notch. The moment a vaguely human form appeared, he pulled the trigger.

For a moment, he wasn't even sure if he had hit his target. Then something inside the tube burst, ripping a huge hole in the side of it. No longer able to support the weight of the metal-encased man, the shaft buckled, then finally collapsed. Hughes crashed to the ground with a blissfully non-amplified scream.

The rumbling stopped, and Stanton turned toward Eschaton. "Okay, let's finish this." The villain had begun to rise but was still on his hands and knees as the Industrialist walked forward and pointed the gun straight at his head. "Do you think you'll be able to magic this out of your brain?"

Eschaton raised his head, his disconcertingly bright smile still intact. "If you shoot me, and even if you manage to kill me, the energy I discharge will surely kill you as well."

"It's a risk I'm willing to take."

"For what it's worth, Stanton, I always thought of you as one of the people whom I'd like by my side when I rebuild my new world."

"And I'd rather be dead than live in your twisted vision."

"I thought that as well." Eschaton nodded, and Alexander Stanton felt something hard and cold slam into his back. For a moment, he'd thought he'd been punched, but as a feeling of numbness spread outward from the point of impact, he realized that it was something far, far worse.

From behind him came a familiar voice in his ear—carried on hot breath laced with the foul smell of tobacco and liquor. "How's that for an affront to the honor of your precious Paragons, you bastard?"

Alexander tried to fire his gun, but his fingers would no longer obey his commands. Eschaton laughed and stood, taking the weapon out of his trembling hand. "Very good, Mr. Clements. *Very* good."

Chapter 14

Ladylike Behaviors

hy do you wear such a terrible costume?" Viola asked Sarah in a matter-of-fact tone.

She had already spent the better part of the morning trying to uncover the Italian girl's softer side, but so far it had proven to be a fruitless endeavor. It was likely, she was beginning to suspect, that there was no sugar and spice in this woman, and if you cut her open you would find snips and snails all the way down to the center of her tough little heart.

As for Viola's outside—the term *scandalous* didn't even begin to cover her attitude toward clothing. Her tastes were by any measure obscene, and although she had technically covered enough of herself that she could avoid being considered naked, her loose-fitting peasant garments seemed designed to constantly be exposing random bits of flesh at any given time—a peep show that seemed to positively radiate with the promise of more.

Sarah was shocked that the woman hadn't attracted the attention of the police, or at least the temperance league. She had been working up to asking Viola what she was thinking, but so far she had barely been given the opportunity to start a sentence. Any moment of silence had instantly been filled with another of Viola's loud criticisms of Sarah. So far she had commented on her manner of speech, her clothes, and the particular seats she had chosen on the ferry as they had journeyed into Manhattan.

The only thing free of critique had been Sarah's hair, and that had been for the simple reason that she had let Viola color it the night before. It had been a battle to make sure that her hair remained a tasteful reddish shade, rather than the harlot's crimson that Viola seemed to prefer.

Going into the enterprise, Sarah had hoped it would provide a way for the two of them to bond, but instead it seemed to have spurred Viola on. She had subjected Sarah to a long and detailed analysis of why being a "rich girl" made her a permanently unsuitable mate for any Italian man—especially her brother. Sarah was, she had learned, also utterly useless and flailing when it came to actually taking care of herself or anyone else in the "actual world outside of her big bedrooms with fancy curtains."

And even if she had managed to put in a comment of her own, it seemed clear that no amount logic or explanation on Sarah's part would make the slightest dent in the Italian girl's mind once it had been made up. Sarah simply *was* a useless child of privilege, and nothing she would do could ever change that, not even the fact that she actually had lived on her own for the last few months.

Once they had reached the island of Manhattan, the subject had turned to the Adventuress's costume, and had remained there during their entire trip to her flat. Sarah was angry, but somehow she was unable to speak without sounding as if she was begging for approval, "I—I was in a hurry. I simply put it together from the things that I could find."

"How can you see to fight anything through a ridiculous mask? You must be blind under there!" Her hands went flying through the air as she talked, punctuating her criticisms with gestures that only managed to make her accusations even more pointed and annoying.

"I can see quite well, really," she replied through gritted teeth. Sarah considered mentioning the fact that the Sleuth had worn the mask for years before she had ever put it on, but any kind of reasoned response was a futile gesture. Viola was a master at verbal fencing, turning any kind of logical response into yet another line of attack, and the girl's refusal to ever respond directly to what was being said to her had begun to make Sarah feel as if she were the one struggling with English.

The current conversation, for instance, had been in response to Sarah's merest suggestion that perhaps having faced off actual villains three times might have made her just the tiniest bit qualified to comment on the actual dangers that they presented. Viola's response was to launch an extended attack on her costume choices.

"My brother knows that your gloves are too big. He told me you almost fell off on the way to the balloon!"

Sarah was, she had to admit, finding it harder and harder to keep herself from simply shrieking at the girl. Neither one of them had given up their age to the other, but it seemed to Sarah they couldn't have been more than a year or two apart. Yet somehow Viola had managed to take on the role of an angry nagging mother, acting as if the very *fact* that she found so much to criticize about Sarah was a terrible burden that Viola had to bear, and that she was doubly disappointed since she had nursed Sarah back to health and put color in her hair.

For a moment, Sarah considered letting her anger get the best of her, but she had already decided to rely on her manners instead; it had always worked for her mother. And if the little harlot was going to pin all the crimes of society on her, she might as well teach the girl that one skill that came with being from the upper classes of New York was very a stiff upper lip. "Perhaps you're right about the gloves, Viola. I'll need to do something about them. Maybe you can help me sew them up a bit."

At least the journey was almost over now. This last argument had seen them to within a block or so of her apartment. Sarah hoped that she might be able to set the beastly girl loose on Mr. Grieves while she went upstairs and finished her business.

Sarah hoped that her things were still there. She had managed to put the fear of God into her lecherous landlord the last time she had been there, but she doubted that it was enough to keep him from disobeying her orders for the better part of the week, especially with Mrs. Brooks clearly breathing down his neck.

Viola's intensity was certainly a weapon of great magnitude in its own right, *when* it was on your side. "I tried them on. They were too big for me, and I don't have your tiny, little rich-girl hands." Viola said it matter-of-factly, clearly challenging Sarah to tell her that she either wasn't supposed to wear them, or that her hands weren't too small—or probably both.

Instead Sarah found herself speechless—trapped by a conversation totally bereft of manners, and dangerously close to unleashing a torrent of uncivil words. She'd already been called "rich girl" one too many times today. And just at the moment she was about to open her mouth and finally give Viola what for, she heard a familiar voice speak her name, "Sarah? Is that finally you?"

When she turned around, it took a confused moment before she recognized the familiar figure of Mrs. Farrows standing beside her in a woolen winter coat.

"Jenny!" Without saying another word, Sarah threw decorum to the wind and ran to her, wrapping her arms around the woman and giving her the hardest squeeze she could.

The housemaid responded in kind, although without quite the same level of intensity. "It's good to see you . . ."

Giving herself a moment to enjoy the reunion, Sarah let go and looked up at her. "But however did you find me?"

"I thought I saw you at the department store a few days ago, but you vanished before I could be sure. I asked if there was a Sarah working there, but no one had heard of you."

"Yes . . . I changed my name," she said with a slight blush.

"And your hair," she said with an obviously disapproving tone. "I was able to get one of the other girls to reveal who you were and where you live, . . . Miss Standish."

"I never thought it would be so difficult to hide in a city as big as New York," Sarah said with a sigh. "Is there anyone who doesn't know what I'm up to?"

"Your father, thank goodness. I'm sure the shock of finding out that his daughter was a department store sales girl would be enough to drop him in his tracks."

"How is he?"

A sharp voice cut her off. "Who's this?" Viola said, giving Jenny a dismissive sideways glance. "One of your rich friends?"

Sarah's etiquette kicked in before she could decide whether or not introducing the two women might actually be a good idea. "Mrs. Jenny Farrows, this is Viola Armando."

Jenny returned the glance and gave a slight curtsey. "Most charmed, I'm sure." She turned back to Sarah, strategically placing her shoulder in Viola's way. "I'm sure your father would also be surprised to see you've taken up with gypsies."

The Italian girl squinted her eyes and stared at Jenny. "Tell your fancy friend that I'm not a gypsy, rich girl."

"She's not a gyp——" Sarah began, but was once again cut off before she could finish repeating Viola's message.

Jenny turned fully toward her now, and gave Viola the withering house-maid's stare that she had used to turn hundreds of young upstarts into crack servants. "Oh, I think I'm well aware of just what *you* are, Miss Armando."

"And what's that?" Viola replied, pushing herself closer until the two women were practically nose to nose. Both of them had their chests puffed out so far that it seemed as if two mountain ranges were about to collide.

Sarah noticed an older gentlemen who seemed mesmerized by the con-frontation, but her stare seemed to be enough to shame him into turning his head and harrumphing away.

"You're an Italian street-tough and a smart aleck; one who has clearly been blessed with more ability than sense," Jenny said in succinct tones.

Viola held her gaze for a moment, nodded, and then took a step back. "She's okay by me. But no more name-calling."

Sarah felt a sense of relief flood over her. While she had hoped that Viola would be able to maintain her effectiveness under fire, she had hardly expected her to be facing off against an opponent as formidable as Jenny Farrows. "Well, my jury is still out on you, young lady, and please don't forget it."

Although she had repeatedly wished that she could make Viola disap-pear, Sarah didn't want Jenny to think that she had simply fallen in with the wrong crowd. "She and her brother saved my life."

The housemaid clucked her tongue. "Can I assume it was from the same kind of ridiculous danger that your father is always getting himself into?"

Sarah nodded and blushed. "I'm afraid so."

"Then maybe I should be apologizing to her."

"Is okay. My brother seems to like her."

"In the name of our Lord," Jenny said, rolling her eyes dramatically sky-ward. "It's all far more than a woman of my years should have to take."

Sarah waited for a moment, unsure of how to respond to Jenny's feminine theatrics until her friend reached out and grabbed her hand. "Now that we've gotten that out of the way, I need you to tell me everything that's happened since that night you ran away. And if not everything, then I'm at least going to need a great many details. I've been terribly worried about you, Sarah."

"There's something I need to . . ." Sarah tried to hold her ground as Jenny marched over to a nearby stoop, but the maid was clearly stronger, and she ended up sliding Sarah two yards across the cobblestone sidewalk. "Hold on, Jenny."

"What's wrong, Sarah? Surely you have time to talk to me after all the effort I put into finding you."

"I'm sorry. I do want to tell you everything, and after I'm done we can go somewhere together and I'll tell you all the details over a nice cup of tea."

Viola gave her a disparaging look, but managed to not say anything, which was an achievement in itself.

"But first I desperately need to get something from inside my apartment." Sarah pointed at a nearby building. "And I need to do that before I can go anywhere, or do *anything* else."

"I see," Jenny replied with a shrug. "And why is this Tuscan ruffian with you?"

Viola reacted like she'd been struck. "Wait, how do you know where I am from?"

"A housemaid deals with all sorts of people over the years, Miss Armando. I doubt there's a German, Italian, or Jew that I can't tell you at least the general area they hail from. And if it's an Irishman I can probably give you the address where they grew up."

Giving Viola no time to reply, Jenny spun to face Sarah. "All right, Miss Stanton, let's take care of your business so I can get my answers."

"This way," Sarah said, guiding her little group up the stairs to the door. As they climbed the steps, she grabbed Jenny's hand and gave it a squeeze. "I'm so glad you're here. I've missed you terribly."

"You should be glad I haven't lashed you up and dragged you back to the house. What possessed you to color your hair?"

"I was hoping it would allow me to hide better," Sarah said as she slipped her key into the door. She was relieved to see that it still worked in the lock. "I should let you know," she said as she pushed it open, "that I've recently had a bit of unpleasantness with the landlord."

"What did you do to him?" Viola asked, clearly keen to judge her actions once again.

160

"I shoved him . . . a bit. He's a bit terrified of me I think."

"He must be a very tiny man."

As they entered the building, Sarah's eyes immediately turned to Mr. Grieves's door. She saw it sliding closed as she stepped in. If he was there, at least he wasn't going to try to confront her again.

Sarah kept moving. "I'm on the third floor."

The three of them trundled up the stairs, Viola managing to make as much noise all by herself as the other two combined.

She wondered if there was anything that Viola was capable of doing subtly or quietly. Perhaps that was part of her hidden charm.

As they reached each landing, Sarah craned her neck to look down the halls and see if she could see any sign of the padlocks, but it seemed that no one had tried to replace them.

When she reached to the door to her apartment, Sarah stifled a gasp. The entrance had been smashed in, and it sat wide open.

Sarah felt angry and heartbroken. No matter how hard she tried to cover her tracks, it was hopeless. Her enemies had no trouble invading her life.

"That doesn't look good," said Mrs. Farrows, echoing Sarah's thoughts with the same eerie accuracy she had ever since they had first met. "We'd best be careful . . ."

Viola pushed through the two of them and slammed the door open wide. "Anyone in here?" she yelled.

"That girl doesn't do anything by halves, does she?" Jenny said, peering through the door behind her.

"Her brother is much nicer."

Jenny frowned. "Boys can fool you, Sarah . . ."

Viola had only taken three steps into the apartment before she let out a scream and was yanked out of view. Sarah and Jenny practically tumbled over each other as they sprang after her.

When they saw what lay inside, they both jerked to a stop. Inside the room, a man was holding Viola up above his head with one of his massive hands. He was ridiculously tall, and yet nonsensically fat, with a bowler hat that was pulled down too tightly on his head. Waxed red whiskers stuck out from either side of his face, drooping down slightly at the ends.

He held her face up next to his, and Viola's body was stretched out across his huge belly, her feet floating just above the floor. She was kicking fiercely, but so far had only managed to connect with empty air.

Sarah could feel her emotions shift, and the next words she spoke came out of her throat in a low growl. "Let her go." A part of Sarah was shocked at just how easily she was slipping into being the Adventuress, although this was the first time she'd felt the hero come through without her having to put on the mask first.

"I'm called the Ruffian."

"They'll call you No Balls if you ever let me go," choked out Viola.

Sarah kept her eyes locked on the man. "One of the Children of Eschaton, I presume."

"Just so," he replied. The tall man laughed and hauled the flailing girl up slightly higher. "Do you read the Bible, Miss Stanton?"

Sarah nodded. "I'm familiar with it."

"It says that those who reap the wind shall sow the whirlwind."

"And I'd say that goes both ways," Jenny Farrows chimed in, her clipped tone barely managing to contain her anger.

There was a stunned look on the man's face as he parsed her words; it appeared he hadn't considered the possibility that biblical retribution might work both ways, "It doesn't matter," he replied with a shake of his head, "because if you come closer, I will, unfortunately, find it necessary to snap this girl's neck." He jangled Viola slightly, and turned his head to the Italian girl's ear. "That is something that I may do anyway if she does not stop struggling." His voice had clear traces of a German accent, and Sarah wondered if Jenny was calculating the location of his birth.

Despite the warning, Viola began to fight and kick. Sarah looked her straight in the eye before she spoke. "Perhaps you should stop. I think this man is quite serious."

Viola went limp in his grasp, "I'll be good . . ." He lowered her down until her feet were just touching the floor. ". . . for now," she said with a snarl.

With the immediate danger passed, Sarah took a moment to look around her apartment. Clearly the man had been in it for some time before they had reached him. It seemed almost as if someone had taken the entire place and given it a good shaking, with everything that remained either smashed to bits or thrown to the floor.

Sarah wondered if the look of shock on Jenny's face was due as much to the state of the place as it was from the threat they were facing. "It doesn't normally look like this," she said by way of apology.

"I should hope not. I'll just assume that this . . . gentleman is responsible for the mess and not you."

"What do you want?" Sarah asked him.

He turned his head and nodded. "It should be obvious. I want the metal man's heart."

"It's not here," Sarah blurted out. As she heard the words leave her mouth, they sounded like a lie.

"This is . . . a shame," the Ruffian said, not seeming to notice her deceit. He took his free hand and wrapped it around Viola's throat. She only managed to let out the beginning of a scream before her words were choked off entirely.

"Stop that!" Sarah said, jumping toward him. An instant later, she found herself being flung backwards, her face stinging from a slap that she hadn't even seen coming.

She crashed into the wall, smashing the plaster, and slid to the floor. As she sagged to the ground, she wondered if the Adventuress's greatest skill was being thrown through the air by villains.

She could hear Viola struggling harder now, and Sarah tried to pull herself up before it was too late. This was Emilio's sister! If she died, he would never . . . Sarah let the thought pass. It was no time to be thinking about boys.

As she lifted up her head to look at the fat man, a strange look passed over his face. His eyes crossed, and his hands fell limp.

Viola scampered out of the way before the Ruffian crashed to the floor. Standing behind him was Jenny Farrows, an iron in her hand.

"The Ruffian indeed!" she said, and gave the man's unconscious form a jab with her foot.

Viola, still coughing and rubbing her throat, joined in, kicking the man with far more intensity. "*Bastardo!*"

"Easy now, young lady," Jenny said, holding her back.

Sarah had seen Viola angry before, but the rage on her face had reached a whole new level. "I'll tear his balls off!" Spit flew from her mouth, and she kicked the unconscious villain with enough force that he let out an involuntary moan.

Jenny grabbed Viola's arm and hauled her back.

"Don't you touch me!" the Italian girl said as she yanked her arm free, but she didn't try to kick the man again.

Sarah tried not to rise to the occasion. "I'm sure you're angry, Viola, but we can't kill him."

"Go to hell, rich lady."

Jenny responded with a tone that sounded both matronly and angry simultaneously. "If you ever plan to be more than a beggar in this world, then you need to understand that there are some rules."

"Here's what I think of your rules." Viola made a spiteful little laugh, marched forward, and tried to push past Jenny, clearly intent on attacking the unconscious villain laid out on the floor. In a thousand years, Sarah would have been unable to describe exactly what happened next: Jenny's hand shot out, and Viola toppled to the floor. The girl spun around and landed on her rump, facing the entirely opposite direction from where she had been heading.

Jenny leaned down over her. "Now let's give the police a call, shall we?"

Viola, clearly not pleased with the situation, smacked Jenny full in the face with a sound loud enough to echo off the walls. "I said, don't you touch me," she hissed.

Jenny appeared unrattled, despite the red mark on her cheek. Using the same hidden speed that she had before, she smacked the Italian girl back. "Impudent child."

Viola put her hand up to her face, her eyes wide. She opened her mouth to reply, and then simply closed it again.

The two of them sat glaring at each other silently, and, looking down at Viola's clenched fingers, Sarah realized that the next move the girl made would not involve an open hand. "Ladies!" she said loudly.

Neither one of them turned to look at her. "Ladies!" she said again, projecting her voice as much as she could without actually shouting. They continued their staring contest, but Sarah could tell that she had at least begun to gain their attention. "You've both come here to help me, and having the two of you fighting like common thugs is only going to give our scary friend here the chance to wake up. Now then, Viola," she continued, marveling at her own confidence, "I need you to grab that washing line and tie up the Ruffian." She pointed to the rope end that was sticking out of a pile of broken dishes nearby. She was relieved when Viola broke her stare to turn and look where Sarah was motioning. "And I'm assuming you have the needed self-control to secure him properly *without* choking him to death."

"He'd be better dead," Viola said as she crawled out from under Jenny's shadow.

"Jenny," Sarah said as the maid straightened up from her confrontational pose, "can you come with me while we go and get what I came here for?"

Jenny nodded and followed her as she walked into the spare bedroom.

As they passed through the doorway into the small bedroom, Sarah heard Jenny curse under her breath. "She's a terror."

"Maybe she wouldn't have been so angry if you hadn't tumbled her onto the floor."

"I've dealt with her type before. Sometimes landing on their arse knocks their brains back into their head."

Sarah tried not to look shocked as she pulled open the door to the closet. She breathed a sigh of relief when she that all her clothes were still hanging there. Perhaps she should have brought her suitcase . . . "This isn't the Stanton house." Sarah pulled the hangers down and threw the outfits onto the bed. "She was almost killed."

"Are you defending her behavior?" Jenny began to pull the clothes off the racks and fold them. "These are nice."

"They're my work clothes." Sarah frowned at them as she thought of her job in the department store. She had missed far too many shifts to think about going back now. "But I don't think I'm going to need them anymore."

"Waste not, want not," Jenny replied, and pointed to a carpet bag on the floor.

"Fine," Sarah said, and pulled up the moth-eaten old sack. "Whatever you're willing to pack for me, I'll take." She leaned into the closet and saw that secret panel was still in place.

Jenny let out a little laugh. "There's the petulant girl I remember."

Sarah looked over her shoulder. "And what's that supposed to mean?"

"For better or worse, I think being out in the world may just have caused you to grow up a little bit."

Sarah tugged out the loose section of the wall at the back of the closet. "I'm not sure how I'm supposed to feel about that, Mrs. Farrows."

Sarah couldn't see the woman, but she heard the familiar snap of a skirt being shaken out. "That's the funny thing about growing up, Sarah; it doesn't matter what your opinion is about it, it happens anyway."

Sarah pulled out the rosewood box. And when she lifted the lid on the container, she breathed another sigh of relief. Pressed into the velvet padding was the lead key that Peter Wickham had given her. She pulled it free and slipped the chain around her neck.

She lifted it up and dropped it into her blouse, feeling the cold metal against her chest. "I have to admit that lately I've begun to feel like two different people."

"Well, even if you're not *quite* as ladylike as you should be, I'm starting to like some things about the new Sarah Stanton."

Sarah said, "I was never all that ladylike to begin with."

"That's as may be, it still suits you. Everything except for the hair . . ."

Viola poked her head in around the door. "I think the Ruffian is waking up!"

Sarah was amused to hear the Italian girl say the man's villainous name in her accent. Were a costume and a new title all it really took to change yourself in the eyes of the world?

Sarah barged in front of Jenny and stuffed the rest of her clothes roughly into the bag. "It's fine. I'll take them all. Let's go."

Jenny took a step back. "After you, Lady Stanton."

Sarah walked past her. She could feel her face becoming a grim mask as the fat man came into view. He was bound and helpless, and he looked up at her with a wide-eyed expression, as if he was surprised by his predicament. Viola had certainly done an impressive job tying the man up. There was a thick cuff of hemp around either wrist. The line then looped down and formed a similar bind around his ankles.

166

He was an ugly man, to be sure, but there was something almost innocent about him, as if he were just a naughty child and not a cold-blooded murderer. He also, unfortunately, reminded her a bit of Grüsser. "What's your real name?"

"Brandon. You girls are making a very large mistake."

"I agree," said Viola, placing her hands on her hips. "We should have killed you when we had the chance!"

Sarah knelt down toward him. She took a breath and tried to act like the more "grown-up" version of herself that seemed to have impressed Jenny. "Is she right, Brandon? Should we have put an end to you? Or are you going to behave?"

He swallowed loudly enough for her to hear the air as it travelled down his throat. "It will make no difference. Lord Eschaton will get what he wants from you sooner or later."

Sarah considered the situation for a moment and leaned closer. She could hear the rope creaking as the powerful man tested his bonds, and from the sound of it, the hemp wouldn't hold for long. "I have a message for Lord Eschaton. Do you think you could give it to him?"

The Ruffian slowly nodded. "I suppose I could."

"I want you to tell him that he needs to stop, because whatever it is that he thinks that he's doing, whatever his plans are, the Society of Steam will put an end to them."

Brandon's eyes grew wide for a moment, and then he let out a laugh. "And you are the Society of Steam? I don't think he'll be very frightened . . ."

"We were good enough to stop you."

The man frowned like a naughty baby. "I'm just not very good on my own, I'm afraid."

"Will you take my message back to him?"

"Yes," he said with a nod. "But I don't think it will help. He wants to destroy the world."

"Thank you." She stood up and turned to the two other women. "It's time to go."

"And how will I escape?" the Ruffian asked them in an almost pleading tone.

"I'm sure Mr. Grieves will come find you soon. Or you'll tear those ropes apart."

"But I am going to tell the police about you as soon as I can," Jenny added, "so I hope for your sake that either way, you're gone shortly."

"We will meet again I think."

"Then next time," Sarah said furrowing her brow, "I'm going to let my friend do what she wants."

Sarah turned and led the women out into the hallway, letting them pass her before she descended the stairs. The carpet bag was unwieldy, but she supposed she was glad for the clothes. "Viola, I want you to give the address of the yard to Mrs. Farrows."

"What for?"

"So Jenny can come for that cup of tea."

"Feh," she said, managing to make her fake spitting motion in the cramped confines of the stairwell before continuing to tromp downstairs.

"I'm invited to a junkyard? How lovely." Jenny stopped and turned up to look at her. "And the Society of Steam? What was that all about?"

"Nothing," Sarah said, and then smiled a little bit. "I just didn't want Lord Eschaton to think that he was facing one little girl." She grabbed Jenny's hands. "I *am* in terrible trouble, Jenny—the kind of trouble that my father usually gets into—and if I'm going to get out of it, I need all the help I can get."

"Your father can . . ."

"No. He can't. Not yet, Jenny. There's something wrong with the Paragons and I don't think he wants to believe it. I need proof. Once I have it, I can go to him."

Sarah shook her friend's wrists and looked her directly in the eye. "And I need you to keep all this a secret . . . for now. Can you do that for me?"

Jenny sat silently for a minute, and then looked away. "For a short while . . . maybe. But you need to be careful. What happened to your mother—I don't want that to happen to you."

"It won't, I promise."

Jenny shook her head. "Don't make promises you can't keep, Sarah Stanton, and don't be a fool." She paused for a moment, and Jenny could see tears starting to form in her eyes. "And I'm coming to your junkyard, if only to see what kind of place that little hellion lives in."

Sarah could only imagine how Jenny would react to the jumble she would find in the Armando household. "I don't think you'll be disappointed."

Chapter 15

Fleeting Good-byes

"**I**f you would just tell us your secrets, we can fly together." Nathaniel ran his hand along the shining wing, and then gave the metal a soft tap with his index finger. The metal rang out in response.

Hughes frowned at him. "Talking to it won't help. Hitting it, either . . ."

"But we're getting close, aren't we?" he replied with a grin. "I can feel it."

"We'll see," the man replied, and bent back over the machine.

The two of them had spent a good deal of time together over the last few weeks. Hughes was an unlikely partner, but together they had begun to unravel the secrets of Darby's technology and restore the new Turbine costume to working order.

The suit had been broken during the battle at the Darby mansion months ago, and had remained that way since that day. Although his previous costume was still fully functional, Nathaniel had known from the moment he had first put it on that this model was clearly superior to the older one. He had felt the power it contained and despaired that he would never get it back.

So far, getting the suit into the air had proved to be a failed endeavor, although the work to make it function had born some fruit. Darby had forced Nathaniel to gain a passable understanding of the principles behind the outfit before he had let him fly it, but the new suit had proved far trickier to decipher than the old one. A number of elements simply seemed to defy explanation as to their working, while at the same time being obviously integral to making it function.

Having reached a dead end on his own, he had asked William Hughes to help him—the man was becoming a proficient student of Darby's designs, and he was surprisingly skillful at charting out the old man's intentions. He had restored a few broken machines to full function since the fire, and Nathaniel was grudgingly glad for Hughes's assistance, and that was something he would not have been able to say about the man only a few months ago.

There were other positive changes since Hughes had lost the ability to fight as the Iron-Clad in the fire; a great deal of his overt anger seemed to have vanished, although off-handed condemnations of everyone and everything seemed to spill out of his mouth at regular intervals, with a large number of them reserved for posthumous scorn for Sir Dennis Darby.

Nathaniel had spent the better part of the morning trying to ignore Hughes's particularly scathing statements about the departed Sir Dennis's "needless complexity" as they tried to uncover exactly what a series of damaged feed tubes were supposed to be feeding.

Nathaniel peered over Hughes's shoulder, checking what he was up to. "I think that's right." All they needed was a single clue from beyond the grave to bring this jumble of mysterious tubes and wires into focus. But the dead tended to stay quiet, especially when they were being continually cursed.

Hughes connected that last wire and leaned back slightly into his harness. The frame reacted by standing up slightly, forcing Nathaniel to move out of the way. The frame itself was an incredible piece of engineering. "I think we're almost ready to give it a try."

"I think that we need to think about it again. The consequences if we get it wrong . . ."

Hughes sneered. "I thought I was the scared old man here."

Nathaniel opened his mouth to remind Hughes that he had already managed to destroy one suit, when he was interrupted by a knock at the door. "Begging your pardon, gentlemen."

The massive purple-and-gray frame of King Jupiter filled the doorway. Nathaniel waved him in. "Welcome!" He felt relieved at the thought of having someone else to talk with.

"Ah, the broken flying suit . . ." Jupiter's presence filled the room beyond his size, making the granite vault feel cramped. There was something awe-inspiring about the man, but at the same time Nathaniel still felt uneasy around him.

Over the last few weeks, the Paragons had done little besides a bit of sparring, and his knowledge about this mysterious gray stranger was still as scarce as it had been the day that he had first appeared before them in the courtyard. In some ways, King Jupiter was *more* of an enigma now than he had been on that first day. "How goes the work?" he said, peering down at the suit.

Nathaniel shook his head. "Slowly." He pointed into the device. "We're still puzzling out where these feed tubes are supposed to go."

"The boy doesn't really trust me," Hughes mumbled.

Jupiter stepped farther into the room and shook his head. "Nor should he. That line you have connected to the main feed is *clearly* designed to vent excess benzene into the exhaust."

Both Nathaniel and William nodded simultaneously as they plotted out what that would mean if it were true, but it was Nathaniel who spoke first, "Of course!" No matter how obscure Darby's designs might appear at first glance, once you understood the intentions behind them, their brilliance and simplicity would shine through. "You are a genius, sir!" He certainly hoped the same thing would turn out to be true about King Jupiter.

The gray-skinned man nodded thoughtfully. "Understanding isn't genius, I'm afraid. It's only the foundation of invention."

Hughes grunted. "I suppose you're right. Was there another reason you came barging in?"

Something dark swept across Jupiter's expression like a cloud, then dissipated like a wisp of dark smoke, "Yes, Mr. Hughes—as a matter a fact, I was going to ask you for some help with a project of my own. I'm still trying to solve that problem in the basement . . ."

Nathaniel tried to hide his enthusiasm for ridding himself of the other man. "I think I can take it from here, Mr. Hughes," Nathaniel told him, still too eager in spite of himself. "I'll hook up the benzene line and we'll run a flight test first thing tomorrow morning!"

Hughes grunted again and slid down into his harness before rolling away from the table. "Let's walk before we can fly."

It was impossible for Nathaniel to know whether he had offended the man, even when he didn't intend to.

"Thank you," Jupiter said as he followed Hughes out the door.

As Nathaniel watched the two men wander off, he realized that he had completely forgotten to inquire as to the nature of Jupiter's project. The man was already a powerhouse without any mechanical devices. "What could he possibly have in mind?" he whispered to the air. He was sure that he would find out soon enough.

The next hour passed in what seemed like an instant, weeks of frustration vanishing as piece after piece seemed to simply fall into place. Nathaniel was confident that this was the correct configuration, and there was no way that he would have the patience to wait until tomorrow to test it out.

He dropped the hatch onto the back of the wing, and was preparing to load it onto a trolley when the building began to violently shake, sending the final screw tumbling from his fingers to the floor, where it vanished into the gloom.

As the vibrations increased, objects began to topple from the shelves, and Nathaniel caught one of the suit's pneumatic cuffs before it could hop off the table and crash onto the floor.

Having secured the wing, Nathaniel grabbed the edge of the table and waited, but if anything the tremors only grew stronger, and more objects clattered and crashed as they leapt from the shelves.

Nathaniel stared down at his suit. It was completely untested and probably still broken, but if this attack represented genuine danger, then he wanted to meet it head on as Turbine, and not run as Nathaniel Winthorp.

He supposed it was possible that he could wear his old, more reliable outfit. But that suit was in Hughes's office, and that was on the other side of the courtyard. There was no guarantee he could even reach it without confronting the cause of the disturbance.

Besides, he knew the first rule during any kind of danger to the Hall was to move to the outside of the building as quickly as possible and find the others. Nathaniel was, he had to admit to himself, less clear on the specifics of the rules that followed after that one, but he was fairly sure that there was nothing in them that specifically stopped a man from pulling out his flask and taking a long pull of whisky while he decided what to do next.

By the time he had satisfied his thirst, the shaking had begun to subside, and Nathaniel, fortified by liquor, decided to take the opportunity to pull on his costume. The coveralls and harness for the new suit lay on an overstuffed chair in the corner. They had managed to provide a soft landing for a few of the books that had fallen from the shelves.

Quickly clearing away the wayward volumes, he began to unbutton his pants and shirt.

Fairly confident that no one was around to hear, he began to hum his theme song to himself. Nathaniel was no musician, and he was sure that if anyone actually heard the anthem, they would have considered it a sadly bowdlerized version of a popular drinking song, which it essentially was. But it always put him in a heroic mood when he sang it.

No one flies higher!

He's filled with desire, to save all the ladies, who will then maybe, give him a kiss, and stoke up his fire . . .

Turbine! Turbine!

The method of attaching the new harness was unfamiliar, and his singing and humming went quickly silent as he clumsily worked the hooks and straps into place.

By the time he was ready to hoist the wings up into the harness, the rumbling had started again. Even with the distraction, the wings slid easily into place, locking into a set of rails that had been well stitched onto the back of the suit.

Despite the streamlined procedure, it had still taken longer than expected, and Nathaniel made a little prayer that the others wouldn't be waiting for him to arrive. Even more importantly, he didn't want anyone to get hurt looking for him.

He tugged hard on a pair of small handles attached to silk-wrapped wires, and the wing split in half and folded up. Pulling the cords downward moved the wings back into a more compact position. In some ways, the ease of storing the apparatus on his back was the greatest innovation.

The old wings had been fixed in place and were always incredibly unwieldy while he was on the ground. Better still, with the wings folded back, Nathaniel could run through doorways without having to scuttle sideways like a crab.

Slipping the flight helmet onto a hook in his belt, he moved through the hallways at a quick trot, his rapid pace reaffirming that his decision to wear the new suit was a good one.

He had just reached the entrance hall when he heard the screaming. At first he was unsure if the sounds were human, but when they started for a second time, there was no doubt that the sounds were coming from a living throat.

For a moment, he was tempted to turn around and find the origins of the anguished yelps. After all, as a hero he was duty bound to protect people in danger, especially if they were his fellow heroes.

"When the Hall is in danger, first move outside the building," he reminded himself, the strict words mimicking just how angry his step-father would be if he discovered that Nathaniel had ignored the rules. Besides, his wings were mostly useless indoors. Once he was outside, he could take to the air and quickly uncover the source of the attack.

His mind made up, he continued across the foyer toward the main door. There was an earthy smell in the air, and dust and colored chunks of plaster littered the floor. Nathaniel looked up to see that large sections of the fresco had fallen away, leaving jagged holes in the mural above his head. He noted with no small irony that it was the image of Darby that seemed to have suffered the most damage.

He felt a slight twinge of guilt as he wondered if perhaps they would finally put his own visage up there when they repaired the damage. He would make a fine Apollo . . .

Reaching the exit, he gave the massive brass doors a solid tug. The metal slab moved an inch, and then made a terrible rasping sound as the corner scraped against the lintel and stuck, letting in only a thin streak of light and stream of cool air from the outside. Nathaniel pulled again, putting more effort into it, but the door wouldn't budge.

Thinking that he might be able to do better with a second attempt, he tried to shove the door closed again, but now it seemed just as unwilling to shut as it was to open.

Nathaniel absentmindedly pulled the flask out of the pouch in his pocket and unscrewed the cap as he pondered his next action. The warmth of the whisky spreading out through his system dulled the panic just a little bit.

Sarah would probably also say that it was dulling his senses, but considering how quickly he could find himself on edge since he had been impaled on the bridge, perhaps a little dullness might be best for everyone concerned.

And then an idea popped into his head. He pressed the palm of his right hand flat against the door, and reached the fingers of his left down until he felt them touch one of the dials on his belt.

Nathaniel grasped it between his fingers, and then paused for a moment, squeezing the dial instead of turning it.

While he had a much better idea of how the system worked than he had previously, there was no guarantee that King Jupiter was actually right about the benzene tube. His first attempt to use the suit might bathe him in a toxic cloud of vaporized acid. "Life grants no opportunities for the meek," he said to himself, and twisted the knob. The turbine on his right side roared to life. He could feel it pressing his hand against the door, blasting his face with a stream of warm air and steam.

He turned it up further. He could feel a dangerous strain in his bones, but after a moment the door scraped loose and slammed shut.

Nathaniel let out a satisfied grunt, and then the building began to shake again. It was deeper and more violent than before, and his fingers slipped free from the control knob on his belt as he tried to maintain his balance.

From above him, loud enough to be heard clearly over the thunderous rumbling and the roaring of his own turbine, came the unmistakable throaty scrape of stone shifting against stone.

He looked up and saw the lintel shift and crack. Nathaniel tried to jump backwards as the massive piece of stone slipped down, but the turbine on his wrist was holding his hand firmly in place against the metal door, as if it had been glued there.

The edge of the door crumpled as the massive chunk of rock bit into it. The metal shook under his hand.

The jolt seemed to free a memory in his brain, and Nathaniel remembered that the previous suit had a hidden kill switch. He pressed his left hand into a fist, and the device instantly shut off.

Nathaniel stumbled backwards, only barely managing to stay upright as he teetered down the broad step that led from the doorway to the main floor.

As he began to recover his bearings, another jolt ripped through the ground. It felt as if someone had managed to lift up the entire Hall and drop it again. Feeling his legs being thrown out from under him, Nathaniel pointed his right hand downwards and unclenched his left.

The turbine reactivated as quickly as it had stopped, and the force of the jet on his wrist halted his fall as effectively as if he'd found an invisible wall to prop himself up against.

After a moment, the shaking once again started to subside, and he reached for the controls at his belt, quickly managing to find the control knob.

He puffed out his cheeks and blew out a long breath to let some of his nervousness pass.

He felt more pleased with himself, in spite of the fact that there was clearly something terrible going on. Not only had the new suit worked, but he'd actually used it in a clever way.

After waiting a moment to make sure the ground wasn't going to start shaking again, Nathaniel took a few steps forward and pounded the brass door with his fist—it responded with a muted thud. Finding that unacceptable, he tugged on the handle with all his strength, but the metal had been wedged into the stone so tightly it might as well have become a part of the wall.

The main entrance was gone, and his only choice was to head back into the building and see if he could find another way out.

As he turned and began walking across the plaster-covered floor, Nathaniel saw the flash of a white-clad figure as it scampered past the doorway that led out from the foyer. He was clearly headed into the main part of the building.

Nathaniel was about to demand that the person stop when he realized that the figure was a familiar one. "It can't be . . ." he told himself, but how could it be anyone else?

Reaching the doorway, he turned and cautiously peered down the hallway to his left. Some of the gaslights had been damaged during the shaking and were burning dangerously high, while others had been shut off—either by design, or from broken pipes behind the walls. Nathaniel had no desire to be burned to death, but he wanted to follow the fleeing figure, and there was enough light that he could see the back his quarry's head as he headed down the corridor. It only took a single good look for his suspicions to be confirmed; what he had seen before was not a hallucination: the White Knight was in the Hall, and he was clearly up to no good.

No matter how well they folded up, it was difficult to be stealthy with a pair of wings on your back. But if the angels could watch over all of mankind without making a sound, then he should certainly be able to follow someone down a rumbling corridor.

But it would be easier with a little help . . . He reached down into his pocket, pulled out the flask, and gave it a shake. Nathaniel opened it and emptied it in a single motion. The whisky burned as it travelled down his throat, and he could feel it igniting his courage.

The White Knight had invaded the building, but he certainly couldn't be responsible for the rumbling . . . The man was more formidable than he first appeared, Nathaniel had seen that when he'd fought the Industrialist, but nothing about him spoke to his being the kind of villain who would be able to breach two-foot-thick stone walls, let alone shake a building to its foundations.

Far more was going on here than appeared on the surface, and Nathaniel would need to be careful if he was going to get to the bottom of it. He also wished he still had the pneumatic weapon that had originally been included with his upgraded costume. That device had, unfortunately, been taken by the Automaton, and the gun had been nowhere to be seen when they had discovered the mechanical man's shattered body in Madison Square.

Hughes had suggested that he strap on a regular six-shooter as a replacement, but a standard revolver lacked the elegance of the weapon that Darby had created for him, and bullets always seemed to be an opportunity for a fatal mistake in a moment of tension.

Besides, he and Hughes had planned to rebuild the weapon once the rest of the suit was working, although that wouldn't help him now. Hopefully he'd be able to find a way to use the powers of the suit to subdue any villains he did come into contact with, and if not, then he prayed that the suit worked well enough that he could fly away.

He followed the White Knight around the corner toward the meeting chamber. He could hear voices in the distance, and Nathaniel could see that the White Knight had paused next to the chamber's open door.

Nathaniel took a step back, hiding himself from view. While he couldn't make out any specific words, from the sounds coming through the door, there was obviously an argument going on in the meeting hall. He pulled out his flask to take one final sip of courage before realizing it was empty. He had barely put it away before he heard the unique sound of the Industrialist's gun being fired.

An instant later, there was a crackle, and then a blast of light bright enough to send shadows dancing down the corridor. It blinded Nathaniel, and by the time the image began to clear from Nathaniel's eyes, the White Knight had disappeared from view.

He tried to run down the corridor, but his wings were shifting awkwardly on his back, and the rumbling had begun again, forcing him to grope the wall for support. Nathaniel moved slowly until he heard two more shots and a scream that could have only come from William Hughes.

The rumbling stopped before he reached the doorway. Looking into the meeting room, he stared transfixed at the carnage within. The image framed by the doorway was like a living image from Hieronymus Bosch.

The room had been shattered and transformed. The meeting table was entirely gone now, the members' chairs broken and scattered around the floor.

Somehow, impossibly, the dais where the president's throne had sat had moved from its previous position and into the center of the room. Sitting on top was a broken column of metal. Something not quite human wriggled on the floor nearby.

The figure was obviously in pain. It looked like a nightmare version of the Automaton, covered in shining steel, but with a shattered tube where its legs should have been. It reminded Nathaniel of something he might have seen at the old Barnum Museum.

But the mechanical freak wasn't all there was to see. The Industrialist was standing in the room as well, his gun drawn and pointed directly at the head of King Jupiter. "I'd rather be dead than live in your twisted vision," he told the gray man.

Nathaniel knew Stanton well enough to know that he must have felt that threat was justified, and that he would have no qualms about pulling the trigger. He found himself almost idly wondering what it was that the new Paragon had done to make the Industrialist consider him a villain.

"I always suspected as much," Jupiter replied, and then he nodded his head. The doorway limited Nathaniel's vision, and when the White Knight stepped into view and stabbed Alexander Stanton, Nathaniel was almost as surprised as the Industrialist was.

"Very good, Mr. Clements, very good," King Jupiter said to the White Knight as the Industrialist sank to the floor.

The man pulled his hood off of his face. "Thank you, Lord."

"And so falls the last leader of Darby's Paragons. And in their place the Children of Eschaton will rise!"

Nathaniel could fully feel the effects of the whisky now, the liquor dulling both his shock and his resolve, and he found himself wishing he hadn't finished the flask. But he was still a hero, and the very murderers and rogues he had sworn an oath to stop were now standing right in front of him.

He took a moment to pull on his helmet and goggles before stepping through the doorway. Once inside, he gave his shoulders a shrug and tugged on the wires on his chest. The wings on his back unfolded and snapped into place.

The gray man looked up and laughed. "Look, Clements, it's Stanton's drunkard puppy come to bark at us. I'm afraid you've come too late to save anyone."

Nathaniel pointed an accusing finger at them. "You'll pay for whatch you've done!" He could hear a slur in his words from too much damn whisky.

"Do you know who I am, boy?" the tall man asked.

"You're King Ju . . ." but even as the name came out of his mouth, he realized just how badly they had all been used. "No . . ." he said slowly. "Zounds! You're Lord Eschaton!"

"You see, Clements," Eschaton said with a dramatic tone. "You were so quick to judge the boy a fool, but he does get there eventually."

Nathaniel opened his mouth to speak, but there were too many thoughts rushing through his head, all of them blurred together by the liquor. He could feel the pieces trying to fall into place, but the picture that they revealed was too dark to believe.

The gray man turned toward him, burning through Nathaniel's drunken shock simply with the power of his stare. "I'd ask you to join us, but after witnessing both Darby and your step-father being murdered by my children, I'm sure the last thing that you're going to do is fight *for* me."

Stanton hadn't moved since he dropped to the ground, but there was a growing pool of blood coming out from underneath him. If there was to be any hope of rescue, it would have to come soon.

Nathaniel held his breath for a moment as he twisted the control at his belt and the turbines on his back hummed to life. When he was sure nothing was going to explode, he let himself exhale. For all the changes Darby had made with the new outfit, it felt even more a part of him than the old one had. He was sure he could make it do what he needed it to.

Leaning forward, Nathaniel clenched both hands into fists. The engines began to whine and he felt himself being lifted up off of the floor and into the air. As he rose towards the ceiling, both Eschaton and Clements craned their heads to track his progress.

He unclenched his hands, letting gravity take over as he dropped rapidly towards Lord Eschaton. He could see the gray man smiling eagerly as he got nearer to him. Nathaniel waited until he had almost collided with his target before firing off a short burst from his wrist turbine. The action threw him sideways, and he placed his rapidly moving foot hard against the side of the White Knight's idiotic grinning face.

The surprised Southerner went crashing into the floor.

The smile left Eschaton's face as he charged toward Nathaniel, clearly intent on disabling him before he could cause any more trouble.

The Turbine flew backwards, increasing the distance between them, then he spun the dial on his belt in the opposite direction and pressed the switches in his hands, instantly reversing direction. He slammed straight into Lord Eschaton. The moment of impact felt unpleasantly close to crashing into a brick wall. But as solid as the gray man was, he still yielded to the superior momentum and was thrown backwards towards the dais.

A hole had been left in the floor where whatever was supposed to cover the pit had not managed to engage. Eschaton, a true look of surprise on his face, fell down through the gap and disappeared from view.

Having found at least a temporary solution to the problem, Nathaniel dialed down the power to his suit and turned back to Alexander Stanton.

He pulled off his helmet and knelt in front of his step-father, feeling that same fear he had the morning that Darby had died in Sarah's arms while he screamed in pain. But he wouldn't let his selfishness win out this time. "Let's go, sir. I need to find you some medical attention."

He was stunned but relieved when Stanton opened his eyes and stared up at him. "Is that really you, Nathaniel?"

"Yes sir. You're badly hurt."

"I know it."

"We need to go."

"*You* need to go." There was a grim look on Stanton's face. "It's too late for me."

"Don't be foolish," he said, attempting to slip his arms underneath the Industrialist's leather coat. He prayed that the blood wouldn't make him too slippery to carry.

"I've seen plenty of men die, and I know what it looks like," he said, pushing his arms away weakly. "No use fighting it when it's my turn."

Nathaniel tried to hoist him up, but barely managed to lift him off the floor. "No! We can escape before Eschaton returns!"

"No, son," he said with a firmness that seemed to deny the truth of his deathly pallor. "I'm done. But we need to talk."

"I won't let you die!"

"It happens to all of us, eventually." He lifted up his hand and pulled off a blood-soaked glove. "Darby, you dramatic idiot—why didn't you just tell us?"

Nathaniel could feel the warm sting of tears starting to form in the corner of his eyes. He didn't try to fight them. "I'm sorry I couldn't save you."

"*Sic transit gloria mundi*—the glory of the world so quickly passes away," he said with a slight smile, putting his hand up to Nathaniel's face. "It's all right, son." The fingers were oddly cold, but it was still the only warmth he could remember from his step-father in a long time. "But I need you to do something for me."

"What is it?" he said, his voice choked by emotion and tears. "I'll do anything."

"Protect your sister."

"Sarah?"

Stanton gripped his shoulder and squeezed, "She knew what was coming, I can see that now. She knew it all along."

He inhaled sharply and coughed out a small spot of blood. "Darby . . . in his will. He wanted Sarah to become a Paragon. Can you believe that?"

Sarah, one of them? It was ridiculous, but exactly the kind of idealistic nonsense that the old man would have dreamed up. "But we read the will out loud."

Stanton coughed. It was a terrible, broken sound. "I had the section removed."

"You lied."

Stanton smiled at that. "I thought it was for the best. But you can tell her if you want."

"I don't even know where she is."

"She's a part of this, and she's a Stanton. There's no turning back for her now." The words were getting weaker. Nathaniel could see that he only had moments to live. "I've tried to be a father to you both, but it's time to grow up. There's work to do." Nathaniel could feel the hand gripping his arm begin to shake.

"Yes sir."

"You're the last true Paragon. I need you to fight . . ."

"I'll try."

"Do more. Win . . ." Stanton's head rolled back, and he could hear the man's final breath slip free from his lips in a shuddering rattle.

Nathaniel sat there quietly for a moment, hoping for a miracle, but none came.

Holding his step-father's dead body in his arms left him feeling strangely empty inside. He had craved Stanton's approval for so long, and in the moment he had finally gotten it, his step-father had simply given him another challenge. Maybe this time he wouldn't fail him.

He unbuckled the straps that held the Industrialist's gun to his body and pulled it free. As he finished unhooking the ammunition belt, a voice yelled out from across the room. "*Gott in Himmel!*" Nathaniel looked up to see Helmut Grüsser standing just outside the doorway, eyes wide, witnessing the same framed scene of hell that he himself had viewed only a few minutes earlier.

"Help me, Grüsser!" he yelled over to the Prussian as he draped the belt over the shoulder. The gun fit awkwardly into the empty holster at his waist, but it would have to do until he could figure out a way to integrate it with the rest of his costume.

"Vas hast du *done!*" said the fat man as he staggered backwards.

Nathaniel stood up and reactivated his engines. It was time to go, but he didn't want to leave the Prussian without a warning. "Grüsser, you need to

182

get out of here—now! King Jupiter and Lord Eschaton are the same man. He's killed the Industrialist and done God knows what to the Hall. We need to go. We need to find help."

Having pushed himself against the far wall of the hallway, Grüsser stood frozen for a few moments without saying a word, the look on his face spelling out his horror and despair. Then he vanished down the corridor as fast as his legs could carry him.

Nathaniel sighed. The man had never been of that much use in a fight, but at least he had been brave. Now that it was bravery that was needed, it seemed he was of no use at all.

He raised his arms and clenched his hands, but instead of powering up, the engines died away. The only sound was simply a strange cackling from behind him that was half laughter, and half a crackling hiss.

When he turned, he saw that the metal-covered half-man had managed to crawl in behind him. Metal columns had grown out from his hands and were attached to the wings on Nathaniel's back. "No fly-y-y-y-y," it said in a broken voice that, for all its distortion, was clearly that of William Hughes.

"Good God, man," Nathaniel said in horror, "what have they done to you?"

"He's been reborn," said Lord Eschaton's voice from somewhere nearby. "My first true child."

Nathaniel felt only an instant of pain, and then the world went dark.

Chapter 16

Words from the Heart

In typical New York fashion, the ferry that Sarah and Viola took back to Brooklyn was the very same one that had been attacked by the Children of Eschaton a few days before.

After the fight at the apartment, all that Sarah had wanted was a few moments for peace and reflection, and when they boarded the ship it had been her intention to simply find a place to sit quietly for the duration of their journey home.

But Viola had quickly discovered the unhappy coincidence, and she had become obsessed with pointing out the poorly patched ceiling that barely concealed where the harpoon had burst into the passenger cabin. She had also discovered a dark mark on the linoleum where the blood from the impaled passenger had stained the floor.

As Viola nattered on, Sarah realized that the Italian girl had many qualities that made her a far more suitable candidate for becoming a Paragon than she would ever be. The Italian girl seemed almost immune to horror and was clearly stronger. She also seemed more at ease in the world than Sarah.

Viola's more "practical" view of men might come in useful as well. The girl seemed to think that all members of the opposite sex existed as either annoyances to be dealt with or objects of desire to be conquered. Sarah imagined that attitude could certainly make it easier to punch a man when the situation called for it.

Lastly, the Italian girl seemed to have an almost limitless sense of curiosity. Once Viola had finally gotten her fill of discussing the battle scars on the boat, she started to pepper Sarah with question after question about Mrs. Farrows.

It was obvious that the housemaid had left quite an impression on the young girl, and Sarah was beginning to gain a deeper appreciation for the technique that Jenny used to transform unruly urchins into crack servants for the Stanton household.

Given a few weeks of exposure, Sarah was quite sure that Jenny would have Viola happily wearing a black maid's dress with a feather duster in her hand.

Just thinking about it had made Sarah realize how much she missed the life she had left behind, whether or not she actually wished to return to it.

Before she had run off, Sarah would have never believed in her wildest dreams—and her dreams had always been far wilder than those of any of the other women she had known—that she would have spent a sunny day in April walking, talking, and fighting with a foreign woman of the streets. Nor would she have believed that she would have found it quite so annoying.

There were, she decided, some very good things about a life that was not entirely punctuated with unexpected adventure.

They had arrived on the Brooklyn docks just before sunset, and used the elevated railway to head north before completing their journey back to the junkyard with a long walk down a dark dirt road. By that time, her back was screaming from lugging the carpet bag full of clothes that Jenny had packed for her. It seemed that Mrs. Farrows had the ability to put people to work without even having to be nearby.

At least the ramshackle building at the center of the junkyard was well lit and inviting. Emilio had created a system of arc lamps and mirrors that flooded the area with a harsh white light that turned night into day. It was an amazing display, and it seemed clear to Sarah that his devotion to electricity was, in its own way, even greater than Darby's.

As they neared the entrance, Emilio flung open the door to great them. He was wearing another one of what seemed to be an endless series of tattered silk robes that almost littered the interior of the house. This one was white, with large red fish running up the side of it. "Sarah! Viola!" He took the bag from Sarah's hand and helped her up into the house.

"Come, come! Sit. Sit!" He pulled open a sliding door and led them into a large parlor that Sarah had, up until this moment, not even realized existed. In the middle of the room, a fire burned merrily in a brazier that hung down from a series of chains attached to a large chimney. There were wires and gears connected to the top of it, and Sarah could only wonder at their purpose.

Tired of thinking, Sarah sat down gently on the couch, taking a moment to sweep her skirts aside. Never one to stand on ceremony, Viola simply flopped herself backwards into one of the sofas and let out a long sigh. "*Fratello, ho bisogno d'una bevanda ed un sigaro!*" She grasped at her boots, slid them off her feet, and threw them behind the couch, where they landed with a heavy thunk.

It was a display that would have been worthy of any upper-class gentleman. Sarah would have found herself even more shocked by her companion if it weren't for the fact that she could no longer muster the energy to continue to be flabbergasted by the Italian hellion.

Instead, Sarah tried to join in with the spirit of the experience by unlacing her shoes and letting herself revel in the fact that for the last few days she had been living a blessedly bustle-free existence.

Emilio walked across to the other side of the room and was preparing something at a small wooden table nearby. "How was the day for you?"

Viola jumped up in her seat with a smile on her face. "We fought *una canaglia*. He was seven foot tall and round like an egg!" She pointed at the marks on her neck and grinned. "*Mi ha strangolato!*"

Sarah didn't need a translator to figure out what it was the girl had just said to her brother, but by her tone it sounded as if she were talking about riding on a merry-go-round, and not being nearly choked to death. It was doubly strange considering the murderous rage that Viola had been in at the time.

Emilio turned and looked back at them with concern in his face. "Then Sarah's friend smacked him with an iron! Bam!" Viola said, gesturing with her arm to show how Jenny had smashed the villain. Emilio just shook his head as he picked up the tray and walked back across the room.

"We only knocked him out," Sarah said.

"And this rich girl let him go!" As Emilio approached, Viola greedily grabbed one of the glasses and the small cigar next to it.

"But you are okay—both of you?"

"We're fine!" Viola shouted, cutting off Sarah before she could thank him for his concern. "And we don't need my stupid brother fussing over us. Now let's drink!" Viola dropped onto the couch a little more gingerly this time, clearly focused on making sure that her glass wouldn't spill in the attempt.

Emilio turned toward Sarah and offered her one of the glasses on the tray. The liquor clung to the sides as it sloshed back and forth.

Sarah reached out to pick one up, and then hesitated. She had been around drink all her life, but she'd never actually tried any before. Beyond the constant muttering of temperance amongst the ladies (although none of them seemed unable to resist a little sip when they thought no one was looking), it seemed to her that the most noticeable effect of alcohol was that it quickly turned perfectly reasonable people into fools.

On the other hand, after the ordeal that she had gone through today, Sarah was beginning to see the appeal of dulling one's senses from time to time.

Emilio nodded at the drink. "Try it! You would like it, Sarah."

"What is it?" she asked, picking up the glass. After giving it a more vigorous swirl, she brought the glass up to her nose and gave it a sniff. The smell was something like incense, with a strong scent of flowers and perfume.

"It is *vermut*."

"It's a kind of Italian wine," Viola added. "Something that old men and my brother like to drink."

From what she knew of the tastes of old men, Sarah imagined that it must be either very weak or incredibly strong.

"*Salute!*" Emilio said, clinked his glass against hers, and took a sip.

Not wanting to be rude, and more than a little bit curious, Sarah tipped a small amount of the liquor into her mouth and held it on her tongue. The liquid seemed to be overwhelming her and evaporating simultaneously, filling her head with flavors and scents that had only been hinted at by her nose.

She swallowed what remained, and it seemed to vanish almost before it could finish rolling down her throat. There was a sudden rush of heat, and Sarah began to cough.

"*Vergine!*" shouted Viola, and began to laugh.

Emilio clucked his tongue and shushed his sister. "*Fai gentile!*"

"You picked a fine girl, Emilio. A tender little blossom to make tin flowers for."

Sarah put her hand up to her mouth and tried to control her coughing fit. Her face felt warm and flushed. "It would be nice," she said to Emilio between gasps, "if there was *something* that your sister could feel some embarrassment about."

Viola's laughter stopped short. "You are braver than I thought, rich girl, but you are still *vergine*." She grabbed a pillow and flung it in Sarah's direction, narrowly missing her head. Instead it slammed into a vase on the side table and sent it crashing to the floor.

Viola frowned. "If it wasn't for your friend Jenny, we'd both be dead."

Her coughing had subsided, and Sarah opened her mouth to reply, but once again she had nothing to say.

Viola stood up, her eyes locked onto her brother. "I am going to bed, Emilio. Try not to let the rich girl hurt herself." She stomped out of the room and disappeared behind one of the curtained doorways.

Emilio sat down on the other end of the couch. "I am sorry. She can be angry."

"Maybe she's right," Sarah said, and took another—smaller—sip of her *vermut*. As infuriating as Viola could be, she was beginning to realize that the girl often had a way of revealing Sarah's fears and putting them directly into words.

During all the time that she had dreamed of becoming a Paragon, Sarah had never really imagined what her life would be like, beyond putting on a costume and facing down vicious villains with bravado and flair. Having grown up around Darby and her father, on some level she *knew* that the reality of it would be more complicated, but she was beginning to think that without a steam-powered gun in her hand, her only true skill was being able to put herself into danger on a regular basis. And now that she had been given a taste of the real thing, her desire to be an actual hero seemed more of a fantasy than ever.

When Sarah looked up, she saw Emilio staring straight at her. She flushed as his eyes met hers, and her breath caught in her chest. The idea of being alone with a man was as impossible as it was ridiculous, and yet it was exactly where she was. He had the barest hint of a smile, and no matter how hard she tried, Sarah couldn't seem to pull her gaze away from his lips.

"You no need sorry, Sarah. Both Viola and I, we had a very hard time before America, but I help you because I want to. Is not your fault."

Sarah finally tore her eyes away and stared at the glass in her hand. "Maybe it is. I think I do hurt the people I care about. I lost my mother when I was a little girl." Had she ever actually *told* anyone that before? The words felt unreal as she said them.

The rumors of her part in the death Lady Stanton were something that she knew always preceded her introduction to any new acquaintance.

Where the first words most people heard when meeting someone new were something along the lines of "lovely to meet you, my dear," young Sarah heard phrases like "Oh, you poor child," or "We're so sorry for your loss." And once she was too old for direct exclamations of pity, Sarah would still occasionally see a look of sadness and suspicion in people's eyes that meant they knew about her sad past.

"She was killed by a villain," Sarah continued, trying to fill the silence. When she felt the hot buzz in the corners of her eyes that preceded tears, she pressed her hands against her cheeks to stop the flow. "It was my fault."

"No." Emilio shook his head and smiled. "You were a little girl. No fault . . ."

"I revealed to the world my father was the Industrialist." Despite her best efforts, a single tear escaped. She quickly rubbed it away with her knuckle. "I was so young, and I didn't know I wasn't supposed to. When the Crucible found out, he took Mother and me hostage."

Emilio sat there quietly while Sarah took a long moment to compose herself. "My father came to our rescue, but in the end he could only save one of us from the Crucible's trap." Her voice cracked slightly, and she took another sip of her drink. Where before it had made her cough, now it seemed to help. "He chose to save me first, obviously, although I'm not sure that he didn't come to regret it."

Emilio moved closer to her, and for a moment Sarah was sure that he was going to kiss her again. When he took her hands into his, she realized how ridiculous she was being. Emilio nodded before he spoke, "I should say . . . tell you . . . I was married . . . in Tuscany. But she is gone now."

Sarah's eyes grew wide. To her Emilio looked so young, but he was clearly older than she was. And if it weren't for her stubborn temperament and lenient father, Sarah would have been married off, herself. There was no reason to think that a boy—a man—Emilio's age wouldn't have been married, but in that instant he seemed much more mature than he had a moment before. "Did you have children?"

He nodded. "Two. Gone away."

Sarah grasped the hand that held hers. "What happened?"

"I was *ladro* . . ." Sarah gave him a puzzled look. "*Criminale* . . . A villain."

"You?" she said with a laugh.

Emilio nodded and stood up. "Watch," he told her, and then leaned over backwards, his back arching down until he had his hands flat on the floor. Then, in a single fluid motion, he brought his legs straight up over his head. "Il Acrobato. You see?"

Sarah couldn't believe it, but as she watched him walk around the room on his hands, she realized that it was no joke. "I made machines and climb buildings." He stood upright and mimed climbing up a rope. "I take people's jewels." He plucked imaginary gems and tucked them safely away into an invisible bag before he sat back down on the couch next to her. She noticed that he had chosen to sit closer to her than he had been before . . . "But the *polizia*, they are smart. They find out who I am."

Of all the men in the world, Sarah had found a repentant villain to have a romance with. For a moment she felt angry and foolish, and then she was suddenly almost blinded by a desire to wrap her arms around him and . . . "I should . . ." Sarah said, and then realized that she had no idea what she should do at all. The situation was so far beyond anything she had ever even imagined. She wanted to escape, but where could she go? To bed? What if Emilio followed her there? What if she wanted him to? For the first time in her life, Sarah Stanton found herself feeling almost naked without the armor of her corsets and skirts.

"You wore a mask?" she said, scooting herself away from him just a little bit as she tried to regain her composure.

"*Sì, sì.* Harlequin." He moved his hand over his face as he spoke. "I was a boy. I read about Americans, and I think is okay to steal for my wife and children."

After Sarah had revealed her father's identity to the world, he had tried to explain to her why he had spent so many years wearing a mask and keeping his identity as the Industrialist secret. It wasn't just for their safety, he had told her, but also that as the Industrialist he was free of human flaws. In the eyes of the people he could be a perfect hero.

Emilio was hardly the first foreigner Sarah had heard of who had attempted to become a would-be Paragon. She had heard of heroes in London and Paris. There was even a small group of men in San Francisco who called themselves the Barbary Boys. Her father said they were more pirates than Paragons, although they sounded quite dashing. Of course, no one but the true Paragons had been given the power of fortified steam.

Sarah looked up and saw that Emilio was moving towards her again, and this time there was no question as to what his intentions were. She told herself she needed to lean back and fend him off, but her body seemed to be moving forward in spite of her good sense, and before she could exert her will, they were kissing again.

She could feel the glass dropping out of her hand, and she had no idea how much, if any, of the liquor was left. Somewhere in the distance, the cup bounced off the rug, and she realized that she didn't care.

Emilio's arm slid around her waist, catching the small of Sarah's back and pulling them closer together. Every one of her senses was suddenly filled with this man, and the taste of him was even more intoxicating than the liquor. A flood of feelings from passion to shame rose up in her so quickly that Sarah suddenly felt as if she were drowning in them.

She wondered if this kind of desire was what Odysseus must have felt when he heard the Sirens' call. Then even that tiny thought was wiped away, and Sarah crushed herself more tightly against Emilio than she had been when their lives had depended on it. It was wrong, and it was wonderful.

From some tiny corner of her mind, a voice screamed out to her. "Sarah Stanton, *control* yourself!" The words were spoken in clipped, strict tones, and she realized the voice she was hearing was her mother's.

Sarah grabbed onto the warning like the drowning Greek sailor she had imagined herself to be, and swam back to the surface of common sense. Freed from passion, she broke free from Emilio's embrace and pushed herself away.

Emilio seemed shocked as he realized that the moment had passed. His eyes were as wide as his face was red. "I . . . Is something wrong?"

Sarah glanced up and tried to say, "Nothing." As she thought more about his question, a laugh spilled out from her mouth. It was only a small chortle at first, but as she tried over and over again to speak, the utter ridiculousness of pretending to be able to cover up *everything* made her laughter come out with more and more intensity until she realized that she was about to cry again.

Emilio had a look on his face—like a child that had been slapped too hard, and was about to cry. "Bella, do I make you sad?"

"No, no," she managed to squeak out between suddenly rising giggles. When she realized that her emotions were no longer under her control, Sarah closed her eyes and lay back against the couch, making no sounds at all except for occasional gasps as she convulsed with mad laughter. "I'm sorry, Emilio." Perhaps it was the freedom to truly breathe after years and years of having corsets wrapped around her chest, but she found herself laughing with more intensity than she could ever remember having done before.

And this time, even when her mother's voice commanded her to stop making a fool of herself, Sarah ignored it.

She wondered if being more open to laughter than to passion meant she was broken somehow, and the thought only made her laugh harder.

Emilio took her hand. "I sorry, Sarah," he said with some shame. "*Sono sciocco.* I wish I had more words for you."

Taking in a huge lungful of air, she held her breath and pressed her hand against her chest until she finally felt the laughter subside. Emilio had already put up with so much, she couldn't continue to laugh in his face.

Taking another breath, Sarah realized that she felt almost as exhausted as she had after the battle with the Ruffian that had happened—had it really only been earlier today?

"You . . ." she stifled the urge to laugh. "You," she tried again, "have nothing to be sorry about Emilio. It's me . . ."

He turned away from her and nodded. "I see."

"I'm," she said, trying to suppress another chortle, "I'm afraid that everything is terribly far from all right for *me* now, Emilio."

"I see," he repeated. The look on his face was even more confused, and she realized that she had, quite without intending to, managed to hurt his feelings. She wondered if Viola would be angry at her for causing pain to her brother, or thrilled that she was learning how to break a man's heart. Either way, it wasn't the kind of woman she wanted to be.

Taking a moment to make sure that the laughter had truly ended, she leaned forward and kissed Emilio. This time she intended to maintain her composure, and although this kiss was far more chaste than the previous one had been, the moment she felt him start to move toward her again, Sarah pulled away. "That's all I can give you right now, Emilio."

He nodded, obviously disappointed. "I think I understand."

Sarah felt a sense of relief, although disappointment lingered somewhere just underneath the surface as well. Had part of her wanted to be ravaged? Had she really become such a wild creature in the few months since she had left society behind?

"Is okay, Sarah." Emilio closed his eyes for a moment, and then stood up. "I want to show you something." He held out his hand to her.

Sarah slipped her hand back into his and let him help her up off the couch, ignoring a sudden impulse to fall back into his arms. "What is it?"

"Your heart—I think I can fix it."

She smiled at that, and then, when Emilio pointed over to the door to his lab, Sarah felt a sudden pang of guilt as she realized that in all the excitement of the day, she had completely forgotten about Tom.

"Come with me," he said. His foreign features and complexion still reminded Sarah of the whispered tales that Sally Norbitt would tell of exotic men—foreign princes who would sweep away society girls and take them to mountain palaces, where they would commit unspeakable acts of lust with their virgin brides.

Of course Emilio was hardly royalty, or, she assumed, prone to unspeakable acts. And Sally could be prone to telling ridiculous lies. But it also seemed like this Italian man had no fear of touching a woman when the mood struck him.

As she let herself be dragged into the workroom, Sarah noticed that Emilio had done more than simply try to repair Tom. The space was much

194

cleaner than it had been on her previous visit. The floor was obviously swept, and while there were still bits and pieces everywhere, he had at least tried to make the place more tidy and presentable. Things that had been simply scattered before were now placed in somewhat orderly piles, and the path on the floor was clear enough that a woman might cross safely in her bare feet.

Reaching the desk, Sarah looked down to see that he had indeed started putting the heart back together. Although a number of gears were still laid out on the table, the rest had been placed back into an open half of the heart in something that approximated order.

Emilio pointed at the empty side of the heart that lay nearby. "Look there!" He reached up and pulled down what appeared to be a brass tube on the end of an articulated arm. It hung down from an apparatus on the ceiling, and when Emilio pressed a button on the side of it, a small but intense flame appeared, revealing a series of glass lenses designed to focus the light onto the workbench.

As Emilio brought the device down closer to the table, the glow focused on the inside of the heart's curved shell, revealing a series of markings etched into the metal. "What is it?" Sarah said, looking closer.

"Is the same question I asked!" Emilio replied, clearly excited. He grabbed another arm from the array, the tension springs on either side of it letting out a merry groan as he pulled it into place. The end of it contained what appeared to be a large magnifying glass. "Can you see?" he asked as he tried to move the lens into focus.

Sarah swatted away his hand and looked through it. "I might be able to see if you stopped fussing."

She moved her head back and forth until the markings became clear. "They're words!" The script itself was tiny and dense—far too small to have been written by hand, especially against the curved brass chambers, and yet, when properly magnified, it was crisply legible. "The gears must lie in a precise ratio," she read aloud. "They are aligned in such a manner that they provide not only the timing, but preserve the character of their motion."

"This is amazing!" she said, turning to Emilio and giving him a smile. Sarah looked again, not understanding any of the actual text, but simply reveling in the familiar cadence and stentorian but slightly poetic tone of

Darby's language. "Every attempt has been made to make the dimensions and chambers as precise as possible. At the same time, the process of transformation is organic, and like all things of nature it is the action itself that creates the perfected individual."

"You see!" Emilio said with a smile. "He tells us!" Emilio asked her after a moment.

She pulled her eyes away from the glittering words and looked up at Emilio. "Definitely."

Emilio nodded. "Is very good." He pointed to a series of books that lay open on the desk. In it were copious notes, entirely in a language that she assumed to be Italian.

Sarah couldn't help but notice that his handwriting was, in its own way, as tight and precise as Darby's had been, although how the old man had managed to shrink his distinctive script and apply it to the walls of Tom's heart was beyond imagining.

"I try to understand," he said as he looked down at the floor, "but so much of it I cannot."

Sarah peered back through the lens and tried to find the beginning of the text. She spotted a large, florid letter *T* and began to read again. "To those who have discovered my words, and would attempt to understand what it is I have created here, welcome. I cannot be sure what your purpose is in opening this vessel, but I assume that it is noble. In your hands is one of the most powerful objects I have ever created. It, more than anything else I have ever done, will change the world. I trust you to make it better.

"But to fully understand what I have created, you must first recognize that science is more than just the discipline of proof; first there must be a theory. To invent the impossible, we must first imagine the improbable. So, to any brave soul who discovers these words, I tell you that a true understanding cannot be reached through science alone."

As she spoke, she realized that it was both thrilling and terrifying to hear Darby's words from beyond the grave. How many other secrets had he hidden away before his death? "Human ingenuity is the art of seeing, and then making. It will never be enough to simply copy something. You must *will* your success into being." Sarah thought back to the key that Darby had worn around his neck—the broken element was proof that even perfection couldn't always guarantee the intended result.

She stood up, took Emilio's hands into hers, and then stared intensely into his eyes. Sarah hoped that the seriousness of her words could keep her passion at bay. "Do you trust me, Emilio?"

He smiled and nodded. "I do, Sarah."

"Sir Dennis and I were very close, although never more than friends. Sometimes I imagined that, if our lives had been just a little bit different, another time . . . that he would have been the kind of man to me that I think you could become. Do you understand?"

"You loved him."

Once again Sarah felt a prickling in her eyes. Of course she had. "I did." Her love for Darby was a childish, impossible thing—far more than just years had separated them. But her feelings had also been powerful, passionate, and real. Sir Dennis had been a true mentor to her, guiding not only her mind, but also her spirit, to places where she could dream of escaping from her father's world and discovering a way where she might begin to make her dreams come true. And now they had. Everyone had secrets and failures, but being a hero meant trying again anyway . . .

"But to understand his genius . . . This isn't just how the heart *works*, it's a way to uncover Darby's methods. Do you understand?"

A look of confusion passed over Emilio's face. "I think . . ."

Sarah grabbed his fingers more tightly. "You can't just fix Tom, you have to *rediscover* him."

"Rediscover?" He took a step back, his arms stretching away from hers. "I am no Darby!"

Sarah smiled and gripped his fingers more tightly. "Exactly."

"I don't understand."

A calmness descended on Sarah. The feeling was overwhelming, almost as if she could feel the spirit of Sir Dennis filling her, directing her in what to do and say. She stood up from the stool and, using her grip on his hands, pulled Emilio back towards her. "That's because you're still missing the most important piece of the puzzle." She felt the presence of the old man so strongly that it took everything in her not to add "my boy" to the end of the sentence. "He would have liked you, Emilio," she said as she began to unbutton the top few buttons of her blouse. His eyes went wide, and Sarah laughed. It was comical how once the idea of sex had entered into a room, it seemed that there was no amount of seriousness that could air it out again.

As she reached down and pulled out the key from around her neck, his expression changed to one of wonder. "What is it?" he asked, and reached up a hand toward it.

"Darby's final secret," Sarah said as she put her hands on either end of the lead key, and began to pull it apart. "And I think," she whispered as she slid off the cap, "it may be the most powerful thing in the world." Exposed to the air, the Alpha Element's strange light began to grow brighter and brighter until the glow filled the space between them. "With it, you can recreate the Automaton."

Chapter 17
A Subjugated Audience

Nathaniel's transition from unconsciousness back into the waking world was sudden and total, propelling him instantly from a comforting place of nothingness into a reality dominated by pain and thirst. He opened his eyes to discover that he was in a dimly lit stone chamber. Nathaniel could remember nothing about how he got there, or even the events had led him into such a sorry state.

The only thing he could know for sure was that there was a throbbing in his head, the pain rising and falling in time to a loud ticking from somewhere in the darkness. The sound reminded him of the old grandfather clock that had stood in the hall of the Darby mansion before it had burned to the ground.

His first instinct was to work to recall at exactly what point during the evening he had—once again—given up his convictions against inebriation, and had actively begun to drink with the purpose of getting drunk. But after a few moments, it was clear that this wasn't just a simple hangover. His head wasn't aching, it had been *hurt*. And despite his ability to consume epic quantities of drink, he had perfected an ability to end up in his own bed—and whatever hard palette he was lying on *now*, it surely wasn't his. In fact, the thin, straw-stuffed mattress barely seemed to qualify as a bed at all.

He reached out to touch the wall next to him, and confirmed that it was cold, rough-hewn stone. Was he in prison? What had he done?

The memories crashed into one another as they washed over him: Hughes had become some kind of monstrous blend of human and machine, and Alexander Stanton was dead—murdered by Lord Eschaton's hand.

Nathaniel sat up, pain making him force out a groan. Bringing his fingers to his head, he felt the dried blood clinging to his hair and scalp. The skin underneath was hot and raw, and if he survived, there would probably be another scar to join the one he had received during his battle with the Automaton.

"*Guten Tag,*" said a voice from the darkness. Its words were cold and emotionless. Focusing into the gloom, Nathaniel could see the round shape of Grüsser enveloping a small chair across the tiny stone room. The Prussian sat up ramrod straight, his shoulders almost perfectly perpendicular to the lines of the iron bars that separated the two men.

"Grüsser, where am I?" After a moment of silence he added, "And what the hell is going on here?"

"*Nichts,*" he said, and turned his head to look at the wall.

"What are you doing? Don't you know what's going on?"

"Ja. Eschaton ist here."

"You need to help me!"

There was no reply. The round man simply sat in his seat, unmoving, and took in a few long, noisy breaths.

The last time Nathaniel had seen the Submersible, he had been fleeing from the carnage in the meeting hall. "What are you doing, man? You're a Paragon."

Grüsser gave a short, quick nod in the direction of the wall and stood up. "Ich do vas Ich must." He spoke in a choked whisper so unemotional that he seemed to be talking to the air as much as he was communicating with Nathaniel.

The Prussian stood up awkwardly, then pulled on a ring attached to the square iron door. The hinges squealed as it swung open. Through the open doorway, Nathaniel saw light from the corridor beyond and realized that he was inside one of the Hall's prison cells. "Grüsser, you're a Paragon for God's sake."

Although the jail had rarely been used over the years, everyone had agreed that they might need to detain villains for interrogation from time to time, and ordinary cells might not be able to contain a superpowered foe. Stripped of his wings and other gadgets, Nathaniel was powerless in every way that mattered. They probably didn't consider him worth the trouble of electrifying the bars, although he wasn't eager to find out.

Feeling a growing thirst, he leaned over the edge of his seat and looked to see if there was any water nearby. A wave of vertigo and nausea rose up through him, and Nathaniel sat back against the wall to wait until the feeling passed. He wondered just how much damage had been done to his head.

The metal door opened again. A tall figure ducked slightly before walking through. "You," Nathaniel mumbled. The man was no longer dressed in his King Jupiter outfit, but instead wore a simple white shirt with crisply creased pants. Even in the darkness he could see the tiny Omega signs stitched in gold brocade across the vest he wore. The silver buckles on his shoes were cast in the shape of the Greek symbol as well.

"Hello, Nathaniel," he said, coming up to the bars. "We've never been properly introduced. I'm Lord Eschaton." He stuck a gray hand through the bars.

Unable to stand up, and trying not to reveal his weakness, Nathaniel let out a tiny, little snort, "And you're the lord of what, exactly?"

The gray man smacked his hand against the wall, letting out a small spark. "Lord of the Paragons, at least."

"You didn't earn that title, you stole it. You're just a cheap thug and a murderer."

Now it was Eschaton's turn to let out a derisive laugh. "You're a naïve child, Nathaniel Winthorp. Do you think that all the fine and gentle members of your precious society gained wealth and power simply by asking for it? There is, I'm afraid, no title ever earned without at least a little bloodshed. And I'm sure you more than most men are well aware of the kind of cruel games that must be played in order to maintain that power once it has been gained."

Between the rage that boiled inside him and the pain washing through his head, Nathaniel couldn't find any words worth speaking in reply. Instead, he lowered his eyes, and saw the stain on his shirt where Alexander Stanton's life had leaked onto him. "You didn't have to kill the Industrialist."

"Clements did that." Eschaton replied. "But he needed to die. The Industrialist was many things, but in the end it is safe to say that his greatest power, beyond any of the ridiculous devices that he wore, was that he had the courage of his convictions—as antiquated and wrong-headed as so many of them were. And when a man like that is diametrically opposed to your vision," the gray man continued, "there is, I'm afraid, only one sure way to stop him."

Nathaniel shifted himself upwards. "Why am *I* still alive?"

Eschaton pointed to the wooden chair that Grüsser had been perched on a few minutes before. "Do you mind if I take a seat?"

"As you like." His words came out slightly slurred. If he was destined to have all the suffering of imbibing with none of the pleasures, then they could at least let him have a drink of *something*—even if only a simple glass of water. Although now that he was awake, the desire for a shot of whisky was growing quickly.

The wood creaked loudly as it settled under Eschaton's weight. It screeched softly as he shuffled it towards the bars. When he got close enough, the gray man stopped and leaned forward. "Now, ask me your question again."

He could barely remember it himself, for a moment. "I . . . I wanted to know why you didn't kill me."

"Two reasons," he said, holding up his thumb and index finger to illustrate his point. "First and foremost, I'm afraid that, as far as convictions go, the only genuine one that I can see in you is the desire to find your next drink. Men bound by addiction are, I've found, far more likely to work with me than against me."

"Like Grüsser?"

Eschaton grinned at that. "You're looking poorly to me, Mr. Winthorp. Are you sure there isn't anything that I can get for you? I'd hate to have you expire before we finish our conversation."

Nathaniel's instinct was to tell the man to go to hell, but the truth was that at this moment his thirst was greater than his pride. "Water," he said.

Eschaton turned his head to the side and yelled out the open door, "Grüsser!"

The Prussian appeared a moment later. He had clearly been waiting for his master's call just outside in the hallway. In the light from the open door, Nathaniel could see that his eyes were wide and staring. He hoped that seeing the death of the Industrialist was still haunting him. "Ja, Lord Eschaton. Was ist du vant?"

"Nothing for me, but your fellow Paragon would like some water." He glanced at Nathaniel and then looked back at the Prussian. "Find him a pitcher, and a bowl and cloth as well. I'm sure he'd like to clean himself up a bit."

The fat man nodded as Eschaton spoke. "Ist der anything else, Lord?"

"That's all for now, but you'd better hurry, I think. Things are beginning to look tight for you. I'm sure you want me to remedy that."

Grüsser raced out of the door at a trot, his footsteps echoing down the hallway. Just as the sound began to diminish, Eschaton turned and yelled out the man's name again. "Grüsser! Get back here." The sound stopped, and then grew louder.

When he appeared at the door, the Prussian was breathless and red-faced. Whatever talent the man had brought to the Paragons, great fitness was not among them. "Ja, Lord?"

"Can you also find a bottle of whisky and a proper glass for the gentleman?"

"Ja." He stood leaning awkwardly against the doorway for a moment, gasping for breath. He seemed to be waiting to see what else Eschaton might have to say to him.

"Go!" the gray man boomed, and Grüsser vanished like a chastened cat, his footsteps going even faster than before.

Nathaniel frowned. He had no great respect for the Submersible, but it was clear that Eschaton's intention was to humiliate him, and he was still a fellow Paragon. "Is that necessary?"

"Yes," the gray man said to him with a nod. "He's hidden behind a mask for so long that he can no longer tell if he's pretending anymore. But we'll fix it in time." He nodded and smiled. "You need to appreciate that there is nothing that I do to the men who serve me that they have not already done to themselves. I just bring it into the open and put it to work for my purposes."

Nathaniel considered this for a moment. "Are you trying to tell me that every man ultimately wishes for his own subjugation?" Having spent most of his life with his nose half-buried in books by the old masters, he had to admit that there was a certain degree of simple charm to the philosophies that Eschaton espoused.

The gray man nodded in response. "I'll admit that it's not the natural human condition. It's simply the outcome that we have brought upon ourselves from the endless arrogance that comes with assuming that we are the children of the divine."

"So you don't believe in God?"

Eschaton leaned back and laughed softly. "Are you shocked that I might question whether there is an intelligent creator who watches our lives from his throne in the clouds?" He shook his head. "The only being I've ever met who was assured of the love of his creator, was the one who never realized that I helped create him." Eschaton lifted up his arms and balled his hands into fists, "until I tore him to pieces."

·Nathaniel took a moment to realize what he was being told. "You helped create the Automaton?"

"I was the midwife . . ." He let out a thundering laugh. "You're lucky you don't believe the Automaton was ever truly alive, Mr. Winthorp, or you'd be facing an ethical dilemma of world-shattering proportions."

Nathaniel knitted his brows together. The man was talking enigmatic nonsense, but . . . "What do you mean by that?"

"By your own definition, I'd be a god!" He leaned back in the chair, and the wood let out another brutal screech under the strain. "Did Darby ever tell you about his unfortunate assistant?"

"I don't think . . ."

"Does the name Harrington ring a bell in your mind?"

"No."

"There is something so wonderful about being as young as you are, Mr. Winthorp. You can simply pretend that the world was always the way it is now, and that the true cost in human blood it took to make it that way is simply a fairy tale that the older generation tells the younger to keep them in line." Eschaton's voice dropped to a whisper, and for an instant Nathaniel could almost glimpse the man he had once been. "But the cost of progress is very real."

Grüsser wobbled back into the room. He held a silver tray in his hands with two crystal tumblers, a pitcher of water, a towel, a bottle of whisky, a shot glass. If anything, he looked even more red-faced and terrified than he had before.

"Grüsser," Nathaniel said, "what's the matter with you?"

The Prussian let out a choking cough.

"It's all right," Eschaton said. "Why don't you show him? I'll take the tray."

Grüsser handed over the drinks, and then slowly unbuttoned his jacket. As he removed it, it became obvious that there was a mechanical device of some sort hidden underneath of his shirt.

He lifted up the blouse to reveal a metal contraption that held a series of metal bands strapped around his body. It was a gorgeously manufactured piece of clockwork, but it seemed to be digging cruelly into the folds of his flesh. The highest of the rings was strapped low and tight around his neck, and seemed dangerously close to cutting into him.

It was obvious now that the ticking that Nathaniel had noticed when he first woke up had been coming from the device strapped to the Prussian, and it was going faster now.

Eschaton stood and placed the tray onto the flat of the chair. The tumblers shook violently, and the pitcher spilled some of its cargo over the side. Some it was taken by the towel, while the rest slipped off the tray, down the chair, and into a small puddle on the floor. Nathaniel wasn't thirsty enough to cry out yet, but he was thirsty enough to notice.

"I call this device my Chronal Suit," Eschaton said, reaching into his pocket and pulling out a large key. "The name is a bit indulgent, I admit, since it only changes the *awareness* of time and does nothing to time itself." The bow end was large and square, and it looked like a larger version of one that might be used to wind up a child's toy. "Turn around, Grüsser."

The Prussian spun in place, exposing a tin box on the back of the device. Eschaton stuck the key into it, then began to slowly turn it. The Chronal Suit emitted an almost comically loud grinding sound as Eschaton wound it. "And truthfully, the only person who fully feels the effect is the wearer. But I think Grüsser is most excellent at communicating his awareness, don't you?"

With each spin, the bands around his neck and chest noticeably relaxed, and Grüsser sputtered and coughed. "He ist ein madman, Nathaniel!" The words came out in a hoarse whisper.

Eschaton turned the key around and around until the mechanism was fully wound. The bands were slack now, but the ticking was louder.

Eschaton pulled the key free as Grüsser massaged his neck. "Please, Lord Eschaton, I don't want to die this way."

"Sadly, Helmut, I don't think we've quite reached the point where I can consider you one of my children . . . yet." He clapped him on the shoulder, and Grüsser noticeably flinched. "How long that will take is up to you." Whether the twitch was born out of fear, or a shock from Eschaton's electrified body, it was impossible to say.

"We found poor Grüsser in the basement yesterday. He had been trying to make his way into the secret passage that Darby built for him to use his submersible. But unfortunately, all the doors had sealed shut during the birth of the Paragon."

Eschaton waved his hand at the door. "All right, Grüsser. You should make it through the night. I'll see you in the morning."

The Prussian took a nervous bow. "Thank you, my Lord."

"And thank you for bringing us the drinks," the gray man replied. "I'm sure Nathaniel will appreciate them."

Grüsser nodded, and then slunk away, moving with slightly less urgency, but more grace, than he had before.

"Now then," Eschaton said, picking up one of the glasses from the chair. "Where were we?"

Nathaniel frowned. "Is that what you have in store for me?"

"No. There's only one Chronal Suit, and it's Grüsser's. To be honest, my first instinct was to simply let you sit down here to rot, stewing in your own sickness and pain while I destroyed the old world around you. I'm sure that once your mind had softened sufficiently it would have been far more amenable to my way of thinking." Eschaton filled a glass with water and held it up in front of the bars. It was close enough for Nathaniel to reach, but he'd have to reach through the bars to get it, and if they were electrified . . .

Nathaniel resisted the urge to try, despite his desperation. He wouldn't let the man torture him so easily. "You truly think I would become that much of an idiot?"

"I think that, given enough time in that cell, you'll begin to recognize that pride and righteousness are not the mighty sword and shield that Stanton taught you they were." Eschaton wagged the glass back and forth, spilling some of the water onto the floor. "And maybe you'd begin to appreciate how easy it is to exploit the weak and unfortunate."

"And what about you?"

"What about me?"

"Don't you want to exploit people? Didn't you exploit Hughes and Grüsser?"

"Neither man was, as far as I know, either weak or unfortunate when I met them. Neither were you, for that matter. And as I told you before, I did nothing to them that they didn't truly want."

"So you say," he mumbled. "And what does Lord Eschaton want?"

The gray man replied without hesitation. "I want to remake the world and save humanity. To pull it back from the brink of its own folly and save the human race from its inevitable extinction."

"And what kind of man is it that believes he can do that?"

"We already know that you would say he is a god. And," he said with a moment of dramatic pause, "I am a compassionate one." Eschaton slid the water through the bars.

Nathaniel, no longer able to control himself now that it was safely in reach, grabbed the glass from his hand and began to swallow it down desperately, the excess trickling down his face.

"Now, while you're enjoying that, perhaps you'll give me a moment to finish telling you the story of Mr. Harrington. Then I'll give you some whisky." He handed Nathaniel the damp towel, moved the tray and its contents to the floor, and sat. "I know it's difficult to imagine that older men were ever as young as you are now, especially in our age of progress and enlightenment. And old men can seem sad, because even after their crimes are conveniently forgiven by history, they must still live with their sins. But I still think you may be interested in hearing this story."

Nathaniel, his initial thirst at least somewhat satisfied, sat up, placed the empty glass down on the floor by the bars, and then took the miniscule journey back to his seat, dabbing at his damaged head with the cloth.

Eschaton waited patiently until he was seated before continuing. "I was originally hired as an engineer by Alexander Stanton. Does that surprise you?"

Nathaniel said nothing. It sounded doubtful, but if he was going to be a captive audience for a madman, he might as well avoid agitating him.

After a moment of silence, Eschaton continued, "I was straight out of the university—a man of simple means, but not without the training necessary to allow me to enter into your step-father's employment."

"What did you do for him?"

"I made toys," he said with a scowl. "Stanton became the Industrialist well before he ever met Darby, and he needed trinkets to prove his power. Or did you think that he made his own hat and gun?"

"I hadn't thought . . ."

Eschaton cut him off. "And when Darby finally appeared, Stanton handed me over to the old man like one man might lend another a pair of shears." He adopted Stanton's upper-crust cadence by way of mockery. "'They're slightly rusty, old fellow, but I'm sure with a little clean and a sharpen, they'll get the job done.'"

"And Darby?"

"He believed he was the only genius in the world . . ." There was a note of sarcasm in Eschaton's voice that Nathaniel hadn't heard before.

Perhaps taunting him might work better. "Why didn't you just quit?"

"And miss my chance to work side by side with the 'greatest inventor of our age'?" He laughed. "As miraculous as Darby may have seemed to you and the Stanton girl, he was ten times more so to me. And for a while it was perfection. I helped him with everything from the perfection of fortified steam to the creation of the Automaton himself."

"But then I slowly discovered that genius is selfish. For someone to be considered a true visionary, it takes not only his own hard work, but also that of everyone around him. And only one man gets all the credit. If I was going to make a name for myself, I needed to create something all on my own."

While he understood the impulse, unlike Alexander and Sarah, Nathaniel had always been content to enjoy the fruits of Darby's intelligence. His frustrations had come more from Sir Dennis's constant tendency to try to *educate* everyone about *everything*.

"I don't mean to be impertinent or rude," Nathaniel replied—although if he hadn't been trapped behind the bars he would have been far more than that, "but what is the point of all this?"

Eschaton frowned. "I know that listening to others isn't the kind of thing you care for, Nathaniel, but if you'll indulge me a little bit longer, I think my intent will become clear."

Nathaniel pointed to the silver platter. "Then, may I have some more water if you're not going to drink it?"

"Patience is a virtue. Once I've finished, I'll give you all the water you want."

Eschaton clearly wanted his every move to seem manipulative and enigmatic, but as far as Nathaniel could tell, it was all the same nonsense. "I have nothing else to do."

"Good." He put his hands on his knees and leaned forward again. "I assume that as a protégé of Dennis Darby, you're familiar with fortified steam?"

"It's what powers my suit."

"It is the secret that gives power to *all* the miraculous devices Darby created for the Paragons. It also was the animating force behind the Automaton."

"I know that."

"You seem to know a great deal, and yet your ability to remain staunchly ignorant in the face of a constantly changing world is outstanding. But," Eschaton continued, "as miraculous as fortified steam is, it is directly effective only when driving inanimate machines. When exposed to living flesh, there is no reaction."

"Darby had said that it was . . ." He paused while he searched for the word. "Inert! And that is, I think, usually considered to be a good thing . . ."

"Good only if you think that the goal of humanity, now that we have struggled to a point only slightly above that of the common ape, should be to remain forever unchanging. A good thing only if the only goal of invention is to ease the burden of our brief journey from cradle to grave, but never transform it. Do you think that this sad condition is where we should *stay*, Nathaniel?"

He shook his head. "You sound like Darby. Always going on about the future, and the possibilities that tomorrow will bring. Why not be content with the present?"

"Because the present never lasts," he said angrily. "And I wanted to discover if fortified steam couldn't be something more than a fuel for mechanical destruction. I wanted to see if there was a way you could access its power *directly*. But until Darby had created the Automaton, I wasn't sure it was possible. After all, if fortified steam could allow a machine to mimic a man, then shouldn't it be possible to create something that imbued a man with the attributes of a machine? Why not create a stronger, more efficient humanity? And that was when I came upon the idea of fortified smoke."

Nathaniel found himself intrigued in spite of himself. "Fortified smoke? What are you talking about?"

"My dream—a caustic gas based entirely on what Darby considered to be the undesirable qualities of his beloved gas. It would be less stable, but capable of interacting with organic matter, and with *flesh*.

"And such a material already existed! It was a by-product of Darby's early processes, but when I asked him about it, he called it a perversion of what he had created. He *forbade* me to investigate any further." Eschaton let out a thundering laugh. "Can you imagine?"

But Nathaniel could envision it. It would have been exactly what he would have expected Darby to say.

"But it also meant that he *knew* the truth, he was simply afraid to the take the next, obvious step."

Nathaniel had heard these kinds of rants before. Many villains considered themselves to be misunderstood "men of genius." But unlike all of the previous madmen he had encountered, Lord Eschaton actually had worked with Darby, and he had already managed to defeat the Paragons. This was more than mere bravado. "But you weren't afraid."

"Not at all—and in that, Nathaniel, we're not so different after all. We both have, from time to time, ignored our elders in pursuit of the vision of our desires."

"Mine only left behind empty bottles, not dead men."

He replied with a smile. "I never said that we were equals." He held up his arm and let electricity crackle over it. "But you could still become so much more."

Nathaniel didn't like the threatening tone in Eschaton's voice. "Are we done? Can I have my water now?"

"Almost—just a little patience." The gray man planted both feet on the floor and reached down to grab the small glass on the ground. He flipped it over and put it on top of the whisky bottle. "Here you are," he said, slipping the liquor through the bars. "This should entertain you."

"Thank you," Nathaniel said glumly. He would have rather had the water, but he reached out for it anyway.

Eschaton's other arm grabbed him and pulled Nathaniel up against the bars. He was surprised, but not shocked. The gray man smiled at him, and let him go. "I can be benevolent."

Nathaniel didn't say a word. He just poured himself a small glass. If nothing else, it would dull the pain of this lunacy.

"At that time I was still confused in my morals," Eschaton continued. "I decided that if anyone was going to be the victim of my experiments, besides some small stray animals of course, it would be myself. So, I set about to create fortified smoke and apply it to living flesh.

"I did my work in secret, utilizing whatever parts of Darby's lab I could gain access to. But the one piece I couldn't create was Darby's Alpha Element: the unique metal that energized the steam and gave it its unique properties. And Darby kept the only sample around his neck."

Darby remembered the key that the Bomb Lance had taken. "*That's* what you stole from him!"

"Not quite. The Alpha Element is useless for creating fortified smoke. But he had created an earlier sample, one that created a steam that was 'impure' and highly poisonous. He claimed to the world that it did nothing, but I knew he was lying. I had seen the results. I had christened it the Omega Element, and I stole it from his vault.

"Once I had taken the Omega Element, I tried dozens of combinations to get what I wanted. And it was when I added coal smoke to the water vapor that my fortified smoke was born. Unfortunately, it also had a devastating effect on organic matter. My intention had been to hybridize a new form that would bring the powers of the smoke and steam together, and so I pressed on. When I discovered a nonlethal blend, I exposed myself to what I had planned to be a small amount of gas.

"But we all make mistakes," he said with a sigh. "And the smoke ate right through the tubing I had built to contain it, and the gas slowly filled the room. By all rights I should have been dead, and for a short time perhaps I was.

"Darby found me hours later and took me to safety. When I awoke, I found that instead of killing me, it had transformed me."

Eschaton leaned back, showing off the results. "It stripped the fat from my body and bonded with my muscle tissue in a way I don't yet fully understand. At first it left me crippled and weak.

"After he realized what I'd done, Darby was furious and terrified. He told me that I was lucky to be alive, but that he could no longer trust me. Once I proved myself capable of walking, he threw me out into the street. I tried to turn to Stanton for help, but he would have nothing to do with me.

"But I had seen the future, and once I managed to regain some health, I refashioned myself as a villain. Calling myself the Clockwork Man, I used my intelligent bombs to rob banks and fund the laboratory I would need to re-create my experiments. But the Paragons soon managed to catch up with me, and even my exploding men were no match for them.

"After that, I simply built devices for other villains. It kept the Paragons busy and away from me while I studied my own condition and gathered my resources."

Nathaniel took his next draught of whisky directly from the bottle, not bothering to pour it into the glass this time. "You said you were crippled in the accident."

"Even without the Alpha and Omega Elements, I was slowly able to improve my body using a regimen of pure smoke and steam. And during those years I was able to uncover more about what had happened to me. But I wasn't able to re-create Darby's metals, and I needed them not only to complete my own metamorphosis, but to continue those experiments.

"It wasn't until I had the Omega Element back in my grasp that I was able to complete my evolution and become the man you see in front of you."

Nathaniel nodded with comprehension. "So that key you stole was . . ."

"The Omega Element, yes." He stood up and leaned down to open a gate at the bottom of the cell door. "But even with it, I have reached the end of my transformation. I was birthed by an accident, and that has limited my possibilities. But I am sure that with the proper application of scientific rigor, even greater discoveries are possible."

When he stood up, there was a dangerous grin on the gray man's face. "And that next step, Nathaniel, is one that you and I are going to take together." He slid the tray through the iron bars, then slammed the gate shut.

Nathaniel dragged himself up off the bench. The alcohol was beginning to do its work, and he was feeling incredibly tired. "I'm not sure what you think I can do for you. I won't assist a homicidal madman."

"I think that you'll find that *genocidal* is the correct word."

Nathaniel reached down and took the water first. "Fine—whatever you want. I'm your prisoner now."

"I never expected you to assist me willingly. But now that I have all the pieces that I need to resume my experiments, the next step is finding a suitable test subject, willing or otherwise."

Nathaniel stood, his eyes widening as the weight of the words sank in. "No . . ."

"No? No?" Eschaton said mockingly. "And why not? You're young and strong—and since the irony of using Alexander Stanton or his lovely daughter is denied to me, I'm afraid that you're absolutely the next best thing."

Cold terror struck Nathaniel, not just from the realization of his fate, but from the knowledge that there was no one left to save him. "You can't do this to me, Eschaton!" And yet, even with the waves of shock, he kept feeling weaker and weaker. What was wrong with him?

"Can't? Stupid boy, I *must*. This has been my plan all along. If I'm going to end the world and save humanity, I'll need to fill the new world with better beings. And while my own transformation has been spectacularly successful, it was also an accident—one that, I have discovered, is not easy to repeat."

Eschaton's voice rose in volume until it was just below a shout. "I am just a crude version of what could truly be humanity's next great state of being. And although not everyone will survive what is to come, the small portion that does will be part of a better world. It will be a place where humanity will become stronger, more powerful, and be freed from the petty concerns of human frailty. And if you survive, Nathaniel, you will be the first *true* child of Eschaton."

Nathaniel wanted to tell the villain that he'd rather die, but instead he found himself sliding down the wall. It seemed that despite his anger, the weight of his injuries was too great. Perhaps he would die after all. Maybe that would be a blessing . . .

It was only as he slumped over onto the bench and fell back toward unconsciousness that it dawned on Nathaniel that the whisky had been drugged.

Chapter 18

The Circus in Daylight

Emilio had been raised in the circus, and while most children would imagine that growing up in a carnival would be a dream come true, the truth was quite different. He had hated that life for as long as he could remember.

The circus was the only life he had ever known, and what thrilled the audience only bored him.

Every morning was a disappointment as the daylight washed away the illusions and revealed the tawdry truths that lay underneath the glamour: clowns were simply broken men with greasepaint on their faces, ferocious beasts were nothing more than sad, depressed animals trapped in cages, and the bombastic ringmaster was the ruler of a homeless tribe of exhibitionists and freaks.

Worst of all was his father. During the nighttime, the man was a hero—The Great Armando—an acrobat flying effortlessly through the air. But when the sun rose, he was simply an aging man praying that his son would take on his legacy before he made the final mistake that would leave him shattered and dead on the ground. Emilio wanted nothing to do with it.

It was staring up at the gaudily painted marquee of the Theatre Mechanique in the light of day that had brought the memories back, and he blinked them away, returning himself to the present moment.

The sign was even more ridiculous than the last time Emilio had seen it. The letters that described the show were painted in red and gold, "The Theater Mechanique Presents: My Adventures in the Clockwork World—A Circus of Steam and Fire, Presented by Vincent Smith."

Behind the lettering was a garish (and wildly inaccurate) rendering of the show's star attraction, the Pneumatic Colossus, along with an improbably kind drawing of Mr. Smith himself.

The mechanical man was depicted as a towering figure one hundred feet high. It belched smoke from the hat on its head and shot flames from the mouth and eyes while Vincent Smith stood below it, righteous and stalwart underneath the onslaught.

Sarah stared up at the sign and shook her head. "My father has a smoking hat . . ."

Emilio nodded. "But this is bigger," he replied, almost matter-of-factly.

"Are you sure this is a good idea?" Sarah asked for the hundredth time. "Can we trust him?"

"Sure enough." Emilio had found the last few days with Sarah incredibly frustrating. Normally, finding the ability to concentrate on work was easy for him, and once he sank into the proper trance, the hours would roll by until Viola came to remind him that it was time for dinner.

But unlike his sister, who always seemed to have something better to do, Sarah hung around him constantly as he worked. At first she had helped a bit, but after a while her endless questions had only managed to slow things down. If Dennis Darby truly had managed to work while she was around, he had no idea how . . .

On the other hand, it wasn't entirely her fault. Even without Sarah's interference, he would have managed to make only so much progress. Once he translated Darby's notes, the ideas had made sense, and he could figure out the processes of the heart's function. But what the mysterious key could do that would bring a mechanical man to life was still a mystery.

Beyond that, the heart had been badly damaged. Even if he understood it perfectly, it would still need repairs and new parts. And every piece had been created with precision that was far beyond the ability of anything he could use or build in his junkyard workshop. There were, in fact, only a handful of people within all of New York who might have the machinery needed to fix or replace the parts with anything approaching the finely tuned craftsmanship of the originals.

And once he had realized that, Emilio's solution was simple: turn to someone who did have what they needed, and hope he might provide some insight as well.

Sarah had been both disappointed and horrified by the idea of asking for help. She had expected great things from Emilio, and his inability to instantly repair and revive Dennis Darby's greatest masterpiece seemed to have not only disappointed her, but had also put a stop to any further movement toward romance after their *vermut*-fueled kiss on the couch.

Not that Emilio was sure he much felt like it, either. There had been some moments over the last few days where things seemed to be veering toward another encounter, but either one or the other of them would quickly steer things in another direction.

And they both had good reasons for maintaining their distance. For his part, Emilio had begun to worry that if they did consummate their feelings, it would only lead to misery for a girl like Sarah.

Compared to Italy, America was, he believed, completely obsessed with sex. The problem was that the expression of it in the New World seemed to be far more about avoidance than discovery, which managed to make romance a dangerous and depressing enterprise for everyone involved, most especially the woman. If nothing else, seduction was supposed be fun *while* you were doing it.

Still, like it or not, this was his home now, and he wouldn't be responsible for Sarah's fall from grace—despite the fact that she was currently clutching his arm with her own, part of an act of deception that they had cemented with a gold engagement ring. Viola had produced it after he suggested that Sarah accompany him on his visit to the theater, disguised as his fiancée.

Even with the disguise, Emilio hadn't been sure that bringing Sarah along with him would be a good idea. Vincent could be temperamental and odd at the best of times. But she had been adamant that anywhere the heart was going, she would have to follow. Having her pretend to be his fiancée would make things easier for everyone.

Sarah had dressed for the day in her best clothes, demanding help from Viola to do up her corsets. Emilio had, once again, been banished from the bedroom, and he could only stand outside as both women tried to outdo each other with the bitterness of their complaints about the clothing: Viola shouting about how much work it was to get it onto the rich girl, and Sarah responding loudly about how painful and constricting it all was to wear properly. He was sure that on some level they had both enjoyed it a great deal.

For his part, Emilio wore a simple but well-tailored suit and a bowler hat. In his left hand he carried a lacquered wooden case by a strong leather handle. There were large brass latches along the top and sides, and hinges on the bottom.

Sarah let go of his arm to try the door. It rattled in the frame, but refused to open. "Should we knock?"

"I have a key," Emilio said, producing it from his pocket. He slipped it into the lock and turned it. "It still works!" he added with a note of surprise.

The door slid back with a rumble, and Emilio shoved it closed behind them.

With the door shut, the only light in the room was what came through from a row of small windows near the ceiling. Beneath them the walls of the room were dressed almost entirely in curtains of dark velvet, lending the entrance a cavelike atmosphere. The floor was a mosaic of small tiles, laid out in concentric circles of white and black. "This way," Emilio said, taking Sarah's hand, and guiding her into a larger room.

Sarah put her hand to her lips when she saw the menagerie of mechanical creatures and flowers that stood on pedestals all over the room.

Each stand contained a small brass plaque inscribed with the name of the specimen, its Latin name, and the fictional country it had been taken from.

Emilio was curious to see what the room must look like when it was open to the public—fully lit, with every one of the devices moving, rotating, spinning, dancing, or jumping. Many of them would also be spitting fire and steam. They were fantastic machines in their own right, but, only a prelude to the incredible devices that would appear on the main stage during the show.

Emilio had found the whole thing a bit ridiculous, but having grown up in the circus, he understood how a good story could excite the audience. "Is not real," he said to her.

"I know," Sarah replied, and gave him the first genuine smile he had seen in days.

Clearly people were not immune to the creatures' charms, even when they were immobile. "*Anura coganus*," she read. She stared at the contraption for a moment, and then clapped her hands together. "It's a frog!"

"*Sì.*" He pointed to a metal fly hanging down on a post only a foot from the ceiling. "It eats that."

"Eats it?"

"*Sì.*" He whistled and pointed as he mimed the frog jumping through the air and grabbing the fly. "Then there," he said waving at the empty pedestal on the far wall.

"Amazing!" Sarah said.

"*Fantastico!*" He raised up his hands in a gesture that was slightly more sarcastic than he had originally intended. After all, if he had worked with Vincent to create entertainment, why should it be a bad thing if people were actually entertained by it?

As they walked, Sarah's eyes caught the statue of the Colossus that stood in the center of the room. It was a scale model, maybe two feet tall, but unlike the ridiculous image that was on the marquee, it was also a fairly accurate rendition. "What's that?" she asked him.

"The Colossus. Is like your Tom, yes?"

"It's smaller."

Emilio laughed. "Is not the real thing."

"No, it isn't." Sarah said as she examined it more closely. "Tom doesn't look like he was made from barrels and pipes." She reached out and touched it. "Does it move?" she asked.

"No. The real one, it moves very well." He lifted his hands up and down as if they were on a string. "Like a toy."

"I'm surprised that Darby never mentioned this show. It seemed like it would be just the kind of thing he would have enjoyed."

"Is open only a short time."

"I see." She squinted at the statue. "I'd love to see what the real thing looks like."

"I show you," he said, and grabbed her arm.

When they reached the wall, Emilio pulled back the curtain to reveal a door hidden behind it. After checking the knob to make sure that it was locked, he rapped his hand hard against the wood. "Vincent!" he yelled out. Waiting only a moment, he knocked again, and called out louder through the darkness, "You there, Vincent?"

They waited for a few seconds in silence before Sarah said, "Maybe he's out?"

"He's an old man." Emilio pointed at his ear. "No hear." Making a fist, he pounded on the door with enough force to make it rattle in its frame. "*Viiiiiin-cent!*" he shouted.

Taking a step back, Sarah looked down. "If he's there, I'm sure he's heard you that time." Her shoulders shook a few times, and Emilio wondered what might be wrong with her.

Realizing that he must have scared her, he put his hand back down to his side and slowly unclenched his fist before putting it on her shoulder. "Are you all right, Sarah?"

She looked up at him and pointed at her mouth. "Viiiin-cent!" she said, in a mock shout, pretending to bang on the door, "Viiiiiiiin-cent!" She followed it with a cackling laugh he had never heard before.

After a moment of shock, Emilio laughed along with her. What was it about this girl? She could be so serious and proper, and then . . .

His sister might think she was just another rich girl, but he had seen her fearlessly attack a man more than twice her size. If the society ladies of New York were all like this, then it was something they were hiding from the newspapers.

He stared into her eyes until the laughing subsided, letting himself enjoy the warmth of the sudden return of his feelings for her.

In response, she tilted her head to the side, and her smile became curious and warm. "What is it, Emilio? Are you all right?" But there was something in the way that she smiled at him that told him she already knew the answer.

Standing there, Emilio realized that he was feeling more than just infatuation. It was something that he hadn't felt in a very long time, and he wasn't entirely sure he wanted to. "Sarah, I . . ." He tried to find the English, but there didn't seem to be any way to express it. Was there only one way to say *love* in English? Was it something he wanted to say?

The moment was broken by a muffled shout of "Damnation!" as the lock in the door in front of them rumbled and clanked. A few seconds later, the door flew open, revealing Vincent Smith standing in the doorway.

The showman looked, as Emilio had expected, like a man who had just woken up from a night of debauchery and drink. It was, in Emilio's experience, how the man always appeared, unless he was on stage.

He was older, right around fifty, with a curly, well-waxed mustache, topped by a pair of piercing blue eyes. His clothes were just a step above what might be worn by someone living out on the street, consisting of a baggy pair of paint-splattered canvas trousers held up with suspenders over a tattered and equally paint-covered union suit that had once been white but wasn't anymore.

All his hair stuck straight out of his head like stiff, white wool, with the exception of his beard and whiskers, which were unkempt, but appeared to be well-manicured.

Emilio had considered warning Sarah about Vincent's eccentricities, but the showman wasn't dangerous, and Emilio's English wasn't nearly good enough to explain how strange he was. He was also worried that it would just give Sarah another reason not to trust the man.

"Zounds! What is this all about?" He looked down at Sarah. "And who are you? The doors don't open until seven o'clock!"

Emilio waved at the wild man. "It's me, Vincent!"

"Emilio!" he shouted as he stepped through the door. He embraced the Italian in a bear hug, lifting him up off the ground. "How are you, my boy? And why haven't you ever come back to see me?"

"I finished work."

"That doesn't mean there wasn't any more. I'm always glad to see you." Vincent's tone was so rich and practiced that it sounded almost unreal. But if the man had ever had another "natural" manner of speech, it had long ago been wiped away by his affectations.

"You told me to leave."

"Did I?" he said with a look of genuine shock on his face. "And why would I say something like that?"

"I make you pay me."

"Well . . ." said Vincent slowly as he twirled his finger in the air, and then followed it with his entire body. "I could see how I *might* have considered that a problem before I actually *opened* the show." He finished his twirl with a flourish, and then stamped his feet down. "But look at it now!" he said, throwing up his arms theatrically. "Ladies and gentlemen, boys and girls, men and machines, I welcome you to not only the greatest wonder of the modern age, but what is also the singularly most *successful* exhibition of mechanical marvels in the entire city of New York—if not the world!"

"Eh-*hum*," Sarah said, over-enunciating the words in a way that made it clear that the interruption was meant to be intentional.

Emilio turned to face her. He was quickly learning that when there was a woman of society around, even one as open-minded as Sarah, there were also a long list of rules that everyone else seemed to be constantly breaking. "I'm sorry. Sorry!" He grabbed her hand and brought her forward. "Vincent Smith, this is . . ."

"Wait, Emilio, don't tell me," the white-haired man said as he took her other hand into his. "I'm sure that I've seen this dazzling young lady somewhere before. Have we met, my dear?"

Sarah gave him a nervous smile in return. "I'd remember you if we had, Mr. Smith."

"Well, I am rather memorable, or at least I do my best to try and be. And of course, many of the women who have seen me up on the stage often dream that they've met me in person—although I can promise you I'm far more charming than I first appear to be, in either case." He bowed and gave her hand a kiss.

Sarah curtsied and took her hand back. Emilio could see that the smile on her face looked oddly frozen, as if that particular grin was something that she called out on command. "As I said, if we'd met before, I'm sure I would remember."

"Perhaps it is *I* who have seen *you* somewhere. Are you an actress?"

"No sir."

"An heiress?"

"Not that I know of."

"Murderess, temptress, or diabolist?"

Sarah's mouth dropped open, but no words were coming out. Emilio leapt into the conversation, "This is Sa . . ."

"Susan Standish," Sarah said quickly, following with a formal curtsey that Emilio thought was the most perfect he had ever seen.

Vincent placed his left hand behind his back, and rolled his right in front of his face as he bent down. "Very pleased to make your acquaintance, Lady Standish."

"My fiancée."

Before Vincent could stand up from his bow, Sarah raised her hand in front of Vincent's face to show off the ring on her finger. It had been crafted from a pair of snakes, one silver, the other gold, entwined together and facing each other with a small gem held in between their mouths. Emilio never ceased to be amazed at the treasures Viola managed to find in the junkyard.

"But," Vincent asked, taking her hand between his thumb and forefinger to take a closer look, "how did you manage to fall into the clutches of this guinea lout?"

"Is enough, Vincent. Leave her alone." Emilio could feel her tension—Sarah was clearly judging the man's every move. He trusted the showman, even if Vincent did his best to avoid paying people the money he owed them.

Still, if Sarah felt that Vincent was worth lying to, Emilio would help her first and ask questions later.

Vincent smiled and looked down. "All right, lad. I'm sorry. I was hoping that you might have come in search of more work, and to be honest I could use your help right now. But if that's not the reason that you're here, then maybe you could tell me what your reasons actually *are* for coming to see me."

Emilio glanced at Sarah, but she seemed content to let him do the talking, no matter how bad his English might be. "We need your help with something."

"And what would that be?"

Emilio reached into his pocket, and pulled out a small brass gear. "Can you fix?" It was not only warped, but some of the teeth had been completely stripped off.

"Interesting," the showman said, leaning forward. "May I hold it, or do you expect me to repair it using mentalism?"

Emilio glanced over to Sarah again, who simply shrugged. He handed it over to the other man.

"Thank you." He held it up against one of the gaslights and nodded knowingly. "It seems simple enough, but I'll need to take a closer look."

Clutching it in his hand, Vincent turned and started to walk away from the door. Then he stopped and glanced down at the box that Emilio was carrying. "You're telling me you came all this way to see me, simply to fix a bent gear?"

Emilio frowned and clenched the handle more tightly. "Is more, but that would help."

Vincent looked at Emilio, then Sarah, then opened his hand to stare at the gear for a second time. "And if I say yes, will you show me what's in that box of yours?"

"One thing at a time," Sarah replied sternly.

"Hmmph." Vincent replied. "Follow me, then." He started to walk away slowly, and then, after a few steps, stopped abruptly. Emilio jerked to a stop, and he could feel Sarah's skirts brushing his legs behind him.

The showman turned to look at them. "And watch your step. It's quite safe when you're out in the audience, but I didn't build the back stage with women's skirts in mind."

As they walked, Emilio was shocked to see how much the place had changed in the last few months. For a time, this theater had been his home away from home—the place where he spent most of his days, and too many nights. And despite Vincent's reluctance to pay, in the end it had been the money he had earned here that had allowed him to purchase the junkyard.

Emilio and Sarah stepped gingerly over a series of small metal rails that snaked across the floor.

Emilio had seen this place when it was an empty shell, but the theater was complete now—a far cry from the constant jumble of half-completed parts that it had been while he had been working here.

"Did you know, Miss Standish," Vincent said without turning to look at them, "that your young man was instrumental in helping to build my feature attraction?"

"The Pneumatic Colossus?" Sarah said, raising her voice enough so that she could be clearly heard.

"Indeed. And what did he tell you about it?"

"Nothing," she replied.

"Wait," Vincent said. He stopped again, raised a hand up over his shoulder, and then turned in place with a dramatic flair. He stared back at Sarah, doing his best to look grimly around Emilio. "Are you telling me that

Emilio Armando brought you to the Theater Mechanique and didn't tell you about the greatest wonder of the modern age?"

"Well," she said, stammering slightly. "I saw his image on the marquee, and the statue in the other room . . ."

"Both of those are nothing—*nothing*—compared to the real thing." He moved closer to her. He had the earthy smell of makeup about him, like an old aunt. "If Emilio doesn't *mind*, perhaps I could give you a sneak preview before we go on with our business. I would hate for anyone to find out that you came all this way and didn't see our star attraction."

"Would that be all right, Emilio?" The tone in her voice sounded anything but genuine, and Emilio doubted she was genuinely asking for his opinion. More likely, Sarah realized it would be better far better if she pretended that her fiancé was the only one interested in fixing the heart.

"Is fine, Susan," he muttered back to her.

"Excellent!" Vincent said. "Wait here." Changing direction, he walked over to the wall and turned a crank. The gaslights burned higher, their glow revealing the full depth of the cavernous stage behind them.

Sitting near the back were numerous creatures, each resting on a small platform, their wheels perfectly placed in the tracks that ran underneath them. There were a lion, a horse, and a hippo, along with a number of other mechanical animals that all appeared similar in construction to the ones that had populated the front entrance, except that these machines were far larger and more complicated.

There seemed to be no obvious rhyme or reason to their order, although Emilio knew they stood according to their appearance in the show. He had helped Vincent build them, and the ones that he didn't work on personally contained obvious elements of his designs.

"Now that you've seen our bit players," Vincent said, walking back towards them, "let's go take a look at our star." Vincent took her hand and headed her toward the back of the stage. "You should come too, Emilio. I've added a few bells and whistles to the Colossus since the last time you were here."

Vincent wasn't completely helpless when it came to engineering these mechanical marvels, but he seemed only skilled at maintaining and repairing the work of others. He was utterly hopeless when it came to innovation. That was what Emilio had brought to the project.

It had been Viola who had convinced her brother to apply in the first place, having heard about someone looking for "mechanical geniuses" from one of her actor boyfriends.

After a great deal of procrastination, Emilio had travelled to New York to speak to Vincent about the job at his small office off Houston Street. Despite his meager accommodations, the showman had been able to describe his vision for the spectacle in the most minute detail. Much of the plan had seemed absurd, and most of the rest was unintelligible to a recent immigrant, but Vincent's passion and infectious enthusiasm were hard to resist. And Emilio understood enough English to know what a generous salary sounded like.

And soon after the project started, Emilio discovered he wasn't the only inventor working on it. There had been a one-armed fellow named Eli, as well. The Jew had a sour disposition that made him difficult to work with, but he was also an incredible engineer despite his handicap, and was capable of quickly constructing mechanisms that challenged even Emilio's ability to understand them. Together they had overcome their language barriers to create a number of objects of true beauty and complexity. Emilio had hoped to work with the man more, and they had discussed opening a shop together when the job was done. Then, one day, he simply stopped coming to the workshop, and Vincent had refused to discuss what had happened to the man.

Vincent stopped them in front of a box standing almost fifteen feet tall. It was at least ten feet along each edge, and it had been painted with an intricate webbed pattern of red, brown, and gold. Emilio thought that it looked like a giant Christmas present, or a monstrous Chinese puzzle box.

"Normally, my dear," Vincent said to Sarah, "you would see the Colossus appear in a far more dramatic manner. The mechanical orchestra would be playing, and the gas and steam lines would be hooked up to bring our mechanical friend to life. I would also be wearing a proper suit and hat." He pulled the metal pin and opened the large clasp on the front of the box. "That's the problem when you see things backstage: it ruins all the magic."

Emilio almost laughed out loud, but stifled it with a cough. If Vincent had been aware that he was talking to the protégé of Sir Dennis Darby, he

might not have been so quick to dismiss her ability to discern between theatrical tricks and genuine miracles of engineering.

"But I will do my best to help you imagine the grandeur of the moment."
The showman took a deep breath, and then bellowed out his words in a deep
and dramatic voice. "And now, ladies and gentlemen, the Circus of Steam and
Fire is proud to present its greatest attraction . . ." Vincent motioned, and
Emilio grabbed the other door. "The greatest wonder of the modern world . . .
the Pneumatic Colossus!"

Chapter 19
Trusting the Rejected

Sarah clasped her hands to her chest as the two men began to pull the box open, revealing what was hidden inside.

The mechanical man was huddled tight, the top hat on his head sunk beneath his knees. The long tubes of his arms were wrapped together and strapped down between his ankles.

The machine reminded Sarah more of a tin toy than a man. His body was made entirely of brass and steel, and his painted-on clothes glimmered in the gaslight.

As she stepped back to take a better look, Sarah's eyes widened. "It is quite . . . something, I have to admit." Seeing the machine like this almost made it appear as if the metal man were being held prisoner, and Sarah remembered when she had seen Tom strapped to the table in Darby's laboratory. She weaved a little bit, and she felt Emilio's hands on her shoulders.

Vincent smiled at her reaction, clearly misreading her shock for awe. "It is impressive, isn't it? And it is far more so once it's fully fired up and walking out on stage, spitting steam from its head and fire from its eyes."

"It does look like him . . ." she muttered. And yet, it didn't . . .

"What did you say, my dear?"

"The Automaton . . ." she said.

The showman laughed. "Ah, you've noticed. It turns out that Sir Dennis Darby's amazing creation went mad and met his demise only a few blocks away from here. They actually found his remains in Madison Square, sitting under the arm of Liberty."

Vincent tapped the machine's head, and it let out a hollow ring. "After that unhappy event, we made a few changes to our design in honor of the fallen Paragon. We like to think of our Colossus here as an homage to both the Automaton and his creator." Sarah wondered if the showman would be shocked if she told him that she had been there when it happened, and that the Automaton's heart was here with them now.

Sarah only realized that she had been staring when Emilio squeezed her shoulder. "You okay, Susan?"

"There's no need to worry, my dear," Vincent said, "I promise that he won't hurt you. We did our best, but this thing is hardly the miracle that the Automaton was—more a steam-powered puppet really. He won't go berserk and attack anyone."

Sarah wanted to defend Tom and explain what had actually happened, but there was no point. The story of the Automaton's demise, as the papers had told it, was of a machine that had gone mad and been bravely, if reluctantly, defeated by the Paragons. In the mind of the public, Tom had died a villain, and now his memory was being used to turn him into a monster.

She tried to take a closer look at the grotesque parody in front of her, but felt nothing but anger. Sarah placed her hands over her eyes. If she didn't have to look at it, she wouldn't . . . "Please, I'm sorry," she choked out, "Could you just . . . put him away?"

Vincent laughed, clearly amused by her reaction to his tin toy. "I'm so sorry, Miss Standish, I didn't meant to frighten you. You're hardly the first young lady to find our star attraction so terrifying. I dare say that we have a few women fainting every night when he actually performs." Sarah doubted that, but she still had many doubts about this man, and once again, Vincent misread her. "Don't worry, we'll make sure he's safely put away."

Emilio and Vincent pushed the doors of the box back together, hiding the metal man back behind his wooden shell. "See," the showman said, slightly winded from the effort, "all gone."

She pulled her hands off her face and sniffled. Thankfully she had managed to hold back any actual tears, or Vincent might think she was crying with joy. "I'm sorry," she said, producing a handkerchief from her pocket. "I must seem such a child."

"Not at all, my dear," Vincent said with a note of what sounded like genuine concern. "Only, I *was* hoping that I could entice you both into coming to see the show tomorrow night. After all, Emilio has never seen the final product of all the work he put in. Although, if just viewing our metallic friend has upset you so much . . ."

Sarah shook her head, angry that she had revealed so much in front of this charlatan. "No, I'm sorry. I'd love to see your show, it's just that . . ." Sarah took Emilio's arm. If only his English had been stronger . . . But his broken language was far more likely to do more harm than good. "I mean to say that I'm sure he's marvelous, it's just that my nerves sometimes get the better of me."

"Women," Vincent said as he started walking again. "You are such sensitive, emotional creatures." He turned to Emilio and gave him a wink. "Now you know why it is that I'm so much more comfortable with machines . . . They are, at the very least, predictable."

Sarah and Emilio followed behind Vincent until he reached a solid wooden door along the side wall. "But enough about the show . . . Let's see what I can do to help you with your problem."

Vincent opened it to reveal a garden courtyard. The space was large, and Sarah saw that it had elements in common with the menagerie at the front entrance. Standing on the concrete paths that lay in between the overgrown hedges and half-dead grass were a number of different machines. These sad creatures were far larger than the ones that had sat near the entrance, but these rusted hulks didn't gleam, and no one had bothered to give them pedestals to stand on. "The rejected," Emilio whispered. "You saved them."

"Just so, my boy—many made by your own hands. These are the concepts and prototypes for the creatures that eventually made it to the stage— gone but not forgotten."

Dominating the courtyard was a squat brick building with a steeply sloped roof constructed from a number of dirty glass panes of odd sizes. "I'm sure that Emilio has told you all kinds of terrible stories about what went on while he worked here," he said to Sarah, once again taking her hand, and walking her down the stairs. "But I'm sure even Emilio is at least a little bit proud of some of his work."

"He's never said anything negative. In fact, the reason that we've come here at all today is that he seems quite fond of you." Perhaps a bit too fond . . . "But I'm sure you know that Emilio's never been one to cast aspersions."

She looked back at the Italian man and smiled. "His English may be a bit . . . limited, but it doesn't make me love him any less."

"He's a lucky man," Vincent said. Letting go of Sarah's hand, he walked up the steps to the front door, then lifted another key from the loop on his belt and slid it into the lock.

She hoped Emilio was impressed at just how much effort she was putting into her role of the bride-to-be, and maybe she did mean her words at least a little bit.

But over the last few days, she had realized that he was far more complicated than she had first thought him to be. He had first become totally obsessed by a desire to fix the heart, and then so utterly tormented when he had failed to be able repair it, that Sarah had actually found herself a bit terrified by his despair.

Even in failure, Darby had always managed to be incredibly even-keeled, but it seemed that Emilio was more like his sister than he knew; his passions were just hidden deeper beneath the surface.

"I think you'll find most men are all a bit hopeless in the end," Vincent told her. "A sad statement on the male of the species, I'm afraid." He held out his hand and motioned for her to enter.

When she stepped inside, Sarah was surprised. It was hardly the achievement that Darby's lab was, but it was impressive nonetheless. The space was more a factory than a workshop, and the room was laid out with benches and equipment sitting at regular intervals along its entire length. Steam lines travelled down the length of each row, powering large machines such as presses and saws that had been placed throughout the space.

Daylight poured in through the irregular windows on the roof, giving the whole thing an airy feeling, although it also meant that the space was close to the same temperature as the outside air. "Isn't it a bit cold in here?" she asked.

Vincent laughed. "The main boiler sits right under the floor. You can ask Emilio if he thinks it's cold in here once we've fired that up."

A terse "*Sì*," was all Emilio said in reply. Sarah was beginning to wonder if she'd done something to make him angry.

As they walked toward the larger benches at the back, something on the wall caught Sarah's eye. She stopped and turned towards it. "What's that?" she asked.

The hanging object was vaguely human-shaped, and sat half-hidden in the gloom. She couldn't quite place it, but there was something about it that was naggingly familiar.

"Is the Wasp," Emilio said. "Is just a sculpture."

Sarah wasn't so sure. The head of it was a leather mask with a pair of large glass lenses on the front of it, and a series of metal louvers that came down over the mouth. The arms were almost comically long, and covered with some kind of complicated machinery from the elbow to the wrist, where there were a pair of bulbous springs. From there, the "gloves" tapered up to a pair of chisels that stuck out at least three feet from where the hands would have normally ended.

There were no actual legs, only a pair of steel braces, and number of flat-tipped metal spikes around a pair of almost comically wide shoes. A series of tubes ran out from the shoulders, connecting to an object that hung on the wall next to it that appeared to be a portable steam boiler.

"It's looks more like a costume than a sculpture . . ." She moved a bit closer. "Were you planning on becoming a Paragon, Mr. Smith?"

Vincent laughed. "Nothing so dramatic, Miss Standish. But you are correct. It was meant to be worn. Now it's just an old prototype. A memory of a previous flirtation with technology."

"Why isn't it out in the garden with the other rejects?"

Vincent stepped up to it and stroked his hand along one of the chisels. It was a casual gesture, but to Sarah's eyes it seemed almost like the kind of loving caress a father might give to his child. "Because I'm rather fond of it, I'll admit." He turned around, standing between her and the suit. "But nothing came of it. It was simply a little idea that I had—a dream of another time." Vincent said nodded wistfully. Then, with a serious look on his face, the showman stared straight into Sarah's eyes. "One that never managed to get beyond its formative stages. Now, if we could keep moving."

"Well, whatever it is, it's very pretty," Sarah added, trying to get a closer look. It certainly reminded her of *something*, but the Wasp had been placed in such a way that it seemed enveloped by more shadow than light.

Vincent's tone softened, but was clearly more urgent. "I'm sorry to hurry you, my dear, but I'm afraid I don't have all day. Perhaps we could get on to your request?" He began to walk toward his large worktable at the far end of the room, and gestured for them to follow.

Sarah frowned. There was something about the costume that bothered her, but nothing, it seemed, that she'd be able to put together right now. Very shortly, it would be time to show Vincent Smith the Automaton's heart, and she still was far from comfortable with the idea.

"Well then, let's take a closer look," Vincent spun open a vice with a single well-placed tap on the spindle. He put the gear into it, and then spun it closed again just as smoothly.

"Now, before I begin, it would help immensely if you could tell me what it is, exactly, that this object *does*."

From the look on Emilio's face, he was at a loss to invent an answer to Vincent's question. She supposed that considering his English, that wouldn't seem too out of place, but one of them would need to come up with something, and very quickly.

Instead, it was Vincent who broke the silence. "Surely it has a purpose?"

"Is a regulator," Emilio sputtered out. At least he was trying to improvise, but it didn't sound convincing to her.

Vincent stared at it with a puzzled look. "You mean it controls a regulator valve?"

"*Sì*," he said curtly. It was all Sarah could do to not roll her eyes and sigh.

"I have to say, it's genuinely remarkable." Vincent reached up to grab a pair of calipers off the tool rack in front of him. "And I'm not even sure what this alloy is *made* of. It's clearly a kind of brass, but there's something else about it . . . Have you tried just flattening it and seeing what will happen?"

"No press."

"He stamped it out of a scrap of metal he found at his junkyard," Sarah said, hoping that might cover their tracks.

"Is that so?" Vincent picked up a magnifying glass and stared more closely at the trapped cog. "Well, it's a very intricate design for *that*. In fact, before whatever happened to it happened, I think this is as close to a perfectly turned gear as I've ever seen." He put the glass down and turned to face Emilio. "You didn't make this, did you?"

Sarah cringed as Emilio shook his head.

"Could you show me the object it came from?"

For an instant Sarah actually felt better. At least they had reached a moment of truth.

Then, with an almost blinding flash, she remembered where she had seen the suit before. Her eyes widened with recognition, and no small look of terror. She grabbed Emilio's arm. "We need to go."

"Is everything all right, my dear?" Vincent asked. "I'm sure that we must be boring you with all our talk of gears and alloys."

"No, it's fine, really." She tugged Emilio's arm and glared at him. They were in trouble, and there was no time to lose. "I just realized we're late for another appointment." She tried to smile. "It's about what's in the box."

Vincent did not look like he believed her.

Emilio stepped forward. "Sarah and I will talk. Maybe a minute?"

"Well yes, of course." Vincent rose up from his stool, and took the opportunity for a stretch before reaching into his coveralls and giving his backside a scratch. "Take your time."

"We need to *go*, Emilio," Sarah said, "Now." She was trying to mute the panic in her voice.

"One minute, Vincent," he said, and took Sarah's arm.

As they walked toward the door, she tried to move faster, but she felt herself being slowed by Emilio's grip.

The moment they were out the door, she pulled herself free, then stumbled down the stairs, barely managing to stop herself from tumbling to the ground.

Regaining her bearings, she walked quickly across the yard until she stood underneath a half-formed mechanical ape, then stopped to wait for Emilio.

"What's wrong with you?" he said as caught up to her.

"That man! Vincent! He's the Steamhammer!"

"Who?"

"A villain! That thing on the wall, it was his costume."

Emilio smirked. "You crazy."

Sarah shook her head. "Crazy?" Who was this man she was talking to? "My father *fought* him. He used the chisels on that suit to crack the foundation of the Hall of Paragons."

"No. He's no villain. I know him, *Sarah*."

Why was he being so stubborn about this? What did he have to lose? "Emilio, you have to trust me. He was buried alive underneath the Hall!" But then how was it he was still alive? Just thinking about it made her dizzy. "But the costume—and he's the right age. And all these machines . . ." If only she could call on the Paragons to make sure. "He's one of them, one of the Children of Eschaton!" How could they possibly give him the heart now?

Emilio put a hand on her shoulder. "Breathe, Bella."

"Don't touch me!" Sarah pulled herself away. "We need to go get that gear back from him!"

Emilio smiled at her. "Sarah, what can he do with one gear?" He held up the lacquered box. "I need his machines to fix this."

Sarah couldn't believe what she was hearing. The Steamhammer was probably slipping into his suit right now. "And what will we tell him the heart *does*, Emilio? That it's a governor?"

"We think of something. Is okay."

"No, it's not at all okay." Sarah laughed derisively and rolled her eyes in a way that was clearly not intended to be flattering. "Emilio, you're brilliant and wonderful in so many ways, but if you think that any man who wears a costume, and then constructs a menagerie of mechanical creatures is harmless, I really don't think you've been paying much attention to the world that you're living in."

"I try to help you." He gave her a look that was as sad as it was confused.

"I know you are, Emilio."

"You don't trust me."

"That's not it at all, I just . . ."

Emilio stepped closer. "Maybe he is Steam . . . man. But I was a villain."

Sarah looked down at her shoes, trying to avoid his eyes. He clearly wasn't playing fair. "I know. But it's different."

She felt his finger curling under her chin, and lifting up her head. "I think is not."

When she looked up into his eyes, there was something like a blush that she felt travel over her whole body. "No, Emilio!" she said, backing away from him. "You won't charm me into trusting him."

"Trust *me*."

"And what if you're wrong?"

Emilio stopped for a second and put his hands to his sides. "I don't have words."

Sarah was getting tired of this excuse. It seemed too easy, and too handy. "And yet your sister has so many."

"Okay. Okay." He took a deep breath and pointed at the box in his hand. "I can't fix, but he can. If we no give him the heart, we have nothing."

"But if he's one of the Children? What if Eschaton gets the heart?"

"I work with him for months. If he was villain, he is not villain anymore." Emilio pointed at the animals in the garden. "He make all this for the show. You see? I make all this *with* him."

Against her better judgment, she was beginning to see Emilio's point. Sarah closed her eyes. "I don't know."

Emilio pointed at her head. "You think all the time from here." He moved his hand until it was just over her heart. "You need to think from here some time." Sarah felt a thrill go up her. Why couldn't he be like this all the time?

"Okay, Emilio," she said softly.

"Okay?"

"I can't fight everybody. I need someone to help us."

He smiled. "Thank you, Sarah. He will help, you'll see."

She tried to smile back, but it felt as if someone had frozen her lips in place. For a moment she was lost, and she looked up to the statue next to her.

The rusted, eyeless features of the face of "the rejected" seemed almost lost and mournful. The corroded beast was, in its way, far more expressive than Tom's emotionless mask had ever been. She could see what looked like tearstains where rainwater had dripped down its red face.

"'I will do everything in my power to prove that your faith in me is not misplaced,'" she said in a half whisper.

"What did you say?"

Sarah held out her hand. "Give it to me."

Emilio looked puzzled. "Give what to you?"

She gestured at the box in his hand. "The heart."

He lifted it up. "What's wrong, Sarah?"

She reached out and slipped the handle from his hand into hers. "Follow me, and be quiet."

"I don't . . ." he said, struggling for the words.

"You don't have to."

In a quick trot, Sarah marched back across the courtyard to the door of the workshop. Her shoes banged hard on the wooden planks as she walked across the floor.

Vincent was still sitting at his workbench, calmly examining the gear. When she was only a few feet away, he spun around on his stool to greet her. "Miss Standish, I'm glad to see that you've come back."

The look on Sarah's face was so tight that it was almost expressionless as she stared into Vincent's eyes. After a few seconds of holding his gaze, she placed the case down onto the table in front of him and opened the brass latches with a snap and waited for Emilio to catch up.

By the time he had reached them, the smile had drained from Vincent's face as well.

"You know who I am, don't you?" she asked.

"I don't understand. Are you someone other than who you told me you were?"

Sarah couldn't quite tell if he was mocking her, and she spoke slower and more loudly this time, enunciating each word. *"You know who I really am, don't you?"*

"What are you doing?" Emilio asked her. "What should he know?"

Vincent glanced up at Emilio and then let out a chuckle. "It's all right, my boy." He looked back to her. "Yes, Miss Stanton, I'm well aware of who you really are. It wasn't until Emilio called you Sarah that I was positive that you were the Industrialist's daughter. Your likeness is fairly unique, and striking."

Sarah wasn't sure whether she should be flattered or insulted. "And you're the Steamhammer?"

His smile broadened. "I was—once upon a time, and long, long ago."

"How did you survive being crushed underneath the Hall?"

Vincent smiled at that. "My much-exaggerated death, you mean?" His expression was almost the definition of a devilish grin. "Your father, with his usual ruthless efficiency, did indeed collapse a wall onto me. It left me with both legs broken, trapped under the earth. But I still had my jackhammers and a small pocket of air. I tunneled through the wall of the Hall, and tumbled to the floor of Darby's lab. The old man took pity on me. He offered to help me, but only if I never put on the costume again."

Vincent looked up, and Sarah could see the beginnings of tears forming in his eyes. "He saved my life, and I kept my promise." He nodded and swept his hand in front of him. "All of this, I owe to that man. When I said the show was a homage to Sir Dennis and his great creations, I wasn't lying."

Sarah nodded curtly, and then turned to Emilio. "So you see, he did have secrets."

"We all keep secrets, Miss Stanton." Vincent said, recapturing her attention. "For instance, I'm sure I'm safe in assuming your father doesn't have any idea of either where you are, or the kind of company you're keeping these days." He gave her a wink that almost made her blush. "And I'd certainly love to hear the story of how you and this very talented boy met each other."

"Another time," she replied, angry at how easily he could manipulate her.

The room was silent for a long moment, and then Vincent continued. "So, Miss Stanton, what's in the box, or do you want me to guess?"

"I have a question first."

"Please, my dear, ask away."

"Can I *trust* you, Mr. Smith?"

"I would think so. You already know all my deepest, darkest secrets."

Sarah stared at the showman for a minute, trying to see if there was any way she could truly decide whether to trust him beyond Emilio's promises.

Bringing Tom back without help was hopeless, and somehow the fact that he had admitted his crimes to her made it feel as if she at least had something to threaten him with. "Yes or no?"

"Yes, my dear, of course. While Vincent Smith continues to live on, the Steamhammer did die that day. I'm not a villain any longer."

His story certainly sounded plausible; extracting a promise from a villain to repent seemed like the kind of thing Darby *would* do. She wondered what the old man would have done if he had refused, and decided it was better not to know. And if Darby trusted him, then . . . "All right, Mr. Smith, you can open the box."

Vincent turned around and put his hands on either side of the front of the wooden case. "Ladies and gentlemen . . ." he said in a mocking whisper. The box split in half along the hinge at the back, revealing the heart sitting on a velvet cushion. "This . . ." he paused for a moment, clearly unable to believe what he was seeing, "this is from the Automaton, isn't it?" he said in hushed tones.

Sarah nodded. She felt nauseous. The fact that he had recognized it so quickly only made her more unsure whether she had done the right thing.

"May I?" he asked, reaching out a hand.

"I suppose so," Sarah replied. It was too late to go back now.

"Darby's handiwork." He slowly caressed the heart with his fingertips in an almost lewd way. "How does it work?"

"We don't know," Emilio said, finally deciding to join the conversation. "We need to fix first, *then* we know."

"I see." Vincent stared at it like it was something he could eat, his eyes narrowing. Sarah only wished there was some way of uncovering what thoughts were *truly* going through the man's head.

She supposed that the Sleuth might have been able to tell. There were more than a few people who had referred to Wickham as the "mind reader," although Sarah knew it was more of a matter of expert observation than clairvoyance. Neither was a skill she possessed.

"Emilio will stay with you until tomorrow, and if you can't fix the heart by then, I'll find someone else." She grabbed the Italian's hand. "That will be okay, won't it, Emilio?"

"Okay." He held her hand loosely, but at least he was going along with it. Emilio was clearly unhappy about having been volunteered to work with Vincent, but she couldn't think of any other way to protect the heart.

"Tomorrow?" Vincent turned away from the heart and looked up at her. "If that's too soon . . ."

"No, no, my dear." Vincent grabbed Emilio by the other arm. "You and me, working together again! What do you think of *that*, my boy!"

Emilio nodded. "Is good." But he didn't sound excited.

He turned to Sarah. "We'll get it done, and then you'll come to the show and see *my* Colossus in action! You can tell me how it compares to the real thing. And you can bring his beautiful firebrand of a sister along as well. What was her name?"

"Viola," he said through gritted teeth.

"Viola, yes. She almost gutted me the last time I met her. Very exciting! And the tickets will, of course, be free for the both of you." Sarah saw his eyes wander back to the heart. "I promise you a most incredible show."

Chapter 20

Burning Sensations

easured from end to end, Manhattan was small—three miles wide from the Hudson to the East River, and eleven miles long, as measured from the Bronx down to the Upper Bay. But the hard numbers denied a fundamental truth about the island. The lower half was packed with construction. It formed a capricious maze of tenements, mansions, feed lots, factories, warehouses, and a thousand other structures crushed together so tightly that there was nowhere to go but up. From block to block, street to street, and day to day, it rose higher and higher into the sky, packing more and more humanity onto the same few square miles of ground.

Anubis saw this city mostly from the rooftops. As he leapt the gap from one to the next, he could be leaping from wealth to crushing poverty in a single bound. And as he flew, suspended hundreds of feet above the ground only by his strength and speed, the black-clad man reminded himself for the thousandth time that the greatest differences were often separated by the smallest distances. He had witnessed socialites gorging themselves in heated dining rooms while just on the other side of a brick wall, starving children were freezing to death. He'd stopped men beating their wives while wedding bells rang in a nearby church, and avenged murders with babies being born in apartments above and below. Good and evil lived side by side in the city, ignored by the innocent until it was their turn.

As a man, it had been his inability to turn a blind eye to those injustices that had driven him to become Anubis in the first place. But once he had put on a costume and began travelling across the rooftops, he had discovered that no single man could end all the suffering. If he was going to change the world, he would need to figure out how, and that was what had led him to Eschaton . . .

"Too much time on my hands," he grunted to himself as he sprinted across the rooftop.

And the fool he was tracking was making his work so easy that Anubis caught himself resisting the urge to let the man wander out of his sight just to see how long it would take to find him again.

His target's name was Chadwick Prescott, and the fool seemed to be under the impression that his whereabouts were unknown to his enemies simply because he had spent three days hiding out in a building on the East Side. Sitting on the fringe of a poor neighborhood, it appeared from the outside to be a run-down tenement, but the inside was well-appointed, and was used by numerous young gentlemen of means as a secret meeting place where a man with a reputation could carry out his illicit activities unseen.

Besides the manager, an old fellow who kept the place clean and locked it up, the only other visitor since Prescott's arrival had been a young woman (either a mistress or a well-paid whore—he hadn't managed to get a close enough look to find out) who brought him food and gave him companionship on a regular basis.

The building was well protected from the front and sides, but Anubis had found it easy enough to enter from the rooftop.

The private apartments were located on the top floor, and when Anubis had found Prescott, the man had been sleeping soundly with a large, unfinished glass of gin on the bed table nearby.

Anubis had quietly and thoroughly searched the building while the man lay unconscious, but the particular object he was looking for had been nowhere to be found, and it wasn't something that could be easily hidden away.

After that, it had simply become a matter of waiting the man out. To that end, Anubis had constructed a small shelter on the rooftop. The structure did a fair job of keeping out the cold and, more importantly, it kept anyone from noticing that a man clad in black leather was sitting inside of it. As he expected, it had only taken a few days before Prescott's need for stimulation had overcome his desire for safety and he had decided to venture outside.

Anubis had tracked him patiently since then, but Prescott was proving to be far better at being dull than he was at staying hidden.

Once free from the house, Prescott quickly established a routine—not only did he visit exactly the same locations at exactly the same time every day, he put on the same outfit, made the same mumbled greetings to the news vendor when he bought the morning paper, and ate the exact same meal—coffee, eggs, and biscuits—at the same café.

Besides the visits from the girl, he spent the rest of his leisure time reading penny dreadfuls along with an occasional attempt at other texts that, from the locations of the bookmarks, he seemed unable to follow beyond the first chapter. Prescott revealed himself to be a man of spectacularly limited imagination and drive.

And yet, having spent so much of his time peering into the lives of so many inhabitants of the city, Anubis could hardly fault the man for it. With a few spectacular exceptions, it seemed that the inhabitants of New York were content to while away their lives in quiet desperation, claiming they did much more, but only managing to raise their eyes upward just in time to catch a glimpse of whatever hurtling doom would end their existence. Humanity, he had come to understand, was not by and large capable of striving for greatness.

And as a child of privilege, Prescott had the added disability of not needing to actually work to stay alive. But to his credit, and probably to his own surprise as much as anyone else's, when he had been offered an opportunity to don a costume and change the course of his life, he had decided to take it. It had been a plan based on subterfuge and lies, and yet Anubis considered Prescott's decision to embrace it an almost commendable action.

But once it had met with its inevitable failure, the spoiled rich boy returned to form—unwilling to gracefully accept defeat and return to his old life, Prescott had tried to steal another chance.

Anubis imagined that his target was probably very pleased with himself, believing that by managing to remain unmolested by the Children of Eschaton for a week, he had somehow managed to successfully escape altogether. But he was as blindly ignorant to the true nature of the men who were tracking him as he was to his own.

The head of Anubis's staff whistled through the air, landing with a clank on the next rooftop as its spines extended outwards. Pulling it tight, he leapt, swinging between rooftops before climbing up the side of the building to pull himself up and over.

Most of the Children would have immediately resorted to violence in order to expedite the retrieval of the costume from Prescott, but Anubis considered patience to be one of the greatest weapons in his arsenal. And it was a skill that he had improved over time, with the breadth of his knowledge about human behavior growing with every person he tracked.

When Prescott cut through Washington Square Park and into Greenwich Village, Anubis was tempted to try to take the shorter route, dropping to the ground, and following him through the shadows.

If the stakes weren't so high, he might have tried it. But he had already spent far too much time waiting for Prescott to lead him to the costume, and he didn't want to scare the man away now that he finally seemed to be getting closer to his goal.

Besides, there were other considerations; Eschaton had ordered them to retrieve the suit days ago, and Jack Knife had told Anubis that the gray man had asked for him personally. Anubis knew Jack well enough to know that he would have gutted Prescott like a fish the first chance he got. Clearly Eschaton was giving the man a second chance, but even his patience would run out eventually.

Anubis breathed a sigh of relief under his mask when Prescott turned and walked down a small lane. If the man was intentionally walking into a dead end, he must be near his destination.

Unlike the uptown neighborhoods that seemed to be changing day by day, Greenwich Village had remained relatively stable in the configuration of its streets. The crooked maze was familiar enough that Anubis barely had to concern himself about his route as he maneuvered himself to the other side of the block.

He reached the rooftop across the alley from Prescott in time to see the man standing by a door to a large brick building. The man nervously looked to his left and then to his right, clearly trying to discover if anyone had followed him.

Anubis shook his head and smiled grimly under his mask. Taller and taller buildings were being built every day, to the point where people had begun to refer to them as "skyscrapers," and yet New Yorkers seemed to have made it a point of pride to never look up.

From the outside, the building was utterly nondescript—a faceless storehouse—exactly the kind of place that uptown gentlemen like Mr. Prescott would never be expected to frequent.

His target disappeared from sight, pulling the door closed behind him with a slam loud enough to be heard from Anubis's third-story perch.

Anubis paused for a second and pulled out the jackal mask from a pouch at his waist, slipping it down over his cowl.

Since the events with the Sleuth a few months ago, he had decided to streamline the outfit in a way that would give his head a little more mobility, enabling him to remove the animal face entirely when he needed to travel light and lean.

That hadn't been the only lesson from that incident, of course. Ultimately his attempt to spare the old man's life had been a futile gesture— Wickham had died in the Darby house only a few days later. And even if the information he had given to the old man had managed to set back Eschaton's plans a bit, it had led to the death of the old man, the destruction of the Automaton, and had placed all the Children under greater suspicion.

Suitably masked for confrontation, he hooked the top of his staff to the edge of the roof and lowered himself down on the spring-loaded mechanism.

Reaching the ground, he scampered across the alley and came to the door. The sign was weather-beaten, but the words "H&R Lott Import & Export" could still be read under the chipped paint. He shook his head at the poorly hidden pun.

Right after the war, the moneyed classes of New York had practiced their depravities almost entirely in the open, but a wave of moral temperance had descended over the city, forcing the gentry to put on a show of piety while their peccadilloes and perversions were driven underground. It was one way the masses could strike back at the powerful, and when one of them was caught by the papers, the wealthy would quickly sacrifice their closest friends to save their own skins. It kept the papers running, and the secrets of the powerful were now deeply buried.

Shame was an emotion that ran deep, and Anubis had noticed that people often felt bitter suffering was often more deserved than outrageous success. Hubris, however, was easy to come by, and even easier to sell. Even a man who took it upon himself to protect the downtrodden might find that he was considered a villain by both the oppressor and the oppressed he tried to save.

Anubis collapsed his staff and stored it away, unscrewing it into three equal sections before fitting it snugly into a set of leather loops on the back of his harness.

Both hands now freed, he pulled out a skeleton key from the pocket underneath his loincloth, and slid it into the door lock.

In sharp contrast to the rest of the door, the bolt was clearly expensive and new, intended to be the best money could buy. He studied the device for only a moment before attacking it. After determining that the imposing appearance of the brass lock was far more for the peace of mind of the purchaser than to actually vex an attacker, it took only a few jiggles of the instrument before the lock gave up its feeble attempt to deny him entrance. It fell open as smoothly and quietly as it would have for someone with a genuine key.

Having seen the well-appointed bolt-hole where Prescott had spent his last few days, Anubis was surprised to discover that the offices of H&R Lott were, at least on the ground floor, those of a legitimate business. A secretary's desk and blotter stood next to the front door, out in front of a number of other desks. On each one was a spindle bursting with stacks of impaled papers, waiting for their accounting.

Closing the front door quietly behind him, Anubis crossed the room quickly and silently, taking care to avoid knocking anything over.

The door at the far end of the office had been left wide open, and Anubis walked through it into the main area of a large warehouse. Piles of wooden boxes were stacked everywhere, straw packing strewn across the floor. The boxes had been clearly labeled both "Fragile" and "China."

A few large pieces of art were standing out in the open, including a number of vases, some of them taller than he was. "Someone has quite a passion for curios from the Orient," he mumbled to himself under his mask.

Seeing no sign of where Prescott had gone, he crouched down and sat quietly for a second, gathering his concentration. The silence was broken by a loud, regular creaking reverberating from the ceiling high above.

Looking for a way up, Anubis saw a steep wooden staircase at the end of the dock. He began to climb it, carefully placing a single foot on the first step. As he slowly transferred his weight onto it, the wood groaned in response. Anubis stepped onto the next highest stair and tried again. This one seemed less alarmed by his presence, and he was able to put his full weight onto it.

Testing each step, and skipping those that wanted to betray his presence, he managed to slowly make his way to the second floor.

As he crept upward, he heard even more thumps and creaks coming from upstairs. The commotion made him wonder what exactly Prescott was planning to do in this place, and if it had anything to do with the object Anubis was looking for. Either way, he was running out of time—he would have to confront the man directly, and if he proved unwilling to succumb to verbal coercion, he'd need to resort to less pleasant methods of getting what he wanted. He was sure that Jack would be pleased.

He poked his head up through the floor and took a look around in the gloom. Anubis had expected the upstairs to resemble the room that Prescott had been hiding in. The reality was far more breathtaking, both in form and scope.

The attic was indeed a secret den, but instead of being a set of living quarters, it resembled a museum. Along all the walls were rows and rows of books and manuscripts. The spaces in between were regularly punctuated by large canvases. Laid out across the floor were sculptures and other objects d'art, ranging in size from tiny ivory carvings on carved wooden pedestals to a massive stone sculpture so large that it had been placed on long beams to distribute its weight. It rose up tall and curved, heading up almost fifteen feet until it stood just below the ceiling, where it expanded at the top like a large mushroom.

At first he couldn't make out exactly what it was he was looking at, as it clearly couldn't be the obvious organ the shape suggested. "Could it?" he muttered to himself. And the more he stared at the erect object, the more it became clear that it was not a metaphor for anything, but simply a massive ode to male sexuality.

Loud footsteps came from the other side of the room, and he could see

Prescott sit down onto the edge of a large four-poster bed. It was surrounded by gaslights that glowed in the darkness and made the bed appear to be an oasis in the gloom.

Clinging to the shadows, Anubis pulled his staff off of his back and slowly reassembled it. Once it was completed, he began to walk towards the bed, taking a moment to take a closer look at a tiny ivory statue that stood on a pedestal on the floor. His eyes widened, struck by the act that a well-endowed demon was committing on a tiny, yet startlingly accurate, depiction of a naked young Asian woman. While it seemed like it should be painful, the look on her little face clearly showed that she was enjoying it.

Anubis shook his head and kept moving, ignoring a similarly graphic act being carried out on a canvas on the wall. Seeing that Prescott was busily removing something from a wooden box, he slid out a random volume from the shelf.

The title was startlingly erotic in nature, crudely concerned with methods by which a man might dramatically increase both his own pleasure and that of his partner in performing acts of lust.

After erotic materials had been outlawed by the federal government, there had been no shortage of speculation amongst the more sensationalist newspapers that the wealthiest members of society secretly kept their most perverted documents in hidden libraries. It always seemed to be more of a popular myth than a genuine truth, and yet here was exactly the secret treasure trove that he had dismissed as nonsense. Perhaps he had underestimated the state of modern journalism . . .

He heard a few loud grunts from Prescott's direction, and he was a bit hesitant about what he might see as he turned to the man. When he did look, he realized that not only had Prescott retrieved his Hydraulic-man costume, he had, with some difficulty, almost completed putting it on.

Anubis had been too distracted by the room, and now he was about to face a man fully armed with acid and flame. He shouted as ran toward his quarry. "Prescott!" The man looked up, startled, just as he had finished hooking a hose to one of the snake heads on his shoulder.

"What? Who is it? What are you doing here?"

Prescott was appropriately alarmed, but Anubis was surprised when he stepped into the gaslight and his target seemed to actually relax. "Is that you, Davies?" Prescott said with a laugh. "I always knew that your predilection for leather would get the better of you someday, but isn't the mask a bit over the top?"

Anubis, annoyed at being mistaken for a wealthy deviant, slammed his staff down on the floor, trying to ignore just how phallic *that* act might appear to be in the context of his location. "I am Anubis!" he said, using the echoing acoustics of the room to his advantage. "I am here to retrieve from you what you have stolen from Lord Eschaton."

At the mention of Eschaton's name, the look on Prescott's face shifted instantly, his smile melting into wide-eyed fright. "Eschaton? No . . . How did you find me?"

Anubis leaned forward, letting the black jackal mask do its work. "I didn't 'find' you, I followed you." He waited for a beat, and then continued. "If you remove the suit *now* and hand it back to me, I may let you live."

Prescott looked angry and whined like a petulant child. "No! I *won't* . . . It's *mine*!" Reaching down to his wrist on the Hydraulic-man's suit, Chadwick pulled a lever, sending a stream of liquid squirting from one of the snake heads. It was heading directly for Anubis's chest, and he jumped away, realizing that he had reacted too slowly even as he moved.

Anubis could feel the splash, and he expected to next feel the acid eating into his flesh, but there was no burning sensation, just the stink of kerosene rising up into his nose.

Realizing that he was unhurt a moment before Prescott did, Anubis lashed out with his staff. The blow struck the other man square in the stomach, and Prescott tumbled backwards onto the huge bed, tearing out one of the curtains on his way down.

The Hydraulic-man attacked again, but this time Anubis was ready for the assault, and he stepped deftly out of the way. The stream travelled through the air, landing on a nearby vase of porcelain "flowers," the blossoms all closely modeled after female anatomy. The pot smoked for a moment, then shattered into a shower of breasts and genitals.

"Leave me alone!" Prescott cried as he clawed at the bed, dragging himself over to the other side. The sheets became tangled in his costume, and he fell onto the floor with a thump. When he stood, a large bolt of silk had attached itself to his shoulder, forming an ungainly cape.

"It's time for Anubis to judge you, Chadwick Prescott!"

Prescott pulled off the sheet and twisted it in his hands. "Judge me? Don't be ridiculous!" The tone of fear was replaced by one of outrage. "I paid Eschaton good money for this costume, and it belongs to *me*."

Anubis knocked the man out of his outrage by jumping onto the bed and shoving the end of his staff into the man's chest. It knocked enough of the air out of Prescott's lungs to make him gasp. "That's not my business. You have stolen what is not yours."

When the man looked up at him, there was a mix of anger and terror in his eyes. "So you're Eschaton's errand boy, is that it?"

Angered by the comment, Anubis raised up his staff to strike the man again. Prescott cringed reflexively. It was satisfying to watch the swagger drain out of him, and Anubis held the blow for a moment.

But there was some truth to what the man was saying. He was here carrying out Eschaton's orders. Was he still working in the service of a higher good?

So far his attempts to undermine the villain had failed. Had he spent so much time trying to infiltrate Eschaton's organization that he had finally become what he had started out pretending to be?

It was worth considering, but not at this moment. "Take it off, Prescott." He let the man's name rumble in his throat for effect as he jumped to the floor in front of him. "Do it and I'll let you live. Otherwise I'll rip it off of your dead body."

"You can try!"

Anubis had been waiting for Prescott to drop the sheet and activate one of the buttons on his wrist. But his focus had left him unprepared for a more direct attack, and he was unable to get out of the way as Prescott crashed toward him, bowling him over. As Prescott ran by, he dragged the sheet over Anubis's head, plunging him into total darkness. Perhaps the man wasn't a complete fool . . .

If Prescott got away now, there would be hell to pay. He would go to ground again, certainly doing a better job of hiding than he had before.

Anubis needed to complete the mission now, or Eschaton would never trust him again—not that he was completely sure if that was still important.

Anubis stumbled after him in darkness, pulling off the sheet just in time to see the huge stone phallus looming in front him. The Hydraulic-man was hiding behind it, moving his hand down toward his opposite wrist as he prepared to attack.

Unable to stop himself, Anubis smacked directly into the sculpture. The object was precariously balanced on the two spheres that made up its base, and it began to tip over.

Focused on the device on his wrist, Prescott was barely able to let out a scream before the huge statue crashed down onto him, pinning him to the floor.

"Get this damn thing off of me!" Prescott shouted. Anubis smiled. He didn't like relying on fate, but if it came his way, he wasn't going to turn it down. And there was something almost poetic about seeing a dilettante like Prescott trapped by an enormous piece of erotic art. He pointed his staff threateningly at the fallen man. "You *will* give me the suit!"

Prescott squirmed once more, and then let out a sigh of defeat. "All right. You've won."

After Anubis used his staff to heave the statue off of him, Prescott rolled over and sat up, putting a gloved hand to his face. The moment it touched his skin, he twitched, and he jerked his fingers away—his flesh was red and smoking where the glove had made contact. After a moment, he screamed.

Anubis looked down to see a growing puddle of smoking liquid around Prescott, and a gouge on the container on his back where the statue had smashed it open. It gave off an unpleasant acrid smell, and he took a step backwards as the puddle rolled towards him.

Without the ability to see the damage, it took Prescott another moment to realize what was happening. When he did, he looked up at Anubis, his eyes filled with horror. "Help me!"

Anubis lifted his staff and popped out its barbs, hoping that he could snag the man and drag him out of the deadly pool. The acid was eating into the floor now, sending up a thickening cloud of heavy smoke. If he was going to have any chance of saving him, he would need to act fast.

Eschaton clearly hadn't been interested in the safety of the wearer when he had created the outfit, and its design didn't do anything to protect its inhabitant from the liquid it contained. Prescott's screams started to rise in pitch.

"Grab this!" Anubis said, poking his staff toward the desperately flailing man.

Prescott reached out towards the pole, managing to wrap his smoking hands around it. Anubis tried to tug Chadwick to safety, although he was unsure just how he could truly "save" the poor man, short of throwing him into a river.

Then, in an instant, something blue flickered and rippled across Prescott's body. Both men were visibly stunned by the speed at which the heat seemed to grow, and the fire was almost invisible until hair and clothing began to burn a bright yellow.

Anubis jumped to safety. He tried to think of a way to save the burning man, but the fire was ferociously hot, and there was, it seemed, no way to reach the flailing figure. He turned to grab the silk sheet that had fallen a few feet away, thinking that he might smother the flames. But by the time he picked the cloth up off the floor, the screaming had stopped.

Anubis forced himself to take a last look, and saw that a hot jet of burning vapor was now spraying out from the container on the back of the suit.

Something clicked in his mind, and Anubis dropped the sheet as he ran past the dying man, racing as fast as he could toward the exit at the far end of the room. He had almost reached the trapdoor when the Hydraulic-man exploded, showering the room with burning liquid, the caustic mixture igniting everything it touched.

As he dropped down through the floor, Anubis turned to look back at the hidden museum. The paintings had ignited quickly. Coupling nymphs, excited satyrs, and frolicking faeries all were turning black as the flames rose hungrily up across the canvases. It was something out of a Puritan's dream.

He watched for a few more seconds as the bookcases quickly transformed into burning pyres and the roaring flames shot up the walls. The heat was already intense, and he could feel it growing dangerously hot underneath his leather costume.

He dropped to the ground as quickly as he could and dashed out of the building. By the time he had run through the offices and back onto the street, the entire structure was ablaze. Someone nearby had already pulled a fire alarm, and he could hear the loud ringing coming from the nearby boxes. It would only be moments before curious onlookers and desperate neighbors would fill the streets. It was time to vanish—quickly.

Holding up his staff, he fired the grapple toward the sky. It landed on the edge of a nearby roof, and Anubis gave the wire a tug to steady it. Instead of the solid jerk he expected, he heard the sound of breaking metal, and the head of the staff tumbled back to the ground, the metal spine having snapped from where the acid had eaten into it.

He cursed under his mask as he reeled in the cable. There would be no easy path to the rooftops tonight.

He dashed into the shadows, pulling apart his staff as he ran. By the time he had finished putting it away, the roof of the building had collapsed, unleashing a pillar of flame into the sky. He hoped that the fire brigades would arrive before the neighboring buildings caught, although time was not on their side.

Seeing no other easy exit, he ran out of the alleyway, pushing past a small crowd of surprised onlookers, some of them wearing nothing more than their nightgowns and bath robes.

He was sure that by tomorrow morning the papers would be full of descriptions of a "man dressed in black, last seen fleeing the scene of the terrible crime." Hopefully that would be the only details they would remember.

Reading those papers would also be a number of young gentlemen who would probably breathe a sigh of relief when they realized that, while the fire had destroyed their precious artifacts, it also meant that no evidence of their perversions would have survived the blaze.

Anubis sprinted for a few blocks until he was sure that there were no longer any prying eyes. Ducking into an alleyway, he squatted down in the darkness and pulled off his mask, inhaling the cool air and wiping the sweat off his face.

He closed his eyes and rocked back against the wall, gulping in the cool air as he tried to banish the vision of the desperate, burning man that he had just left to die.

Chapter 21
Ganging Up

Sneaking up behind the knife-wielding thug, Jack raised his birch cane up high, and then smashed it hard across the back of his opponent's right leg. The boy yelped, stumbled down to his knees, and yelped again. Jack attacked again, giving the thug another blow across his back that sent him face down onto the cobblestones. "Now then," he said loudly, "I'm hoping that you boys will have the good sense to take advantage of the kind offer we made you, and give us back our home."

The gang that had taken over the Children's courtyard during their absence called themselves the Blockheads, and they wore wooden top hats to prove it. Their headgear was, Jack thought, impressively and expertly made—constructed from thin sheets of wood that had been meticulously steamed and bent into the right shape. No easy task . . .

Jack hadn't really been surprised to find that there were new residents when they had finally come back to reclaim their abandoned hideaway. The location was hidden, but was also too perfect to go unoccupied for long.

But this gang had been better organized than he had expected for such a young crew, and getting them to leave was turning out to be a chore. Still, they were proving no match for Jack Knife and his boys.

The boy on the ground looked up and snarled at him. "This is our turf, you British bastard!"

"It was ours first!" he said angrily. "And I'm not British!" He hit the downed thug again, this time striking him directly on the top of his wooden hat. The thin wood splintered under the impact of Jack's cane, and when he struck the boy again, the cane left a bloody gash on the top of his head. "Go!" he shouted, and raised his birch stick back up into the air. This time the Blockhead leader scrambled to his feet and ran.

The most frustrating thing was discovering that they had never needed to leave at all. The Children quickly vacated the space after the incident with the Sleuth, fully expecting the Paragons to come roaring in, looking for revenge. But the invasion had never happened, and a few days later, the old man had burned to death when the Darby mansion had gone up in flames.

Soon after that, Jack received a cryptic message from Lord Eschaton—but truth be told, he found all the gray man's messages fairly hard to decipher. Between the usual ranting and other gibberish, the note said that the Paragons were no longer a concern, and that Jack and the boys could safely take back their ground.

Unfortunately, the space had since been occupied by the Blockheads. With the Ruffian still recovering from his failure to stop a group of girls—something Jack still didn't quite believe—he had needed time to gather enough of his boys to take the courtyard back.

As he watched their leader run, Jack gripped the wood of his cane so tightly that his knuckles turned white. Whacking at people with a club was hardly his style, and his fingers were itching to grab at the knives in his jacket and put the cowardly bastard out of his misery. It wasn't until the thug ran into the maze that the urge passed.

Looking around him, Jack felt a sense of fatherly satisfaction—the rest of his boys were doing an equally good job of teaching the rest of the young gangsters not to mess with the Children of Eschaton.

"All right, Blockheads!" he yelled, loudly enough that he was sure everyone could hear. "If you've been too busy to notice, I just whipped the arse of your leader and sent him running away with his tail between his legs." He unhooked a button of his jacket and let it fall open, revealing the rows of gleaming steel blades secured into the lining underneath.

Jack smiled. He had their attention now! He dropped his cane to the ground and pulled free a handful of his blades. In rapid succession, he threw five of them, one after another.

The first four each landed in a different wooden hat, making loud "thunks" as they did so. It was a sound that Jack could only imagine would be well amplified inside their heads.

The fifth blade whizzed past the face of its target as he twisted out of the way, slashing through his cheek as it went. The man was large—a bearded fellow with a hairy chest so big that it was practically bursting out from underneath his starched white shirt and red velvet jacket. Blood welled out of the wound, pouring down his face, but to his credit, the man didn't make a sound.

Jack reached into his coat to grab a second handful of knives. "Now, if the rest of you are smart enough to follow your boss's example, I may let you live. But first I want to see you throw those ridiculous hats to the ground."

The gang members paused. Jack knew it would be shameful for them to give up the one thing that gave their sad lives meaning in this world. Clearly they needed further encouragement. "I won't ask again, and next time it won't be the wood that I'm aiming for."

The large man with the bleeding face bowed his head as he grabbed the rim of his wooden bowler. He lifted the hat off his head and stared at it for a moment. "You like to play with knives," he said in a soft tone. "So do I." He flicked his wrist with a practiced motion, sending the hat spinning through the air.

As the hat twirled, Jack saw the glint of a metallic edge hidden in the brim, and he understood the burly Blockhead's cryptic comment. Jack tried to duck, but even as he started to drop, it was clear that he would not be able to move out of the way in time. Watching death hurtling toward him, Jack felt something close to a sense of peace that he would die from a blade.

His calmness was interrupted by a black blur inches in front of his face. The object struck the wooden chapeau from the side, knocking it out of the way at the last instant.

Jack recognized the staff as it clattered to the ground nearby. It belonged to Anubis, and while he was glad to have his head remain in one piece, he wasn't pleased by the thought that he might owe the black-clad man any kind of debt.

But he'd deal with his rescuer in a moment. His first order of business was to make sure that the rest of the Blockheads understood the mistake their largest member had just made.

He flung two knives at the bearded man. Unable to dodge a second time, Jack's target took the blades deep in his burly thighs, and he dropped to the ground with a grunt. The hate in his eyes seemed undiminished by the pain.

"Grab him!" Jack shouted, and two of his men took the big man's arms.

Jack reached the hobbled Blockhead with only a few long strides. He stared into the angry slits of the Blockhead's eyes and smiled. "I could have killed you just now," he told him.

"You should have," the burly man replied with a deep growl.

Jack had to admit, despite having a similar physique to the Ruffian, there was something about the *depth* of the man's intensity that set him apart—it spoke to a skill he could use. "Maybe I don't want you dead . . . yet."

"S'not how I feel about you," the Blockhead said, narrowing his glare.

"That's obvious." Jack stared back at him quietly for a second, and then looked over to his men. "Tie him up and throw him into one of the huts. Let's give him the big fellow a chance to think about his sins before we punish him."

The man said nothing as the Children dragged him away.

Lifting his arms, Jack turned to the remaining Blockheads and addressed them directly. "Now, if the rest of you can behave yourselves, I'm looking for a few new Children, so come back in a couple of days—empty-handed—and we'll talk."

Truth be told, he'd been impressed with the raw abilities of the Blockheads, and after the difficulty he had finding the group he'd put together today, it couldn't hurt to pump up his own ranks. If his instincts were right, and they often were, things were about to get a lot more dangerous for him and the boys, and there wasn't just strength in numbers, there was security as well.

As the last of the opposing gang members walked out of the courtyard, Jack looked around at his remaining men and nodded. "A good day's work, boys! The Children of Eschaton are back in charge!"

A tired cheer rose up from his crew. Looking around, he realized that the Blockheads hadn't done much to improve the place. But at least they hadn't done too much to damage it, either. Most of the small shacks were still in place, and the brazier was burning merrily. "Now, let's get this shit-house back in shape."

It wasn't until he tried to sit down that he realized what was missing. "Where in the hell is my barrel?"

"It'th over here," shouted out a young lad through his missing teeth. Jack looked up to see him pointing to the edge of a trash pile where the barrel had been unceremoniously dumped.

At least they hadn't burned it. "Well then, Donny," he said, with a note of displeasure in his voice, "put it back where it belongs."

Cutter jumped in and began to clear away the garbage. The man was eager to help, as always. Cutter did everything with gusto, although his almost dwarfish stature made him less useful for tasks that demanded skill and grace. Cutter's skills lay in his almost psychopathic love of knives, although his abilities were quite unlike Jack's. His passion was wielding a blade, not throwing it. And unlike Jack's throwing knives, he liked his long and sharp.

Jack had first met the man when he had tried to relieve Jack of his purse. But the instant Cutter saw Jack's skills with a knife, he had dropped his own blade and offered his services instead. He'd proved to be a valuable soldier, if not always so good at restraining himself . . .

Finishing his survey, Jack turned his attention to Anubis. "Hello jackal-man," he said, finally acknowledging the presence of his black-clad rescuer. "How are you today?"

"Well enough."

"Nice of you to finally show up," he said.

"I must have dropped my staff saving your neck."

"Donny, get the man's staff for him."

"We haven't seen you around here much lately," Jack said, staring directly into the jackal's mask.

"I haven't been around."

"So, how goes the mission?"

Anubis shifted with obvious discomfort. "The Hydraulic-man is dead."

"Really?" he said, drawing out the word. "I thought you were going to let him live."

"I didn't kill him."

"'Didn't kill him' as in 'I didn't kill him,' or 'didn't kill him' as in 'all I did was stick out my foot and the horses did the rest'?"

Donny reappeared with the staff, and handed it back to him. Jack noticed that the weapon looked a bit damaged since the last time he had seen it. "Or maybe as in 'I threw my staff at him.'"

Anubis stared at him, unmoving and quiet. "Something like that."

"So you did have something to do with it."

"He burned to death."

"And the suit?"

"Burned with him."

"You were supposed to bring it back to me."

"The whole building burned down."

Jack shook his head. There was no doubt Anubis was talented, but there was a moral streak in the man a mile wide that made him close to useless. It also put him at odds with the rest of the Children as often as not, but Lord Eschaton continued to have faith in the jackal long after it had become obvious to everyone else that he was as likely to undermine their plans as he was to support them. "And I don't suppose you have any proof of that? I mean, considering how resistant you were to actually take this mission, and how it would suit your bleeding heart to let your quarry escape, and then say he died in a fire, with no trace left of the man or his suit."

Anubis nodded and reached into his armored vest. Jack tried not to visibly stiffen as he did so. It always paid to be on his guard, but he didn't want to appear as if he were afraid of the jackal, even if he was. But if Anubis had been planning to attack him directly, he would have made his play long ago.

When he pulled out his arm, it held one of the silver snake heads that had been part of the Hydraulic-man's suit. "Here's my proof."

Jack took it from his hands and gave it a closer look. The object was melted and burned from a heat that had been intense enough to fuse bits of ash and coal directly into the metal. "And what if you faked this, with Prescott's help?"

"Then I did a very good job."

Jack squeezed his hand around the metal chunk and pondered his options. "You're more trouble than you're worth." It was hard dealing with men of conscience when you didn't have much of one yourself. "I don't know why Eschaton doesn't let me kill you."

Anubis stepped forward. "I can think of two reasons."

Donny and Cutter had finished rolling his barrel back into place, and Jack was tempted to lean against it as they talked, but there was a long, dark stain on the side, along with an odd smell that made him think the wood would need a good scrubbing before he touched it again. "All right," Jack said, clapping his hands together, and speaking loudly enough to let his voice reverberate around the square. "I want everything back the way it was by tomorrow—just in case any of those idiots show up again." He actually hoped that some of them *would* show up. By then they'd either have the burly one with the red beard eating out of their hand or strung up like a Christmas turkey. Either way, the big fellow would stand as a warning to the rest of them . . .

Feeling satisfied that the work was proceeding properly, he turned back to Anubis. "Now, what were we talking about?"

"The two reasons you don't want to kill me."

"And those were?"

"First," Anubis said after a pause, "even if you don't like my methods, I get the job done."

Jack chuckled at that. Anubis had started out as an excellent partner, and both of them had been equals in the ranks of the Children, but as Eschaton's plans had progressed, Jack had, more than once, found himself cleaning up after Anubis's tendency to leave any job that required a bit of violence half-finished and call it done. "Your 'methods' were the reason we had to abandon this hideout in the first place." He stuck out his finger and poked against the golden ankh in the middle of Anubis's leather chestplate. "And *that's* why you ended up having to save me from being scalped by a man with a wooden hat!"

"I didn't let the Sleuth go."

"So you keep saying, but somehow I find it less believable every time you do. And whether you let the man go or he escaped, you were supposed stop him by any means necessary. Instead, you stopped me!"

"I'm not a murderer."

"No, I understand." Jack held up the silver snake's head. "You're just an enabler to murder."

"I tried to save him."

Jack smiled. "Really? That's a pathetic excuse. But it really didn't happen all by itself, did it?"

Anubis tilted his head toward the ground. "No."

Jack held open his jacket. "You know, if I ever was put on the stand, I could tell the jury it was my beautiful little knives that did all the killing, but somehow I don't think that would keep my neck out of the noose."

Jack could hear the sound of Anubis breathing heavily under his mask. "I watched him burn. He died in agony."

At least he was getting to the jackal. He wished he could see the man's eyes and know just how deeply he'd wounded him. It was Jack's experience that men died more easily than expected. Every living creature tried desperately to cling to life, but when the end finally came, it always came in an instant.

When Jack had been younger, he had found it difficult to watch people die, but with age he began to realize that no matter what the form a man's death took, they all went to the same place. Sooner or later, he reasoned, Anubis would recognize that as well, even if it was Jack's hand that showed him. "But you said there were two reasons. What was the second one?"

"*Eschaton* doesn't trust you, either."

Jack frowned. "Who trusts anyone? You think I trust you?"

"No. But it might make us allies."

Jack laughed. He was about to call the man a fool, but the words didn't leave his mouth. It wasn't, he had to admit, completely wrong. "What are you getting at, Anubis?"

"The enemy of my enemy is my friend."

"Lord Eschaton isn't *my* enemy."

"He isn't your friend, either."

Jack thought about that for a second. "Neither are you . . ." But the gray man was still the closest thing he had to any kind of friend at all. Before Eschaton had appeared, Jack's life hadn't really amounted to all that much.

Jack had been born in London, and his parents had been royalty of some sort, but not royal enough that it mattered when the money ran out. Looking for a second chance, they had decided to try their luck in the United States. It had turned out to be the worst kind of luck, with both his mother and his father killed by a runaway horse-cart.

The wagon had careened onto the sidewalk, and passed less than an inch above the young boy's head as it smashed into the midday crowd, tearing his mother's hand from his with the blow that killed her.

After that, Jack's modest inheritance had been slowly embezzled away by a string of so-called aunts and uncles who had handed him off from one relative to the next, showing him the barest minimum of love and affection until the money had run out.

By the time he turned fourteen, there were no more relatives and no more money, and he had become a ward of the state. Jack had quickly rebelled against the cold care of the orphanage, and when he decided to run away, no one bothered to come after him.

Living on the street forced him to rely on his meager skills to get by. But for all his naïveté, when it came to survival, there was one skill that had served him well: ever since he had been a boy, Jack was a dead shot. As a child, he had often knocked sparrows out of trees with nothing more than a rock, and his father, while he was alive, had encouraged his son's skills in marksmanship, giving him access to a variety of weapons, including bows and slingshots.

Throwing rocks was good enough to keep him alive, for a while at least. But as he grew bigger, so did his enemies, and simply being able to distract or wound his targets was no longer enough. The only way to be safe was to make sure that if he put someone down, they would never get up again. Soon after that, he discovered that a blade was better than a stone.

But even after he had mastered a throwing knife, Jack had learned that there were limits to what a blade could do to get you out of trouble. For every man you killed, it turned out, there was another who would come looking to avenge his death.

Jack was on the run when the gray man had caught him. He had been hired to take revenge on one of Lord Eschaton's costumed clients. The murder itself hadn't been of interest, but when he saw what Jack could do with a knife, he had pulled him out of danger and into the Children. He'd called the boy his "wild dog," and he told him that if he could learn just a bit of cunning to go with his skills, Jack could become a wolf. If, Eschaton had once explained, he could let go of his anger and simply hate everyone with an equal passion, Jack might become a leader of men. The gray man had offered him a chance to become more than just a thug on the run, and Jack had taken it.

Eschaton had cleaned him up and given him the jacket filled with perfectly balanced knives, along with his new name.

And for a while, it had been enough.

But soon he was being passed by for advancement by men like Rapid Fire, Bomb Lance, and Doc Dynamite. And while those men had worked by Lord Eschaton's side, Jack was still out on the streets. Not that he couldn't understand *why* he was there—but he wanted more.

So maybe Anubis could help him. The man *was* a wild card—too honest to be trustworthy—but it wouldn't hurt to humor him. "I don't need any friends," he told the jackal.

"Everyone needs a friend, sooner or later."

"I don't see you having any." Sooner or later, the jackal would make a mistake and give Jack a good reason to kill him. Or maybe he really did have something to offer. Either way, there was no reason to antagonize him. And the two of them were alike in some ways. "And you need to stop getting in my way."

"And you need to stop sticking a knife into everyone who makes you angry."

Jack chuckled at that. Now Anubis was sounding like Eschaton. "We'll see. Meanwhile, we have other work to do."

"New orders?"

"You're just in time."

Anubis didn't move or respond. He just continued to breathe at him through his leather mask. The sound of it was incredibly annoying, but he declined to comment on it in the name of their newfound alliance. "You need to lead Donny and Cutter over to a theater in Union Square tomorrow."

"Not you?"

"Not me." He smiled. "I've got a gang to rebuild, no thanks to you."

"What am I supposed to do?"

"Eschaton has tracked down the Stanton girl, after Bomb Lance and le Voyageur failed."

"And he wants us to get her."

"Exactly. And she has the mechanical man's heart, as well." He looked the jackal up and down. "Think you'll be up for it?"

266

Anubis nodded slightly. "I won't kill her."

"Always the bleeding heart." He nodded in the direction of Cutter. "The dwarf only knifes women who try to hurt him first."

"Is that a joke?"

Jack shook his head. "It's a fact. So," he said, accenting the last word hard enough to make it sound like a threat, "can I trust you to get this done?"

Anubis nodded. "I'll be here tomorrow."

"Before dark, if you'd be so kind. And," he said, holding up the snake's head, "no excuses."

"As you say." Anubis turned and began to walk away. Jack saw that there was something wrong with his suit, a gap where a hole had been burned through the leather. What it revealed made him smile.

Chapter 22

The Life and Death of Machines

Vincent had clearly put in a great deal of effort to make sure that from every corner of the theater, and on either side of the stage, the faces of the pneumatic man stared down at the crowd from the walls. Sarah tried to ignore how similar the likenesses were to Tom's long-shattered porcelain features.

From her seat near the front of the auditorium, Sarah had to admit that the show was visually impressive, even if the story was nonsense, and served mostly to introduce a menagerie of mechanical creatures.

The show focused on a safari through the "lost clockwork world of darkest Africa," led by the heroic Vincent Smith. The young adventurer was hot on the trail of the legendary pneumatic man, a giant living machine that was also the ruler of all the mechanical creatures.

Vincent himself acted as narrator to the supposedly "true adventures" of his younger self. Dressed in an immaculate costume of white breaches and a red jacket with long tails, he stood at a podium at the edge of the stage, explaining both the origins and the dangers of the different creatures he faced during his journey, while occasionally manipulating the controls that brought them to life.

Within the play there was an actor who portrayed the younger version of Vincent. He was dashing and debonair, and (Sarah guessed) far more handsome than the actual man had been at that age. He was also clearly a trained acrobat who had spent the last half hour dodging and weaving the horns, hooves, claws, and talons of the different mechanical monsters that he faced on his journey.

Currently he was madly running away from a rampaging metal hippopotamus that had been terrorizing a tribe of mechanical Pygmies known as the "iron men." Portrayed by little actors in metal costumes, they were

269

throwing spears at the creature, and so many had pierced its tin hide that it had begun to take on the appearance of a giant angry porcupine.

Sarah looked over to see how Emilio and Viola were enjoying the show. The Italian girl was obviously enraptured, hollering and clapping, shouting to urge the Pygmies on.

Emilio seemed less animated but equally engrossed by the show. He was holding his sharp face firmly in his hands, and was obviously entranced by seeing his machines on the stage. Clearly his time back at the theater had rekindled his interest.

Sarah stared at him, watching the show reflected in his eyes. For a moment, it almost seemed as if she could see the wheels actually turning inside of his head.

Sarah kept looking, wondering if he would even notice her attention. And at the moment she was about to give up on him, his eyes flicked in her direction. Having seen her, he turned toward her and smiled.

Sarah smiled back, but her expression felt disconnected and false. It was as if someone else had taken over her face and was smiling for her. It was, in a word, mechanical.

Accepting her wan grin, Emilio nodded and turned back to watch the show. Sarah sighed. What did it mean that he couldn't see into her heart?

Or maybe he just didn't *want* to see any deeper . . . The Armandos were as happy as they'd been since she met them, and she supposed that there was no reason they shouldn't be enjoying themselves. But try as she might, Sarah couldn't let herself relax.

Instead, she shifted uncomfortably in her seat. It wasn't entirely nerves: it had been a while since she had been in a bodice, but she had wanted to look a little more dressed-up for the occasion.

She had hoped it would help her feel a bit more comfortable—embraced by a taste of the life that she had left behind. There was even a decently fashionable hat on her head that Viola had magically produced from her wardrobe, although with the mood of the Italian girl subject to sudden shifts, Sarah hadn't dared to ask how she managed to come by it.

Viola had also dressed up, although her dress was far more revealing than any proper lady would wear. When she had asked Sarah's opinion, Sarah had simply replied that it was "flattering," although she had bitten back the word *scandalous* in order to say it.

Viola had told Sarah that she was, under no circumstances, allowed to bring her costume along with her, although there were a few things in her bag, if the need arose for her to defend herself.

Turning her attention back to the stage, she watched as the mechanical hippo swayed woozily, dripping copious amounts of black gore. The Pygmies had surrounded it and were poking at the dying creature repeatedly with their spears. She found herself feeling sorry for it, and then reminded herself that it wasn't alive, or even a living machine like Tom. It was simply a puppet—expertly manipulated, but lifeless.

But emotion won out, and Sarah found herself relieved when a moment later it collapsed with a groan, jetting out a large spout of pink steam from its back that was a clear signal that the beast had been vanquished. At least she would no longer have to watch it suffer.

The curtains swung closed, and the limelight swung back onto Vincent. "Having worked together to slay the beast, we had forged a bond of trust. The iron Pygmies, so keen to butcher me only a few hours before, were now eager to point me in the direction of the pneumatic man. I had proven that I might be able to free them from his tyrannical rule.

"But they would be unable to accompany me on my journey. The tiny metal men were too small and heavy to try to climb the sheer cliff face that separated me from my goal."

Sarah wondered to herself how the pygmies would know where to tell Vincent to go if they couldn't get there themselves, then she chided herself for being so particular.

She knew that if she could let herself relax and enjoy the show, time would go more quickly. It reminded her of Christmas mornings before the adults were awake, except with an underlying sense of dread.

It wasn't the show itself, of course. Since the moment that she had placed Tom's heart into Vincent's hands, she had discovered an uncomfortable tightness in her chest that refused to go away.

And it was obvious that Emilio wasn't completely unaware of her nervousness. His solution was to tell her to stop worrying, which only served to make her even more concerned.

She looked up at the stage and stared at Vincent Smith. No matter what he was now, the man *had* been a villain. No matter how hard she tried to believe his claims of repentance, it was impossible to ignore the fact that the last hope for Tom was now entirely in the hands of a man who had once fought against the Paragons—and had tried to bring the entire Hall down on top of her father!

Trying to alleviate her fears, they had arrived to the show early, but that had only made things worse. Vincent had greeted Viola with a lusty hug (which she returned). Then he handed them three tickets and told them that they should enjoy the show.

When Sarah demanded that Emilio tell her about his progress on the heart, he smiled and told her that after the performance was over, they would retire to the workshop. "Don't worry Sarah! Is good!"

She had considered demanding that he show it to her immediately. But like it or not, things were clearly out of her hands, and Emilio trusted Vincent totally.

Sarah caught herself clutching nervously at her blouse, her fingers tracing the outline of the key around her neck. Not wanting to appear like a nervous child, she folded her hands together into her lap and frowned.

Ever since she had picked up Tom's broken heart from the remains of his body, she had allowed herself to hope that if she restored that single part to working order, they would be able to rebuild the rest of him. And if anyone had bothered to ask her, she would have told them that she believed it with every fiber of her body—although she would not have been able to articulate why she thought it was true.

Now that she was on the verge of that being a reality, doubt had begun to creep into Sarah's own heart. Truth be told, she understood almost nothing about what it was that had animated the mechanical man beyond the marvel of the Alpha Element. Even Darby had often remarked that he was never fully able to comprehend what had brought Tom to life, nor had he ever been able to replicate it.

"And so I began to climb the mountains of mechanical mystery," Vincent said from the side of the stage. The curtains parted to reveal a craggy cliff face constructed from steel and brass. The handsome actor was already climbing up it, hand over hand.

With each step he took, the wall slid underneath him, allowing him to stay in place while he continued to ascend upwards. It was an impressive effect, and Sarah could tell it was something Emilio hadn't seen before. His lips were pursed in a grim line that Sarah had come to realize meant he was in a deep state of concentration, trying to unravel a mechanical secret.

Out of the corner of her eye, Sarah noticed movement along the far aisles. When she turned to take a better look, she saw two men. Both wore scruffy jackets of brown worsted wool, with cloth caps pulled down tightly over their heads. One was tall and thin, the other no taller than a child, although he clearly had a man's bearing. They were both hunched over as if they had something to hide, trying so hard not to be noticed that for a moment Sarah thought they were actors preparing to surprise the audience.

When they disappeared through a curtain at the left side of the stage, an uneasy feeling started in the pit of Sarah's stomach. It began to grow until she could no longer remain in her seat.

"Emilio!" she said, poking the rapt Italian in his shoulder.

"*Sì!*" he replied without turning to look at her, and then lifted a hand to point at the stage. "They slide up from below—like a puzzle."

Sarah frowned and shook her head. He was clearly going to be of no use unless she had something to show him. "I'm going to the water closet." Emilio's only response was an absentminded nod.

Sarah pulled herself out of her seat, remembering at the last moment to take her bag. It contained something that Emilio had made for her, and even if the purse was too large to be genuinely ladylike, just holding it made her feel a little safer.

She softly begged forgiveness from the other theater-goers as she shimmied past them towards the aisle, her dress managing to get in everyone's way as she went.

When she finally escaped her row, Sarah realized that in order to access the curtain she had seen the two men disappear through, she would first need to walk all the way to the back of the theater and cross over to the far aisle.

She moved as fast as she could, reaching the back of the theater and rounding the turn before the blare of heavenly trumpets and a collective gasp from the audience drew her attention back to the stage: young Vincent had finally reached the top of the mountain, and the mechanical wall was vanishing downward as a gleaming metal city rose into view.

Men in white stood at the top of the cliff, their faces covered with silver masks that were clearly meant to be reminiscent of the face of the pneumatic man himself. Tom's visage was everywhere tonight, it seemed.

Sarah turned her gaze back to the floor and stomped along, following the red carpet until she finally reached the heavy red curtains that framed the doorway. Pulling them apart, she stepped inside.

The little chamber beyond was quieter, and when the thick curtains fell back into place, they muffled the sounds of the show. There was a door in front of her. Sarah opened it and began climbing up a small set of stairs.

At the top was the backstage area she had visited when she had been here last. The theater was alive now, buzzing with actors and stagehands moving as they prepared the different mechanical animals for their appearance on the main stage.

A few of the stagehands looked at her as she walked in, but most of them seemed too busy to take any real interest in her, and no one came to question her sudden appearance.

Sitting in the back was the pneumatic man. He was unfolded now, his arms and legs attached to the wires that would give him the illusion of life, almost prepared for his moment of glory on the main stage.

There was literal fire in his eyes now, along with a trail of steam that rose up from the stovepipe on his head. It truly did remind Sarah of the Industrialist's hat—she wondered what her father would think of that.

Sarah looked around to see if she could find the men she had followed, but they were nowhere to be seen. She took a deep breath and plunged into the mayhem, dodging and weaving through the organized chaos all around her until she reached the door to the garden. Like the previous entrance, this one had also been left ajar. These were men clearly without manners . . .

Sarah's eyes went wide when she saw what was on the other side—as beautiful as the courtyard had been during the day, at night it was even more so. The rusting machines that had seemed so sad and neglected in the day-light were now given new life by flames inside of them that made them glow yellow and red.

Sarah was so entranced by the flickering creatures that she was startled when she heard a voice from nearby. "Let me try, Cutter!" It wasn't until she heard one of them speaking that Sarah even realized that the men she had been following were now standing directly in front of the workshop door, the short one attempting to break in.

"You know as much about picking locks as you do about pulling off a girl's garters," said the man working on the lock.

Sarah crept behind a glowing statue in the shape of a large grasshopper, the tips of its antennae giving off a cheerful yellow light.

The heat radiating from it kept her from getting too close, but it was a welcome relief from the cold night air. "I alwayth find a poke ith as good ath a grope," the taller man replied.

"Donny, you've got a lot to learn about women," the other said with a nasty chuckle.

The taller of the two men was squatting in front of the door handle, fid-dling with the lock while the shorter one looked on. "I'll get it, Cutter, jutht give me a chanthe!"

"You're useless, but go ahead," the short one replied and moved out of the way.

The tall one continued to lisp while he worked. "Anubith said we weren't thuppothed to cauth a futh, and you had uth walk thtraight through the theater."

"How often do you get to a see a show like that, Donny? 'Specially with all them fancy machines like that?"

"It wath thomething, all right."

"I would have liked to have seen more . . ."

A loud clack came from the lock. "Got it!" the tall one said as the door swung open.

The lisping man tried to barrel straight into the room, but his partner's hand snapped out and grabbed his coat. "Take it easy, Donny. Who knows what traps he has in there."

"But Vinthent told uth the girl would be here . . . He told uth about the heart."

Sarah felt her stomach flip despite the tightness of her corset. She hadn't trusted the old villain and she'd been right all along. "But he's not one of *us*," the short one replied. "Lord Eschaton got him over a barrel, and he's just tryin' to save his skin. Never trust a desperate man, Donny."

Sarah breathed a sigh of relief. Perhaps it wasn't too late for her to get the heart back.

"Jack alwayth thayth never trutht anyone."

"Well I say follow me, and keep your dirty paws off anything you see in there until I say so."

"Of courthe, Cutter . . ."

The two men crept inside, once again leaving the door open behind them. At least they were consistently bad-mannered.

Sarah waited for a moment to be sure they weren't coming back, and then she crept out from her hiding place and up the stone stairs to the doorway.

It was mostly dark inside the shop, and before she entered, Sarah reached into her oversized black purse, drawing out a pistol that Emilio had given her after her last trip to the city.

The weapon had been fashioned after her description of the pneumatic gun from Tom. But without the power of fortified steam, this weapon was nowhere near as powerful, and instead of the devastating puffs of air that her previous weapon had used, it simply fired wooden bullets. The pistol was spring-powered, and was capable of firing up to twelve shots before it needed to be rewound and reloaded. Emilio had promised her that it could take down a man without killing him, but unlike her previous weapon, she would need to aim it.

As she walked up the steps and looked through the door into the darkness beyond, Sarah prayed that no one noticed her looming shadow as it rose to cover the soft wedge of light that stretched into the workshop from outside. If the men inside saw her . . . She ignored her nerves and plunged in, the door rotating open quietly on well-oiled hinges.

In the darkness, the workshop seemed larger than she remembered, with the gloom managing to give the machines inside a sense of sharp menace that they had lacked in the daylight.

She could see the two men standing in front of something along the left wall, still completely oblivious to the fact that they were no longer alone. "Ith that it, Cutter?"

"A little patience, Donny . . ."

Slipping through the door, Sarah snuck behind the center row of tables, then ducked down and began to creep along as silently as she could manage.

Almost immediately, her corset began to rise up, clutching her chest and constricting her simultaneously. Unable to slide up to her neck due to Viola's tight lashing, the bottom of the garment instead dug down into her thighs. Sarah shook her head as she recognized the familiar feeling of being victimized by fashion.

She reached up and grabbed at the top of a table with her left hand to help steady her as she moved painfully along. She could feel her right palm getting damp where it gripped the weapon.

"What ith that, Cutter?"

"Not our problem. Let's keep moving."

Sarah peered under the table. She could see the legs of the men as they headed from one table to the next, looking for the heart.

"Not here," Donny said.

"Nor here," replied Cutter.

Sarah prayed that they would find something interesting to look at before they reached the end of the row. Perhaps she could grab it before they did . . .

When she had left the heart with Vincent, it had been laying on his workbench, and even if he had moved it around to work on it, she couldn't imagine that it had gotten very far. Moving as quickly as she could, she reached the last table in the row and peered around the edge of it. Sarah stifled a yelp: the heart was on the large bench at the far wall, suspended in some kind of vice.

Just as she prepared to make a grab for the device, the two men rounded the corner.

"Found it!" Donny yelled gleefully. Catching a glimpse of him before pulling her head back, Sarah realized that the tall one wasn't much more than a boy—sixteen at the most.

"Yes you did, Donny, you did indeed."

Sarah took a deep breath and looked down at the weapon in her hand.

"How do we get it out?" Donnny asked.

"Unscrew those bolts and it should fall right into our hands."

The opportunity to grab it and run was now long gone. If she was going to get Tom's heart away from these two, it would need to be through direct action.

She clutched the weapon tightly as she tried to work up the courage needed to jump up and shoot at the two men.

"I'll do it!" Donny said enthusiastically as he started reaching out for the elaborate frame that Vincent had fitted around the object.

Cutter batted his hand away. "Slow down, boy! We don't want to tear it apart."

The threat to Tom gave Sarah the extra surge of courage that she needed. Standing up, Sarah saw that both men had their backs to her.

She took aim at the short man first, figuring he was clearly the more intelligent and dangerous of the two. "It always pays to be careful." The moment he touched the frame, he began to shake violently, and then collapsed to the floor.

"Cutter!" his friend shouted.

"Oh!" Sarah gasped.

Donny spun around to face her. "Who the hell are you?" he asked through a mouth full of missing teeth.

Sarah gave no reply. The fight in the balloon had taught her the importance of acting instead of talking, and she fired off four shots as quickly as her finger could pull the trigger.

Her nervousness made it difficult to aim, but two of the bullets struck Donny in the chest. Each one knocked him back slightly, but none of them had the effectiveness that a single shot from the pneumatic gun might have had. "That hurt!" he said, and began to close the gap between them. On his face was a look of anger and menace that made her think that perhaps it would have been better to face Cutter instead.

His arm shot out and grabbed her roughly. "I athked who you are, lady. Have you come here to thow Donny a good time?" The smile on his face would have been grotesque even without any missing teeth. As it was, it was terrifying.

Sarah was trying her best to overcome her fear so that she could escape, but the fingers digging into her wrist were fighting for her attention.

Raising up her right arm, Sarah put the gun up to her attacker's temple and fired again. This bullet hit him straight on, walloping against his skull with enough force that even she could hear the echo.

For a moment, Sarah wasn't sure what was going to happen, and then Donny let out a curse. "Dammit, that hurt!"

She shot him in the head a second time.

This time the man released her arm, and the only noise he made was a groan as he dropped to the floor.

"Was that a good enough time for you, Donny?" Sarah said, giving the fallen man a good kick to the ribs before she stepped past him and over Cutter to reach the heart.

The device was suspended in a frame of steel rods. The ends were padded with velvet and had been designed to hold the heart in place for repair without scratching the surface. Sarah thought that detail was probably Emilio's handiwork.

She looked carefully around the edge of the frame until she found a wire. Sarah grabbed it and pulled, and when the cord tore away from the wall, it spat out a small shower of sparks that bounced across the table and lit up the dark room like a tiny bolt of lightning. Once again, her skills at being stealthy were proving to be poor, but she had already managed to win the fight.

Reaching out gingerly, she touched a finger to the metal heart. She sighed with relief when there was no effect.

Wrapping her hands around the heart, Sarah gave it a tug, but it refused to budge. She pulled harder, but it resisted, held solidly in place by the clamps. Letting out a frustrated huff, she began to undo the remaining thumbscrews that held the metal sphere in place, grunting as she strained to loosen them.

After three of them had been undone, the heart tipped forward. Sarah cupped her hands underneath it, and it rolled down into her palms. It was cool and heavy against her skin, and holding it gave her a feeling of calm that she hadn't had in days.

Sarah opened her purse and tried to place it inside, but there wasn't enough room to fit it in. As oversized as the purse had seemed when she had chosen it, it was too small to contain everything she needed. "Silly girl," she muttered to herself.

Shaking her head with frustration, she put the heart back on the table along with the pistol, pulled out her father's metal-lined gloves, and then slipped the heart inside the bag.

Sarah knew she would look ridiculous wearing the Industrialist's gloves without the rest of her costume, but she had no other choice unless she wanted to leave them behind. As she slipped them on, a smile crept across her face—she couldn't help feeling like a bit of a bandit with her gun in one hand and the bag in the other.

She was halfway to the studio exit when the door swung open wide, revealing a figure in black standing in the doorway. For a moment, she thought it might be Emilio come to her rescue, but even in the darkness it only took her a moment to realize that the startling profile couldn't be him. His face had the features of a wolf, a snarling mouth hanging over a glimmering golden ankh on his chest.

The villain raised up a hand. "Stop, Sarah Stanton."

Sarah raised up her gun and fired. The bullets bounced off the man's black leather costume, clearly doing little or no damage. If she ever had the chance, she really would need to talk to Emilio about the effectiveness of his weapon . . .

"Please," said the man in the wolf mask, stepping closer.

"Stay back!"

"I'm trying to . . . Ungh!"

Sarah smacked him as hard as she could with her purse, realizing an instant later that she had just used Tom's heart as a bludgeon.

It had been an effective weapon. The impact knocked the man clear of the door, and he slumped to the floor. "I'm sorry, Tom," she whispered, praying to herself that she hadn't just managed to undo Vincent's and Emilio's repairs in a single blow.

With the doorway clear, Sarah ran out across the courtyard until she reached the backstage door. She was gasping for breath, her heart pounding in her chest. At least she'd had the good sense to wear boots instead of fashionable shoes, otherwise she would have completely collapsed from the effort.

Sarah flung the door open with enough force that it caused a nearby stagehand to jump. But after she pulled the door closed behind her and threw the bolt, she had no idea what to do next. It was possible that she could head for the exit and try to get the attention of Emilio and Viola, but what good would that do? They were already facing at least three of the Children of Eschaton, and there was a good chance that more would follow . . . If she tried to warn them, it might only make things worse than they already were.

Her other option was to run—head right out onto the stage and scream for help. But that could cause a commotion, possibly a stampede. After the events onboard the ferry, the last thing she needed on her conscience was another massacre.

What she needed was a place to hide while she gathered her thoughts. Looking out across the stage, she saw the Pneumatic Colossus still sitting in the corner, steam spitting from his joints and the hoses rising up out of him.

Sarah ran toward him and shoved herself down behind his back, her corset once again attacking her thighs. This close, the mechanical puppet was hot and moist, and stank of the lubricating oil that had been mixed into the steam.

As she felt the greasy moisture seep into her clothes, Sarah heard her mother's voice inside her head, lamenting the fact that Sarah had just managed to ruin her last good dress. She supposed that Viola would be thrilled to see the remainder of her "rich girl" clothes oil-stained and ruined.

"Focus, girl!" Sarah whispered to herself. She was in trouble and she knew it. It certainly wouldn't take long for one of the Children to find her here. She did, after all, have the very object they were looking for in her hands. And she could expect no help from Vincent.

But was the heart even fixed? Sarah took off her gloves and pulled the object out of her bag. Vincent and Emilio had done an admirable job of making it look as if it were repaired. It appeared far more like it had when she had seen it in Tom's chest in Darby's laboratory. Emilio had even replaced the plug that held the Alpha Element with something similar to the one that Eschaton had pulled out of it.

When she unscrewed the plug, she saw that the base of it was a receptacle for the key around her neck. Emilio clearly had a very good memory.

From nearby she could hear a loud rattling, and shouts from the stage door. It would be only a few moments before the Children of Eschaton found her.

Sarah pulled the key out from her blouse and removed the lead covering. "Tom, I hope you're still in there."

The Alpha Element seemed to almost be devouring the steam around it, glowing brighter than she had ever seen it glow before.

She shoved the front end into the plug. It fit perfectly, and Sarah quickly began to screw it back in. With each turn, her excitement grew, and her hands were trembling.

Halfway in, the plug caught, the threads mashing together. Sarah swallowed, and instead of forcing it, she untwisted it half a turn and tried again. This time the plug found its groove and turned all the way in.

Having screwed it as far as it would go, Sarah held her breath for a moment. She wanted something to happen, some sign that Tom was still alive, even in his reduced state. But the device in her hands remained motionless.

A feeling of despair rose up in her, making her feel desperate and childish. What was it she was expecting to happen? There had been no guarantee that repairing the heart would restore Tom to life.

"Miss Stanton?" The voice that came from nearby had the same deep timbre she had heard the wolf-man use in the workshop.

As Sarah looked desperately around to try to see where the voice was coming from, she discovered a hatch where the legs and the waist of the Colossus came together. Perhaps she could hide the heart there? It was better than having one of the Children snatch it from her.

Twisting open the latch, she lifted up the hatch to discover a gearbox inside. Spinning cogs controlled a series of rotating shafts that spidered out into the limbs of the mechanical man, allowing the giant puppet to move its hands and feet.

She shoved the heart up into it, the gears jamming against the metal as she pushed hard to make it fit inside. Steam and grease covered her hand when she removed it, and her fingers slipped a few times before she could shove the latch back into place.

"Miss Stanton, you have nothing to be afraid of." Sarah looked up to see the snarling face hovering above her and felt that it was very doubtful he was telling her the truth. She pointed her gun up at him.

"If you wanted to be calm and reassuring, you've picked the wrong mask," she told him.

"My name is Anubis. I only judge."

Accepting that she was beyond the point where she would be able to fight her way out of her predicament, Sarah put the gun and gloves back into her bag. When she was done, she held up her hand, but the leather-clad figure didn't move.

"Don't you have any manners?"

"I'm afraid I don't . . ."

"Can you help me up, please?" she said, taking a tone of authority. Whoever this man was under his mask, he clearly hadn't been raised in society.

"Of course," he said, and offered his hand to her, palm upward.

Sarah took it, her greasy fingers barely hanging onto his gloves as she stood. "Thank you." Throwing all convention to the wind, she wiped her sleeve against her brow. If she hadn't been convinced that the dress was a total loss before, the damp black smear she left behind on the cloth confirmed it.

"Wherth is she?" said another voice. "I'll kill her!"

She looked up and saw Donny's broken-toothed face approaching.

"Leave her alone," Anubis said.

"No." Donny walked straight towards her. The pain of the slap he gave her came almost as much from surprise as it did from the actual blow, which was not inconsiderable in its force. She felt her head rock from the strength of it. "I've had enough of your mouth." The broken-toothed boy raised up his hand to strike her again, then held it there, a simple and obvious threat. "Now tell me where the heart ith."

Anubis turned to face him, but there was no emotion visible under his black mask. "If you do that again, I'll knock you down."

Donny faced Anubis defiantly. "And if you were on our thide, I'd thtill have all my teeth!"

When he turned back to her, Donny's face was puckered into a sour grimace, like a pouting child. His hand lashed out again, but this time something stopped the blow.

Donny turned to face the man in black, his wrist caught in Anubis's black-gloved hand. "You've lotht your mind. Jack will kill you."

From somewhere nearby, Sarah heard a familiar grinding sound.

"I've had enough of him, and of you." Anubis said as he slowly twisted the man's arm, forcing him down to the floor. "I was hoping to accomplish more by being one of the Children, but too many people have suffered while I waited for my opportunity. It ends now."

"Traitor!" Donny yelled at him. "I knew it all along."

"You were right." Anubis held up his fist, clearly intent on hitting the other man. But the threatening hand withered and fell to Anubis's side as his gaze fixed onto something behind her.

The grinding noise grew louder. Sarah turned to see that the Pneumatic Colossus had begun to rise. Its legs were slowly unfolding underneath it as the machine rose up from the floor, its head rolling upward like a puppet being lifted by invisible strings.

"Tom," she whispered. Looking up into its fiery eyes, she realized Vincent had been right; the machine was far more impressive when it was spitting fire and steam. But she would have never believed it if someone had told her that the Pneumatic Colossus would speak her name.

"SARAH," it replied, and the word poured out from the grate under its face in a cloud of white vapor.

Chapter 23
A Shaken Man

Emilio turned to Sarah to point out that he had created the mechanized cherubs currently saving "Young Vincent" from toppling over the edge of the cliff. Instead he discovered an empty seat. As he looked for her silhouette in the dark theater, he vaguely recalled Sarah telling him that she was going somewhere, but he couldn't quite remember where it was she was going to go, or how long ago she had told him she was leaving.

"Have you seen Sarah?" he whispered to Viola in Italian.

Her eyes were intensely focused on the stage, and she didn't move them to talk to him. "Shhh," she said, raising a finger to her lips, "I'm watching." From her tone, it was clear she expected no further disturbances.

Under other circumstances he would have been pleased that Viola was so enraptured by the show. While he had been working on Vincent's mechanical creatures, she had often mocked him. "It sounds terrible," she would tell him. "Who wants to see a bunch of tin monkeys running around on stage?"

But now that she was actually there, his sister was totally lost in the spectacle, and he was sure that she would deny having ever said a discouraging word about it.

Emilio loved his sister, but her selfishness was his least favorite part of her. When Viola was a little girl, their mother had taken to calling her "my little mule," due to her stubbornness. It was still a fitting description.

Viola was the most in love with what loved her the most, and the fires of that passion burned very hot. They also needed constant fuel, and she could be hopelessly in love with a man one week, and then barely be bothered to remember his name when the next one came along.

He shook his head and tapped her on the shoulder again. "Sarah is missing."

"What?" This time she glanced at him for a moment. "Don't be ridiculous. She's probably gone to make water. She'll be back soon."

Up on the stage, a cluster of the small angels were about to enter into desperate combat with a flock of brass vampire bats intent on extracting every last drop of blood from the intrepid adventurer.

He watched Viola gasp along with other members of the audience as the flying creatures clashed in midair. One of his mechanical angels was torn to pieces, leaving only a small cloud of feathers to flutter onto the stage. It had been a good design. "I'm going to look for her."

"As you like." Viola muttered at him. She clearly had no interest in joining him.

Emilio stood up and shuffled out of the aisle as discreetly as possible. He knew where he was going to check for her first. Given Sarah's ability to find trouble, and her nervousness about the fate of the mechanical man's heart, she would have headed to the workshop.

He reached the end of the aisle, and then turned to watch the conclusion of the battle between the angels and the bats onstage. Young Vincent and the remaining angels were working together now, and the explorer fired a large blunderbuss that seemed to blast half of the black creatures off the stage while the rest flew up into the rafters.

Seeing the mechanical angels flapping, and hearing the rising noise of the audience's thrilled applause, Emilio couldn't help but take a bit of pride in his creations.

He had certainly built nothing as interesting since. After his time with Vincent, he had spent most of his days isolated in his workshop, hoping to create something that would get him noticed by the Paragons, or at least get him work as an apprentice.

But now that he'd seen people watching the show, Emilio had begun to wonder if his attitude toward craftsmanship was too provincial and measured. Perhaps Americans appreciated spectacle more than craftsmanship.

Heading to the back of the theater, he walked through the main doors and back into the menagerie. The mechanical animals had been shut off for the night, and the room was quiet and empty except for two men who were standing near the mechanical frog.

One of them was clearly wearing an adventurer's costume. There was a hood over his head and a noose knotted around his neck. It would have been terrifying except that the outfit seemed to have been cut for a slimmer figure . . .

The other man wore a dingy oiled duster and was smoking a cigar. From the Stetson on his head, Emilio could tell that he fancied himself a cowboy of some sort.

Both he and Viola had talked a great deal about how exciting it would be to see a cowboy when they arrived in America, but it had turned out that in New York City they were few and far between.

When they saw Emilio, the men whispered to each other, then turned to face him. "Can we help you?" the man in the noose said in a Southern accent so thick that it was difficult to understand.

Emilio held up his hand to just about Sarah's height. "Have you seen this girl? She has red hair, and wears a black dress."

"Sorry pal, we ain't seen the filly yer lookin' for." The cowboy also spoke with an accent. It was a western drawl that seemed impossibly authentic, and his words rolled out with a blast of cigar smoke. Emilio did his best not to cough as the cloud surrounded his head.

"You are a real cowboy?" Looking at the man, Emilio knew that he probably shouldn't be asking him that, but he had to. "I never met a real cowboy before!"

"Are you a real dago?" The man replied. "Because I've shot plenty of those . . ." He slid back his duster, revealing a well-used Colt pistol in a holster at his side. "And I wouldn't mind shootin' a few more."

As he looked down at the weapon, Emilio couldn't help but notice that the man had a yellow letter *D* sewn into each of his boots.

The man in the white costume just stared straight at him through the eyeholes in his hood. "You better run away, my guinea friend, because otherwise I think *my* friend is going to shoot you."

Emilio knew better than to hang around men who were showing off their guns. He began to back away slowly, doing his best to look meek and mild, and certainly not at all like the kind of person who would know that these men might be members of the Children of Eschaton.

When Emilio reached the backstage door, he turned the handle, but it was locked. He knocked on it nervously.

"Waitaminit . . ." said the cowboy. "Didn't Murphy say something about one of the men on the balloon being an Italian?"

Emilio tried to twist the handle again, but it was still just as locked as it had been a moment before. "Now that you mention it, he did," replied the Southerner.

For a moment, Emilio considered trying to escape back into the theater, but perhaps he could still talk his way out of trouble, and running might mark him as guilty of something. On the other hand, his English made it almost impossible for him to try to talk his way out of *anything*.

The two men began walking towards him. If they were attempting to terrify him, it was working. The cowboy loomed up at his left side. "Where ya in such a hurry to get to?"

The man in white appeared on the other side of him just a moment later. He smelled of liquor. "And that girl you're looking for—what's her name?"

"Sarafina," he said smoothly, and then tried not to wince as he realized just how big a mistake he had just made.

Up close, the cowboy seemed bigger, meaner, and far less of a caricature than he had been before. "Yeah? That wouldn't be Sarafina Stantontini, would it?"

"No, sir. Sarah Bugiardini." Emilio found himself wishing he had brought his shield with him, or that he had at least made another spring-loaded gun like the one that he had given to Sarah.

The one weapon he did have wasn't designed to stop two men, and as he began to lift up his arm, he wondered which of them he should consider to be the most dangerous.

"Now it's Sarah?" the Southerner asked. "I thought you said her name was Sarafina?" Emilio suddenly found his back pressed up against the door, the men too close for him to use his weapon . . .

"I sorry . . . Sarafina. You say Sarah, and you make me very nervous."

"A real cowboy makes everyone nervous," the man in the duster said with a smile.

Emilio tried to grin back, but he was sure that whatever expression appeared on his face must have looked far more like terror than pleasure.

Just as the man started to reach for his gun, Emilio felt the door unlatch behind him. The second it opened, he shoved himself through, clearly catching the young stagehand by surprise. "I must go to work. Sorry, gentlemen."

Before either one of them could react, Emilio slammed the backstage door shut and threw the bolt home.

The stagehand scowled. "What the hell are you doing?"

"I'm Emilio Armando, I make the animals."

"Well, there's a show going on back here right now, you'll need to come back later."

"No, no. I know Vincent. He wants me to take a look at the monkeys."

"One of the *monkeys* is broken?" The boy rolled his eyes. "Nobody tells me anything. Then I guess the question is where *were* you? They're supposed to go onstage in five minutes."

There was banging on the door, and he could hear a Southern accent through the wood. "We'll be waiting for you when you come out, dago."

"And what's all that about?" asked the hand, turning as if he might unlock the door again to ask them.

Emilio grabbed the boy's arm and pulled him the other direction, leading him toward the cacophony of the backstage area and away from the pursuers. "They want tour. I say no."

"New Yorkers," the stage hand said, shaking his head as if this kind of thing happened all the time.

"Is a crazy city. Now, where do I find the monkeys?"

"Straight over there."

"Thank you." As the boy was walking away, Emilio yelled after him. "You not see a girl back here? Red hair, this tall?"

"Sorry, pal. No one here but us monkeys." The stagehand laughed at his own joke and scampered away.

Emilio walked toward the place where the animals were kept, hoping that he could sneak out to the workshop without being seen. As he got closer to the trolleys, he heard a sharp snap and glanced up. What he saw above him stopped him cold.

Unaided by any chains or ropes, the Pneumatic Colossus was rising up from the floor on its own power. Standing directly in front of it was Sarah. She had her hand up to her face, and her eyes were set in a defiant, angry stare at a tall man in a tattered wool suit. Standing next to him was an even more imposing figure. He was clearly yet another adventurer, dressed in an all-black costume. Emilio sighed. Sarah's capacity to get herself into trouble continued to be undiminished.

Emilio was already running to her rescue when he heard the wheezing sound of Sarah's name coming from the machine. One of the pneumatic man's long arms reached down and batted away the man in the tweed coat.

The man tumbled across the floor, finally landing in an unconscious heap against the talons of a large golden eagle.

Having taken care of one problem, the Colossus attempted to try the same thing with the man in black, but the adventurer managed to deftly hop out of the way of the swinging metal limb.

The mechanical man fell forward onto its other arm, the metal torso now hanging directly over top of Sarah. It was impossible, but he seemed to be protecting her.

"Sarah!" Emilio yelled out to her. "What's going on?"

Her eyes widened when she saw him. "Emilio! The heart," she said, pointing upwards. "It's inside of him. It's Tom!"

Emilio tried to understand what she had just told him, but it made no sense. She had brought the Automaton back to life? Whatever had happened, it was clearly dangerous for Sarah to remain trapped underneath that machine. "Get out of there!" he yelled at her. "Come to me!"

The Colossus swung its face around toward him. Its appearance was monstrous, with steam pouring out from the grill at its mouth. The eyes were glowing with fire.

Staring into the hellish gaze of a machine that he had helped to create, Emilio was unable to say more than "Stop," as it scooped Sarah up, managing to clumsily and yet almost tenderly cradle her in its arms, staring at Emilio the entire time.

"No, Tom!" Sarah shouted. "Let me go!"

"SAFE . . . SARAH!" it boomed, looking down at her.

Emilio found himself distracted, trying to imagine what mechanism the machine was using for speech. He quickly decided that it was the using steam tubes in its body to create a series of audible "burps" that allowed it to talk. But how had it learned to do that so quickly?

He angrily shook his head. He needed to rescue Sarah, and this wasn't helping.

The machine did something else impossible: rising up to its full height, the Colossus leapt into the air. It jumped straight over Emilio, the numerous tubes that provided it with steam and gas trailing wildly behind it. Emilio looked up and calculated that the moment the machine came crashing back to Earth, so would the hoses.

Even as he took his first step out of its path, Emilio already knew that there wouldn't be time for another. Although he had imagined the blow would come from above him, something smashed into his side instead, slamming him out of the way.

He landed on the ground with a thud. The air was bashed out from his lungs as something large and heavy landed on top of him, pressing hard into his back.

Emilio could hear the sound of people shrieking above his own desperate gasps for breath. The Colossus must have reached the main stage, sending the audience into a panic. Emilio wondered what would happen to him when the creature moved. Would he be dragged to death by the hoses that were draped over him?

The screams of pandemonium grew louder, and he could feel the heavy vibrations of the mechanical man's footsteps through the floor. But instead of the expected sensations of being torn to pieces, he felt the weight rolling off of him. There was another booming voice, but this one was clearly human, and it was talking to him. "Are you all right?"

As he finally managed to take a breath, pulling air back into his lungs, Emilio wasn't really sure if he had all the information he needed to answer that question, let alone the wind to form an answer.

Taking a moment, he began to move his arms and legs, checking one after another until he was sure that they were all in working order. Once he was satisfied that he was still in one piece, he sat up. The moment he did so, he felt a pair of hands grab his shoulders, roughly dragging him away from the wriggling steam hoses that lay nearby.

The face of a jackal peered down at him. There were two black holes where its eyes should have been. Perhaps he had died and was already on the way to hell. "*Kýrie, eléison*," Emilio whispered. Perhaps this was the visage of the demon that had been sent to bring him there.

"I am Anubis. Are you ready to be judged?"

"Am I dead?"

"Not yet."

As Emilio's vision began to clear, he realized the man above him was the costumed adventurer who had been standing next to Sarah, and not a creature from the underworld. "Thank you."

Anubis's head shuddered as a wooden beam impacted with it from behind. The man moved woozily for a moment before crashing down onto Emilio, unconscious.

"Are you all right, my boy?" Vincent grabbed the black-clad figure and rolled him roughly onto the floor. "For a moment I thought that man might have done you grave bodily harm!"

Emilio sat up. "He saved me!"

"Do you see this?" he said, waving the jagged piece of lumber in his hands. This close, the stage makeup on his face made him look like a madman, although Emilio supposed that was always true of Vincent. "Up until a minute ago, this was a piece of my stage!"

The showman held out his hand, and Emilio took it. "But what does that have to do with him?"

"He's one of the Children of Eschaton."

"How do you know that?"

"Because the villains were *blackmailing* me. They wanted me to give them the Automaton's heart! You really need to keep up."

"The Automaton! Sarah!" he said. A hundred thoughts collided in Emilio's head at once.

"She's out there." He pointed his stick beyond the curtain. "I don't think the pneumatic man means to hurt her, but if we're going to save her *before* he finishes tearing apart my theater, I'll need your help."

If Vincent had been blackmailed, then he had planned to give the heart to the Children. Had Sarah been right all along? "Why, Vincent?"

"The rest of my staff has run away, and I know that you've faced some of these men before."

Emilio shook his head. "No. Why did you bring the Children here?"

Vincent frowned. "I'm sorry, Emilio, I truly am." He suddenly looked older than he had before. "But there aren't that many men in New York whom one can turn to when looking to repair the heart of a mechanical man."

Emilio nodded. "They came before us?"

"They did. And I was one of them once, a long time ago."

"Why don't you tell me?"

"Because they threatened everything I had. I just wanted to be left alone. I'd forgotten that once you've played heroes and villains, you can never truly escape." There was a wistful look in the old man's eyes as he looked around his theater. "I should have known better . . ."

He turned toward Emilio and smiled. "But never mind all that now. It's something you have to discover for yourself, I think. Now let's rescue your girl."

They began to run toward the back of the theater, following the steam hoses. Near the back wall they attached to a series of brass pipes that stood straight up out of the ground. Next to it was a wooden hatch. When Vincent threw it open, a blast of steam rose up out of it. "That's not good," he said to no one in particular.

Vincent began to climb down into the hole. "All right, Emilio, I'm going to try to cut off the machine's supply of steam."

"You think that will stop it?"

The showman looked at him and smiled, shaking his head slightly. "You spent a day working with me on it, and you haven't figured out what the real function of that creature's heart is yet, have you?"

"It makes Automaton live?"

"Of course, but *how*?"

Emilio felt like he was being scolded by a teacher, and he didn't like it. "I don't know."

"Ask Sarah Stanton. I'm sure she'll tell you." Vincent stopped for a moment, only his head remaining aboveground. "Or we'll discuss it later. Right now there's no time to waste if we're going to stop this thing. And I need you to go get my costume from outside while I'm down here."

"What?"

"My Steamhammer outfit—in the workshop." His head followed the rest of him down into the hole. "You'll need to hurry!"

After a moment of indecision, Emilio headed for the courtyard door. There was, he supposed, no better plan for him now than to follow Vincent's orders, and it was where he had been headed in the first place.

He had just made it down the steps into to the garden when a shuddering explosion from inside the theater shook him out of his reverie. "Sarah?" For a moment, he considered going back inside, but there was little he could do to stop the mechanical man even if he faced him.

The door to the workshop had been left wide open, and Emilio ran through it, stopping to turn up the gaslights.

As the room brightened, there was a shout. A squat figure rose up from floor. The man was surprisingly short, and as he stood up he stretched out his neck and body. "I feel like I was kicked by a damn horse." He noticed Emilio. "Who the hell are you?" the man asked.

"Emilio. Who are you?"

"They call me Cutter," the man said, pulling out a long, nasty-looking knife.

Staring at the blade, Emilio wondered if there was anyone in the theater who *didn't* want to attack him. At least this one was alone.

Emilio lifted up his arm and then extended it fully, keeping his fingers pointed toward the floor. He could feel the brace underneath his jacket lock into place at the elbow.

"What are you doing?" Cutter asked him, but Emilio didn't say a word. Better to concentrate rather than waste his time.

Emilio slapped his upper arm using the palm of his left hand. A single, massive spring-powered bolt flew out from the sleeve. It covered the distance between the two men in an instant. The large wooden head of the projectile hit the man hard in the jaw, and he dropped back down onto the floor.

For a second Emilio wondered if he had killed him—although having a few less Children of Eschaton in the world might be good for both his own health and Sarah's.

Rotating his arm straight up, Emilio felt the device under his coat unlock, allowing his elbow to once again move freely. It wasn't a bad design—if he could find a way to make it more useful in close quarters, and fire more than a single shot.

When he heard the man let out a groan, Emilio grabbed a roll of twine from one of the workbenches and quickly lashed Cutter's hands and legs together. He was glad the short man wasn't dead, despite any tactical advantage it might have offered him.

He doubted his knots would hold the man for long, but if Cutter escaped after Emilio had gotten the costume, it wouldn't matter much, as long as he disarmed him first.

After doing his best to tie the man up, Emilio retrieved his bolt and the man's knife. The blade was savage-looking, although it had obviously been well cared for—and well used. Emilio almost felt guilty when he shoved it into a vice and snapped it in half.

Having dealt with the villain as best he could, Emilio pulled down the costume from the wall. The suit was heavier than it looked, the chisel arms made from solid steel.

Up close, he could see that the thick glass lenses on the mask had been designed so that they could open and close, and even though they had been well polished, there were still chips and gouges in the surface of them.

He flung the costume over his shoulders, grabbed the portable boiler by a handle near the top of the device, and headed for the exit. As he stepped out the door, Emilio could hear that Cutter was awake and shouting out a stream of curses. They grew louder when he saw his broken blade.

Outside, by the light of the rejected, he could see Vincent peering out through the courtyard door. "Emilio?" he said in a half shout.

"I'm here!" he yelled back.

"Hurry up, boy. They're blowing the place to hell and back in there!"

He raced across the courtyard, moving as fast as he could with the unwieldy device in his hands. "I sorry. The Children of Eschaton are everywhere."

Vincent dragged him through the entrance and slammed the door shut behind him. The showman grabbed the boiler from his hands and began to check it. "I've tried to keep this thing in working order, but it's been a while since anyone has actually used it."

"When you were a villain . . ."

Vincent looked up at him and smiled. It was both mischievous and fatherly, with a look in his eye that seemed more genuine than his usual showmanship. "I wasn't just any villain, my boy, I was the Steamhammer—the man who shook the very foundations of the Hall of Paragons!"

"And now you think you can do this again?"

He laughed as he pulled the suit off Emilio's shoulders. "Not me, lad. I've grown too old to go mucking about with this suit now. It would rip me to pieces." He held it up it up toward Emilio, "You're going to wear it."

"What? No. You crazy!"

"Maybe." Another thundering boom shook the building. "But if you want to save the girl, this is your best chance."

He wanted to complain, but he realized that Vincent was right. He couldn't face a metal monster with his secret gun. "All right, all right," Emilio said, kicking off his shoes and stepping into the metal leg braces. The boots were too large for him, but not by much.

As Emilio pulled off his jacket and revealed the mechanical bolt thrower attached to his arm, the grin on Vincent's face grew wider. "I had a sneaking suspicion that you were the right man for the job." He helped Emilio undo the straps and pull it off. "Now let's get the rest of this on."

Emilio pulled the codpiece and leggings up over his suit while Vincent knelt down in front of the boiler and fiddled with a series of brass taps. "Getting this up to pressure used to be the most difficult part, but I've made a few improvements to it over the years." He flicked a few switches, and the water inside of the glass sphere began to bubble and swirl. An electrical device was heating the water rapidly, and some kind of black smoke was being released into the chamber.

Emilio had no idea what the purpose of the smoke was, and he could think of any number of flaws with bringing electricity and water that close together at the same time. "Is it safe?"

"My boy, you'll be wearing an untested steam accelerator on your back. You need to have an adventurous attitude." He let out a maniacal cackle, deeply out of character with his usual theatrical façade, and it was anything but comforting. "Now get suited up and we'll get this on you."

Emilio slipped his hands into the canvas arms and grabbed the handles inside. There were triggers on each one that had been clearly designed to turn them on and off.

As Vincent hefted up the device and slid it onto Emilio's shoulders, he could feel the heat of the boiler against his back. The wasp-faced helmet came down over his head, and Emilio felt as if he was seeing the world through someone else's eyes. It had been a long time since he wore a mask, and it was an uncomfortably familiar feeling.

But it was also different from when he had been Il Acrobato. The goal then was to hide his true identity from the world, not to try to boast that he had become someone even more powerful. But inside this costume . . .

"How are you in there?" Vincent's voice was muffled by the helmet.

Emilio nodded. "Is okay!"

"Good. Good! Now give the arms a try. I've got it on a low setting, but be careful—if the hammers aren't pressed up against something when you activate them, the vibration could break your arms."

Emilio nodded again. He pushed the jackhammers against the ground, then pressed his thumbs gently against the activation switches.

The jackhammers shook like two angry beasts made entirely of sound and teeth—hungry to destroy the world. The feeling was both shocking and incredible at the same time. After just an instant, he released the triggers.

"How was that?" Vincent asked him.

Emilio had no idea, except that he had been transformed from a simple man into something else. Was this really what he had wanted to become? Was this what he was working toward in his laboratory? He wondered how it could possibly end well.

The ground underneath Emilio shook again, but this time he had nothing to do with it. He slammed one of the chisel arms back onto the ground to steady himself.

When he turned to see the source of the noise, Emilio watched in horror as the Pneumatic Colossus tumbled back through the curtain and crashed into the stage in front of them. The drapes ripped away, and the cloth completely covered the metal creature. There was no way for Emilio to tell if the metal monster still had Sarah in its clutches.

He felt pair of hands on his back, shoving him forward. "Go, my boy! Save the girl and my theater! Do me proud," Vincent shouted after him.

Emilio stumbled toward the mechanical man, unsteady in the heavy frame, doing his best to avoid the shrapnel that littered the ground.

He could see the folds of fabric billowing as he got closer, and somewhere underneath of them there was someone clearly trying to escape. "Sarah!"

Emilio stumbled as he ran. His hands clutched the handles of the chisels, and he was careful to avoid accidentally pressing the triggers. He stood there for a moment, trying to figure out what he could do, when the edge of the curtain lifted. Sarah, clearly shaken but otherwise unhurt, freed herself from the tangled fabric.

When she looked at him, she seemed terrified by what she saw, clearly thinking that Vincent had returned as the Steamhammer.

"It's me, Sarah! It's Emilio!" he shouted, hoping that his voice would penetrate his mask.

Then he heard a familiar western drawl from somewhere in the theater. "Whatever you are, I hope you're planning on getting out of the way . . ."

Emilio turned and saw that the cowboy was standing there, smiling up at him as he pulled on the cigar in his mouth, making the ember glow bright red. He brought a stick of dynamite up toward it, and the fuse began to sparkle. "And you'd better do it fast."

With a calm and practiced swing, the man flung the lit explosive straight toward the stage. It flew in an elegant arc, landing perfectly on the curtain, only a few feet away from Emilio and Sarah.

Chapter 24

A Long Intermission

A nubis opened his eyes, but the world was still pitch black. For a moment he wondered if the blow that had knocked him unconscious had blinded him as well. It was a minor panic, born out of fear, but as consciousness returned, he realized that his actual situation wasn't nearly that bad.

Reaching up, he adjusted his jackal mask, aligning the eyeholes so that they fit properly over his eyes. The world around him swam back into view. He was still exactly where he was when he had been hit.

The blow had left a stinging pain in his head as a reminder. It was sharp and searing, as if whatever struck him had embedded a nail straight into his brain. He reached up to touch a new lump not too far away from where he had been hit by the Stanton girl earlier.

If this was the kind of damage that people took simply from being in the proximity of a Paragon's daughter, then their reputation was well deserved. In fact, it seemed that there was less physical danger to be had from the Paragons themselves than being near to their progeny.

A loud yell penetrated his pain. For a shout of panic, it was incredibly restrained, but he instantly recognized it as Sarah Stanton's voice—she was screaming to be put back down.

It was coming from nearby, but he couldn't see either the mechanical man or the girl. Something rustled, and Anubis saw that the hoses that had almost killed the Italian man were still wriggling. Somewhere on the other end, the metal creature must still be attached to them.

Pulling his staff from its holster on his back, he screwed the segments into place. Sliding off a wooden cap from the bottom of the shaft revealed a sharp metal point. He lifted it up and then stabbed it hard into the side of the nearest tube. A jet of steam sprayed out, and he jumped back as he received a blast of white vapor. It was scalding hot, but once again his suit saved him from the brunt of the damage.

"You!" someone shouted.

Anubis looked around, trying to locate the source of the voice.

"Over here! Now pay attention, Wolf-Man, or whatever your name is!"

"I'm Anubis," Anubis replied, finally locating the source of the voice. It emanated from the white-haired head of Vincent Smith sticking out from the floor.

"Fine, fine—but I need you to stop all that right now."

"You hit me."

"I did," the man admitted almost gleefully. "And I'll do it again if you don't stop attacking those cables and let me get on with what I'm doing down here."

"I won't let you do that again," Anubis said. He tried to look imposing, but it seemed that the last blow had left him with a wobble in his step.

"Yes, yes. I can see you're quite fierce," Vincent said with some sarcasm. "But perhaps you can go and help your friends capture a helpless girl and leave me alone while I try to save my theater."

"I'm not one of the Children," he said, and then wondered why he had. Why was he trying to convince this man of anything?

"You came with them. You threatened me."

"I'm not one of them *anymore*."

Vincent smiled at that. "You can't ever just walk away."

Anubis stood a little taller. "I plan to stop them all."

"Good luck," Vincent said, as another of Sarah Stanton's screams pierced the air. "But if you're not going to kidnap Sarah Stanton, perhaps you should save her. Either way, you can leave those cables alone." The white-haired head disappeared back underneath the floor.

Taking a deep breath, Anubis turned around and stumbled out toward the stage. He was still dizzy, and if he couldn't find some untapped fortitude—and quickly—he wouldn't be able to stop, or save, anyone.

As he pulled back the front curtain and walked out into the auditorium, Anubis saw that the audience and crew had abandoned the theater. At least someone had had the good sense to turn up the gaslights before they'd left.

The Pneumatic Colossus, Automaton, or whatever it was now, stood near the front of the theater, its back to the stage, legs planted in between the fourth and fifth row. It looked like a gigantic, malevolent tin toy, with wires and steam streaming out in random directions from all its joints.

It took Anubis a moment to discover the location of Sarah. She was still in the creature's arms, but it had split open its left limb into a metal sling, and it had her cradled inside of it.

"Put her down, ya dumb machine, before you make me shoot ya both!" The thick drawl was unmistakable, and he could see Doc Dynamite and the White Knight standing in the aisle, facing off against the metal monster.

The Pneumatic Colossus's head jerked back as the cowboy fired off his guns, smacking the metal head with four bullets.

When it turned back to face them, it unleashed a jet of flame from its mouth. Both men jumped out of the way as it scoured the space they had been standing in. The attack left a row of chairs on fire, filling the air with an unpleasant scent of burning horsehair.

Vincent had wanted him to leave the hoses connected while he worked on whatever plan he had in mind, but clearly the gas line was what gave the creature the ability to breathe fire, and to Anubis it seemed obvious that it also presented the greatest danger to the theater itself. Anubis muttered an apology under his breath as he stabbed at the hoses with his staff.

Each one let out a hiss when it was punctured, and it only took an instant for the spout of flame coming out of the Colossus's mouth to sputter and die along with its burning eyes.

Anubis jabbed a few more holes into the hoses for good measure, but any small hope he had that cutting the creature off from its power source might cause it to cease moving were completely in vain.

Equally as futile was the thought that his attack had gone unnoticed. Without moving its head at all, the mechanical giant simply reached its right arm all the way behind itself and began groping around, ignoring any limitations a human limb might have had. The arm seemed far too short to reach him, until the material at the joint stretched and split. Then the grasping metal fingers shot towards him like a harpoon.

Too woozy to try jumping out of the way, Anubis swatted at the hand with his staff. The arm was lighter than it appeared, but it was still heavy enough that the weight of it threw him backwards. The tin limb swung off in the other direction and landed with a thud on the stage. Rods and wires shifted and writhed like snakes where they had been exposed at the broken elbow.

He heard Sarah Stanton yell, this time clearly enough to make out the words. "Stop it, Tom!" The Automaton seemed to ignore her and reeled the wobbling limb back into place.

Anubis swallowed a shout as the head of the Colossus turned to face him. Its eyes were dark now, leaving only a pair of soot-covered sockets with a series of bullet holes perfectly stitched in between them.

Anubis had to admit that Doc Dynamite's skills with a gun were almost as impressive as Jack's with a blade—for all the good it had done.

His head was pounding and his feet were unsteady. Anubis rallied himself and held up his staff in front of him. "Listen to the girl, Automaton. Stop this nonsense!" He glanced around, determining which way to jump when the mechanical man attacked again.

Anubis wasn't disappointed when the Colossus raised its right arm into the air, then smashed it down toward him like a flail. He jumped left and felt a nauseating flash of pain in his skull as he flew through the air.

Despite his attempt to gauge his leap beforehand, he landed hard and inelegantly on the ground, barely keeping his staff in his hands. A fresh jolt of pain shot up from his left foot, warning him that he had come close to breaking something.

Anubis wondered what he would find when he had the chance to sit down and take stock of just how much damage had been done to him in the last half hour. But first he had to avoid being crushed to death by a thirty-foot-tall mechanical man . . .

"Are you all right?" he heard the Stanton girl yell down to him.

He turned and looked up at the machine. Even with its unmoving face, it somehow gave him the feeling that he was being sized up by an angry dog. "I'd be better, but someone hit me in the head." He frowned under his mask, angry that he'd let the pain make him drop his persona.

"Perhaps if you hadn't been *chasing* me, Tom might not feel the need to protect me!"

Anubis felt a flash of anger through his pain. "I'm trying to save you!"

She looked back at her captor. "Tom would never hurt me."

At least their conversation seemed to be keeping the creature at bay. "Are you sure this is the same machine you knew?"

The look on the girl's face grew more concerned, her doubts floating to the surface.

Just beyond the Automaton, Anubis could see the White Knight pulling out a long strand of wire rope from his belt. The braided steel line had a large metal ball at one end, and the pudgy villain threw it at the metal man, wrapping the cord around his tin legs.

The creature's head snapped around to face the new threat. Anubis lifted his staff, aimed it at the metal giant, and pulled the trigger. The tip of it shot outward, making a solid clanging noise as it impacted with the metal skull.

The Colossus whipped back around to face him again, angrier than it had been before. The right arm rose up, but this time it stayed there, waiting for him to jump before it attempted to swat him. The machine was learning . . .

"Any time now, White Knight," Anubis shouted through his mask. If there was a good reason why Clements hadn't already tugged on the wire and brought the creature down, he couldn't look away to discover what it was. The tiniest break in his attention would give the mechanical man the opportunity he was waiting for.

"Don't provoke him!" Sarah screamed, but if the girl had any genuine control over the Automaton, the theater wouldn't have been burning.

"Damn thing's stuck!" he heard the Southerner shout back.

"Then just pull on it!" The stand-off between man and machine could last only so long, and there were no happy possibilities in his future if something didn't happen soon.

Almost miraculously, the Colossus wobbled slightly, and its head turned again.

Seeing his opportunity, Anubis ran straight at the metal man.

The creature seemed confused as Anubis propelled himself into the air. He landed hard against the back of the machine's left leg, the impact smashing the air out of his lungs and setting off a wave of pain in his head so powerful that for a moment he found himself literally blind from the agony.

Anubis tried to hold on as tightly as he could, but the machine man was falling over. His hands slipped free, and Anubis fell for only a moment before he felt his back crash into something. Whatever it was he had hit let out only a single deep note before it shattered underneath his weight. Anubis felt the staff being ripped from his hands as he dropped into a tangle of wires, brass, and wood.

When his descent stopped, he hung there for a moment, blinded by pain. In the distance, he could hear the sounds of tearing cloth, splintering wood, and screams.

Turning his head, he saw that there was a violin next to his face. He had fallen into the mechanized orchestra pit, and the instruments had collapsed under him. The wire strings from the broken piano held him in the air.

Looking up, he could see the Colossus's metal legs a few feet above him, the creature having sunk into the stage.

Anubis tried to clamber out, but besides the pit being a tangled briar of instruments, pipes, and other broken mechanisms, he was beginning to realize that the numerous impacts his head had been subject to over the course of the evening were coming very close to overwhelming him completely.

When he had dragged himself to the edge of the pit, a brown-gloved hand reached towards him. "Need a little help?" Doc Dynamite was smiling behind the cigar in his mouth.

"What about the Automaton?" Anubis replied as he took the offered help and dragged himself out.

"Seems he's down for the count."

A few feet away, he could see the White Knight frantically playing with the mechanism that controlled the other end of his wire cord. "I can't get the damn thing off of me!"

Anubis, thinking he could help, stepped toward the Knight, but he felt a hand against his chest, stopping him. "Wait a second," Doc Dynamite said. "We still got business to attend to."

Anubis followed Doc Dynamite's gaze up to the stage. Sarah had managed to crawl away from the Colossus, but something was already stirring under the thick folds of cloth that had covered it as it fell. "Not for the count."

"Guess not," the cowboy replied.

Meanwhile, another man in a costume had entered into the scene. Anubis recognized Vincent's Steamhammer costume from the wall of the workshop. It looked even more insectlike now, with two long metal shafts coming out from his arms, one of which he was waving at the girl. "It's me, Sarah! It's Emilio!" he yelled out in a voice clearly too young to be the showman's.

But Doc Dynamite didn't seem to notice. "Whatever you are, I hope you're planning on getting out of the way . . ." Doc Dynamite inhaled deeply, making the ash of his cigar glow bright. In a single practiced motion he brought a stick of dynamite up to its ember. The fuse sparked to life the instant it touched it. ". . . And you'd better do it fast."

Bringing his arm around in a lazy arc, he chucked the explosive into the air. It landed perfectly in the lap of the fallen Colossus.

"We might want to duck," he said to Anubis.

They both dropped to the floor a second before the dynamite exploded in a deafening roar.

Anubis's head and ears were ringing as the smoke from the blast cleared. Looking up, he could see that Clements was now flailing more than ever—desperately trying to free himself from the chairs he had fallen into when the explosion had severed the other end of his metal rope. The remaining wire had finally reeled back into the device on his arm, stopping where the ruptured end refused to go back into the hole.

"Let's go!" Doc Dynamite yelled loudly enough to be heard even through the ringing in Anubis's ears. "You grab the girl and I'll finish blowing that thing apart."

"We need to get the heart."

Dynamite laughed. He shook his head and pulled out another stick of dynamite from his bandolier. "Eschaton can go to hell if he thinks I'm givin' that metal monster an operation. If there's anything left after I blow it to pieces, we'll scoop 'em up and give 'em to him."

Anubis nodded. He was in no shape to try to argue. At least it wouldn't be his fault this time.

Underneath the velvet cloth, the Colossus was struggling more violently now. The remains of the stage were collapsing around the metal man as it tried to find the purchase it needed to pull itself up.

Walking past the end of the orchestra pit, Anubis hauled himself up onto the stage near where Sarah Stanton was standing. Every movement was agony, and he wanted nothing more than to find someplace where he could lay down and sleep.

Instead, he pulled himself to his feet and walked unsteadily towards the girl. Standing next to her was Vincent. He wondered what bad advice he was giving her now.

The old man took a step toward him, and he held up his hand. "Not now," Anubis said firmly, and the man stopped in his tracks.

"Sarah Stanton," Anubis said. He was still trying to use the deep voice he had mastered to strike terror in his foes, but what came out of him sounded wavering and unsure.

She stepped forward with a look in her eyes that said she was clearly unafraid of him. "What do you want? If you've come to try to steal me away, I can assure you that I won't go quietly."

Anubis grabbed Sarah's arm and pulled her close to him. "Trust me," he whispered into her ear.

Sarah looked up at him with a furrowed brow. "Why should I?"

He gave a quick nod in the direction of Doc Dynamite and the White Knight. "Because I don't want to let them get their hands on you."

Sarah tried to pull her arm free, and Anubis was surprised to find that he still had the strength to hold onto her. Sarah seemed shocked as well. "Let me go!"

He looked at Sarah again and shook his head. He had made many sacrifices by becoming one of the Children, and many more while he had waited for the right moment to strike. Now he realized that the right moment would never come. And while Eschaton had been planning and plotting, there hadn't been lives at stake. But now the madman's plans were being put into action, and people were dying.

Whatever fate Eschaton had in mind for the girl, it certainly wasn't one that Anubis could ignore. Now was the moment to strike, and it always had been.

"Bring her down here," Doc Dynamite yelled to him. "We need to go."

Anubis looked back at Sarah. "Did you have a plan," she asked, "or am I supposed to let you continue to manhandle me until you come up with something?"

He was in no condition to fight against two villains. Maybe it was time to take the girl and run . . .

But his need to choose was postponed as the ground shuddered underneath him. The man in the insect costume was driving his chisels into the stage, forcing it to collapse around the Automaton.

The mechanical man was attempting to swat the Steamhammer, but he proved surprisingly adept at avoiding the creature's attacks. Or perhaps the machine had simply sustained too much damage.

The Steamhammer stepped under a metal arm and drove the chisels deep into the creature's shoulder, and after an instant the arm dropped away entirely.

"Good boy!" Vincent yelled out.

Sarah pulled her arm free and pressed her hand over her mouth. "No, Emilio! Leave him alone!"

The Colossus freed his remaining arm from the curtain and took another swat at the Steamhammer. Emilio crossed the chisels and managed to catch the limb between them, even as the force of it knocked him down to the floor.

"That's going to be bad," he heard Vincent say behind him. "Very bad, I think."

There was a thundering vibration that threw everyone to the ground, and the chisels and arm shattered simultaneously.

When Anubis looked up, he saw that the Steamhammer was no longer moving. The Automaton helplessly flailed its remaining stump.

Doc Dynamite picked himself up off the floor and pulled out another stick of explosive—larger than the one he had used previously.

"Dynamite! You need to stop! You'll kill the Steamhammer," Anubis yelled at him. The man was clearly not concerned with anyone's survival, even his own—although somehow he always managed to end up coming out of his explosions unscathed.

The Doc lit the fuse and looked up at him. "Go to hell, jackal," he said.

But before he could throw it, a red-headed woman appeared behind him. "You go to hell," she said, and shoved Doc Dynamite's arm. "That's my brother."

The stick flew only a short distance through the air before vanishing into the tangle of instruments and machinery in the orchestra pit.

"Run, Emilio!" Sarah screamed, but before anyone could manage to take more than a single step, the dynamite exploded.

Anubis huddled himself into a ball, his hands wrapped around his head, praying that nothing sharp would strike him as a storm of metal and wood flew through the air. The stage underneath his feet buckled from the blast, and pieces of the shattered instruments rained down around them with the occasional strangled musical note.

After a few seconds, Anubis looked up, his attention caught by the sound of splintering and cracking that seemed to becoming from all around.

The Pneumatic Colossus was thrashing its broken limbs furiously, trying to free the remains of its shattered body from the stage by any means possible. It succeeded in flipping itself over, and propped a stump up onto the stage.

Just as it rose up, there was an ominous groan. This time not only the stage, but the foundations beneath it gave way. As the ground crumbled, the Colossus disappeared from view, tumbling down into the bowels of the theater.

The man in the Wasp costume was nowhere to be seen.

Anubis turned to see the Stanton girl running past him toward the massive hole. Almost without thinking, he reached out and grabbed her, his fingers gathering up a handful of her dress. "Stop." She jerked to a halt, letting out a strained gasp as her own clothes forced the air out of her lungs. "It's too dangerous."

She turned to him with fury in her eyes. "Who do you think you are?" She reached out and slapped his face, though it didn't do much except startle him underneath the leather. He had half expected her to knock him unconscious. "Now let me go!"

"Only if you promise not to hurt yourself." He was trying to be gentle with her, but it was getting more difficult to do anything with control.

"I'll make no promises to you."

Vincent stood. There was blood on the white sleeve of his costume where a chunk of flying metal had bitten into his arm. "I think you should let her go."

Anubis waited a moment, considering the possibilities, but he needed allies more than enemies, and he released his grip.

"Thank you, Vincent," Sarah said, "I appreciate that."

"But he's not wrong. You do need to be careful, young lady," the showman added.

Now that he had a moment to compose his thoughts, Anubis looked out into the audience, seeking out his two "allies." He found the White Knight almost immediately. The man was crawling along the floor toward the exit, his suit badly tattered. By the way he was moving, he was either hurt or had yet to recover from the explosion.

Doc Dynamite and the red-haired girl were both still flat on the floor, and were completely unmoving—knocked out cold or dead and cooling.

"I think we should get off of the stage before the rest of it collapses," Vincent said with great weariness in his voice, and jumped down.

Anubis tried unsuccessfully to stifle a grunt of pain as he landed on the ground.

Sarah followed, demurely showing off her skills in skirt manipulation— she descended in a manner that made it appear as if jumping off of stages was exactly what dresses were designed for.

Sarah reached out and touched Anubis's arm, but he yanked it away. "You're hurt."

"A little," he said gruffly. "Someone hit me in the head—twice," Anubis reminded her, surprised at his own petulance.

"I'm beginning to feel sorry about that, but at the time it seemed you were with the Children of Eschaton, and . . ."

He held up his hand and dropped his voice to a whisper. "And the longer they continue to think that, the better it will be for all of us." He looked around again.

"But how long can you fool Eschaton?"

The girl was smart, just as the Sleuth had been . . . But perhaps he could do more for her than he had managed to do for him. "I don't need you. You're only a trophy. Eschaton wants the mechanical man's heart most of all."

Sarah stared into his mask, managing the most passable imitation he had ever seen of someone looking straight into his eyes. "You'll have to kill me before I'd give it to him. You know that, don't you?"

"I don't know anything," he said looking away. She *couldn't* have seen his real face, and yet he still felt embarrassed and exposed. The pain was weakening him, letting more of the man under the mask leak out . . .

"I don't mean to interrupt," Vincent said, clearly intending to interrupt them, "but Emilio is missing, and I think we need to find him before the Automaton finds us."

"First we take care of the injured," Anubis growled back. If he spoke slowly, he could manage to almost sound as if he were unhurt.

Walking over to where Doc Dynamite and the girl lay on the floor, he saw blood spattered across the ground. The cowboy seemed to be unpierced. Anubis grabbed Doc Dynamite's shoulders and rolled him over. The man let out a loud groan. "Now that's what I call a *ride*."

"Are you all right?"

"If I still got two arms and two legs, then yeah."

Anubis nodded and stood. Sarah had already reached the girl. "Oh no," she said. "No!" she said again, the panic in her voice rising as she dropped to her knees.

Anubis kneeled beside Sarah, in front of the fallen woman. There was blood on her face, pouring out from a ragged cut that ran from her cheek to her mouth.

He was glad that the Italian girl was still unconscious. He knew that waking up with a wound like that would be no kindness to her, and would leave a permanent scar.

Doc Dynamite's gruff voice came from behind him. "That the *whore* what ruined my aim?"

Sarah looked up with an expression of pure anger, but before she could open her mouth to speak, Anubis stood up in front of her, blocking the cowboy from reaching her or the girl. "She's hurt. Perhaps you could take a moment to . . ."

He felt a pair of hands in his side, pushing him out of the way. "Whatever you used to get Jack and Eschaton to buy your lies, it don't work on me."

Anubis shifted his weight and grabbed the man's arms. It was a weak attack, and if he had been fighting an opponent with genuine martial skills, they would have laughed at his graceless form and broken free, but the cowboy's skills were all bullets and bombs. Anubis shoved him backwards. "Leave her alone."

"I warned you," the cowboy said, yanking his arms down and managing to tear free from his grasp with nothing more than brute force. Anubis cursed himself silently in his head—that should never have been able to happen.

310

By the time he could respond, Doc Dynamite had already pulled out his pistol and was waving it at him. "I should do everyone a favor and shoot you both."

Sarah's look of defiance only grew sharper. Anubis had great respect for the girl, but he knew Doc Dynamite wasn't bluffing: he'd rather shoot than to have to put his iron away cold.

Anubis was about to tell the Stanton girl that she needed to be quiet when someone else spoke out. "Good God man, haven't you done enough damage?"

The old man took a dramatic pose and held up a hand to punctuate his points. "What's wrong with you people? Threatening defenseless women?" He pointed a finger at Doc Dynamite and leaned in toward him. Doc Dynamite just smiled in response. It was a curious, tight-lipped grin. "I was a villain myself back in the day, but I had more sense than . . ." His speech was cut off by the sound of a gunshot.

Anubis didn't know much about the cowboy's past, but he did know that the man had indeed been an actual doctor, and his surgical precision remained with him. The bullet wound in Vincent's chest was slightly to the right of center—perfectly placed so that the lead projectile would miss the sternum and pierce his heart.

A cold look of shock came over Vincent's face when he realized that his time was over—his expression a tragic mix of helplessness and resignation. "Oh my," the showman said, and then dropped to the ground.

The cowboy turned the gun on Sarah. "Now, do either of you have any more you want to say, or are you going to shut your mouths and come with me?"

Sarah's lips were pressed so tightly together, it almost seemed as if she were smiling.

Normally this would have been the exact moment that Anubis would have chosen to strike, plucking the gun out of the villain's hand faster than he could pull the trigger. And if he could have done so confidently, he would have. But after all the blows he had taken, he could no longer be sure of his reflexes. "Eschaton wants her alive," was all he could think to say.

"I don't think he actually cares all that much for this little thing any-more, 'specially now her daddy's dead."

"What?" Sarah said. "What did you say?"

The smile that appeared on Doc Dynamite's face was so deeply satisfied that it looked like the man was in love. It was as if he had just stepped into a warm beam of summer sunshine on a cold winter's morning, and it pulled the scar on his cheek into a tight white line. "Nobody told you? You're an orphan now."

Sarah shook her head, her eyes wide. "You're lying."

"Sorry to be the bringer of bad news, darling. The White Knight gutted him, and Eschaton buried him. Happened a few days back. Anubis'll tell ya."

She turned and looked at him, judging him. "You knew?"

Anubis had always suspected that the cowboy took pleasure in the pain of others, and here was the proof. He nodded and looked away. "The Industrialist is dead."

Dynamite pulled the hammer back and pointed his revolver straight at her head. "Now come on, little lady. You wanted to be a Paragon so damn bad, and here's your chance. So why don't you show me how the Industrialist's little girl is going to get revenge for her dead daddy?"

"This isn't necessary." Anubis tilted his head forward. Perhaps he could bully the man into . . .

Dynamite turned to look at Anubis just long enough to throw him a threatening glare. "I'll get to you, jackal. There's words need to be said between you and I, but you can sit tight until I'm done with the girl." He wobbled the gun slightly to emphasize his point.

Sarah was visibly quivering with frustration, anger, and rage, and Anubis could see that tears were forming in the corners of her eyes. "Damn you!" she shouted at him, but she made no other move.

Doc Dynamite started to laugh. "That's all right, sweetheart. You tell the doctor where it hurts." His laughter came out with a rasping sound, and for a moment it blended almost perfectly into the rumbling cacophony that was slowly rising up from the stage. Dynamite fell silent as the noise continued to grow.

After a few seconds, it became more organized, transforming from a deep rumble to a discordant jumble of notes and booms, almost like the noise an orchestra would made as it tuned up for a performance. The Pneumatic Colossus was rising up from the orchestra pit. It spoke with a voice that sounded like pure anguish. "STAY . . . SAFE!"

As the machine rose up, a cloud of bright steam poured out from the gleaming pile of metal that made up its body. The head was still mostly the same, although its eye sockets now each contained the head of a cherub. The body underneath was even more monstrous, and seemed to have been pulled together from almost random elements from the pit. It was still vaguely human in form, but built from a disturbing mosaic of instruments and mechanical animals. Rows of metal wings flapped along its shoulders, and one arm ended in the snapping jaws of a rhino's head. "STAY . . . SAFE . . . SARAH!" it said, louder this time.

"Keep away!" Doc Dynamite yelled back at it, jumping behind the girl. She struggled to fight him off, but the cowboy wrapped an arm tightly around her waist, pointing his gun directly at her head. "Now back off, or I swear I'm gonna send your girlfriend straight to hell."

The mechanical man leaned over and reached out its arm. A rhino head peered at them, steam pouring from its mouth.

Now that it was closer, Anubis could see where the Colossus's head was altered from the original design: the faceplate had been split into crude sections, and the thick hoses that had once connected it to its source of steam and gas now ran out from underneath the metal skull and across its body, wrapping around a framework of pipes.

There was a mouth underneath its head, and it moved when it spoke. "I," it said in a rumble of steam and woodwind glissandos, "WILL . . . KILL YOU."

"You already woulda if you coulda," Doc Dynamite replied, "but I've got the girl." Anubis almost admired the cowboy's bravado, but he wasn't sure it would save him this time.

Sarah kicked and struggled, clearly sure that Dynamite wouldn't kill her while she was his hostage. "Tom! Don't worry about me, I'll . . ."

There was a sickly sounding crack as the bottom of Doc Dynamite's revolver landed hard against the side of Sarah's head. It was another blow applied with medical precision—her eyes fluttered closed, and her head lolled to one side. "That's better," he said, dragging her limp form farther away from the stage.

"Now, monster, if you want to see your girlfriend alive again, I need you to back off."

The creature rose up higher, extending up from the orchestra pit on a column of pipes and wires. It leaned forward on its odd, snakelike body, closing the distance between them.

Anubis's mind was racing. He should have tried to disarm Doc Dynamite when he had the chance. But his inability to act had allowed things to spiral out of control. If he tried now and failed, the consequences could be far, far worse—for both him and the girl.

The ground underneath their feet began to shake, and Anubis grabbed onto one of the theater seats to steady himself. At first he thought the quaking had been something caused by the Colossus, but it continued to grow in intensity, and even the Automaton seemed to be having trouble maintaining his balance. Metal bird wings and other pieces of the scrap that he had used to construct his body were sliding off like scales as the edge of the pit started to collapse, and he had to extend his neck higher and higher to keep his head aboveground.

Doc Dynamite was doing his best to hold onto Sarah, but he was being similarly overwhelmed by the vibrations. Seeing his opportunity, Anubis jumped at him.

His legs betrayed him, and he landed short of his target. Anubis reached out desperately for the gun, and when he felt his hand close around the barrel, he thanked God for at least one bit of luck today.

Two shots barked out, close enough to make his ears ring, and he could feel the heat of the shot through his gloves.

He gave the weapon a yank to the side, and it pulled free from Doc Dynamite's hand.

His first instinct was to throw the gun away. Anubis had a strong distaste for the way a pistol could give the cold confidence of a murderer to the weakest man, but unfortunately, today the weakest man was him. He took the weapon and pointed it directly at Doc Dynamite's head. "Enough!"

"All right, partner," the cowboy said. He raised his hands up into the air, letting the girl crumple to the floor at his feet. "But last time I checked, you and I were supposed to be on the same team."

Someone screamed out Sarah's name, and he glanced over to see the Steamhammer running toward her, ripping off the mask to reveal Emilio underneath.

"I stop the monster!" he yelled.

Unable to help her with the remains of his shattered metal arms, the Italian began to pull off the suit as quickly as possible, the ornate boiler on his back landing on the floor with a clank.

There was a blur of motion in the corner of his eye, and Anubis looked back in time to see Doc Dynamite's hand coming toward him.

Anubis jumped back and landed with a wobble. "Don't make me shoot you."

"You're not a killer, boy. And that's too bad for you." Doc Dynamite took a step forward. "And even if you were, you have no idea how much explosive I got underneath here. One wrong shot and," he held up his fist and popped his fingers open. "Boom!"

The cowboy, moving closer, slapped the gun out of Anubis's hand, sending it skittering across the floor toward the orchestra pit.

Both men leapt after it, but it was obvious to Anubis even as he flew through the air that he wouldn't be the one to reach it first. He had been sloppy, and now he was paying the price.

Using his momentum, Doc Dynamite managed to wrap his hand around the pistol, but Anubis was able to grab onto the cowboy's arm and use his weight to push it down.

There was no doubt who was the stronger of the two men, and beyond sheer force, Anubis had youth and training on his side. But he was, in the end, still human. The punishment he had taken had more than evened the odds between them.

Doc Dynamite was slowly lowering the gun toward him. Even though his life was at stake, Anubis seemed unable to stop it.

As the barrel moved over Anubis's head, Doc Dynamite smiled. "*Adios, amigo.*"

Chapter 25

Passing Judgment

S arah swam out of her haze and looked up to see that Emilio was holding her in his arms. She could vaguely recall that things were very bad, but if there was so much danger, how was it that she had fallen asleep?

There was some kind of metal frame strapped to his legs. "What are you wearing?" she asked Emilio groggily.

He looked at the suit and seemed to be almost as surprised as she was. "It is the Steamhammer. I wear it to help Vincent."

"Vincent is dead." She was angry for herself for being so blunt, and then she remembered that her father was also dead. Sarah pushed the emotions away. There was still too much going on; grief would have to wait.

As Sarah sat up, she saw the Colossus's head rise back up out of the pit. Somehow it still reminded her of Tom, but she would have been hard-pressed to admit that it was still him. Anubis had been right, she couldn't be sure just how much of the original remained . . .

"Sarah? What's wrong?" Emilio said with concern. A limb extended from the side of the pit. It looked vaguely like an arm, but it was constructed out of mechanical rubble, built from animal parts and instruments. At the end of it, where there would normally be a hand, instead it had the head of one of Vincent's mechanical rhinos, its mouth stretched open impossibly wide. It hovered in the air, and Sarah realized that Anubis and Doc Dynamite were grappling underneath it.

The cowboy had a pistol in his hand, and Anubis had pinned down his arm. For a moment, it was unclear who would win the battle, and then Doc Dynamite began to shift the gun toward Anubis.

Sarah tried to will herself up off the floor, but Emilio held her down. "You must rest."

The gun had now lowered toward the center of the jackal mask. "*Adios, amigo*," Doc Dynamite said, wearing the same evil grin that had crossed his lips just before he shot Vincent.

Anubis let go and leaned back. "I'm at your mercy."

"I ain't got . . ." Too fast for vision, the Automaton's limb struck. The gun fired, but the rhino head had caught Doc Dynamite in its jaws, and it jerked him up into the air.

The cowboy, kicking desperately, emptied the remaining bullets from his gun into the mechanical man's head, but they had no effect. "NOW I WILL . . . KILL YOU." A blast of steam came from the Automaton's mouth as it spoke, the vapor shrouding the struggling man.

"Let me go, freak!" Doc Dynamite threw the empty weapon at the creature. It bounced off the Automaton's metal head as harmlessly as the bullets had a moment before.

Tom responded by lifting Doc Dynamite higher into the air. It held him there for a second, and then curled back, clearly intent on smashing him into the ground.

"No!" yelled Sarah.

"SARAH?" it boomed. The head turned to face her with a mechanical jerk.

The cowboy had already started to pull out a stick of dynamite when the rhino handed him off to a curling tentacle that rose up from the pit. Doc Dynamite let out a scream as it looped tightly around him, and the unlit stick dropped harmlessly to the ground.

She started to get clumsily to her feet. "No, Sarah!" Emilio told her. "You are hurt!"

Sarah glared back at him. She understood the impulse, but she didn't have the time for it. "I'm not a damsel in distress, Emilio. You can either help me up or let me go."

Emilio lifted her to her feet.

"Thank you." She looked at him and gave him a quick kiss. "I'll be all right. Now get out of that ridiculous costume and tend to your sister. She's hurt and needs your help."

Sarah turned away and took a few steps closer to the pit. "Is that really you, Tom?" she said, looking up at the Colossus's face.

318

"STAY . . . SAFE, SARAH."

She recognized the words now. They had been the last words that the Automaton had said to her at the doctor's doorstep. "I'm trying to, Tom. But I need you to put that man down first. He'll pay for his crimes, but *you* can't be his executioner." She stepped up to him now, and the enormous metal face began to lower down toward hers. "Let us help you."

"HE WAS GOING TO . . . SHOOT YOU." There was an unmistakable change in the timber of Tom's voice—something softer and more human— more like the Automaton that she remembered. It was as if he had been asleep and was beginning to wake up.

"And you saved me, Tom." She reached up to him. "You've saved me so many times." She could feel tears in her eyes now. She had managed to hold them back since that day in the apartment, and now was not the time to start crying.

"I'M SORRY . . . SARAH. I AM . . . DIFFERENT NOW."

"But you're back." She reached out a hand to touch the tin face in front of her, and she wondered if Tom could actually feel anything through his metal skin. "Let me help you, Tom. You need to put the man down."

The head nodded, and the coiling limb dropped the cowboy onto the ground. He landed limply and didn't move.

It was possible that he was already dead, but it was still better than having Tom fling his body across the theater.

She knew that the Automaton had killed before. Darby had been a man of great personal warmth, but, like so many of the other men she had known, he was also capable of being utterly ruthless when the situation called for it. Tom had been the tool of that wrath on more than one occasion.

The mechanical man had even been sent out to deal with various police actions from time to time, although whether he had ever acted directly against the populace was never spoken about in the papers, nor was it something Sir Dennis had been willing to discuss with her when she had asked him about it.

But Tom had already been changing when he fell to Lord Eschaton. He had been on the verge of becoming more—what, exactly? *Human* seemed like the wrong word. *Independent? Moral?*

Even so, Sarah had no way of knowing just how much of the Tom she had known still existed in his heart, and how much had been lost with the Alpha Element that Lord Eschaton had stolen away. Where did his soul lie?

But whoever this creature was, it knew her name, and it had tried to protect her. That had to be enough for now.

Men were dead, and Viola was hurt, possibly quite badly. And the Children would still be coming after her, and they still wanted Tom's heart. They needed to leave, and time was getting short.

"Tom, can you free yourself from here? Can you come with us?"

There was a sound of shrieking metal as limbs heaved. It tried a few times, then stopped. "PERHAPS. BUT IT WILL TAKE . . . TIME."

No doubt the police would be arriving soon, and the Paragons would come after that.

Or would they? She turned to Anubis. "If my father is dead," she said the words matter-of-factly, but it felt like someone was stabbing her in the heart, "what has happened to the Society of Paragons?"

Anubis stood still for a moment before answering. "King Jupiter is in charge now."

That was a name she had never heard before. "And who is that?"

Another long pause. "Lord Eschaton."

Sarah felt faint. "In charge of the Paragons?" And finally, like a dam bursting, the tears began flowing. She had wanted to be an adventurer so badly, but that world hadn't been full of death, deceit, and monsters. Why had her chance only come when the world had fallen apart? And how had it all fallen onto her shoulders?

She had expected to begin sobbing, but the anticipated flood refused to come. She wiped the tears away and looked up. "Tom, you must find a way to move quickly! I still need you!"

The head nodded, and then reared up. "I AM NOT ENTIRELY IN CONTROL OF . . . MYSELF."

"What does that mean?"

"I DO NOT KNOW."

"What do you mean?"

"I WANT TO . . . LIVE!" Her anguish felt like a knife wound in her stomach. Then she felt a hand on her shoulder. She looked up, expecting to see Emilio, but instead it was the black mask of the jackal-faced man. "Tell him to give you his heart."

"What?" Sarah said.

"If the Automaton can't move, then we take the part that matters and rebuild him."

"That's ridiculous."

Anubis moved closer to her. The Automaton reacted warily, but also didn't attack. "If the heart is what Eschaton wants, then you can be sure it's the only part that matters."

"And *you* won't steal it from me, Child of Eschaton?"

"It is, as you said, not what I want." His voice was weak and wavering, and he could barely stand up, but something about him still seemed strong.

"What do you want?"

"To stop Lord Eschaton, and to redeem myself."

Sarah nodded. "You can't do that all by yourself."

"Somebody told me that once, and I didn't listen."

Sarah turned back to Tom.

"Tom . . . I . . ." Asking him to rip out his own heart was ridiculous. Wasn't that exactly what Lord Eschaton had done? Did the fact that she'd be asking him to do it to *himself* make it any better?

"I TRUST YOU . . . SARAH STANTON."

"I'm sorry Tom, I don't . . ." but the rest of her words were cut off as the ground underneath them began to tremble.

Sarah resisted the urge to scream as Tom's face collapsed, the sections of his head falling away to reveal nothing but metal and unspooling cable underneath. A moment later, most of it had disappeared down into the pit. It seemed Tom's entire body was disintegrating.

A steel arm rose up and moved toward her. It stopped only a few feet away, and Sarah saw that at the end of it was the heart, framed by more cables, wires and cogs. It seemed out of place—the strict structure of Sir Dennis's handiwork, surrounded by a hodge-podge of metal, wet from the steam that hissed around it. And yet it seemed more truly alive than it had before.

Sarah reached up and grabbed it, but it wouldn't budge. She turned to Anubis. "I'm going to need your help."

He nodded, and grasped the metal frame. They both began to tug, rocking it back and forth. Wires and hoses ripped away, and the sound of it reminded Sarah of a scream. Sarah could feel that there were more tears on her face, but she refused to acknowledge them as a sign of weakness. It was good to be human, and it was good to care.

The heart tore free and Sarah turned it over, clutching it to her chest as she unscrewed the stopper that held the Alpha Element. She could feel the heart stop as she pulled it free. She put the unmoving mechanical organ on the floor, and slipped the glowing metal back into the key around her neck.

"That's good work," said a familiar drawl. "Now if you don't mind, I'd like you hand it over to me."

Sarah looked up at Doc Dynamite. He was holding a small stick of dynamite in one hand and a lit cigar in the other. He stared straight at her, and for an instant Sarah wondered just how many women a younger version of this cruel man had turned into roundheels just with his wicked smile and a wink from his gorgeous blue eyes.

He lit the long fuse and held the explosive up in the air. "If I can't have it, we can all go together."

Sarah saw a black-clad foot appear between the cowboy's legs, and the man's usually squinting eyes went wide from the pain of the impact in his groin. Anubis plucked the dynamite from Doc Dynamite's hand, and pinched out the fuse between his gloved fingers.

"Doctor Dynamite, I have judged you. You and the rest of the Children of Eschaton are condemned to destruction."

"I'll kill you for that, Wolf-Man," choked out the cowboy, his hands cupped around his crotch.

"I look forward to you trying." Anubis smacked him hard in the jaw and the cowboy collapsed to the floor. "And I've been looking forward to that."

Sarah looked up at him. "You remind me of my father a little bit."

"You might not say that if you knew what was under this mask."

Sarah wondered what he meant. She was sure that she would accept him no matter how disfigured he was. "We want the same thing, you and I."

"Perhaps, Miss Stanton, although I think you may have better reasons."

"Maybe, but it isn't a contest." She cocked her head and held out her hand. "Emilio has a junkyard, in Brooklyn—when you're ready."

He took it and gave it a shake. "All right. I'll find you, Sarah Stanton."

"And I expect that next time I'll see you, you'll show me your real face."

Anubis turned and ran up the aisle, then stopped and turned before he reached the back doors. "You have a good heart, and your father's spirit, but are you ready to fight a war?"

"Lord Eschaton has hurt or killed almost everyone in the world that I ever cared about," said Sarah as she clutched the heart to her chest. "I think I'm getting there."

"You still have a great deal more to lose," he said.

"Sarah!" Emilio was clearly in a panic. "Viola is hurt! Her face . . . is very bad." His hands were red with his sister's blood.

"I know a doctor, not too far from here. I think he can help her."

As she turned to help Emilio, Sarah heard the booming voice of Anubis filling the theater. "I have judged you, Sarah Stanton, and found you worthy!"

"I'm glad someone thinks so," she said quietly, and turned to go help Emilio.

Acknowledgments

A first book is written in a kind of vacuum. It's you, a few close friends, and a lot of hopes and dreams.

Second books, it seems, take a whole lot more people . . . Here's some of the people who helped make it happen.

Thank you to:

Ken Vollmer for reading the damn thing, giving me great feedback, and being my biggest fan!

Kristene Markert, who paid a price and helped anyway.

Joe Cangelosi for giving Emilio and Viola something to say in Italian.

Lou Anders for believing in this whole crazy thing and giving it room to breathe.

Justin Gerard for creating covers that I am not worthy of.

Jay Lake for going above and beyond the call of duty for someone he barely knows. Thank you twice!

Cherie Priest, Mary Robinette Kowal, and Gail Carriger for all being absolutely lovely in every way, and treating me like an equal before I really deserve it.

Ken Levine for years of good advice and showing me that honesty and hard work are the best way. (Perhaps now that your name is in here, you'll read the damn thing.)

Douglas Rushkoff for knowing it was what I should have done all those years ago.

Andrew Fuller, who listened to everything I had to say, and helped me find a place to stumble into when it all went pear-shaped.

Adrianne Ambrose, for being my favorite writing pen pal, and always there with a good word.

Gabrielle Harbowy for catching one million mistakes, and making them elegantly disappear.

Joan Bowlen, for showing up at just the right time.

Peter Overstreet, for making me realize that steampunk time was here, and then telling me what year to set it in.

And to everyone else who put me up, and put up with me while I wrote this thing:

Bruce Scanlon & Kathy Guidi

Kristina Nelson

Peter Zimmerman

Laurenn McCubbin

Nicholas Stohlman

Jay Goodman

Mary Ray & Mike Zyraki

About the Author

ANDREW P. MAYER was born on the tiny island of Manhattan, and is still fascinated by its strange customs and simple ways.

When he's not writing new stories, he works as a video game designer and digital entertainment consultant. Over the years he's been at work in the virtual mines, he has created numerous concepts, characters, and worlds, including the original Dogz and Catz digital pets.

These days he resides in Oakland, California, although he's been travelling a lot *lately*. He currently spends way too much time on the computer, and not enough time playing his ukulele.

You can find his musings on writing and media at www.andrewpmayer .com.